I0700735

Jojo Unplugged

Jamie Orr

This is a work of fiction. Names, characters, places, and incidents either are the product of the author's imagination or are used fictitiously. Any resemblance to actual persons, living or dead, is entirely coincidental.

Copyright © 2023 by Jamie Orr

Verdell Publishing

All rights reserved. No part of this book may be reproduced or used in any manner without written permission of the copyright owner except for the use of quotations in a book review. For more information, contact:
Jamie@SwingJamie.com
SwingJamie.com
JojoUnplugged.com

First paperback edition February 2023
First eBook edition February 2023

ISBN: 979-8-9877780-0-5 (paperback)
ISBN: 979-8-9877780-1-2 (eBook)

Cover design by Colton Orr

To my mother, Ruth Orr, who delighted in sweet, loving stories. I'm grateful she had the chance to read this book.

CHAPTER 1

———

JOJO

JOJO KEPT one eye on the stage manager as she waited behind the curtain for her cue. Onstage she could hear the friendly, top-of-the-show banter between the co-hosts of *NYC Today*. These morning talk shows were always breezy and light, which normally was a perfect fit for Jojo. But today she was working hard to keep her energy up. *You can do this*, she told herself. She bounced on her toes and shook her hands out. *Smile.*

In truth, she was exhausted from the recent tour and jet-lagged from the flight back from Amsterdam. Normally, she would warm up a talk show audience with a song, but her band had gone on vacation the moment they stepped off the plane. She was doing her best not to resent Carson, her boyfriend-slash-manager, for this poor bit of scheduling. But regardless of how she felt, she wasn't about to let it show. It'd be over in fifteen minutes and then it was sweet vacation time.

Okay, here we go, she told herself.

The stage manager raised her hand and mouthed, "Five . . . four . . . three . . . two . . . one."

Jojo clicked on an electric smile and waved as she emerged from stage right. She got an instant boost from the studio audience as they erupted to their feet. She was in her own backyard, and these were her hometown fans. Some had lined up as early as 6:00 a.m. to get inside, while many more were still on the sidewalk watching the video feed. She felt a surge of energy, and just like that, her smile went from pasted on to the real deal. Jojo *loved* her fans.

She tried to spot Carson. He was usually in the front row, but it was hard to see past the stage lights.

The cohosts stood to greet her. She shook Ryan's hand, but as she reached for Kylie's, she was swept into a warm hug.

"It's great to have you back, Jojo. And don't even bother sitting down. I want everybody to see this fabulous jacket of yours. It's vintage, right?"

Jojo flashed her an appreciative smile for the easy conversation starter. "It's the London skyline." She turned slowly, showing off landmarks like Big Ben and St. Paul's outlined in colorful beadwork against the jet-black fabric. "I found it in a market stall in Notting Hill, and they told me it was probably made in the 1950s."

"Very classy," Ryan said, as they settled on the U-shaped yellow couch. Jojo was grateful she'd paired leggings with the jacket. Dresses and skirts could be tricky on these couch interviews.

"And you're looking radiant, as always," Kylie said.

"Well, kudos to your stylists. They take good care of me." In truth, they'd barely touched her. This was her work—the way she left home most mornings. High-fashion wigs and makeup were her trademark—her glitz and glitter, as Carson called it. And unlike most performers, she didn't leave her onstage persona at the edge of the stage. Most days, she felt like she was performing twenty-four seven.

"How many times have you been on the show?" Ryan asked.

"I've lost track—at least four or five. Of course, I'm on the Upper East Side, so it's super convenient."

"I've seen some pics on your Instagram feed," Kylie said. "Your apartment's gorgeous."

Jojo bobbed her head in agreement. "The sad part is, I've been on the road so much that when I got home last night, I couldn't remember the security code." The remark got a laugh, though it hadn't been funny at the time.

"Can we say your lifestyle has changed," Ryan asked, "since your first appearance on the show?"

Jojo smiled modestly. "I'll say! Back then, three friends and I were squeezed into a two-bedroom in Brooklyn. We furnished it for practically nothing. It's amazing how much free stuff people leave on the curb. And if you remember my song 'Girlfriends,' we shot half the music video at one of our favorite flea markets and both my roommates were in it." Jojo feared she might be rambling, which meant Carson would be getting restless. He liked her to stay on message. *Talk about the tour and the new single.*

Kylie was one step ahead. "So, you just came off a five-month tour. That's got to be physically grueling."

"Yeah, beneath all this foundation, I've got some serious shadows under my eyes." Jojo raised her eyebrows as if sharing inside information. "But there are perks. The fans were amazing, and their enthusiasm and support keeps me going." She gestured to the audience and blew them a kiss. Sure enough, cheering and clapping filled the space and Jojo clapped right along with them.

"It's got to be intense," Ryan said once the noise died down. "I saw a video of you performing 'Come On Over' in Seattle, and everyone in the stadium had their hands in the air." As if on cue, he and Kylie raised their arms and started swaying. Jojo joined in and belted out the chorus straight up *a cappella.* Soon everyone was waving and singing. She loved these little highs.

During the commercial break, Carson ran on stage. "You guys are killing it. But if I could offer one note . . ."

Jojo cringed. She knew his impromptu appearances in the middle of shows were only barely tolerated.

"I just want to make sure you leave time to talk about the single. I was promised that would be the focus."

"Definitely," Ryan assured him. "Saving the best for last."

As the stage manager frantically escorted Carson back to his seat, Jojo mouthed, *Sorry*, but Ryan and Kylie shrugged it off.

The show was live again, and Kylie took the reins.

"You must be proud of your latest album. In the first six months, it's already outsold your first two. And you just released another single."

"'Sweet Side' will be the fourth and final single off this album," Jojo said. "Originally, the label only budgeted for three, but I think they were blown away by the amount of support for this song. Some die-hard fans were lobbying for it online."

"The power of loyal fans," Kylie said wistfully. "And now it's the fastest rising song on Billboard."

"It's a big departure for you," Ryan said. "I don't recall you doing a cover before."

"That's true. I've either written or cowritten everything up to now."

"But this, of course," Kylie said, "is a classic Matt Heston song. Was that a risk?"

"Absolutely. My label was dead set against it for the longest time. I wanted it on the last album but obviously lost that battle. Record execs are always worried about going 'off brand,' so this time around, I made a deal. I'd record it and if they didn't like it, I'd never bring it up again."

"I'll bet they're happy now," Ryan said. "It's touched a nerve of nostalgia for a lot of folks and possibly that's why it's debuted so high on the charts."

"At twenty-four," Jojo said, not bothering to play it cool. She'd been sweating this one out and the relief was still fresh.

From the wings, the show's producer was making a circular motion with one hand and Ryan picked up the signal. "We've got a surprise for everyone. We dug back in the *NYC Today* archives and found an absolute gem. I'd never seen this before and would bet a lot of people haven't. It's a live performance, right here in our studio, with Matt Heston singing"—Ryan paused for effect—"'Sweet Side!'"

This *was* a surprise. There wasn't much video of Heston that Jojo hadn't seen, and she certainly hadn't seen this.

The large studio monitor leapt to life and there he was, looking the way she remembered him at twenty-five. He was boyishly lean, with thick, tousled hair obscuring part of his face. Heston had a brand of reserved confidence that had charmed an entire generation of girls.

He was on the stage with his band, and after a few instantly recognizable chords, started singing softly, his eyes downcast as though the song was too personal to share. But as he neared the end of the first verse, he looked up to the camera and any appearance of shyness was replaced by an intensity that still gave Jojo shivers.

Out of the corner of her eye, she saw Ryan give a thumbs-up to the producer. With the discovery of this old clip, excerpts from today's show might even go viral.

When the song ended, the focus was back on her.

"Those are some big shoes to fill," Ryan said. "Heston's version of 'Sweet Side' is so iconic it's practically woven into the American soundtrack. You must have known people were going to compare them. Are you worried?"

Petrified, she was about to say but thought better of it.

"Before the album was released, I was anxious. But so far, it's been well received." She held up both hands with fingers crossed. "And I think my recording's different enough that it's clear I wasn't trying to copy the original."

"You've definitely made it your own," Ryan said. "Heston was always a bit edgy, whereas you've captured a more celebratory feel—especially with the music video."

Kylie was nodding effusively. "The video's simply amazing.

But it still feels like a gutsy move on your part. With all the great songs you must get pitched, why were you willing to put so much on the line for this one?"

Carson had prepped her to expect this kind of question and yet, Jojo wasn't totally sure of her answer until the words began to flow. "I've always loved Matt Heston's music, and back when I was teaching guitar, he was super popular with my students." She paused, realizing that didn't answer the question. "But if you ask anybody about the music that's had the greatest influence on their lives, they're likely to name a song or artist who was big when they were in high school. Those are the years when emotions are raw and senses are heightened and everything feels so . . . so *crucial*."

She usually avoided long-winded answers during interviews, but she was on a roll and Kylie and Ryan weren't cutting in.

"When I first started writing songs, I felt pretty discouraged with the results. Then I heard 'Sweet Side' and something clicked. It's as if that song unlocked a world of lyrics for me."

She hoped she hadn't gone overboard on the honesty. There was always a sense of vulnerability that came with getting personal, and if she'd opened up too much, there'd be some bizarre memes by the end of the day.

"I'll bet every one of us has a song like that," Kylie said and then looked at Ryan. "Hey, that's a great show idea!"

"I could get into that," he said, while picking up another cue from the producer. "So, Jojo, what's next on your agenda?"

The segment was winding up and Jojo was feeling lighter. "When I walk off this stage, I'm officially on vacation."

"Congrats," Kylie said, beaming like she truly meant it. "You deserve it. Any special plans?"

"None whatsoever."

"Ahhh . . ." Ryan sighed. "That's my favorite kind of vacation."

CHAPTER 2

MATT

MATT WAS TILTING his miter saw to forty-five degrees when movement outside caught his eye. He went to the dusty shop window and brushed it with the cuff of his shirtsleeve.

"Hell no!" he muttered and was out the door in two strides.

A young woman and a cameraman were halfway to the house, and he ran to intercept them before they could reach the front door and hassle his daughter.

"You're on private property," he yelled across the yard. "Please leave!"

"Hello, Mr. Heston?" the woman called out, while the man beside her shouldered his camera.

"Please respect my privacy. I've got nothing to say."

"We're only here to ask one question. I promise, it will just take a minute."

It was never just one question. There'd be a follow-up and then another and another . . . He made a beeline for the front door. He'd learned over the years that the less he interacted with these people, the better.

But they were relentless. "Your fans just want to know how it feels to have one of your songs climbing the charts again."

"I have no idea what you're talking about. You've obviously got the wrong guy."

"Didn't you write 'Sweet Side?'" The woman was matching him step for step. "Haven't you heard it yet? As of this morning, it broke into the top twenty on Billboard." She stuck the microphone directly in his face.

"Lady, I listen to country."

He had just reached the porch steps when she held out her phone and he heard the song. It was his lyrics and melody, but the singer was female and the arrangement very different. As determined as he was to get into the house, he suddenly found his feet riveted to the spot. Even on the tiny speaker, the song was obviously well produced—though maybe a bit slick for his taste.

"Is this the first time you've heard it?" she asked.

He wasn't about to make her day by admitting to that on camera, though the truth was probably written on his face.

"Who is that?"

"Jojo. It's her latest single."

His disdain was visible as he repeated her name. "Jojo? Did they run out of last names?" He knew perfectly well who Jojo was, but there was something so pretentious about stars who went by one name only. "Well, you can tell Jojo it's overproduced. I wrote that song for my wife. It's supposed to feel intimate. What's with all the orchestration? Jojo would do well to go back into the studio and strip it down to the bone. Then I might be able to hear the lyrics."

Damn. He could see the smug satisfaction on the reporter's face. Instead of a simple *no comment*, he'd given her the soundbite she wanted. And now it wouldn't end with these two. Tomorrow there'd be more vans and more cameras and more bloodsucking reporters.

He pushed past the microphone and into the house, cursing himself, and slammed the kitchen door.

"Dad, what are they here for?"

He jumped. "Jeez, Gracie. Don't sneak up on me." Clearly, she'd been there for a while, peering around the edge of the curtain. "And don't let them see you."

"They're walking back to their van," she said. "The lady's on her phone."

"Probably talking to her boss and telling him to reserve two minutes on tonight's news."

"Two whole minutes. Nice job, Dad."

When had his twelve-year-old gotten to be such a wise guy?

He peeked around the edge of the curtain. This hadn't happened for a while, and he'd begun to think the press was losing interest. Except for the occasional "Where Are They Now" story, their lives had started feeling normal.

Matt went to the kitchen sink and poured a glass of water. How was it possible one of his songs could make it into the top twenty and this was the first he was hearing about it, especially when the biggest Jojo fan on the planet was living under the same roof?

He looked at his daughter. "Honey, is there something you've been wanting to tell me?"

"About what?"

"Oh, I don't know. Maybe that Jojo has a new single?"

"Oh, that." What was with the blasé tone? He stared her down until she folded. "I knew you'd be upset."

"Why would you think that?"

"Well, aren't you?"

He sat at the island and thought for a moment. Okay, he could see why she'd been hesitant.

She pulled out a stool and sat across from him. So many milestones were passing. For a long time, getting onto the kitchen stools required a bit of climbing, but she'd shot up in the last year. She propped her elbows on the counter, resting her chin on her hands.

"Lucky for us," he said, "you inherited your mother's mellow temperament. Sometimes I can . . . run a little hot. It's just that when I get ambushed, I hate looking like a backwoods hick who's completely out of touch."

"Well . . ." she hesitated, "I kinda thought that was the image you were going for."

"Very funny. I wish you'd take this seriously."

"I am—but face it, Dad, the only paper you read is the *Banner* and about the only time you go online is to check the weather."

"Not true. I also order stuff for the shop."

It was her turn to stare him down.

"Okay, okay," he confessed. "I'm not exactly Mr. Pop Culture, but that's even more of a reason I depend on you. You interact with people at school and you're online a lot. You're basically my eyes and ears on the music scene."

Her shoulders slumped. "I was going to tell you. I was even thinking of telling you tonight. It really hasn't been very long. 'Sweet Side' is the highest debuting single of the year."

He suppressed a chuckle as she rattled off the factoid like a deejay.

The discussion might have ended there, but something didn't add up. "Did Jojo just release a new album?"

Gracie hung her head. "Okay, busted. The album came out months ago. But 'Sweet Side' wasn't supposed to be a single, so I thought you wouldn't find out." It sounded like she was finally being honest. "I know you wrote it for Mom, so it's always going to be hard for you to hear it. But what's the big deal? Other people have sung it and Jojo's might be the best cover yet."

He didn't like to think this had been weighing on her. She was right about Jojo not being the first, but apparently those other recordings didn't go anywhere because the royalties never amounted to much.

He got up and went to the window again. "The van's gone."

"Will there be more tomorrow?" she asked.

"Maybe, if the song keeps climbing." He turned to the old,

corded phone hanging on the wall. "I think I'm going to call your Uncle Thad."

"I thought you never talked to him."

That stung. Not because it was untrue, but because Thad had deserved better. He'd been an exceptional manager, keeping one eye on the bottom line and the other on the welfare of Matt and his band. They'd come to feel more like family than friends, thus the honorary title of uncle. In the end, the breakup of the band had cost him as much as it cost Matt.

"Well, I guess it has been a while, but I've always considered Thad an important person in my life. That's why we asked him to be your godfather."

Gracie slid off her stool. "Say hi for me and tell him I like the birthday cards." She left the kitchen, and he waited until he heard her on the stairs before picking up the receiver. He was surprised he remembered the number after so many years.

"The Sawyer Agency. May I help you?"

"Does Thad still work there?"

"Can I tell him who's calling?"

Matt hesitated, unsure Thad would even take his call.

"It's Matt Heston."

"Mr. Sawyer is expecting your call, Mr. Heston. I'll put you through."

Unbelievable. Was he that predictable? Matt started pacing, the twisted phone cord following him back and forth. He wasn't certain how this was going to go down. Some wounds don't heal, and the way he'd bailed on Thad and the band at the height of their success had probably been the deepest betrayal of Thad's life.

"Hey, Matt."

"Hey, Thad."

The older man sounded unchanged, and Matt felt himself being pulled back in time. In the music industry, most agents were big talkers. But Thad had always been a man of few words.

"How's my goddaughter?"

"Gracie's good. She's twelve now. You've been nice about remembering her birthdays."

"She always sends a thank you, which is more than I get from my own grandkids."

A silence hung between them.

"I wish I knew her better."

Another jab to the heart, though Matt doubted it was intentional.

"I'm glad you called," Thad said and the space between them started to thaw. "Have you seen a little bump in your royalty checks?"

"Not much."

"Well, it's probably too early. There's always a delay. Since 'Sweet Side' has been on the album for about six months, you should see a nice increase in your next check, but the real payout will come from the single."

"Are you still my agent?"

Thad laughed. "Technically speaking, you never fired me. You just stopped taking my calls."

"Sorry about that. I was pretty messed up."

"We all were," Thad said. "The whole thing was messed up, but you sound okay. Better anyway."

"So, about this deal with Jojo," Matt said. "Did they run it by you first?"

"You know it doesn't work like that."

"Well, how does it work?"

Matt could practically hear Thad shaking his head. "People have been singing your songs for years and now you want to know how it works?"

"Well, it's a hell of a lot different when some guy sings one of my songs in a bar in Austin, Texas. The next morning, I don't have reporters camped out on my lawn."

Thad seemed amused.

"It's not funny," Matt said. "It's a hassle."

"The kind of hassle every kid I rep dreams of. I've never understood it. You put out two albums and then disappeared and somehow the press turned you into the goddamned Salinger of the music biz."

"You're right," Matt said. "It doesn't make sense. There's plenty of people more famous, so why can't the tabloids go bother them? And it's not just me they bother. Last fall, a guy approached Gracie. I was off somewhere running errands and wasn't gone long." There was a stillness on the line. "I'd asked her to rake the leaves out front and a guy walked right into the yard. Said he just wanted to ask a few questions about her mom."

"Jeez, Matt."

"I got home, and the guy took off, but Gracie was really shaken." His pulse quickened just thinking about it. "It took every ounce of self-restraint not to chase him down the street."

"I'm so sorry. I had no idea," Thad said. Something must have caught his attention on the other end. "Hey, why are you on *E! News*? Hold on, I'm going to turn up the volume."

Matt cringed. He couldn't hear every word, but he heard enough. Was that really the way he sounded? It didn't take long before Thad had seen enough.

"Oh, Matt." He sounded discouraged. "I hope you didn't just shoot the goose that laid the golden egg."

"She caught me off guard!" Even in Matt's head, the excuse was pathetic.

"Well, hell. You, of all people, should know how to handle the media by now. The bad news for you is these guys love to poke the ferret, so you'll probably have a regular feeding frenzy tomorrow."

Matt didn't appreciate being the ferret in this story and he didn't need Thad reminding him he'd handled it badly.

"But as you probably know, controversy sells. So, you may actually be a media genius."

Matt shifted the subject. "You still getting a piece of the royalties?"

"Yup."

"Well, you deserve it."

"I believe I do."

Thad had every right to be prickly. He had to be approaching retirement and, financially, things would be a heck of a lot better if everything hadn't imploded.

"My phone's lighting up," Thad said. "I'm going to have to go. Take care." He didn't wait for Matt to say goodbye or apologize.

An apology was so overdue, it was more likely to open old wounds than do any good.

CHAPTER 3

JOJO

JOJO DIDN'T HAVE any family living in the city, but she had the next best thing—Leah and Tom Skoby, and their two spirited little boys. That evening, her driver dropped her at their apartment building in the East Village and her bodyguard walked her to the door of the lobby. Inside, as the elevator opened, a middle-aged couple stepped out and did a double take but thankfully kept moving. She got on and pushed the button for the third floor.

On the ride up, she turned her phone off. It was the only way to keep the outside world from intruding. The elevator doors slid open, and she headed down a hallway, spotting two small faces watching her from a half-open doorway.

"I see Tristan and I see Josh," she said in a singsongy voice.

"Auntie Jojo!"

As she reached them, the boys glommed onto her legs like barnacles. Their mother appeared, drying her hands on a dish-towel, and gave Jojo a quick hug. She seemed a little harried.

"It's not that I don't want to hear how Amsterdam went, but for fifteen minutes can you be my savior and keep them out of the kitchen."

Jojo laughed. "I got this." She was already heading for the boys' bedroom, doing a zombie walk with a giggling monkey clinging to each leg. "Is Tom home yet?"

"Running late," Leah called back.

Jojo loved the familial energy, the smell of dinner cooking, and the adorable faces looking up at her. In their eyes, she was a magical character who showed up in fanciful wigs and makeup a couple times a month for dinner and in dance videos choreographed by their mother. The two women had collaborated on six projects.

Ten minutes later, the boys were teaching her how to roll Play-Doh with a rolling pin when Tom peeked in. "Hey, boys. You having fun with Auntie Jojo?"

"Daddy!" They ran to maul their father for a few lively seconds and then, just as quickly, ran back to the play table.

Jojo rose from her perch on a child-sized chair and gave Tom a hug.

"No Carson tonight?" he said.

"'Fraid not. Just the spinster aunt."

"What's a spinster?" Tristan asked. He was now rolling his Play-Doh into a long snake.

"A spinster is the exact opposite of Auntie Jojo," Tom said. He headed back into the hallway. "I've got to get changed, and Leah says if you keep them busy a little longer, you can have our next-born."

Jojo laughed. "Sounds like a deal."

She was fairly certain they'd made up their minds to stop after Josh, but a little girl would be so much fun.

Tom hadn't seemed disappointed Carson wasn't joining them, and she hadn't offered a reason. Earlier that morning, after they'd left the *NYC Today* studio, there'd been another fight over the schedule—the third in as many weeks. But this time felt different because Jojo dug in her heels. The tour had been grueling, and she needed to recharge. And as amazing as her life might appear from the outside, it had become routine and predictable, which was starting to show in her songwriting.

"I need to change things up, and I need a rest," she'd said. "It's nonnegotiable."

"Sure. We'll see," was Carson's reply, an apparent misunderstanding of the word *nonnegotiable*, which was the sort of thing that frustrated her. She remembered a time when they could talk for hours about marketing and stage design and tour schedules. But now they were both so busy Carson had gotten in the habit of just telling her where to be and what to do, with little or no discussion. Rather than risk infecting the Skoby household with their tension, Jojo had suggested she and Carson spend some time apart tonight.

Dinner was served informally in the kitchen, a casserole dish on the sideboard and dirty pots and pans still on the stove. Jojo adored the revolving art show on the refrigerator door, including family photos and the recent addition of a T. rex in green and orange crayon. It was a sharp contrast to Jojo's almost sterile kitchen.

Later—after dinner and after she'd read the boys two bedtime stories—she found Tom and Leah in the living room.

"Oh, look, Tom," Leah said, "it's the nanny."

Jojo slumped onto the couch and kicked off her shoes. "Yeah, how did that happen? And is it true they each get to pick a separate goodnight story? Or did I get hustled?"

"You know you love it," Tom said, "or you would have called for reinforcements."

It was true. There was something deliciously sweet about reading to two little boys as they snuggled up beside her and hung on every word.

"Why didn't Carson come tonight?" Leah asked. The question seemed innocent enough, but it yanked Jojo out of her mellow mood.

"Oh, no reason, really." She traced her finger along a pattern on the couch. She looked up to see Leah waiting expectantly for more. "Just a little friction." She hoped that would be enough, but still there was silence. "Look, I don't want to bore you guys with the details of every little fight we have."

A look crossed between the couple.

"I saw that," Jojo said. "What gives?"

Leah sighed, as if explaining something to one of her sons for the hundredth time. "We're not going to say anything negative about Carson, since we still have to get along with him every time you bring him around."

Was this Leah's idea of *not* saying anything?

Always the diplomat, Tom stepped in. "Carson's not a bad guy —in small doses."

This was the closest Tom had ever come to criticizing him. The two men always seemed to find something to banter about, but she suspected it wasn't as easy as Tom made it look. Carson had a habit of feeling like he had to impress Tom. The last time, it had been the endless list of gadgets on his new BMW.

Leah's eyes were boring into her as only best friends can get away with. "So what was the fight about this time?"

Jojo wasn't sure she had the energy to rehash it. "He just keeps filling up my schedule. I'm supposed to be off this month, but then he booked me for the festival in Montreal in three weeks and then there was this morning's appearance on *NYC Today* and I know he's trying to move up my studio time—"

"Kind of like he's not hearing you," Leah said. "And you're just noticing this?"

Leah's digs at Carson usually came in the form of brief sniper attacks, but tonight she wasn't backing off.

"Are you angry with Carson or with me?"

"Oh, I'm done being angry with Carson," Leah said. "This is all on you, girl, because you are way too smart to be putting up with that man. You complain about the way he treats you, but you do nothing about it. It's like underneath this thing you two have going on, you've forgotten *he* works for *you*, and not the other way around."

It didn't seem that simple to Jojo. When Carson discovered her, she was singing in bars and small clubs. He was the one who saw the potential in her. He created her now-famous Jojo image, had presented her to the world, and made her a star. She felt like she owed him. And then there was the matter of sex, which they dove into headfirst when they were both giddy with the newness and excitement of her ascension. For a while, it seemed it might grow into something deeper, but now it felt more like a habit she didn't know how to break.

"We know it's complicated," Tom said gently. He was always the more conciliatory of the two. "That's why we've got a proposal for you."

This was starting to feel like an intervention.

"We want you to have the cabin for the month," Leah said. "On the condition you go alone and don't tell Carson where you are." Perhaps realizing she still sounded combative, Leah's voice softened, and she moved to the couch beside Jojo. "I'm worried my friend is disappearing. I don't think you realize how controlling he is."

Jojo felt a compulsion to defend herself, but as she looked from Leah to Tom, all she saw was compassion. Leah might be hot-blooded, but she was one hundred percent in Jojo's corner and Tom was as levelheaded and kind as any man she'd ever met. And deep down, she admitted they weren't telling her anything she didn't know.

She lost her will to argue and thought again about their place in Vermont. She'd been invited on several occasions but had always been too busy—the eternal story. The idea of being on her own in a quiet retreat in the middle of nowhere was enticing, but she wasn't even sure how she'd get there. "I don't even own a car." The statement came out of nowhere and was so ludicrous none of them spoke for a moment. Then suddenly they laughed, and the tension broke.

That Jojo was on the *Forbes* list of the Wealthiest Women in

Entertainment yet didn't own a car struck them as particularly funny. Of course, she had a chauffeured car parked right outside, but she didn't know whether she owned it or if it was provided through a service. She was fairly certain she owned her tour bus— at least her name was written on the side. But maybe it was leased or rented. At any rate, she wasn't going to drive her bus to Vermont.

Ever the practical one, Tom spoke up. "Do you even have a driver's license?"

"Of *course*," she said but then wondered if it might have expired. The act of retrieving it from her wallet and confirming that it was valid was enough to set plans in motion.

Leah dialed a rental car company and handed her the phone. "Just do it."

By the time they were done, Jojo's escape from Manhattan was carefully planned, right down to disabling the tracking app Carson had installed on her phone. In the process, she noticed there were several messages from Carson, which was typical. She quickly shut the phone off again. Whatever it was, it could wait.

At the end of the evening, Tom went to find the key to the cabin and the two women waited by the door.

"I know you usually rent the cabin out when you're not there," Jojo said. "So I want to pay."

"Forget about it. How many jobs have you thrown my way?"

Jojo knew they would never cash a check, so she'd have to come up with another way to thank them. "One other thing," she said. "You've mentioned before Matt Heston lives up that way, and I was thinking maybe I should reach out to him. Especially now that 'Sweet Side' has been released as a single."

Leah raised her eyebrows. "Is that why you agreed so easily?"

"Of course not!" *Or was it?* It might have been at the back of her mind, but only as the tiniest little seed of a thought. "I don't see a problem. It's totally appropriate for one professional to reach out to another—singer to songwriter."

"Oh sure," Leah teased. "It has nothing to do with a teenage crush?"

"There was *no* crush. Only a deep appreciation for his music."

Leah looked unswayed. "Aren't you forgetting he has a daughter? If you're trying to keep a low profile, that could complicate things, especially if she's a fan."

Of course, Jojo knew there was a daughter, but wasn't the child very young? She'd been a toddler when her mother died, so . . . oh heck, that would make her eleven or twelve. "Point taken," Jojo conceded. The last thing she needed was close contact with a preteen who might have a bunch of web-savvy friends and a TikTok account.

"Just keep a low profile," Leah said. "And lose all of this." She made a sweeping gesture from the top of Jojo's wig down to her shoes.

Jojo frowned. "Sometimes I get the feeling you're not crazy about my look."

"Au contraire. It's the only reason this plan's going to work. Today you're a butterfly and tomorrow you'll turn into a caterpillar. Not a soul will recognize you."

Jojo wasn't sure she liked the analogy. She'd felt like a caterpillar most of her life—through school and when she first moved to New York. It was the total makeover Carson had engineered that allowed her to spread her wings and be noticed. She couldn't recall the last time she'd gone a full day as her old self.

"I'm really serious," Leah said. "No makeup or this plan won't work. You can't avoid town altogether because the local grocery doesn't deliver. So, when you shop, keep it quick—in and out."

Tom reappeared and handed Jojo the keys. "The little one's for the padlock on the boathouse in case you want to kayak or paddleboard."

Leah put out both her arms for a hug, which was so tight they squeezed out a tear or two.

"It's not like we can't still talk," Leah said. "There's Wi-Fi and cell coverage."

"We'll talk every day," Jojo said as she backed into the hall. "And thanks. I love you guys."

A few moments later, as she waited at the elevator, she heard quick footsteps behind her and turned to find Leah, hurrying to catch her and looking worried. "I'm afraid Carson will change your mind. Please don't let him." Did Leah think Carson held that much sway over her?

The elevator door opened and Jojo stuck her hand out to hold it. "I promise I won't even talk to him until I'm out of town." She held her phone up. "See, it's off."

Leah didn't look convinced.

The elevator pushed against Jojo's arm and she stepped on. "Don't worry. I'll call when I get there."

On the drive back to the Upper East Side, Jojo pushed the button that opened the privacy window between her and the front seat. "Hey, guys. I hope you got dinner."

"Dinesh knows all the best Indian spots," Russ said. "But don't let him choose how hot."

"Yeah, I learned that the hard way." Jojo smiled into the mirror, but Dinesh kept his eyes on the road. "I've got exciting news for you gentlemen. You'll still get paid, but I won't be needing your services for a while." She explained only what they needed to know, including the fact she'd be back briefly in three weeks before flying up to Montreal for one show.

"Will you have security where you're going?" Russ asked.

She decided it was easier to say yes than convince him she would be perfectly safe by herself in the middle of the Vermont woods.

"Just one request," she added. "If Carson asks questions—"

"We never had this conversation," Russ said.

Dinesh raised his eyes to the mirror, and she could read his loyalty. "We work for you, ma'am."

She settled back in her seat but left the window between them open. Carson might sign their checks, but Dinesh and Russ considered her the boss.

As they approached her building, Russ broke the silence. "Keep driving." Then he turned to the backseat. "It's an especially large crowd tonight. We can circle the block if you still want to use the front door, or we can use the private entrance."

Small groups of fans hanging around the building were common, but whenever one of her songs got hot, the crowd swelled. Usually, Jojo didn't shy from the public, but she was already shifting into vacation mode.

"Okay, let's skip the front door tonight."

The elevator took her to the seventeenth floor and opened into the marble foyer she shared with two other apartments. To the right was her door and, inside, blissful peace. She was tempted to sit down and relax but knew she'd regret it later. It was always better to get right to the chore of peeling back the layers of her public façade.

The nightly ritual started in the wig room. Jojo lifted the straight blond hair from her head and placed it gently on an empty mannequin head among the dozens of others that lined the shelves. As she pulled off the wig liner, her natural chestnut curls sprang to life as if happy to be free. She would deal with them later.

Next stop was the makeup room, where she sat on a stool at a long marble counter. The lashes came off first and then the nails. When she was on tour and didn't have the luxury of time, acetone was her go-to nail remover. But she didn't like the way it dried her skin, so at home she used a remover that worked more slowly but was less harsh. In about twenty minutes, her nails were clean and natural.

In the bathroom, she started with coconut oil to remove her makeup and then a gentle soap to remove the oil. She finished with a thin layer of moisturizer.

Restoring order to her hair was a simple task. Since it was usually under a wig, she kept it short—just off the neck. As a child, she envied girls with straight hair, while hers was a tangle of unruly curls, which her mother tried in vain to tame with barrettes and headbands. It wasn't until a friend in high school told her to "lose the hairbrush" that she discovered there could be order within the chaos. From that point on, she began to make peace with her assorted waves and ringlets.

Now with the evening regimen almost complete, she reached for a spray bottle and gave her head a good spritzing. Then, running her fingers up from the base of her scalp, she lifted and kneaded clumps of curls until buoyancy and balance returned to her short bob. Sometimes she worked in some styling cream, especially in the winter when her hair was drier, but tonight, it was fine as it was.

If she wanted to—and she occasionally did—she could now take the elevator down to the lobby and walk outside, directly past the paparazzi, and no one would look twice at her. Leah hadn't been exaggerating about Jojo's ability to blend in. And if she could do it on the streets of New York, she could certainly do it in Vermont, where no one would expect her.

Jojo went into the living room without turning on the lights and sat on the large wraparound couch. When the realtor first showed her the apartment, she walked straight across the hardwood floor to the full-length windows and fell in love with the skyline.

She closed her eyes and thought about tomorrow. Carson was sure to flip out. He was always preaching about the fleeting nature of fame and planting the fear that if she slowed down for even two seconds, the next rising star would take her place. Maybe his kind of motivation was okay in the short run, but she couldn't maintain this pace forever.

Perhaps she could put a positive spin on it and sell this trip to Carson as a working retreat. With her next studio date still set for late July, it seemed reasonable. Four weeks of songwriting, mixed with swimming and walks in the woods, sounded like a workable compromise.

She heard Leah's voice in her head. *It's like you've forgotten he works for you.* It was true and high time Jojo stopped worrying about keeping Carson happy.

After a few deep breaths, her mind wandered again, this time to the video they'd played on the show that morning. Matt Heston had been her favorite singer-songwriter from about the time she was fifteen until he suddenly quit his band three years later. In hindsight, it was odd she'd been so into him since he was more alternative rock, and over the years she had moved toward hip hop and pop. But back then, she was still figuring out her style, and something she absolutely worshipped were his lyrics. She could sit and read a Matt Heston song like other people read poetry.

"Sweet Side" had been on his second album and she had listened to it for hours at a time, dissecting the words and chord progressions. Of course, she'd also learned to play every one of his songs and sang them so often that occasionally her parents had to declare a Matt-free evening for the sanity of the family.

Her thoughts returned to the present and the need to pack so she could have everything downstairs by seven fifteen in the morning. There was no need to take more than a few bags and a couple of guitars. One was a beater she didn't mind taking outdoors, and the other was her cherished Sam Rubio. Sam's guitars were legendary, and he'd made this one with her in mind.

A rental car would be dropped off behind the building by seven thirty and she'd leave immediately. She had the address for the cabin and would program it into the car's GPS, not her phone, which was still turned off. She'd tell Carson where she was when—and if—she was ready.

It was all choreographed like a scene from a spy novel, but it would be worth it if, by tomorrow afternoon, she was sitting on a dock and dipping her toes into a cool lake.

CHAPTER 4

MATT

MATT HEARD GRACIE coming down the stairs and closed his laptop. "I thought you'd be asleep by now."

In the recent warm weather, she'd switched from her flannel pajama bottoms to sleep shorts, which were looking *too* short. With camp starting in a few days, he wondered about some of her other summer clothes.

She sat beside him on the couch. "I could hear you playing that interview."

"Sorry, I should have used headphones." He drummed his fingers on the laptop. He'd looked half crazed in the video and was still beating himself up over it.

"I watched it, too," Gracie said. "And everybody around here knows you're not like that. You're a perfectly normal dad."

"That's high praise. Thanks." Maybe she was right. Who cared what the rest of the world thought? Westbury was his world, and most of the townspeople shared his disdain for the press. They would understand.

"To set the record straight," he said, "I wasn't obsessing over just one video all evening. I thought in fairness, I should check out some of Jojo's stuff. Did you know if you google her, you get over three hundred million results?"

"Wow, Dad. I must have been upstairs a long time."

"Seriously, I probably watched thirty videos and I've barely scratched the surface."

"You know that thing I said about you being a normal dad?"

"Uh-huh."

"Well, not so much now."

He caught her drift. This probably wasn't something he'd mention to the guys at the lumberyard. "I'm not exactly Jojo's typical fan, am I?"

"If you're going to watch her videos, you need to be accompanied by a minor."

"Very cute." Normally, he might have sent her back to bed by now, but school was out and she didn't need to be up early for anything. Plus, he enjoyed the company. "Do you want to see my favorite?" he said.

"You already have a favorite?"

He opened the computer and went to a YouTube video entitled "Road Weary Blues." It was a live video shot in Phoenix on Jojo's second world tour.

"Oh, I've seen this one. This song is totally you, Dad."

Surprisingly it was. Most of Jojo's music was too pop-y for his taste, but this one was different. It was a song about being on the road in the vein of Bob Seger's "Turn the Page." Every singer-songwriter has written at least one road song, after spending a few hundred hours on a bus with unwashed band members and too little sleep. The lyrics were somber and laced with a touch of loneliness.

As a performer, this was the type of song Matt would have put in the setlist right after something high energy. It was such a powerful feeling to lift an audience up to where they were soaring, and then, with the next song, bring them in for the huddle.

At the end of Jojo's video, Gracie snatched the computer from his lap. "Okay. My turn."

While she looked up one of her favorites, the melody of "Road Weary Blues" continued to haunt him with memories of his own touring days and the close-knit fellowship with the band and crew. He had so many vivid memories, but they faded as the next video played.

Gracie's favorite, or more likely her favorite of the moment, featured a dozen incredibly fit dancers moving to the song "Hands Off My Booty." After thirty seconds and enough hip thrusting to permanently damage his eyeballs, Matt reached over and snapped the lid down.

"Jeez! What's that rated?" Then he saw her grin. "So, you think that's funny? Well, the joke's on you, missy. No more YouTube until you're twenty-one."

"*Whatever*. I'm just impressed you lasted thirty seconds."

Did all dads go through this when their daughters got to a certain age? "Honey, is that really what dancing has become?"

"I haven't even been to my first dance yet. Ask me in a year or two."

She laid her head on his shoulder. How quickly she could switch from the older side of twelve to the younger side.

"I also watched Jojo's 'Sweet Side' video," he said. "It's pretty good."

"Pretty good?"

"Okay, it's kind of amazing. It's like watching a mini epic film. She got some famous Italian movie director to do it. I can't believe the money those people throw around."

"I know it's your song and all," Gracie said sleepily, "but I like the way she sings it."

"Well," he said, "after about the twentieth time, it started to grow on me."

"Good thing you don't obsess about stuff, Dad." Apparently, she could be sleepy *and* sarcastic.

"Yeah. Good thing." And then he added softly, "We should get you upstairs."

"Okay."

She drowsily led the way, and he followed. After she got into bed, he drew the covers up and turned out the lights. She was fading, and he wasn't sure she was still listening, but he said it anyway, "Your old man learned something today."

"What?" she mumbled.

"I learned I really miss my friend Thad."

"He seems nice."

"Yup. He really took me under his wing back then."

She was already half asleep, and he wondered how much she would remember in the morning. The light from the hallway was spilling halfway into the room, and her face was mostly in shadow.

"Goodnight," he whispered, and closed the door.

CHAPTER 5

JOJO

Jojo was on I-87, an hour north of the city, and her spirits were already lighter. She had escaped. She had actually done it. She figured she'd put enough distance between Carson and herself that it was safe to turn her phone back on. Whatever he might come up with to fill her schedule today or tomorrow no longer mattered, because she had forward momentum on her side.

Almost immediately it rang, and of course, it was him. Was it psychic ability or was the man hard-wired into her devices?

"Babe. What the hell? I've left you a zillion messages."

"Sorry." Why did she say that when she wasn't? "I've had my phone off."

"No kidding. Anyway, I'm sending you a link."

"I'm in the middle of something," she said. "I'll watch it later."

"You'll want to see this right now. We've got to put a strategy together."

Forget it! she thought but was already pulling over to the shoulder. Cars were whizzing by, and she wasn't even sure this was legal. She saw the link he'd sent and clicked.

She recognized Matt Heston right away. His face had filled out a bit, but if a man could improve with age, he definitely had.

"Are you watching?" Carson said.

"Yes. Just give me a sec." She was trying to keep the irritation out of her voice.

There was a reporter trying to interview Matt about "Sweet Side," though it was clear he didn't want the attention. When he finally faced the camera, he made it sound as if Jojo had stolen the song. *What the hell.* It was in the ASCAP library where anybody could purchase the rights, but some of her fans wouldn't know that. He was being totally unfair and flat-out wrong, but the part of his rant that hurt the most was when he accused her of cheapening a personal song with an overproduced arrangement. How could a man spew so much venom in one brief video clip?

"Okay," she said to Carson, no longer as light-hearted as she'd felt only minutes earlier.

"Talk about ungrateful. With all the royalties he'll be raking in, he should be thanking you."

She scrolled through the comments, only half listening.

"People are taking sides," he said. "Like it's some kind of singing contest. I told you this was a bad idea."

Really? When "Sweet Side" debuted at twenty-four, he'd thought it was brilliant.

Jojo breathed out slowly. She worked hard to stay controversy-free and mostly had succeeded. But now this—of all things. In part, she'd felt like recording Matt's song was a way to pay homage to his legacy and this was the thanks she got.

"The label wants to know how we're going to respond," he said. "The single's still got momentum, but this could kill it in a heartbeat."

"Oh, come on. You know as well as I do that if anything this will help." She didn't mean it to sound like spin, but Matt's comments were likely to unify a large part of her fan base. Most were passionate about defending her.

But the criticism from Matt that bothered her most had nothing to do with musical rights. *Overproduced* was a dreaded word in the business and the critics might echo it. Another reason the word bothered her was because he might be right. Before they went into the studio, she had vacillated between doing a lighter version, closer to his original, or going big. The latter would allow her to put her own stamp on it. In the end she went big, and the decision was entirely her own. Commercially, it appeared she'd made the right choice, but it hurt that Matt Heston disagreed.

"He hates it," she said. "From the sound of it, he even hates me."

"What?"

"Matt hates the recording. He hates the arrangement. He hates everything about it."

"Who cares? You can't seriously put any stock in this clown's opinion? He's been living in a hut in the woods for ten years, listening to the birds chirp. He's not exactly in touch with today's sound."

He's not a clown, she muttered under her breath. "But you said the guys at the label are worried."

Carson didn't respond for a moment. He often contradicted himself and then glossed over it. A semitruck sped past and her car rocked in its wake.

"Where are you?" he asked. "My phone can't locate you. We have to put together a messaging strategy and run it by the label before we start tweeting."

Did she have to confront this issue right now as well? "I'll be out for a while."

"Okay, so where should we meet up?"

She was already feeling like crap, so she decided to go all-in. "Carson, I'm not in the city."

"Then where the hell are you?"

"Upstate. I just need to get away and chill for a while." Then she remembered her plan. "It's basically a song-writing retreat."

"Without me?"

That was a laugh—the idea of chilling with Carson.

"Being on my own is the way I recharge. Have you really not noticed that about me?" She could picture him now, scrolling through messages and multitasking, even as the discussion turned serious. "I need this time for me, and I need time to write. I've only got nine partially written songs for the next album."

By making this about the album, she hoped he would take it less personally. She had no desire to crush his ego. She needed him firing on all cylinders, especially now that he had to deal with the fallout from this Matt Heston interview.

"The break will give us time to do what we each do best," she said. "For you to focus on the business side while I focus on the creative side."

"So where are you headed? I can't believe you set this up on your own. I didn't even think you had a credit card."

Did he realize how insulting he was? Of course she had a credit card, but she'd intentionally left it at home. It was too easy for him to track her charges, so this would be a cash-only trip. The very fact she had to cover her tracks like this was another in a long list of annoyances.

"I figure I'll drift a bit," she said, determined to reveal nothing. "I'm looking for inspiration—I'll see the sights, stay in some cheap motels, and remember what it's like to be normal again."

"Did you say you've only got nine partially written songs? You realize we're in the studio in three weeks."

"Four! I'll be back in four weeks." She was overheating. "And if you try moving up the schedule, I swear to God . . ."

Deep breath. Just cool down and don't make any threats you can't take back.

"I'll be back in four weeks," she repeated, this time more calmly.

"Are you forgetting Montreal?" he said.

Damn, for a moment she had briefly forgotten the one unbreakable interruption he'd shoehorned into her supposed vacation. "I'll be there for Montreal—it's just one weekend. But from now on, I want you to run the schedule by me before making commitments. I mean it—every single show. I get final say." She'd said it before, but this time she meant it.

"Okay, okay! I get it." Perhaps he sensed how close she was to hanging up. "So, here's an option you might not have considered. How about you and me on a sandy beach—a semi-private island? Just the two of us."

Was nothing getting through to him?

She muted her phone and—just as another truck sped past and shook the car—screamed at the top of her lungs. She couldn't do this anymore. It was time to stop being a coward and be honest with him as well as herself. She took her phone off mute.

"Carson, I hate doing this over the phone. I should have done it yesterday when we were together. I'm so sorry I didn't." She was speaking too fast and slowed down. "I'm just going to say it. I think we've grown in different directions. Neither of us is the same person we were when we met."

"What are you talking about?"

"I want to break up—not professionally, of course, just this personal thing we have on the side. I'm not even sure what to call it. Everything else will stay the same. You'll still manage everything. When it comes to business, you're indispensable."

For a while, there was only the sound of the traffic.

"Is there someone else? Is that why you're leaving the city? Is he with you?"

As if she had time for another man. "I'm all alone."

"Maybe you're overtired?" He was making it worse. "You haven't been yourself lately. As your manager, I'm thinking you shouldn't be alone right now."

Her voice turned icy. "Carson, are you suggesting I'm ending our relationship because I'm having some kind of breakdown?"

"No, of course not. But you haven't been sleeping well lately."

"That's only when I'm with you."

"But—"

"I know this is hitting you hard," she said. "So before either of us says something we regret, I'm just going to hang up. We'll talk again in a few days. I'm truly sorry, and I hope you're okay."

She hung up and turned off her phone again before he could call back.

Chapter 6

Matt

THE SMELL of bacon lured Matt downstairs to the kitchen, where he found Gracie at the stove. This was hardly the norm, not that he was going to complain.

"One egg or two?" she asked.

"Two, please." There was coffee in the pot, and he got a mug from the cupboard. "I'm impressed. Maybe I'll make a habit of being the last one down."

"Don't get too used to it," she said. "I'm just trying to get you in a good mood before you look outside."

"Too late. I saw them from upstairs."

There were two vans parked at the edge of the road. Even at the height of his career, this attention never made any sense. How was it that Matt Heston hurling insults into a camera trumped all the *real* news going on in the world? Sometimes he felt like going out on the porch and yelling, "Get some perspective!"

"We're almost out of cream," Gracie said. "Could you put it on the list?"

Matt made a note on the small pad stuck to the side of the refrigerator. He was all too happy to change the subject. "Are you going to be riding your bike to camp this year?"

"Unless it's raining."

"Sounds good," he said. "What about your guitar?"

"I'm thinking of keeping the old one at camp. It's a pain taking it back and forth."

"What about on talent night?"

"Then I'll use Mom's."

This was another reminder of how quickly Gracie was growing. Once she realized her left hand was large enough to wrap around the neck of Natalie's guitar, it became her favorite. Not only did it connect her to her mom, but it also had a nice action. Matt appreciated how Gracie was protective of it and cautious about where she took it, often defaulting to her old 3/4 guitar at camp or when meeting up with friends to play.

She slid eggs and bacon onto his plate and then onto her own. "Can you talk to Chief Harper again? I thought the news people weren't supposed to come into the yard."

"I'll call him, and maybe he'll come by and remind them."

"One guy even went into the woods behind the shop," she said.

"It's all that coffee they stand around drinking."

Gracie screwed up her face. "That's disgusting. I picked those flowers back there." She grabbed the vase sitting between them and threw the flowers into the compost bin.

She seemed more bothered than usual, and Matt realized this level of attention was new for her. She was more accustomed to the occasional lone reporter who hung out by the road with a telephoto lens or the creepier type who knocked on the door, asking to use the phone because his or her car had broken down. It had been years since an actual news crew had shown up and he doubted Gracie remembered those days.

"Honey, don't let this get to you. As soon as 'Sweet Side' tops out, they'll lose interest and disappear."

She looked at him as if he'd said something nonsensical. "*I'm fine. I'm just afraid you'll get into another argument.*"

"Oh." A pang of guilt hit him squarely in the gut. She wasn't worried about herself; she was worried about him. But what should he have expected after yesterday's little exhibition? "What if I promise to be on my best behavior?"

She looked skeptical.

"I can be a very congenial guy . . . when I put my mind to it."

Her expression didn't budge, and he attempted to lighten the moment by acting wounded.

"I'm crushed," he said. "I'll have you know, back in the day, I was known as *Mellow Matt.*"

She practically choked on a bite of eggs, but at least he glimpsed a smile before she covered it with her napkin. Then, as if the conversation was over, she turned her attention to her phone and started scrolling. Normally, he would have told her to finish eating first, but he was still bothered by what she'd said.

Perhaps he was going about this all wrong. Watching his angry face on yesterday's news clip had made him wonder if that's why the press kept coming back. If he was friendlier, they might consider him less interesting.

"Did you know you're trending on Twitter?" she said, interrupting his thoughts. The blank look on his face must have been answer enough. "There's a survey where people can vote on whether they prefer your version of 'Sweet Side' or Jojo's."

How did people find the time? he wondered. "I'm guessing I'm not doing so well."

"'Fraid not. Jojo's ahead by a lot. But it's not really fair. I doubt most of your fans even know how to use Twitter."

"Ha, ha. Very funny. But can we change the subject?"

"Gladly."

That was too easy, he thought, and sure enough, she pertly folded her arms as if she were up to something. He suspected this was her idea of looking adult and he had to suppress a chuckle.

She picked up an envelope that had been lying in front of her. "I want to know about this check that came in the mail yesterday."

He considered this less funny. "So now you're opening my mail?"

"Isn't it my mail, too?"

"When was the last time you received a letter?" he asked. "And I know for certain the bills aren't addressed to you."

"It's the royalty check, isn't it? And it's a lot bigger than usual."

"So, you have been opening my mail." He reached for the envelope and pulled out the contents. ASCAP statements came quarterly, and this one was definitely the best he'd seen in a while. "Seriously, honey, if it's addressed to me, you shouldn't open it any more than I should open yours."

"But it's part of my education. If I'm going to be a professional musician, I need to know how ASCAP works."

Unfortunately, she was serious. "Wouldn't you rather talk about being a lawyer or engineer? Or how about a veterinarian? They're pretty cool."

"Daaaddd . . ."

He scratched his head. How could he say no to that face? "You already know the basics," he said. "What else do you want to know?"

"Is this check bigger because of 'Sweet Side?'"

"According to Uncle Thad, it's a percentage of album sales before it was released as a single." She knit her brow and he guessed he wasn't explaining it very well. "You know, I bet Uncle Thad would love answering your questions and he's really the expert."

Not that Matt was trying to get out of the discussion, but this was potentially a nice way for Gracie and Thad to connect.

It looked like the wheels were still turning in Gracie's head. "So, now that it's a single, will the next check be even higher?"

"Probably, though it's never wise to bank on it."

"Then can we get a horse?"

"A *horse*? No, we're not getting a horse. Mrs. Mayer lets you ride at her place whenever you want."

"If I muck out the stables."

"And if you get a horse, you don't think it'll need mucking? Besides, any extra money goes straight into your college fund." Which Matt had every intention of starting one of these days.

Gracie wrinkled her brow. "But I'm not going to college. I'm going to be a singer like you and Jojo."

"Hey, there's no sentence that includes *me and Jojo*, and there's no universe in which you don't go to college."

"Dad"—she paused a moment—"I know you're not a mean person."

His head was spinning. "Are we still talking about horses?"

"No, we're back to talking about Jojo."

It was much too early for his brain to be working this hard. He decided he needed more coffee.

"Don't you think you should apologize?"

"To Jojo? For what?"

"For totally dissing her song."

"Jojo's a huge star, much bigger than I ever was. She's got people patting her on the back all day and telling her how amazing she is. And if she even heard what I said, which I doubt, I'm sure she couldn't care less what I think."

Gracie didn't look convinced, but instead of arguing the point, she got up and carried her dishes to the sink. It appeared she was letting it go for now, but he sensed the issue wasn't dead.

Chapter 7

Jojo

About twenty minutes over the Vermont line, Jojo entered Westbury Village and the state route she was on abruptly turned into Main Street. It was only two blocks long, with a few side streets. The car's GPS told her the lake and cabin were a couple miles east of town. It was tempting to go straight there, but she was hungry and there'd be no food. She turned around in the feed store parking lot and went back to the only grocery she'd seen.

Before getting out of the car, she looked in the mirror and did a mental checklist. Natural eyebrows: check. Clear lip gloss and just a trace of blush: check. Her natural brown curls softly framing her face: check. Her eyes lingered on the mirror, bemused by the complete transformation. The hair was undoubtedly the biggest change since most of her wigs were straight and swept up or pulled back from her face.

Finally, she inspected her nails. They were her own, though she had brushed on a clear coat that morning. Heck, a girl had to live a little. This was vacation, not a walkabout.

One last thing. Before getting out of the car, she put on her sunglasses, but they practically screamed, *Hey! Look at me!* She took them back off and put them in the glove box.

She was surprisingly nervous, perhaps because there would be no do-overs or second chances. *Get a grip*, she told herself. If she could pull this off in New York, it should be a breeze in Westbury, where absolutely no one expected to see her.

As she headed into the store, she grabbed a cart. If people noticed her at all, she hoped she looked like another one of the summer people in her olive skinny capris and a white tank top.

At the deli, she ordered a sandwich for lunch and picked up a box of instant mac and cheese for dinner. She'd get back on her usual regimen tomorrow, but today she was celebrating. She picked up some fruit and, figuring there was probably a coffee maker at the cabin, chose a bag of French roast.

When she got to the dairy section, she picked up eggs, cheese, and yogurt and then remembered cream for the coffee. A young girl in denim shorts and a yellow T-shirt reached into the cooler first and pulled out a pint. Their eyes met briefly, and the girl said, "Cool."

Oh, come on! Jojo thought. But then the girl touched the silver guitar pick hanging from a thin chain around her neck. Instinctively, Jojo touched her own pendant and began to relax.

It was the universal symbol among Jojo fans—her signature piece of jewelry—and young girls around the world had adopted it as a way of spotting one another. She shouldn't have put it on that morning, but it was a habit.

"Favorite song?" the girl asked.

A voice inside Jojo warned her to be friendly but keep it brief.

"Well," she began, thinking it over, "I've been in the car all morning and a few minutes ago, I started singing 'Road Weary Blues.'"

The girl's eyes got wide. "OMG! I can't believe you just said that. Last night my dad and I watched a video of Jojo singing that exact song in Phoenix on the second world tour."

Jeez, maybe she needed to be more worried about being recognized in Westbury. "Your *dad's* into Jojo?"

"Well, not exactly. I think he only likes certain songs. I played him the video to 'Hands Off My Booty' and he shut it down." She snapped her fingers.

"Yeah, that's not a big hit with dads," Jojo chuckled.

"The message is actually really positive," the girl said. "But I don't think he was listening to the words."

Talking to this young fan was the most fun she'd had all day, but it was probably time to move along.

"Aren't you going to ask me my favorite song?" the girl said.

Oh yeah. Fan etiquette kind of demanded it.

"Absolutely, what's yours?"

"Well, I know all the buzz right now is on 'Sweet Side' and it's a cool song and all. But lately I've been into 'Baby Don't Bench Me.' And I know Jojo was really singing about this guy who suddenly drops this girl, like for no reason. But it also made me think about the way friends treat each other. Friends totally do that sometimes. Do you know what I mean?"

Jojo nodded. "It's really awesome how you can listen to a song and find your own personal meaning in it. I think that's why Jojo never tries to explain her lyrics."

"I've totally noticed," the girl said. "Wow, I can't believe I just came in for cream and we had this amazing conversation. You're really cool. I wish we could talk more, but I've got to go. Bye!"

"Bye," Jojo said.

It was over and done so quickly, but halfway down the aisle, the girl stopped and looked back. "I'm gonna write a song about this." And with those parting words, she lifted the cream high above her head like a fist pump, spun around, and marched away.

CHAPTER 8

IDA

IDA BURROUGHS CAME out of the restroom at the grocery store. She didn't like leaving her post at Matt's place, but there was no way she was peeing in the bushes like the guys. If she missed out on some big scoop, so be it.

But as long as she was here, she might as well grab some lunch at the deli counter. It had been an incredibly slow day, and she was beginning to wonder if coming to West Podunk, Vermont was a waste of time. But this was the nature of the game—hours of waiting for a five-second photo op that would pay the bills for the next month. Few had the patience for it; or maybe the better word was stubbornness. But an exclusive photo with the right story was like pure gold. She was hoping for a fresh angle—something different from the played-out *Matt Heston the Hermit* story. Another grainy shot of Matt walking from his shop to his house was a total snooze.

She ordered a pastrami on rye, knowing full well it would come up short of her usual New York deli. And as she waited, she glanced around at the shoppers. *I'll bet half these people know Matt,* she thought—maybe grew up with him or even dated him in high school. Now *that* might be a good angle.

She watched a middle-aged man in Carhartts throw a package of beef jerky in his cart. Definitely a local.

A young couple walked by, looking like they were dressed for tennis at their Greenwich country club. Definitely not local.

It was harder to figure out the girl and the young woman having an animated conversation by the dairy cooler. Both were pretty. The older one had on capris pants that looked too tailored to be off the department store shelf, so probably not local.

After getting her sandwich and picking up a diet soda from the cooler, Ida got in line at the checkout. Only one register was open, and it had to be the lunch crowd because several guys in work clothes were in line with sandwiches, chips, and even more beef jerky. What was with all the jerky?

She noticed the young girl from the dairy aisle was just ahead of her, apparently on her own. Might as well start with her.

"School out yet around here?"

The girl looked at her, perhaps wondering if they knew each other. "We got out last week."

"I have a daughter about your age," Ida lied. Subtext: *I'm a mom, so it's okay to talk to me.* And it worked.

"What's her name?"

"Beth, but we're just up for the summer. I'm sure you don't know her. Anyway, I thought she'd be thrilled hanging out at the lake, but she's already bored. What would you suggest for stuff to do around here?"

"Does she like horseback riding? Because Mrs. Mayer gives lessons."

Ida nodded as though her fictional daughter might enjoy that.

"And there's Camp Maycroft. It's a day camp. This will be my seventh summer there."

"Do they have horseback riding, too?"

"Yeah, it's a big deal there. They have all the other normal camp stuff, too. And every other Wednesday, we have a talent show. That's my favorite part."

They were edging toward the checkout. This didn't seem to be going anywhere, but over the years, Ida had learned the power of persistence.

"What's the talent show like?"

"The kids do all sorts of acts like music, skits, magic." The girl seemed totally into her camp. "This year I got permission to start a dance group and I usually play guitar and sing, too. That's kind of my thing."

Ida kept nodding, pretending to be interested. They were at the front of the line now and the girl turned to the cashier, who was a few years older. "Hi, Tina."

"Hey, Gracie. Pretty crazy at your house today. How'd you get past the reporters?"

Ida's radar turned up a few notches.

"Out the back and around behind Mrs. Taylor's house."

"Smart," Tina said. "That's $2.79."

Gracie Heston, Ida thought. What were the odds? But in a town this size, maybe they were pretty good. She couldn't recall anyone doing a story on the girl. In fact, not much was known about her.

Gracie paid and put a pint of cream in her bag.

"Have you ever been on the news?" Tina asked.

"Are you kidding? Dad won't even let me sit on the porch when they're in the yard."

"What a drag," Tina said, handing back some change.

As Gracie was leaving, she turned back to Ida. "Your daughter should definitely check out Maycroft. Bye."

After Ida paid for her own items, she double-timed it into the parking lot and looked around for Gracie. "Hey, excuse me." The kid was putting her earbuds in and didn't hear until Ida almost caught up with her. "Sorry to bother you again. Does that camp of yours run all summer?"

"Sure," Gracie said. "There's a new session every two weeks. It's down by the lake."

"I know it's probably too late for this session," Ida said, weaving her story on the fly, "but I was thinking of taking my daughter to see it. In fact, Beth's also into music, so maybe she'd enjoy your talent show."

Gracie lit up. "She should totally do that. The first one's in a couple weeks. You should call the camp and get a tour and a schedule and everything."

This was one helpful kid.

"Can the public come to the talent show?"

Gracie shrugged. "Well, I know families come—my dad'll be there. And I'll bet you can get a pass if your daughter's thinking of being a camper."

Jackpot, Ida thought. This was like going to Vegas and winning on the first pull.

"I've got to get home," Gracie said. "Hope to see you at talent night."

Ida had no intention of going back to Matt's house now. She couldn't risk Gracie seeing her among the reporters. Anyway, she'd found her angle.

CHAPTER 9

JOJO

As Jojo pulled out of the parking lot, she spotted her young friend from the dairy section. Her earbuds were in, her head was bobbing, and her shopping bag was swinging. She had an irresistible spirit, and it felt like a sign that Jojo had come to the right place.

Her attention was drawn to a police car, its lights flashing, about a hundred yards ahead. It was parked on the side of the road with several other vehicles, mostly vans. No one was stopping traffic and there was no sign of an accident. She slowed and saw people standing about but nothing to explain what they were doing.

As Jojo continued along Lake Road, she caught glimpses of water through the trees. According to the GPS, she was close, and as she rounded a corner, there was the painted sign at the end of a driveway that read SKOBY. How nice to have the freedom to put out a sign without concern for paparazzi or overzealous fans. Sometimes she envied Leah for having just the right amount of fame. Loads of people loved and respected Leah's work, but she didn't have to hide.

The long gravel driveway led to a modest two-story cabin on a fieldstone foundation. It was clad in gray shakes and had a porch running around two sides. The building was tucked among mature hemlocks, and through the foliage, she could see the lake shimmering. Leading down to the water were stone steps descending to a boathouse and dock. Somehow, she had pictured an open vista, but this was even better—more intimate and, best of all, more private.

In three trips, she carried everything in from the car, certain this was the lightest she'd traveled in recent years.

The living room and kitchen were one big space, and upstairs there were three bedrooms. Leah had told her to choose whichever she wanted, so she set her bags in the corner room facing the lake and driveway. Returning to the kitchen, she unpacked the groceries and then considered her options. She could eat lunch on the porch or take a walk around the property. It was rare she didn't have to worry about a schedule or navigating a sea of fans. If she wanted to be truly decadent, she could take a nap. It had been a long drive, and the green, overstuffed couch was inviting. She lay down, only intending to rest for a few minutes, but soon was fast asleep.

———

When Jojo awoke, the sun was low in the sky and the interior of the cabin was dim. For a moment, she felt disoriented and flicked on a lamp. How was it possible she'd slept six hours? And was the gnawing sensation in her stomach from hunger or stress?

Having found the courage to break up with Carson, she'd hoped for a sense of relief but now was worried about the backlash. Despite his personal failings, at least he knew his way around contracts and tour logistics and personnel. He'd be an idiot to quit, but she'd wounded his pride, and he might do it just to spite her. Then she'd have to get back to the city and scramble to find someone who could run the business. The learning curve would be immense.

Her phone sat on the coffee table, taunting her to check messages. No doubt Carson had already left a dozen or more.

Stop it! This anxiety was self-induced. Carson had no power over her unless she gave it to him. The best way to handle this was with a cooling-off period—a few days without contact. She wouldn't check messages or take his calls. He might not like it, but after all, she was on vacation.

She got up and opened some windows in the living room and kitchen to let the place breathe, then ran upstairs and did the same. The cabin had a wonderful, old-timey feel with lots of knotty pine, comfortable-looking mismatched furniture, and a well-worn braided rug in the main room. There was a window seat along one wall and the bookshelves were chock full of light summer reading.

Jojo walked outside and down to the dock for her first sweeping view of the lake. The surface was calm and mirrored the pinkish hues of the setting sun. Along the shoreline were cabins peeking through the foliage. Directly opposite were some larger buildings that might be part of a resort or summer camp, but there was no sign of activity.

According to Leah and Tom, there wasn't much boat traffic before July 4th, when most of the city people started arriving. At the moment, it was blissfully quiet—a couple of kayakers in the distance and a man and young child fishing from a dock. This was exactly the solitude she had dreamed of.

She pulled out her phone and turned it on. As expected, there were messages from Carson, but she ignored them and called Leah.

"Hey girl," Leah said. "I was starting to worry."

"I took the longest nap of my life. Is this a good time or are you putting the boys to bed?"

"They're in the bath. Boys, say hi to Auntie Jojo."

She could hear them shouting. "Tell them I love them. By the way, can you guess where I'm standing?"

"Let's see." Leah paused, barely two seconds. "On the dock, watching the sunset."

"Oh my god. Have you got security cameras?" Jojo glanced back at the boathouse.

"No cameras—we're just psychically connected. Plus, it's where I'd be. It's a shame you can't see much of the lake from the cabin. Tom and I have talked about cutting a few trees."

"No. It's perfect the way it is."

"I'm glad you feel that way. It's my favorite place." Leah's words had a wistful sincerity, and Jojo realized she'd never seen her friend outside of her fast-paced New York habitat.

"There isn't much else to report," Jojo said. "All I've done so far is sleep and look at the view."

"That's all you're supposed to do. It's the whole point."

"There's something about being here. It feels like somebody pressed the pause button on my life."

"Perfect," Leah said. "That's what I want to hear every day."

"You sound like a therapist," Jojo said. "And I'm going to sign off because the sun just slipped behind the mountain and I'm starving."

"I've got to go, anyway. The boys are turning into prunes."

They said goodbye and Jojo took one more look around the lake. It was almost unreal to remember she'd awoken that morning in the heart of the city and now was standing in this tranquil place. The first star was hanging above the horizon and swallows were darting about, inches above the water.

As she trudged up the hill, she realized she hadn't mentioned the breakup. With the boys in the tub, it wasn't the right time, plus she still felt torn about it. On a personal level, she was relieved, but on a business level, she was more than a little anxious. She would need to vent soon, though, and that would require listening to Leah gleefully gloating about being right.

———

The next day, Jojo slept until mid-morning, which wasn't surprising after reading half the night. The culprit was a novel with a pink-and-white cover she'd found on her nightstand. She often poked fun at Leah for her addiction to chick lit, but this one had hooked Jojo within a few pages.

After breakfast, she carried a mug of coffee and her Blueridge guitar out to the porch. She hadn't made it this far in the music business by being lazy. Vacation or not, there were songs to write. She wanted at least thirteen by the time she went into the studio, and it was always wise to have a couple more in her back pocket.

During the tour, she'd reached various stages of completion on nine songs. Her keyboard player had cowritten two of them. In addition, she had a demo of a melody Peter Marsh had written for her. It had a great dance vibe but still needed lyrics.

The Adirondack chairs on the porch had big clunky arms that weren't designed with guitars in mind, so she brought out one of the kitchen chairs. Finally, she had no more excuses and got to work, starting with the Peter Marsh melody. She'd come up with a hook the night before when she read the phrase "my one and only." She switched it up to be "My One and Lonely."

After a couple of hours and a couple mugs of coffee, she needed a change of scenery and went down to the lake, carrying her guitar and notebook. There were only a few puffy clouds in the sky, and a light breeze ruffled the water. A sailboat was tacking across the widest part of the lake, and she spotted a few sun bathers on other docks. Though the trees made it difficult to see individual buildings around the lake, she counted about thirty docks.

For the next hour she continued working on the song but eventually grew tired of sitting cross-legged and lay back on the sun-warmed decking to watch the clouds sail by. She'd hoped that by getting out of New York, she'd leave most of the tension behind, but her brain was still agitated, and it wasn't just from the breakup.

She picked up her phone and checked Twitter. *Big mistake.*

Matt's comments had ignited a firestorm and people were taking sides. She hated this kind of drama.

Her phone rang—it was Leah. "How's the Vermont weather?"

"Perfect. Now if only I could say the same for my state of mind."

"Let me guess," Leah said. "You've been talking to Carson?"

"Not today." She took a deep breath and dropped the big news. "We broke up."

"Say what?!"

If only she could see her friend's face.

"This is huge! How do you feel?"

"I'm still trying to figure that out, but my biggest fear is he might quit?"

"Are you kidding? His entire ego is tied to your success. If he wasn't your manager, he'd be nothing. A big zero."

That seemed harsh, and not exactly reassuring. "I can't run everything without him."

"So what if he quits? You hire a new manager. Personally, I'd recommend a woman—less chance of you sleeping together."

That advice would have been useful a few years back. "Go ahead. Make jokes, but Carson is hardwired to win at any cost."

"And you're not?!" Leah's tone was somewhere between incredulous and annoyed. "You waged a one-woman war to get 'Sweet Side' on the album. You're as hardwired to win as anybody I know. The difference is, you're not a bully about it."

Jojo let that sink in. "This is why I need you in my corner."

"Then believe it," Leah said. "Oh, before I forget, today's the solstice, so you're going to get some visitors tonight."

It was a relief to change the subject. "What visitors?"

"There's a day camp across the lake called Maycroft. I teach some workshops there every summer. It's traditional on solstice night for a bunch of kids and alumni to go around the lake in canoes, kayaks, rowboats, whatever, and serenade people at their docks."

"So, you want me to hide?"

"No need. It'll be dark by the time they reach your side of the lake, and they don't come that close. Nobody will recognize you and it's too special to miss. I'm actually jealous I can't be there."

Jojo's interest was piqued. Besides, a group of singers under the cover of night sounded less risky than her trip to the store, and that had gone well.

"Okay, I'm game."

"They'll only stop if you put a light at the end of the dock. There's a kerosene lantern around somewhere—either in the boathouse or maybe on the porch. Light it just before sunset."

Kerosene lantern? What century had she traveled back to? "I guess I can figure it out."

"Google it. You'll thank me."

After their goodbyes, Jojo lay down again, feeling the full warmth of the sun on her face. It was blissful. She needed this even more than she'd realized.

CHAPTER 10

MATT

MATT SAT by the campfire and held a stick with a couple of marshmallows over the flame. On one side of him was a heated discussion about the proposed renovation of the town offices and on the other side, a group of parents were speculating about Maycroft's future. Mr. and Mrs. Yates had operated the camp for decades but were close to retirement and no one was in line to succeed them. Like Matt, half the adults in town had attended the camp as kids. It would be a sad loss if it closed and the land went to developers.

There'd been a brief time in his life when he had money and could step up and help when a worthy cause presented itself. The volunteer fire department still drove a pumper truck that bore his name and he'd started a fund to help kids in the school band rent instruments. But his days of charitable giving were long past.

When Natalie's cancer got bad, she begged him to finish out the tour. Even when she was very sick, she'd worried over their finances. She was smart and always thinking ahead, especially if she wouldn't be there to help.

He could have flown home between concert dates for a day or two at a time. That's what everyone advised, but he believed in his heart he should be with her every day, even though both sets of parents were helping. So, when he quit and came home for good, she'd been angry, and in the end she'd been right. Because she lived long enough to find out he was being sued by the last eleven venues on the tour. Insurance paid some of their losses, but he covered the rest out of his own pocket—a combination of money he had in the bank and payments from future royalties. It had taken five years to settle the debts and by then, the royalty checks had shrunk dramatically.

"Let's finish up those marshmallows," Mr. Yates called. "The sun sets in ten minutes."

Matt looked around the beach and spotted Gracie with some friends. She was on a mission tonight to recruit kids for the dance club. Mrs. Yates promised rehearsal space as long as the club had at least five members.

Adults and kids were heading toward the water's edge, where about thirty kayaks and canoes were lined up. He didn't relish the next few minutes, which were likely to get dicey. Gracie had reached an age where she preferred hanging with her friends, which meant there'd be an open seat in his canoe and Sue Patterson had hinted about filling it. She and her husband were recently separated, and Matt had no desire to step into that hornet's nest.

Right then, Gracie peeled off from her group and came over. "You ready?"

"You mean we're sticking together?" He didn't bother to hide his pleasure.

"*Duh.* It's tradition. Besides, I like how you do most of the work."

The evening was looking up. "I always suspected you were just dipping your paddle."

"Don't worry—I've got bigger muscles this year." She flexed both arms, then lowered her voice. "I want to stick with you. Half these people can't sing."

He laughed because it was true. Solstice was big on community spirit, but less so on talent.

As they walked to the canoe, Matt could see people around the lake gathering in small groups at the end of their docks. It was common practice for some of the lake people to invite families from town and make a party of it. During the first week of summer, a lot of the cabins were still empty, but it looked like they'd be singing at about fifteen docks, meaning they'd cycle through their favorite camp songs a couple of times.

Directly across from Maycroft, a woman was lighting her lantern. Even at a distance and in the fading light, she looked fairly young and appeared to be alone.

"Dad, you okay?" Gracie was holding out a paddle for him. "What are you looking at?"

He picked up the stern and slid the canoe into the shallow water. "Just counting the docks with lights."

She looked across the lake. "Do you know her? Hey, maybe she'll play along when we sing."

"What do you mean?" He looked again and saw the woman had picked up a guitar. If he wasn't intrigued before, he was now. He held the gunwales steady while Gracie climbed into the bow, an odd smirk on her face. "What?" he asked.

"Oh, nothing. You just seem distracted."

It wasn't worth rising to the bait. As soon as Gracie was seated, he got in and used his paddle to push off. All along the beach, boats were launching. It was tradition to head west first and go counterclockwise around the shoreline. The weather was perfect—warm, with only a slight breeze. He felt lucky to be here with his daughter and neighbors. It was one of those small-town moments he appreciated more with time.

CHAPTER 11

JOJO

JOJO WATCHED as the flotilla left the camp and headed along the shoreline. At the pace they were moving, it would be a while before they reached her. As an outsider, this felt a bit like eavesdropping. She was envious of these people, bound by friendship and tradition. The closest she came to that feeling of community nowadays was the camaraderie with her band and crew.

Even though the first full day of her vacation had been pleasant and productive, there was a touch of melancholy at the edges, and she wasn't sure why. It might have been caused by any number of things—her life was in flux; her friends were far away; and the future held so much uncertainty. Feeling wistful, she dragged her guitar pick across the strings and played a few bars of Otis Redding's "Sittin' On the Dock of the Bay."

She knew a lot of the old standards from her years teaching and "Dock of the Bay" was one of those songs every guitar player learned at some point. It was one of Jojo's dreams to write at least one song in her lifetime that people would still be singing in fifty years.

As the evening grew darker, she let the guitar sit quietly in her lap. A crescent-shaped moon looked down on the lake and a light breeze carried a melody from the approaching boats. She could make out most of the words—something about friendship around a campfire.

The lyrics, the communal spirit, the twinkling of lantern lights . . . She understood now why Leah was sentimental about this solstice tradition. It was the perfect way to welcome the summer.

She counted thirty boats, give or take. Some carried only one person and others had two or three with ages ranging from children to grandparents. As they paddled toward her dock, she hoped Leah hadn't left out any details. Was she supposed to offer cookies, like people did for Christmas carolers?

They started a new song shortly before reaching her and though she didn't know the words, the melody was the traditional "Danny Boy." Without thinking, she strummed a few chords until she found the right key and then switched to a finger roll, just as the boats fanned out around her. She felt more at ease now, as though she were part of the group, rather than an audience of one.

When the song ended, she thanked them, and several people wished her goodnight before setting off again. But one canoe broke from the group.

"Hi," said a young voice. "Remember me from the store?"

As the girl's face came into the lantern light, Jojo felt her spirits lift. "How could I forget someone whose father watches Jojo videos?"

"Say what?" said a surprised male voice at the back of the canoe. "That was supposed to be a secret." He sounded more amused than annoyed.

"That's my dad, and I'm Gracie."

The canoe edged closer and brought the father into the light. "I'm Matt."

Jojo felt a wave of heat. It was him. Her heart raced, and she felt flushed. Her physical response confused her. Only two days earlier he'd been disparaging her music, but the warmth in her cheeks had nothing to do with anger. She was usually cool under fire and had mixed with plenty of famous people, and not once had her body betrayed her like this.

Annoyed at the way she was acting, she pulled herself together. She could only hope the darkness had obscured her reaction.

"I'm Joelle," she said, sticking with her favorite alter ego. They might have shaken hands but for the few feet of water between the dock and the canoe.

If Matt was amused by her reaction, he didn't show it. "So, when did the two of you meet?" he asked.

"Yesterday, at the store," Gracie said. "We both had the same necklace."

Jojo touched her chest where the necklace should be but realized she'd removed it. "I took it off when I went swimming."

"Yeah, I worry about that, too," Gracie said. "Is that a Blueridge?"

Her face still flushed, Jojo glanced down at the guitar. "Impressive. You obviously know your instruments." Her eyes kept wandering to the back of the canoe. She should have acknowledged recognizing Matt the moment he drifted into the light. If she'd done it right away, it would have felt natural, but doing so now seemed awkward.

"There's one in the music room at school. But mostly I play my mom's Martin."

The child was totally at ease and her father seemed comfortable letting her do most of the talking. His face was very different when he wasn't snarling at a camera. Tonight, in the soft flicker from the lantern, he looked as though he didn't have a trouble in the world. There were still traces of his former boyish charm. His hair was a bit scruffy, but he was clean-shaven and there was the hint of a smile at the corners of his mouth.

"I don't think we've seen you here before," he said.

"It's my friends' cabin. Tom and Leah Skoby."

"You know Mrs. Skoby?!" Gracie said. "She's the most amazing choreographer ever."

Jojo laughed. "I'll pass that along to her." She noticed the rest of the singing fleet had reached the next dock, but Matt and his daughter weren't in a hurry to catch up. "Are you also a dancer, Gracie?"

"Just a beginner. I took Mrs. Skoby's workshop when she visited camp last summer."

Funny, Leah hadn't mentioned it. "So you know each other."

"It was a big class. Half the camp took it. Now I'm trying to start a dance group so we can dance more."

"That's awesome." Even as she spoke, Jojo knew she wasn't giving Gracie her full attention. Her pulse had slowed to normal, but she was still having difficulty squaring the two versions of Matt. The detail his daughter had mentioned in the store about him liking "Road Weary Blues" only added to the confusion.

"I like to dance, too," Jojo offered, trying to keep the conversation going. "But I'm not nearly as good as Mrs. Skoby." Leah would howl to hear Jojo call her *Mrs.*

"Well," Matt said, "we just wanted to thank you for accompanying us on your guitar. Nice job picking up the key like you did."

Huh. He would notice a little detail like that. And was it just her imagination or was he watching her as closely as she was watching him?

"And thanks for serenading me," she said. "Leah told me it would be a treat, and it was."

Matt was already swinging the canoe around. It would be a while before they caught up with the group.

"See ya!" Gracie said.

"Hey, Matt," Jojo called after them, "don't stay up too late watching music videos." The remark slipped out and surprised even her.

"If I do, I might have to order one of those necklaces."

"Please don't," she heard Gracie say. "That would be weird."

So Matt Heston had a sense of humor. It didn't fit his public image.

They were silhouetted by the moon as they drifted away, and she could still hear their paddles dipping in the water when Gracie's voice carried over the quiet lake.

"She's really nice, Dad. You should have talked more."

"Honey, your voice travels out here."

Jojo smiled. He seemed like a sweet dad.

As the shock wore off, she wondered how serendipitous this meeting had been. She had a sneaking suspicion Leah knew that Matt and Gracie would be among the singers.

CHAPTER 12

JOJO

JOJO GOT AN EARLIER START the second day and was writing by 9:00 a.m. Twice her phone rang, and both times her stomach twisted as Carson's name appeared. He left messages, and she could feel the gravitational pull to check them. *What if it's business? What if it's an emergency?!* But then she reminded herself, with Carson, *everything* was an emergency. It took some willpower, but she hit delete without playing the messages.

When the phone rang again near lunchtime, she almost didn't check the screen but was glad she did.

"Hey, Leah. What's up?"

"Guess who I just spoke to?"

Jojo groaned. "I'm guessing my ex. Is he pissed?"

"Not at all. The little snake—sorry, am I allowed to call him that?"

As frustrated as Jojo was with Carson, she needed to walk a fine line. "Don't forget, he's still my manager, so let's play nice."

"Well, you might feel differently when you hear what he did. He acted totally cool and pretended to shoot the breeze for all of ten seconds and then he says, 'Oh, by the way, I've got to FedEx some demos up to Jojo and she must have bad cell coverage. What's the address of your place up in Vermont?'"

Jojo's stomach tightened. "How did he figure it out?"

"Don't sweat it. I could tell the slimeball was bluffing. So I said, 'She better not be in Vermont because I've got a family of five renting the place this month.'"

"Did he fall for it?"

"He started backpedaling so fast. Something about a bad connection and he must have misheard."

Jojo breathed easier but knew Carson wouldn't give up. "Do you think he's calling everybody we know and pulling the same stunt?"

"Probably. But I think he's crossed Westbury off the list, at least for now."

"Thanks, Leah. You're the best."

But it was still unsettling on so many levels. Carson was snooping around and lying to her friends. By trying to find her, he was doing the exact opposite of what she'd requested. *Some vacation,* Jojo thought, while trying to quell this latest wave of anxiety.

Wanting to change the subject, she shifted gears. "I'm glad you told me about solstice. It was amazing."

"Ahhh . . ." Leah sighed. "I'm so jealous. Were there many boats this year?"

"Seemed like a lot. By the way, Gracie Heston is a huge fan of yours." Jojo inserted the news casually and waited for the reaction.

"Gracie Heston? Is that Matt Heston's daughter?"

"Yup. She knows you from your workshop last summer."

"Huh. I only knew the kids by their first names and the parents never came around." Either Leah was putting on a great act or she was truly surprised. "Was Matt there, too?"

"Yup."

"I don't believe it! All the coolest stuff happens to you."

"So, you didn't know they'd show up?"

"I swear, I've never met any of the singers." Leah sounded

sincere. "It must be your magnetic personality. Or maybe just because he's single and you're cute."

Jojo ignored the last comment. "Sorry for doubting you. It's just that when Matt appeared out of the dark, I was thinking, what are the odds?"

"I want details. What's he like?"

"Not at all like I expected," Jojo said. "He's easy-going and friendly, and the way he interacts with his daughter is so incredibly sweet. He was even funny." Saying it out loud was stirring up some of the same feelings again.

"I take it you didn't call him out for attacking you?"

"His daughter being there saved him from my wrath."

She heard Leah snort, apparently not buying it. Confrontation wasn't exactly Jojo's style, which at least partially explained why the situation with Carson had persisted for so long.

"Anyway, I played it safe," she said. "We were both incognito. He was just a guy named Matt, and I was just a girl named Joelle."

"Good job, you. The less drama, the better."

"But it's strange," Jojo said, "how different he was from his interview. It's almost like he's two people."

Leah cracked up. "You're one to talk, *Joelle*."

"Okay. Point taken."

"So . . ." Leah said, with an air of anticipation, "do you think you'll see him again?"

Jojo had thought about it, but right now, protecting her anonymity was a priority. "I doubt we'll cross paths again, and all I really wanted was to meet him, and now I have." That felt like the prudent response—now she just had to convince herself it was true.

"Bummer," Leah said. "Now we won't have anything juicy to talk about."

Jojo heaved a dramatic sigh. "There's always the weather."

"That's my cue to sign off," Leah said. "Talk tomorrow?"

"I'll be here."

In the afternoon, Jojo did a serious grocery run and stocked up for the next week. It made sense that the fewer times she shopped, the less chance there was of being recognized. And yet maybe she was worrying needlessly because she wasn't getting any double takes or odd looks. She was blending in just fine.

Back at the cabin, she was unloading her bags from the car when Gracie came riding up the driveway on her bike. This was their third meeting in as many days, but obviously this time wasn't a coincidence. *Don't panic,* she told herself. She'd been around the girl enough now without being recognized.

"Hi," Gracie said. She stopped a few feet away and stood there, straddling her bike. Her shorts and blue T-shirt seemed a size too small, as though she'd been going through a growth spurt. "Want some help?"

Despite the risk, it was hard to resist that precious smile. "Sure, you're just in time." As Gracie leaned her bike against a tree, Jojo noticed a guitar in a soft case strapped to her back. "Do you carry that back and forth to camp every day?"

"Nope. But since we both play and we both like the same music, I figured we could jam."

Jojo almost laughed. Oh, to be young and confident that the world simply worked like that. But maybe she'd stumbled into Vermont's own *Brigadoon,* where instruments magically appeared and people broke into song. "Are you pretty good?" she asked.

Gracie picked up two bags, and they both headed toward the cabin. "Dad says I'm good. I play acoustic, electric, and keyboard. And I'm passable on bass and drums. How about you?"

It sure didn't sound like Gracie was stopping by for lessons. "You've got me beat. I just play acoustic, electric, and keyboard."

Gracie waited by the door while Jojo fished in her pocket for her keys. "That's exactly what Jojo plays."

Damn. This kid was like a walking Jojo Wikipedia page. The thought set off an alarm. If Gracie saw her autographed Sam Rubio guitar, it would be game over and Jojo was almost certain she'd left it on the living room couch. "Can you set the bags on that chair and go back for the last two? You can also leave your guitar out here. The porch is a good place to play."

While Gracie ran back to the car, Jojo flew inside and spotted the Rubio. She put it in the case and tried to slide it under the couch, but it wouldn't fit. She ran to the pantry and put it inside just as Gracie came through the door.

"This is nice," she said, looking around.

"You can put those bags on the table." Jojo glanced around the living room and kitchen for more clues that might give her away but didn't spot any. "I'll just put away the stuff that goes in the fridge and then we can play. If you want a chair, you can take one of these out to the porch."

"Okay," Gracie said, picking up one of the kitchen chairs.

A few minutes later, they were on the porch. Jojo had her Blueridge and Gracie had a student-sized guitar she said was easier to carry on her bike.

"How do you like to do this?" Jojo asked, as they tuned up. She probably needed to have her head examined, but part of her really wanted to do this. Rarely did she get to hang out and simply be normal. Not to mention, she saw a part of herself in this child. If Gracie could play all those instruments, she had to be passionate about music, much as Jojo had been at the same age.

"Can you play both rhythm and lead?" Gracie asked.

"Sure."

"Then I'll pick the first song," Gracie said, "and play lead. You play rhythm and sing harmony. Then you'll pick the second song, and we'll switch parts."

It sounded like Gracie had done this before. The idea of alternating parts was tempting, but singing lead was way too risky.

"Would you mind if I stick with backup? I haven't been singing harmony lately, and it's a skill I don't want to lose."

"That's cool. I hardly ever sing lead with Dad because when we perform, we usually sing his music."

"So, you and your dad do concerts?" It sounded like Matt was passing the family tradition on to his daughter. How had this escaped the attention of the press?

"We only perform around here," Gracie said. "He used to be famous, and people like to hear his old songs, so we never do anything contemporary."

Jojo suppressed a smile. Personally, she still thought of Matt's music as contemporary but knew from her own fans how most kids considered any music older than three years to be *ancient*.

She was more relaxed now with the way they'd divvied up the parts, though she still would have to dial back the vocals—a little more Joelle and a lot less Jojo.

Gracie started with track one of Jojo's first album and they went from there, with Jojo choosing the second track and then Gracie the third. *Were they seriously going to run through the entire album?* Suddenly, Jojo was blanking on the fourth track, but then it came to her just as it was her turn.

There were no breaks between songs other than an occasional "nice" or "awesome." And whatever key the song had been recorded in, that's what they stuck with, note for note, like the original. This kid was amazing.

It felt like one of those games of who blinks first. Jojo should have had the advantage, but on tour they sometimes extended songs or changed things up just to keep them fresh. So, on the eighth track, she was racking her brain to recall the original key. Fortunately, her fingers remembered.

They were in the middle of the twelfth track when one of their phones rang. For a while, they ignored it, but when Jojo realized it wasn't hers, she stopped. It was both a disappointment and a relief.

"Could that be your dad?"

Gracie broke out of the zone. "What time is it?" She pulled her phone out and grimaced. "Hi, Dad. Yeah, sorry. I stopped to see Joelle and got distracted . . . Okay, I'll be right home."

"Was he worried?"

"Maybe a little." She was already putting her guitar in the case. "This was wicked cool—playing together, I mean. I've never met anybody who could do that."

"I'm sure your dad can."

"With older stuff, I guess."

Jojo couldn't recall the last time she'd jammed like this for the pure fun of it. She sensed Gracie was in a hurry and followed her down the porch steps. "I hope you're not in trouble."

"I should have checked in. But I didn't think we'd play so long."

Jojo wondered how this looked to Matt. She had little experience with kids and wasn't sure what was expected when one showed up on your doorstep. "You can blame it on me," she said. "Tell him I was having so much fun, I begged you to stay."

Gracie looked doubtful that her father would believe it. They reached her bike and just as she was getting on, Jojo made a snap decision.

"Why don't I drive you home? That way, I can smooth things over with your dad."

Gracie's eyes widened. "Really?!"

It hit Jojo that this was exactly what she'd advised herself not to do, but it was too late. "I think the seats go down in my car. Let's see if we can fit your bike in."

The bike was small and fit easily. Jojo ran back to the cabin to put her guitar away and lock up and soon they were headed into town.

"I hope your dad's not angry." Visions of Matt fuming in front of the camera were still fresh in Jojo's mind.

"He's pretty mellow," Gracie said. "Unless you're a reporter. You're not, are you?"

Jojo laughed. "I think that's the first time I've gotten that question. But no, I'm not."

"Didn't think so. They've been coming around again because he wrote 'Sweet Side.'"

"I saw him on the news. I guess he's pretty mad at Jojo right now."

"Kinda," Gracie said. "But mostly he doesn't like the attention because he worries about me, especially when I'm home alone."

Jojo hadn't even considered the parenting angle of dealing with the press.

"Do you live right in town?"

"Yeah, it's up there on the left. The one with the Heston Cabinetry sign out front."

There it was—the house where she'd seen the police car and a few other vehicles on her first day in town. She'd already driven past it three times without noticing the sign. Odd how the tabloids always made Matt sound like a recluse, yet his house was on Main Street. But why should she be surprised about anything the paparazzi wrote? She pulled into the driveway and parked. There were two buildings—one appeared to be the cabinet shop and the other a traditional two-story New Englander with a large front porch. At the moment, she didn't see anyone skulking about with a camera.

As they got out of the car, Matt emerged from the shop. He cut a very different image in the full sunlight than he had the night before. For one thing, he was a lot taller when he wasn't hunkered down in a canoe, and he looked rather sharp in jeans and a blue-and-white checked shirt with sleeves rolled up to the elbows. Jojo was relieved to see he was smiling but curious about the red hula-hoop in his hand.

"I almost forgot about the contest!" Gracie said, jumping out of the car and getting her guitar from the backseat. "Are we late?"

"No, we've got plenty of time. Don't run with your guitar."

She was already halfway to the house. "Can you get my bike? I'll be right back."

"Does she ever slow down?" Jojo asked.

Matt shook his head. "I wish I had half her energy."

Now that he was standing in front of her, Jojo suspected these weren't Matt's work clothes and it appeared he might even have run a brush through his hair.

"Tonight's the first farmers market of the year," he continued, "and there's going to be a hula-hoop contest."

Jojo nodded at the hoop by his side. "I see you've been practicing?"

"I wouldn't last five seconds," he chuckled, leaning it against the truck. "But Gracie can go for ages. It's not for another hour, so we're getting dinner first from one of the vendors."

As they went around to the back of the car to get the bike, Jojo realized he didn't seem in the least bit out of sorts about Gracie's side trip to the cabin.

"It was really nice of you to drive her home," he said.

"I felt badly. We started jamming and I can't even describe it. The time just flew."

"I know the feeling. We play almost every night."

"That explains a lot," Jojo said. "I could barely keep up."

She opened the back of the car, and as he leaned in to pick up the bike, she noticed his shoulders had broadened over the years. There was probably a lot of heavy lifting in his line of work. As he set the bike down, she caught herself staring and turned away to close the hatch.

"Anyway," she said. "I'm really sorry if you were concerned."

He laid the bike off to the side on the grass. "It wasn't a problem. Sometimes I act more worried than I am, just so she won't get lax about checking in. But honestly, I figured she was with you. Last night on the way home, you were all she talked about. You made quite an impression when you ran into each other at the store. And then seeing you again at solstice, she figured it was a sign you're destined to be her new BFF." He gave her a rueful smile. "Those were her words—not mine."

"That's really sweet," Jojo said, finding his smile somewhat distracting.

"I'm glad you think so. Sometimes Gracie's enthusiasm turns her into a mini steamroller. But don't worry. I'll put the brakes on—gently, of course."

"That really isn't necessary." Jojo touched his arm without thinking. "When I said it was sweet, I meant it. I don't mind her stopping by, and if I'm busy, I'll tell her."

He looked at her doubtfully. "Promise?"

"Promise." It seemed their conversation had settled into an easy-going back-and-forth. "Besides," Jojo added, "Your daughter might end up helping my career. I think she's going to be the next big thing."

He laughed. "That's what she tells me. She's determined to be the next Jojo."

Her conscience shot her a little zinger. It was one thing to lie about her identity with strangers and people she was unlikely to see again, but this was starting to feel like a potential friendship. Matt seemed like a decent guy and deserved the truth. Even if he didn't take it well, at least she wouldn't feel guilty. She was on the verge of confessing when the door slammed, and Gracie came sprinting across the lawn.

"Is Joelle coming with us?!"

Matt gave Jojo a hopeful look and her previous thought sailed right out of her head.

"There'll be all kinds of food," he said. "And you can't come to Westbury and miss the hula-hoop contest." He was very convincing, and she could feel the last vestige of her resolve to play it safe melting away. She glanced from Matt to Gracie, and the child's wide-eyed enthusiasm clinched the deal.

"Are we taking the truck or the car?" she asked.

"Yay!" Gracie said.

Matt passed the hula-hoop to his daughter. "We're walking. It's not far."

Jojo got her purse and Matt fetched a blanket from the truck. There was no sidewalk, so they walked along the edge of the road, heading toward the center of town.

Gracie rolled the hula-hoop as she walked. "Dad, you should have heard us today. It was amazing. I finally met someone who plays as well as you but has better taste in music."

He growled like a bear and tried to grab her, but she was light-footed and skipped ahead, laughing and taunting him.

"You're getting old and slow."

It was hard to believe this was the same girl who, an hour earlier, had sounded almost soulful when they'd played "He's Gone for Good."

Matt let out one more growl. "Just for that, I'm not buying you dinner. I hope you brought your own money."

"Joelle will loan me some. We're besties now."

Jojo threw up her hands. "I'm staying out of this."

"Wise choice," Matt said. Then he gave her a questioning look. "So, what's your story? You must be pretty good to impress my daughter." So much for hiding her light under a basket, not that she'd actually tried very hard.

Jojo had a stock answer that was basically the story of her first couple of years in New York. "I'm a music teacher—guitar and keyboard. But I also write songs, which is why I'm here for the month. Leah and Tom were nice enough to give me the friends and family discount, which basically means they're letting me stay for free."

"It's nice to have rich friends," he said.

Jojo had never thought of her friends as rich, but if Matt did, it sounded like the rumors were true about his finances.

"Do you sell your songs?" Gracie asked.

"So far, I just write them for me." Again, this was basically true.

"I can help," Gracie said. "I'm really good at hooks."

Matt chuckled. "She actually is."

"Are you coming over again tomorrow?" Jojo asked.

Gracie looked to her dad.

"As long as you don't overstay your welcome." It tickled Jojo to hear this slightly stern dad voice coming out of Matt Heston. She'd always seen him as a rebel against parental authority.

"Then I'll be there," Gracie said, as she pried her phone from a rather tight pocket. "What's your number, just in case?"

Jojo felt a flutter of panic, but then remembered Gracie would only see her number, not her name. Matt, however, seemed to pick up on her hesitation.

"Just in case what?" he asked.

"I don't know," Gracie said. "What if it rains or something?"

He sighed, as if conceding that made sense.

"I don't mind, if you don't," Jojo said. He shrugged, and she gave Gracie her number.

"But absolutely no unnecessary texting," Matt added. Then, catching himself, he turned swiftly to Jojo. "Sorry, that wasn't intended for you."

"I suspected as much." She grinned, amused by his gallantry but certain she could protect herself from a mere wisp of a girl, even if that girl had overactive thumbs and a penchant for texting.

Before she knew it, they'd reached the market. It wasn't huge but took up most of the town common. Booths and food trucks were bustling with business and at the center was a bandstand where a man played fiddle and a woman played mandolin. Matt looked at Jojo for a reaction. She sensed some pride on his part—perhaps for his town and perhaps for this little slice of idyllic country life.

"Is it here every week?" she asked.

"Until October. There'll be more vendors later in the season. Not much has ripened yet."

"I love it. Thanks for inviting me."

They wandered between the booths, where people were selling cheese, local meats, maple syrup, wooden bowls, and early crops like lettuce and peas. They stopped at one booth so Jojo could buy asparagus, and then at a food truck brightly painted with the words Curry Heaven and were about to buy dinner when Gracie objected.

"We can't eat before the contest. I'll throw up."

"Maybe *you* can't," Matt said, "but Joelle and I can. We'll get you something afterward."

"I can wait," Jojo said. "As long as you can."

Matt shrugged and looked at Gracie. "Okay, ladybug, you win."

"Daaaddd!"

"Sorry," he said, looking guilty. "Let's go listen to the music."

As they moved through the market, heads occasionally turned, but they weren't focused on Jojo. These were Matt's people, and he often nodded back and even acknowledged a few by name. Jojo was getting a kick out of the whole thing. Not only was she getting to hang out with her adolescent idol—which, even for a star of her stature, was a little surreal—but she was also getting a taste of freedom. She could never have walked through this market dressed as Jojo without stopping to pose for selfies every ten feet.

Matt caught her smiling and gave her a curious look. "Did I miss something?"

"Just happy I came."

His eyes lingered on hers. "Me too."

She felt a tiny thrill but quickly dismissed it. He was just being friendly—a good ambassador for his town.

They found an open spot in front of the bandstand and spread the blanket. There were families all around, and small children ran and tumbled while bluegrass music played. After a few minutes, Gracie spotted some friends, picked up the hula-hoop, and ran over to practice.

"Gracie and I sing here once or twice a season." It was the first time he'd mentioned being a performer, and Jojo was glad it was finally out there.

"I have a confession," she said. "When you paddled over to the dock last night, I recognized you, but I wasn't sure of the etiquette."

He seemed amused. "Like whether it was okay to ask for an autograph?"

"That was definitely it," she said, playing along. "Because you know I can get twelve bucks for it on eBay."

"Damn, it used to be twenty." There was a bit of mischief in his eyes. "We could do a selfie right here. What can you get for that?"

She suspected the tabloids would pay a fortune but not for the reason he thought.

"I can't figure you out," she said. "How can you be so relaxed? I thought you had to hide out in your house most of the time."

He laughed, but she could swear his eyes darted over the crowd. Even if most of these people were locals who respected his privacy, there was always the possibility of some curious observer with a camera.

"For one thing," he said, "we can't live our lives shut up in the house, and I don't want Gracie missing out." He paused before deciding to continue. "The attention comes in waves. In the beginning, it was crazy, but then the gaps got longer and in the last couple of years, life's been almost normal. Until a couple of days ago . . ."

His voice dropped as he trailed off, and she didn't need an explanation. "Sweet Side" had put him back in the spotlight, where he didn't want to be. She felt a pang of guilt but reminded herself she had done nothing wrong.

He looked at her rather seriously. "I'm not sure why I feel comfortable talking to you like this. Maybe it's because you're a fellow musician. At any rate, I sense you're not the type to go blabbing to the press."

He paused again, and she realized this was more a question than a statement.

"Of course," she said. "I would never . . ."

"It's just that I've been burned before." He looked somber. "A few years back, this girl I went to high school with, and barely knew, sold a story to one of the tabloids. She made it sound like we hung out a lot and described me as a moody, troubled teenager. I mean—*what the hell*?"

Jojo waited, expecting there must be more, but there wasn't. "That's it? That's your tabloid sob story?"

He looked taken aback.

"You are way too thin-skinned to be a celebrity, Mr. Heston."

She wasn't sure she knew him well enough to call him out, but she couldn't resist. She was halfway serious and halfway ribbing him, but what she really wanted was to share some tabloid stories of her own. Some stories with real teeth.

He knit his brow. "Did you just call me Mr. Heston? How old are you, anyway?"

"Don't change the subject, *Mr. Heston*. And I'm over eighteen, in case you were actually worried." She doubted he was serious.

"Well, that's a relief," he said. "And it wasn't the story itself that hurt, it was more that she broke the code."

"Code? Is this some kind of backcountry thing?"

He laughed. "It's not like she's at the bottom of the lake. But people around here respect each other's privacy. You don't go telling stories on your neighbors."

Okay. She could see that. But in the grand scheme of celebrity hardship, his story was definitely on the tame side.

"Is she still around?"

He shook his head. "Took the money and ran. Her family's still here, and I get along with her father. He's a good electrician and we cross paths on job sites."

So much for the simplicity of small-town life, she thought.

"I've come to the conclusion," he said, "in the world of tabloid journalism—if you can call it journalism—there's a stock cast of characters. There's the former child star who parties too hard. There's the anorexic model who only dates billionaires, even the married ones. And then there's the popular musician who, due to sad circumstances, quits at the pinnacle of his career to live in obscurity." Matt shrugged. "Of course, that's my role. But I'm willing to bet there's a few editors out there asking their staff, 'Can't we find someone else to play this part? Because Matt Heston is getting a little long in the tooth.'"

Jojo almost asked to see his teeth, but that would have bordered on flirting.

"It wasn't *that* funny," he said, as she tried to wipe the grin off her face.

Even she had wondered in the past about why the press fixated on Matt, when there were plenty of other famous ex-musicians to write about. But the fact was, his story possessed all the dramatic elements the paparazzi loved. There had been tragic loss, a young child left motherless, broken contracts and lawsuits, and a huge rabid fan base that, for a long time at least, circulated rumors of Matt's return.

They were quiet for a while. Their eyes even met once or twice as if trying to read the other's thoughts, but at no point did Jojo feel uneasy. The lawn was filling up and the couple playing bluegrass had bumped up the volume.

Matt inched a little closer to be heard over the music. "About last night—when we met at your dock. Thanks for not making a big deal."

"Well," she said, drawing in a deep breath as if about to deliver a dissertation, "prepare to be annoyed, because I can't go on indefinitely without saying something. Just for the record, I do like your music and admire your talent as a songwriter." She left it at that, suspecting that with Matt, less was more.

He grinned. "If you wrote music reviews, *Rolling Stone* would be a much shorter magazine."

Just then, a woman's voice came over the PA system. "Hi, everyone. It's time for the big event—the annual farmers market hula-hoop contest!" As the crowd cheered, thirty or forty hula-hoopers, from little children to grandmothers, spread out in the open space between the audience and the bandstand. The woman who had been playing mandolin switched to banjo and, along with her fiddling companion, broke into "Foggy Mountain Breakdown." The hula-hoops gyrated, and the audience cheered for their favorite contestants.

Jojo was instantly caught up in the fun. They whooped and whistled for Gracie and her friends. At one point, she turned to Matt, only to discover he was staring at her. He smiled, and she smiled back. The unplanned evening had taken a very pleasant turn.

CHAPTER 13

MATT

MATT LOOKED up from his bowl of half-finished oatmeal. "Are you still planning on going over to Joelle's after camp today?"

"Yup," Gracie said. "But I know we have to go to Manchester, so I won't stay too late."

They were planning to hit the factory outlet stores for some summer clothes. Suddenly, everything of Gracie's seemed too small. They'd gone through her dresser and closet to make sure there weren't some larger clothes hiding somewhere, but found nothing. They also needed a birthday gift for her friend, Cammy. The party was tomorrow. Once again, Matt had put everything off until the last minute.

"Do you know what you want to get Cammy?"

"Earrings or a bracelet."

Thank goodness she had that figured out. He wouldn't have had a clue.

"Can we ask Joelle to come? I'll bet she'd like Manchester. All the New York tourists shop there."

It had crossed his mind, but asking Joelle to join them two nights in a row would send the wrong message.

"I think we need to focus on your clothes and Cammy's gift, and I doubt she'd find it much fun. Maybe on the weekend."

Gracie didn't argue, but for once, he almost wished she had. He'd laid in bed longer than usual that morning, thinking about their outing to the market. After the hula-hoop contest, they'd gotten dinner and then returned to their blanket by the bandstand. The musicians were packing up and most of the audience had left. Gracie had burned off a lot of energy during the contest, but she still had enough to grill Joelle on her opinions about all things pop-music related. He'd mostly listened, having little to offer, and had noticed Joelle wasn't wearing a wedding band. He was trying to guess her age when she gave him a bemused look.

"Are we boring you, Grandpa?"

His turncoat-of-a-daughter had sniggered, and he shot them both a crotchety old frown. Gracie rolled onto her back in stitches, but Joelle had surprised him with a slew of questions about the artists who most influenced him. It turned out her knowledge of musicians straddled at least two generations.

Later, when they got back to the house, Gracie went inside while he and Joelle stood for a while beside her car.

"How long are you staying?" he asked.

"A month."

He whistled under his breath. "That's some serious vacation time." He'd figured a few days or a week at most and was happy to be wrong. "I can't remember the last time I had a break like that."

"Not even when you came off a tour?"

Usually he resisted thinking that far back, but he didn't want the evening to end and would have grasped at any topic to delay saying goodnight.

"Yeah, I guess that would be the last time I had anything close to a month off. The guys and I were addicted to the road. Performing back then was like mainlining adrenaline, so our manager would practically have to kick our butts home to get us to take a break." Matt smiled to himself, remembering what a mother hen Thad had been. "I didn't appreciate those times at home as much as I should have, but looking back . . ."

Joelle's face clouded as if she were sorry to have brought it up.

"Don't worry. I'm not that fragile," he said, touching her hand briefly where it rested on the hood of the car. Then he forced a smile. "Would you believe I'm usually the life of the party?"

She laughed, and just like that, the mood lightened again.

"Thanks for a really special time," she said. "And for dinner." It sounded like the evening was winding down. "Next time, I'm buying," she added.

So, there would be a next time. He felt the urge to kiss her goodnight but wondered if it was too soon. He glanced toward the house. "Do you think Gracie's watching?"

"Side window," Joelle whispered through a tight-lipped grin.

If the spectator had been anyone but his daughter, he might still have gone for it. But he sobered up before making a fool of himself. He opened her door and, as she moved to get in, her fingers trailed lightly down his arm, ending in a gentle squeeze. He could still feel the tingle, but now, as he replayed it in his mind, he wondered if he was reading too much into it.

"Earth to Dad?"

"Yeah?" he said, re-emerging from the memory.

"Do you think a girl can have too many earrings?"

"Didn't Cammy get her ears pierced the same time you did?"

"Yeah."

"Do you have too many earrings?"

"No, but I don't have as many people giving me stuff. She's got a big family."

That was true. The Christmas tree at Cammy's house always had a lot more presents under it and birthdays were probably similar.

"Honey, there's something else I was thinking you should buy tonight when we're shopping." She brightened expectantly, though he doubted she'd like where this was going. "Your shirts aren't too small just because you're getting taller."

Her face drooped, and he was at least grateful he didn't have to spell it out.

"Cammy's mom said she'd take me."

"Oh, okay. Really?" He felt relieved, but only for a moment. They should have taken care of this before she started camp, and he didn't like the idea of waiting even a few more days. If Cammy's mother had noticed, then probably every twelve-year-old boy at camp had noticed. He hadn't even brought up the bathing suit issue and didn't want to think about how she was squeezing into last year's suit.

"You know, honey, it's probably not complicated."

"Dad, I've got this." She got up and put her bowl and glass in the sink.

He realized he was about to lose her. "I'm sure there'll be sales ladies who can help."

She picked up her guitar case. "I don't want to be late. See you later." The door slammed, and he was alone.

He rubbed his forehead. *That could have gone better*.

CHAPTER 14

JOJO

ALL DAY, Jojo's mind had been jumping around. Whenever she tried to focus on a song, she'd soon discover her thoughts drifting back to the night before or flitting ahead to whether Gracie would show up again. Kids often changed their minds. And even if Gracie stopped by, it was unlikely to lead to another encounter with Matt, which might be for the best.

She was embarrassed at the way she'd touched him as they said goodnight. She'd meant it to be more friendly than flirty, but it might have crossed the line. What if he had a girlfriend? It hadn't come up, and he certainly didn't act like it, but still . . .

The afternoon was hot, and she cooled off with a swim before going inside to wash her hair. Now, as she ran her fingers through her wet curls, she looked at herself in the mirror. Not having to deal with wigs and nails and makeup was saving her at least an hour each morning and maybe another half hour each night. The evening before, she had jumped into the car with Gracie so fast she hadn't given a thought to her appearance. That simply wasn't like her.

It was tempting to pick up the eyeliner and apply a touch, but she resisted. She'd noticed plenty of women at the farmers market with little or no makeup. It was an entirely different culture here. In the end, she left her face au naturel and went downstairs.

In case Gracie did show up, her Sam Rubio was hidden upstairs under her bed. She went out on the porch where there were still two kitchen chairs and returned to working on a song.

It wasn't long before she heard a bike on the driveway. Looking up, she read Gracie's body language and detected a change. Her usual smile was absent, and it looked like she was fighting gravity as she dragged herself up the porch stairs.

"How was camp today?" Jojo asked.

"Fine."

"There's drinks in the fridge."

"Okay."

With only two words and not even a hello, Gracie went inside to the kitchen. By the time she came out again, Jojo had laid her guitar back in its open case.

"Do you want to play or talk about it?"

"Play." Gracie set her drink down and opened her case, but then started talking. "I need summer clothes, so Dad's taking me shopping."

"That sounds like fun." But Jojo sensed there was more.

Gracie's eyes were fixed on the floor. "It's so embarrassing. He wants to . . . shop for bras."

"Ohhh," Jojo said, the pieces falling into place. The too-small clothes. The absence of a mother. This had to be a challenging time for a single dad and his daughter.

"I remember how it was for me," Jojo said, a forgotten memory bubbling to the surface. "I came home from school one day and there was a package of training bras on my bed. Later my mom asked if they fit and that was it." So even her own mother had skirted around the conversation.

Neither of them spoke for a moment.

"Dad's taking me later today."

Jojo wondered if one of the store clerks might help, but few stores offered that level of service anymore.

"My friend's mom said she'd take me sometime, but I'm going to a birthday party tomorrow and, well . . . what do you think?"

It was the first time in her life a child had come to Jojo for advice, and she wasn't feeling very wise. "I'm not the best one to ask, but it might be nice to have it for the party."

Gracie sat back in her chair, still struggling with the logistics, and Jojo sympathized.

"Do you have any relatives who can go with you?"

The child shook her head and then looked up shyly. "Would you come?"

It wasn't a surprise. She'd sensed Gracie might be working up to that very question. If she were twelve years old and without a mother, Jojo might have improvised in the same way. The problem was it felt like overstepping. It might be wise to stay out of it, but the poor girl really seemed distressed.

"I'll tell you what," she said, then cringed at what she was about to do—*again!* "Later on, I'll drive you home like I did last night, and I'll talk to your dad—alone, if you don't mind. Sound fair?"

Gracie brightened and then switched gears as though the conversation had never happened. "I did bring my song journal, but would you mind if we just play like we did yesterday and not work on new stuff? I don't think my head's in it."

It sounded like they were in similar states of mind. "That works for me."

They picked up where they'd left off on track thirteen of Jojo's first album and played for close to an hour until a pickup drove up the driveway.

Gracie checked the time on her phone. "I wonder why Dad's here. It's still early."

Jojo set her guitar down. "Wait here. I'll talk to him now." She ran down the stairs as he got out of his truck. "Did we go too late again?"

"No, not at all. I knocked off early and thought I'd come by to listen. Afterward, we're heading up to Manchester to the outlet stores."

He was all smiles and upbeat—just the way he'd been when they said goodnight. It looked like he'd changed out of his work clothes and cleaned up—probably because they were going shopping.

"We'd love an audience," she said. "But first, I want to run an idea by you, and it's important you say no if I'm out of bounds. I don't want to come off like a busybody."

"Let me guess. She asked you to join us."

Jojo nodded.

"And I'm also guessing she wants me to stay in the truck while you take her shopping for"—he dropped his voice to a whisper —"*unmentionables*. That's what her Gram calls them."

Jojo smiled at the outdated expression. "She didn't specifically say you had to stay in the truck, but she might appreciate it."

"I doubt this was in your vacation brochure. And I warned you, she can be persistent."

"It isn't like that," Jojo said. "To be honest, I'm here by myself most of the day, which is good for writing, but too much alone time and I'll go stir crazy."

That seemed to convince him. "Well, we'd love to have you. And truthfully, it would help."

It hadn't taken much persuading, so she decided to push her luck. "Just one condition. You bought dinner last night, so tonight it's on me."

He chuckled but didn't actually agree to her terms. "We can argue about it later, but right now, I want to be entertained."

As they went up the porch steps, Jojo gave Gracie a covert thumbs-up and her young face practically glowed.

"Want to hear us play, Dad?"

"That's why I'm here." He gave her a kiss on the top of the head before sitting down in one of the Adirondack chairs.

"How about 'Forever Yours, Forever Mine,'" Gracie said.

Jojo responded by hitting the first chord, but it was Gracie who came in strong on lead vocal.

If I never dream of you again,
If you never live inside my head,
At least we had this space in time
Forever yours, forever mine.

The music had a vibrancy that hadn't been there before. Accustomed to playing for thousands, Jojo was surprised to find herself anxious playing for Matt. Before coming to Westbury, she had wanted him to like her music, but now she wanted him to like her. She began to put too much into it and had to pull back. *Mellow. Just keep it mellow.*

If I always have this broken heart,
If we're always meant to be apart,
At least we had this space in time
Forever yours, forever mine.

CHAPTER 15

MATT

MATT HADN'T EXPECTED this level of intensity from the duo—the air vibrating with their harmonies. Gracie had always taken their sessions seriously, but he'd never seen her this dialed in. This was the style of music she loved, paired with someone who shared her passion. For the first time where Gracie and music were concerned, he felt . . . inessential. Not only could she make great music without him, she could soar higher. He knew he should be proud, but there was also a twinge of loss. A new chapter in Gracie's life was beginning—one where he would play a smaller role.

As for Joelle, Gracie hadn't exaggerated. She played as if the guitar was an extension of herself. Her left hand slid effortlessly up and down the fretboard, while the pick in her right hand struck a mix of individual notes and chords. She was clearly a pro.

He had come by early, expecting some good amateur porch music, but he was getting a lesson in humility.

The song ended, and it took a moment before Gracie and Joelle broke their focus and turned to him.

"Wow," he said. "I had no idea, Gracie. This is by far the best you've ever sounded—your playing, singing, everything. Joelle, I don't know how you did it, but you woke something up in my daughter. How much have you guys worked on that song?"

They both laughed.

"That was our first time," Gracie said.

"So far," Joelle said, "we haven't sung anything twice."

"I practice a lot," Gracie said, and Matt nodded, having had every Jojo track burned into his brain. "I do it on GarageBand, one line at a time, with a metronome so I can slow it down if I need to."

"That's a lot of commitment," Joelle said.

"I'm guessing you know a thing or two about that," Matt said. "I figured you were good, but you're insanely good."

"Thanks." She graciously accepted the compliment with no false modesty.

"You mentioned teaching," Matt said, "but I'm guessing you've also performed and maybe done some session work."

"All the above."

"What's session work?" Gracie was putting her guitar away, which reminded him they needed to get going.

"Let's talk about it on the drive. The stores don't stay open very late tonight."

They took the truck, and Gracie rode in the jump seat. They talked about the music industry, and for once, Matt didn't have to field all the questions. Joelle brought a fresh perspective, and she was no neophyte to the business.

As they approached Manchester, Matt interrupted. "As fascinating as this is, we need to switch to shopping mode and make a plan."

"I can get everything at TFO," Gracie said. The "T" in the name stood for *teen*, but it could just as well have stood for tween. Gracie and her friends had been buying most of their clothes there since they were about ten. "Dad, where are *you* going shopping?"

"The focus is on you tonight, and I'm helping for at least part of it. I want to make sure there's none of those short shorts I've seen some of your friends wearing. You'll outgrow them before the summer's even over."

He didn't bother to look in the back seat but suspected she wasn't happy. Joelle was staying out of it. He pulled into the outlet parking lot and found a spot right in front of TFO.

"Can I at least go in and look around first?" Gracie said. "Pleeeaaase?"

Matt got out and slid his seat forward. "Have fun. We'll keep an eye on the window if you need us." They watched as she went into the store alone. "A year ago, she was fine going anywhere with me. Half the time, she'd even hold my hand."

Joelle reached across the console and patted his hand. "It's okay, Mattie, you can hold my hand whenever you want."

"Jeez, no one's called me Mattie since I was about six." Any initial awkwardness of getting to know one another was apparently behind them.

"How much time should we give her?" he asked.

"How about ten minutes? And what if I go in first and you come a little later?"

She made it sound like they were planning to storm the beaches, but he was relieved to have some adult female assistance. "That sounds like a great plan." He meant it too. Sure, he and Gracie could have muddled through, and maybe gotten help, but this was easier.

"Just so you know," Joelle said, "clothes shopping isn't easy at her age. 'What will other girls think? What will boys think? What will Dad think?' It's a lot for a twelve-year-old."

He was certain that as a young boy, he hadn't given a single thought to his clothes. Most of the time, they had magically appeared in his dresser. But he knew girls were different.

"I hope you're not regretting coming along."

She leaned back in her seat and tilted her head toward him. "I feel oddly content. I can't decide if it's because I'm on vacation or because I enjoy hanging out with you guys."

It was a bold statement. She had a habit of saying what she was thinking, so he did the same.

"Is it true men are more approachable when they have a child?"

She thought for a moment. "Maybe, and I suppose it takes some of the pressure off. For example, I'm not sitting here wondering how the night will end. I'll go back to the cabin, and the two of you will go home. So, there's at least the appearance of things going slower."

"But in reality . . .?"

"Can I be totally honest?" she asked. Though he nodded, she still seemed uneasy. "In reality, it feels a little like playing house."

On the drive, he'd begun thinking the same thing. "Maybe I should have discouraged this."

Joelle shrugged. "Gracie needed help, and I had so much fun last night, I wanted to hang out with you guys again."

She seemed not to hold back and her openness was rubbing off on him.

"Since we're being honest," he said, "I was a bit jealous when I heard the two of you playing earlier." He searched for the right words, but those beautiful brown eyes were a distraction. "Gracie and I have always had this amazing connection through music. Ever since she could hold a guitar, it's been *our* thing. But this afternoon, when I heard the two of you, I got a reality check. I don't think playing and singing with Dad will ever be the same."

Joelle turned to face him straight on. "I would never want to do something that comes between the two of you."

"It's okay, seriously. If it wasn't you, it would be someone else. And frankly, it could be worse. It could have been a boy."

She frowned. "That doesn't make me feel any better."

"It's the natural progression of things," he said. "Little girls grow up and need their dads less and less. I knew it was coming but didn't expect it so soon."

Perhaps he shouldn't have brought it up because it clearly bothered her, and she wasn't buying his paternal stoicism.

"This conversation isn't over," she said. "But it's time I go in. Wish me luck."

"I'll be watching," he said. "Just give me a wave when it's time for the fashion show. Oh, one other thing, remind her she needs a bathing suit."

CHAPTER 16

JOJO

JOJO PASSED through the glass doors and was greeted by a giant banner hanging from the ceiling. It was her. She'd been the official face of TFO for over a year and the last time she'd been in one of their stores, it had been the flagship on Fifth Avenue for the kickoff of this year's summer line. Normally, this was the last place she would go when trying to avoid attention, but in the past couple of days, she'd started to get a buzz from taking risks. Apparently, Joelle could go anywhere.

"Isn't she amazing?" Gracie was nearby, holding a stack of clothes and staring at the banner with total adoration.

"Do you mean her music?"

"Everything. Just look at her. She's so awesome."

"But you know," Jojo said, "it takes a lot of makeup and time to look like that. Without all the glitz, she could walk right past you and you wouldn't even recognize her."

"You're funny," Gracie said, not buying it. "We've got to hurry. They close in forty-five minutes."

"Seriously?" Jojo glanced at her watch. Why were they just getting here if the store was closing?

"Is Dad staying outside?"

"For a little while. So let's look at bras first and then bathing suits."

Gracie was already ahead of the game and held up a plastic hanger with a youth-sized sports bra. "My friend wears this kind. If I try it on, will you tell me if it fits?"

Jojo nodded, and they headed back to the dressing rooms. She stayed in the outer room while Gracie went into a cubicle and then emerged moments later in shorts and the sports bra.

"Did you know," Gracie said, "some girls wear these without a shirt?"

"Yeah, good luck with that."

The child smiled at her figure in the mirror. "Dad would freak."

"It looks like a good fit," Jojo said. "I'd get at least three."

Picking out a bathing suit was harder. The first one Gracie tried was a string bikini.

"Wouldn't a one-piece be easier at camp?" Jojo asked. "Seriously, they stay in place a lot better."

Gracie frowned and then faced the mirror, shifting her weight from one foot to the other so that her hips shifted from left to right. "But it looks so cute, and all the girls are wearing them."

Jojo doubted that, though she probably tried the same line on her mother. "If you show that to your dad, he'll probably insist on a one-piece. But if we can find a two-piece that's a little more G-rated, he might go for it."

There was reluctant acceptance, and Jojo ended up making a couple of trips to the girls' bathing suit section. In the process, she ran to the front window and signaled Matt, before heading back to the dressing room. *This is insane,* she thought, noticing the time again.

"Your dad's on his way, so you better pick one."

Gracie could be quick when motivated and made her choice by

the time Matt poked his head tentatively into the outer dressing area.

"Is it safe to come in?"

Jojo glared at him. "Only if you have a good excuse for bringing us here right before closing."

He looked a little shamefaced, but not nearly as much as he should have. "Sorry. I forgot to mention that."

"Dad. What about this one?" To Jojo's dismay, Gracie had changed back into the bikini. Now Matt was probably going to think she'd okayed it. The look on his face was a tragic mix of surprise and embarrassment, right before his eyes dropped to the floor. But before Jojo could say anything, Gracie started laughing.

"Just kidding, Dad. Joelle said you'd hate it." She disappeared back into the changing cubicle as quickly as she'd appeared.

"I swear I had nothing to do with that," Jojo said.

"I believe you. It's just that I hardly recognized her." The poor man looked as though he'd just aged a few years.

With time running out, Jojo couldn't imagine why Gracie would waste it on her little prank, until she reappeared in a cute tankini with solid teal boy shorts and a striped top. The relief on Matt's face was almost humorous. That's when Jojo suspected Gracie might have known exactly what she was doing, because from that point on, Matt readily agreed to everything.

As they made their way to the front of the store, a voice came over the intercom and announced they'd be closing soon.

"Have you picked out a present yet?" Matt asked. He had a fist full of hangers in one hand.

"There's earrings at the front counter," Gracie said.

"Then run ahead. We'll catch up."

Jojo had a stack of shorts and shirts in her arms and to anyone watching, they must have looked like a couple of parents out shopping with their daughter.

"I can't thank you enough," he said. "I was dreading this, but it seems like it went okay."

"Except for your bikini-induced heart attack back there?"

"Yeah. I wasn't ready for that. Last summer, she still looked like a little girl."

There was a woman at the front counter helping Gracie, and as they approached, she looked up and gasped. It was that all-to-familiar look of recognition and Jojo's heart sank. The salesclerk was probably in her late thirties or early forties and not at all someone Jojo would have thought to avoid.

"My sister and I are huge fans. Would it be okay if I get a selfie?"

The woman was already coming around from behind the counter, and Jojo's body tensed. Everything was about to change until Matt spoke up.

"No problem," he said. "Joelle, do you mind?"

For a moment, everything got weird as the woman handed Jojo her camera. "Can you take two or three just to be safe?"

Matt stood beside the woman and smiled. As Jojo lined up the shot, she saw her own face on the screen, smiling down from the giant banner. She lowered her aim before snapping three pictures. As she handed the phone back, she forced a smile, but her heart was still thumping. She almost laughed out loud, but no one else would have seen the humor.

Gracie was thumbing through the display case of earrings, seemingly oblivious to the photo shoot. "I can't decide on Cammy's present." She looked distressed as she held up two pairs.

"Do you think she'll want to wear them at camp?" Jojo asked.

"Probably."

"Then I wouldn't go with the dangly ones. Every time she pulls a sweatshirt off or changes clothes to go swimming, she might end up losing one."

"Then maybe these," Gracie said. She held out the card with tiny horseshoe-shaped studs. "She's horse crazy."

Jojo agreed, and Gracie placed them on top of the clothes pile.

"Ring 'em up," Matt said to the sales lady.

They headed out of the store exactly on the hour, with an employee locking the door behind them.

"I just have one question," Jojo said. "Who the heck goes clothes shopping forty-five minutes before the store closes?"

"Dad does. Pretty much every time."

"It's super-efficient," Matt said.

Jojo looked from one to the other. "You mean that was on purpose?"

"If you've got three hours to shop," he said matter-of-factly, "then it'll take three hours. But if you've got only forty-five minutes . . ."

"You're insane," Jojo said, not bothering to hide her exasperation. "I can't believe you're actually proud of yourself." She looked sympathetically at Gracie. "Just in case your father never told you, there's this thing called the weekend when the stores are open all day."

Matt groaned, but there was clearly a twinkle in his eye. "Don't tell her that. Gracie loves speed shopping. Don't you, honey?"

"Actually, it's kind of stressful, Dad."

"But you used to think it was fun." Matt looked a little chastened. He opened the driver's side door and put Gracie's shopping bag behind the seat.

Jojo decided to drop it. After all, every family had its quirks. "At least we accomplished our mission," she said. "But please don't tell me the restaurants are about to close, too."

"Eating is one thing Dad does slowly," Gracie said. She seemed more relaxed now that their mission was accomplished.

They left the truck in the parking lot and walked around downtown, mostly window shopping, but they also went into The Northshire Bookstore so Gracie could pick out a birthday card. There were several options for dinner, and they ended up at Nipper's Cafe for cheesesteak sandwiches. They talked about songwriting and Gracie's dance group, and even about how the cabinet business was doing. When Gracie went to the restroom, Matt set his elbows on the table and rested his chin on his hands. He suddenly had a devilish glint in his eye as if he was up to no good.

"We could take off and stick Gracie with the check."

Jojo mimicked his pose and stared back conspiratorially. "That would teach her to leave home without money."

He shrugged in agreement. "She could pay it off washing dishes. That would give us just enough time"—he paused and raised his eyebrows suggestively—"to take a walk."

She laughed. "You think you're sooo cute."

This was a far cry from the Matt Heston she'd seen in the press. Articles usually described him as "serious and brooding." So who was this guy and why such a difference? She was tempted to ask, but the mood was deliciously pleasant, and she didn't want to risk disturbing it.

Dusk had settled by the time they left the restaurant, and Gracie fell asleep on the ride home. She looked younger, slumped down in her seat, her head cushioned by an old blanket.

Jojo looked over at Matt and noticed his features had softened in the waning light. With Gracie asleep, it felt almost like they were alone. The moment was perfect, and she was overcome by a swell of tenderness and a sense that her heart was expanding.

Catching her gaze, he reached for her hand and they linked fingers. There was no need for words. She stared ahead into the night, remembering some lines from one of Matt's songs.

> *It's you and me and the open road*
> *Just hold my hand and don't let go.*

By the time they reached the cabin, it was dark. Matt eased the truck to a stop, glancing in the mirror to be certain Gracie hadn't stirred. He kept the engine running, and they got out quietly, the moment charged with a sense of anticipation.

As they climbed the steps, he spoke in a low voice. "Gracie's got that birthday party tomorrow, so I'm a free man for dinner."

"Are you asking me out? Unchaperoned?" It would be totally different—just the two of them. This would be an actual date.

"I realize three nights in a row is probably a little . . ." His confidence seemed to waver, and she felt the moment slipping away. As crazy as three nights in a row might be, she didn't want to wait a day or two to see him again.

"I think we can get around this on a technicality," she said. "Last night and tonight weren't actual dates. In one case, you were showing me the farmers market and this evening I came along as a shopping consultant."

"Good point," he said, more than willing to accept her flimsy logic.

"So, yes, to dinner," she said.

He moved closer. "I was thinking of keeping it simple. I could bring a pizza."

"Sounds nice." She would have agreed to anything, given the spell she was under. "We can eat on the porch. It's beautiful in the evening and there won't be anyone clamoring for autographs or selfies." They hadn't yet discussed the earlier incident, and he smiled a little awkwardly.

"Sorry about that. I hope it wasn't too weird."

"No. It was totally cool. Like getting the authentic Matt Heston experience."

Their words had the pretense of casual conversation, but he was close enough now to kindle a fire. She kept expecting him to make a move, and just when she thought she might have to help things along, he brought a hand up and casually brushed back a strand of her hair. Then finally . . . finally . . . he leaned down and their lips met.

She closed her eyes as her fantasies collided with reality.

She'd imagined the two of them like this, but never really

believed it. The bliss lasted several seconds and when their lips parted, it was only by inches as his mouth hovered above hers.

"As much as it kills me," he whispered, "I have to go."

"Hmmm . . ." she moaned, wrapping her fingers around his belt.

"You're making this hard," he said, nuzzling her cheek. "You're going to have to let go." He kissed her once more before prying himself loose.

She watched until the truck disappeared before heading inside. After flicking on a light, she stood motionless for a moment, her mind still buzzing from the sensation of his lips on hers. *I just kissed Matt Heston.* She twirled around and collapsed onto the couch. Bottom line, he liked her—the real her—not the celebrity. And she liked the way he made her feel, all giddy and high. Her rational brain said it was too early to be falling for him. Yet the feeling was there, and she couldn't turn it off. Nor did she want to.

Her phone rang, and she rolled onto her back to read the screen before answering.

"Hey, Leah."

"Hey, girl. Did you get my message?"

"Sorry, I was busy kissing Matt Heston." There was a moment of delicious silence while Jojo waited for the fireworks.

"Oh . . . my . . . God! I knew it, I knew it, I knew it!"

"You did not," Jojo said. "Because I didn't even see it coming."

"But I heard it in your voice when you described that whole meet-and-greet at the dock. Anyway, tell me everything."

Jojo tried to keep it brief, but a lot had happened since their last conversation. She had to start from Gracie's first visit, and it took a while before she reached tonight's kiss.

"Damn, girl. You've been busy."

Even Jojo was slightly floored once she'd recounted it all. "I can't believe that all fit in two days."

"At the rate you're going, he may propose tomorrow."

"Knock it off. It's all been super casual, except maybe the kiss . . . and the hand holding . . . and the way his shoulders fill out a nice dress shirt." She was practically melting into the couch.

"Huh," Leah said. "Sounds like someone's got a crush."

That word felt totally inadequate, but she doubted she could convince Leah. And sure, she'd been swept off her feet before, only to come crashing back to earth when the excitement wore off. But at twenty-eight, Jojo hoped her man radar had improved. And never in her dating experience had a guy checked off as many of her boxes as Matt. Of course, there remained one major hurdle. He had no idea who she was.

She gritted her teeth and forced herself to say it out loud. "I still haven't told him."

"I was afraid to ask," Leah said.

"Hey, don't judge me. You agreed it was the right thing."

"That's before you kissed him! That's when I thought you might just run into him once or twice."

Jojo pressed her face into the seat cushion and groaned. "You're right. I should have said something, but we were having such a nice evening and he smelled so good. And if I do tell him, is it fair to expect him not to share it with Gracie? That's like asking him to lie to his daughter, which feels messed up. And who knows, maybe I can trust Gracie not to tell her friends." Jojo's head was spinning.

"There is another option," Leah said, adopting a calmer tone. "It wouldn't hurt to slow down. Have you even told him you recently broke up with your boyfriend?"

The conversation was totally killing her mood. "We've hardly had any time to ourselves, and I wasn't about to discuss my breakup in front of his daughter."

"Fair enough. But if you keep seeing each other, he'll find out about Carson eventually and wonder why you didn't mention him. Better to get it out there."

"Okay, okay," Jojo said. "I'll tell him about Carson."

"Don't do it just for him. Do it for yourself. A lot's been going on and talking about it might help."

Before the call, Jojo had been in a blissful fog and would have happily remained there. But maybe she needed this kind of reality check, and wasn't that what friends were for?

"Just remember," Leah said, "we both know you'll never settle down in Westbury, and he'll never uproot his child and move to New York."

"Whoa," Jojo said, feeling like they were getting off track. "That's way down the road."

"Just saying—before you go outing yourself, make sure you've thought about what a future together would look like." Finally, Leah eased off. "What's happening tomorrow night?"

"Gracie's going to a birthday party and Matt's stopping by with a pizza. Nothing fancy."

"He's coming to the cabin? Just the two of you alone?" And just like that, Leah's judgy voice was back.

"It's no big deal. He's being considerate by trying to avoid reporters and fans—which, I might point out, is one of many things we have in common. Besides, it'll probably be a quick date. I doubt kids' parties last that long."

"Long enough to boil an egg," Leah muttered.

Jojo was afraid to ask.

"I worry about you," Leah said. "For someone who's touted as one of the sexiest women on the planet, you know practically zip about men. I want you to read some of those romance novels I've got around the cabin. You need a crash course in relationships."

Jojo didn't mention she'd been up late reading the last couple nights. And the sexiest woman label had nothing to do with real life.

This wasn't the kind of advice she'd hoped for and she feared if the conversation continued, she'd only get more defensive. Leah meant well but didn't know Matt.

"I'm exhausted," she said.

"I'll bet."

Jojo rolled her eyes. "Goodnight, Leah. And even though you're a buzz kill, I still adore you."

"Same. And take care of yourself."

CHAPTER 17

IDA

IDA WAS STANDING on Gothic Bridge in Central Park, waiting for a hansom cab to come along the carriage path and pass below her. This was a good vantage point for a shot of the occupants—but only if they looked up. So far, two other carriages had passed by and in both cases, the couples had obliged.

The driver had tipped her off that he'd be giving a ride to a certain well-known tennis player and his latest paramour. It wasn't a likely feature piece, but some editor would find it useful as filler material.

Her phone vibrated, and she decided there was time to take the call—the carriage wasn't due for a few more minutes.

"Ida, it's Carson. Carson Skinner."

"You're the only Carson I know. At least the only one who calls me. What's up?"

"Just checking in."

That was obviously a lie. He only called when he wanted something, so she waited, forcing him to continue.

"Let's just say it's a slow day. Thought I'd see if you're hearing any rumors out there."

"About your girl?"

"You know how I like to stay ahead of the curve."

"I've got nothing fresh that you haven't already heard. The word on the street is that she was worn out after the tour. Then Matt Heston trashed her song and that put her over the deep end."

"It's total crap," he said.

"I figured as much, but it's great clickbait."

"You people suck," he said.

"Tell me something I don't know." Another carriage was approaching, but it wasn't her driver. "So, where's your girl hiding out? She's pulled quite the vanishing act."

"Dull as it sounds, she really is on vacation."

From his tone, Ida almost believed him, but she suspected there was more to it. Carson wasn't his usual cocky self.

"Hell of a business," he said, "when the truth is the last thing anybody believes."

"I've gotta run," Ida said. "My cab's here."

"Thanks for nothing."

"Back at ya." She hung up and got ready for the shot.

CHAPTER 18

MATT

MATT STOOD at the bathroom sink shaving. He was bare chested but had on his best jeans. Gracie peered through the half-open door. She was wearing some of her new clothes for the party—shorts and a T-shirt.

He checked out her wardrobe choice in the mirror. "Will that be dressy enough?"

"We're going to play some games outside. So, Cammy said to dress caszh."

"Me, too," he said. "I think I'll go *caszh*."

She frowned. "I hope you're going to wear a shirt."

"Of course, I'm wearing a shirt, you doofus. I was thinking of the one with blue checks."

"No way!" she said, as if he'd proposed wearing a lampshade. "Joelle's already seen you in that one."

"When?" He rinsed the traces of shaving cream from his face.

Gracie grabbed a towel off the hook and handed it to him. "At farmers market."

He looked at her doubtfully. "You can't seriously remember the shirt I wore two days ago."

She thought for a moment. "When I was practicing for the

hula-hoop contest, I watched you guys talking and I noticed the blue in your shirt looked nice with the blue in her shirt."

It seemed a strange detail to commit to memory. He was about to ask her about it when he checked his watch and noticed the time. "We've got to get moving."

"I'll pick one out for you," she said, doing a quick about-face in the hallway.

He followed her into his bedroom and watched as she went straight for a mostly white button-down with thin vertical black stripes.

"This one," she said, pulling it off the hanger and handing it to him. It wasn't worth asking why. He simply put it on.

"Did you wrap Cammy's gift yet?" he asked.

"Yup. It's down in the kitchen."

———

After he dropped Gracie off at the party, Matt picked up the pizza and headed to the cabin. Childless evenings were rare, and dates even more so.

All day, he'd been chuckling over shared moments from the past couple of nights. Joelle had a quick wit and was fearless about speaking her mind. She challenged him constantly and pulled no punches when they disagreed. And he loved it—the sparring, the tough questions, and especially the cute way she sometimes scrunched up her brow and glared at him, like when calling him out for the apparent sin of speed shopping.

Tonight, he wasn't sure what to expect. Although things were going well, he still knew very little about her. They'd skipped some normal conversation and backstory since Gracie was usually around, and he hoped they could fill in some missing parts tonight. He hadn't even asked if she was seeing anyone, though after that kiss, he was guessing no.

He'd also been thinking about her comment that shopping

together felt like "playing house." She often spoke bluntly—a quality that was sometimes jarring, but generally better than beating around the bush. He'd agreed, and now that they'd both acknowledged it, there was no immediate need to rehash it.

It was true; things were moving quickly, and that was often unwise. But Joelle was like an addiction, and he couldn't help himself. In the past, he'd always kept his love life and home life separate. Dating had been easier when his parents were living with them, and his mom and dad could watch Gracie while he went out. But somehow, he'd let his guard down and Gracie was as invested in this relationship as he was. That was the only part he regretted so far.

He glanced at the pizza box and then set his eyes back on the road. *Stop overthinking.* He should enjoy tonight and trust that Gracie would be fine. She was old enough to understand Joelle's visit was short term, though it wouldn't hurt to remind her from time to time.

Joelle was sitting on the porch as he drove up and at the sight of her, his misgivings vanished. As he got out of the truck, she set down a wine glass and stood up. This was the first time he'd seen her in a dress. It was in a bold floral print with spaghetti straps and hung to mid-thigh.

"Howdy, mister. Are you my pizza delivery boy?"

"That's pizza delivery *man*," he said, as he climbed the steps. "It's still hot, though it may not be for long."

"How about putting it here?" She picked up her wine glass from a small table between two chairs.

He set the box down and turned back to her. Except for the spaghetti straps, her shoulders were bare, and the dress was cut to a *V* between her breasts. Her skin was perfect and lightly tanned.

"That's a pretty dress."

She spun effortlessly, and the hem flared out. "Why, thank you for noticing." She was so at ease. A beautiful woman like Joelle probably dated a fair amount, whereas he was feeling out of practice.

"I almost didn't pack any nice clothes," she said. "I figured I'd be alone the whole time."

"Well, I'm glad you did. Not that you don't look nice normally." Jeez. He was suddenly fumbling for words. "I mean, you always look nice."

"You look good, too." Her arch tone gave the impression she enjoyed keeping him off balance. She led the way inside. "Now, let's get some plates and something for you to drink."

He was halfway across the living room when he noticed the kitchen cabinets. They were knotty pine—a popular mid-century style, but it was the details that caught his attention. They were familiar.

"This is such a classic camp kitchen," he said. His professional curiosity led him to a small drawer. "Do you mind?"

"Are you asking permission to check out Leah's drawers?"

He smiled, then carefully pulled it all the way out. It was full of spatulas and whisks and serving spoons, and he turned it around to see the back. "Take a look."

She came closer and read the stamped letters. "K. N. Heston."

"My grandfather. He started the business." It was a treat to find some of Pop's early work. "I bet he built these around the fifties or sixties. How long have the Skobys owned the place?"

"I think it was right before I met Leah. Maybe five or six years."

Matt reinserted the drawer and slid it home. "Are you guys close?"

"We talk most days. She's my bestie, but don't tell Gracie. *She's* still my Westbury bestie."

He frowned. "Guess I won't ask where that leaves me."

"Ohhh," she said, as if comforting a wounded puppy. She sidled up closer. "Let's see if we can put a little salve on that ego." It came out as a whisper as her mouth inched closer. Suddenly, they were kissing again. It was more intense this time, and it lasted until they both surfaced for air. She dropped her arms and stepped back.

"Pizza's getting cold," she said offhandedly, as if she hadn't just rocked his world. "I'll get plates. Drinks are in the fridge."

He was tempted to reel her back in and doubted she'd resist, but decided instead to play it cool and went to the refrigerator.

"I'm not sure when Gracie will call, so I'm just going to have a soda. Do you want more wine?"

She was standing behind him, and he could feel her eyes on his back.

He turned and held up the bottle. "Is this what you're drinking?"

"Yes, thanks." She held out her glass, and he refilled it.

He felt conscious of every movement—both his and hers. It was almost like slow dancing for the first time. He put the bottle back in the refrigerator and then watched as she reached for two plates in one of the upper cabinets. As she raised her arm, the hem of her dress crept a little higher.

Just as he was beginning to overheat, he was distracted by a crack in the glass door of the cabinet. He reached past her and ran his fingers over the fracture. It felt stable—probably not a hazard.

"I haven't noticed that before," she said. "Funny how your eye went right to it."

"Occupational habit." He opened the door and looked at the back. "It's an easy fix. I'll put in tempered glass this time. It'll be safer, but I can't cut tempered glass in my shop. I'll have to order it."

She looked at him, half amused. "You're sweet. It's probably been broken for years, but if you really want to fix it, make sure you put it on my tab."

"Don't worry about it. Pops would want me to do it."

They ended up on the porch, sitting side by side with the pizza and drinks between them. It had been warm all day, and the sun was still well above the horizon.

"Margherita," she said, picking up a slice. "Well done, you."

"When I went to order, I realized I didn't have a clue what you like, and I didn't have your number."

"So, you asked Gracie?"

"Yeah." He looked at her suspiciously. "Did she text you?"

Joelle laughed and nodded. "How is it you can see a woman three nights in a row and still not have her digits? Here, give me your phone."

He opened the screen on his cell and handed it over. Her thumbs flew over the keypad as nimbly as Gracie's. On a fret board, his own fingers were equally agile, but he'd never transferred those skills to the phone.

"Do you want mine?" he asked as she handed it back.

She rolled her eyes. "No, silly. The guy is supposed to call first. You really are clueless about dating."

He liked the way she razzed him sometimes. "Maybe that's because I don't get much practice."

"No way." She looked skeptical. "I'll bet your wanted poster is hanging in half the boudoirs in the county."

He nearly choked on a bite. "Boudoirs and wanted posters? I feel like I just walked into a spaghetti western. The truth is, all those stories about lawsuits and settlements scared off most women."

"Maybe that was a blessing," she said. "It separates the wheat from the chaff when you take money off the table." She grinned. "And in case you're wondering, I'm the wheat in this parable."

"And here I took you for a gold digger."

She looked amused. "Money and kidding aside, what about the Heston mystique? Nobody can take that away."

True, nobody had taken it away, but sometimes he wondered if he'd thrown it away. "I'm afraid the Heston mystique is buried under years of sawdust. But I appreciate the sentiment. And I wasn't lying when I said I don't date much—probably not once since my parents moved." He wasn't exaggerating, but from her expression, he wasn't sure she believed him. "How about you?" he asked. "You're attractive, talented, and not a bad kisser."

Somehow, she managed to smile and look uncomfortable at the same time. "I was with a guy for about four years. Officially, the breakup was recent, but we've been growing apart for a long time."

He wondered how recent and if it had anything to do with her coming to Vermont, but before he could ask, her phone pinged.

"Sorry. I meant to turn it off." She glanced down, then hesitated. "It's from Gracie. You mind?"

"Of course not."

Jojo chuckled, then held her phone up. "It's a pic of Cammy wearing the earrings. Apparently, they were a hit. I'll give her a thumbs-up."

It seemed odd that Gracie was messaging this grown woman as if they were school friends. Then again, Joelle had played a part in picking out the gift.

"I hope she's not texting you too often," he said.

"It's only the second or third time." Joelle didn't seem in the least bit concerned, so he dropped it.

"You mentioned your parents earlier," she said. "Did they live with you?"

"More like we lived with them. We moved in after my wife died. Gracie was three, and I was a mess. Mom took over the parenting, and I checked out for a while." He rarely talked about that time, but tonight the words were coming easily. "I'm not proud of the way I behaved. When you have a kid, you should step up no matter what."

"Sometimes our families step up for us," Joelle said. It was a simple statement with no sign of judgment.

"Yeah, but moving back home is a slippery slope. It started out with Mom making our meals, but soon she was doing my laundry and taking care of Gracie, and I was sleeping late and taking long, self-indulgent walks." He sometimes thought about how much better Natalie would have handled single parenthood if she were the one who had lived. "It wasn't my proudest moment."

Joelle didn't respond—just continued eating and listening.

"I don't know why I'm rambling on like this. I should have given you the option of the short answer."

"It's all good," she said. "Don't forget, I've met Gracie, so I know there's a happy ending."

She had a point. The story was less dreary in hindsight. Back then, everything had seemed dark.

"For a couple of months, I sure couldn't see that ending," he continued. "Then one evening Dad said he needed help with a cabinet install the next day. He didn't ask. He simply told me to be in the shop at seven."

"Smart dad."

"I think he would have done it sooner, but for a while, everybody assumed I was going back on the road with the band."

Joelle raised her eyebrows, but he pretended not to notice. He wasn't ready for that conversation. Not tonight.

"At any rate, I went to work the next morning and I've worked in the shop ever since."

"What about the parenting bit?" she asked. "When did you turn into Super Dad?"

He laughed. "That's still a work in progress, but things improved once I felt useful again. Then one Saturday, I woke to Gracie jumping on my bed and saying she was hungry. 'Go find your Gram,' I told her, but it turned out they'd taken off for a couple days to visit friends in Barre." He chuckled at the memory. "All they left was a note."

"Sounds like a dose of old-fashioned therapy," Joelle said.

"That it was. Gracie and I survived the weekend, and from then on, I started acting like a father again. But Mom still gets a lot of the credit."

"Where are they now?"

"Scottsdale. My dad's knees were giving him trouble. Too

many years of crawling around installing cabinets. So now they've got a nice one-floor condo, which his knees and back appreciate. And my mom didn't mind saying goodbye to the cold, though she misses her granddaughter."

"How did Gracie handle it?"

"I thought she was fine at first, but I think she misses having a woman in the house." That sounded awkward, and he hoped Joelle wouldn't infer anything from it.

Matt's phone pinged, and he saw it was Gracie. He doubted the party was over yet. He read the message twice, feeling at first surprised and then a little unsettled.

"Everything okay?"

He did his best to act unfazed and decided to share only part of the message. "Breaking news. Apparently, Cammy's mom prefers my version of 'Sweet Side.'"

"That's not surprising. There were bound to be one or two." Joelle grinned at her own joke.

He was growing accustomed to these sparring matches. "Nice that you find yourself amusing."

"Did Gracie poll her friends as well?"

"She probably didn't want to hurt my feelings, but now that you bring it up, how would you vote?"

"It depends on my mood. Your version is mellow, and Jojo's is"—there was a long pause as she dug around for the right words —"not so mellow."

"Spoken like a true diplomat."

"Is something else bothering you?" she asked. "Was there more to Gracie's text?"

Apparently, he wasn't good at hiding it. He considered making something up but figured Joelle would see through that as well.

"She also asked how our date is going and whether you like my shirt. She even put a dozen heart emojis at the end." That bothered him the most. "She's at a party, surrounded by friends, yet she's on her phone texting us."

Joelle nodded sympathetically. "I get why you're concerned, but don't read too much into it until you talk to her."

"Am I overreacting?"

She shrugged. "Who knows what goes on in the head of a twelve-year-old? And would it be so bad if she's simply happy for you?"

They'd been having an enjoyable evening, and he didn't want to change the mood. He thought he'd shaken off those earlier reservations during the drive over, but they were still dogging him.

"It's my own fault," he said. "I should have dropped her off and come over without telling her where I was going."

"Yeah, but then you couldn't have dressed up and worn that delicious shirt." She raised her eyebrows, as if trying to add some levity.

"Don't get me started on the shirt," he grumbled. "You'll probably think it's silly, but I was planning to wear one with blue checks."

"The one you wore to the farmers market?" Joelle asked.

He scratched his temple. *Women.*

"Yeah, that shirt. But Gracie wanted to make sure I made a good impression."

Joelle guessed where this was going. "So, she nixed that shirt and picked this one."

"Yeah, she's clearly rooting for us. And she's made other references, too. I just can't shake the feeling that the longer this goes on, the worse she's going to feel when you leave."

"Maybe you're not giving her enough credit," Joelle said. "Even if she is only twelve, she knows relationships take time. I realize it's early days, but I truly like you, Matt, and I can see a situation where we keep seeing each other, even after I leave for home. If that happens, I could come back to visit from time to time and you guys could visit me in the city. It would be a blast, and I bet Gracie would love it."

Joelle had just answered two questions: She wasn't looking for a summer fling and, apparently, she didn't have a boyfriend squirreled away in New York. As Matt digested these revelations, she misinterpreted his silence.

"Oh my. That came out sounding as if I've mapped out our entire future."

He smiled and put a hand on her knee. "No worries. I appreciate the frankness. We would never have a conversation like this if I didn't have a daughter. So, you get nothing but bonus points for honesty."

She appeared to take him at his word and seemed relieved.

"But I want to be upfront," he said. "I've tried the whole long-distance thing. It's hard at the best of times and sometimes downright painful."

"When you were on the road with the band?" she asked.

He nodded. "At least Natalie and I had marriage vows to hold us together . . . and a child. I saw some guys fall in love, either back home or with a girl they met on the road, and then struggle to make it work. And these were decent men. But couples need regular, steady connection. Without it, feelings cool off."

"Did that happen between you and Natalie?" Joelle asked. "Did your feelings cool off?"

It was a deeply personal question, but they'd already dropped any pretense of light conversation.

"There were times when I was distracted—consumed with my career and not thinking enough about things back home. But I never cheated if that's what you're asking. My parents loved Natalie and would have killed me. Whenever I'd talk to my dad from the road, he'd always say stuff like 'You do right by your family, son.'"

Joelle chuckled. "Did your mom ride your case, too?"

"Oh, yeah. If Dad was all about honor and duty, Mom was more like, 'Don't you dare break that girl's heart.'"

This time, they both smiled.

"That's perfect," Joelle said. "I like family stories like that. It gives me hope for the world."

It was a nice sentiment, and he suspected it was a glimpse into her own character.

"Since I've never been married," Joelle said, "I realize it's a poor comparison, but I've never cheated on a boyfriend. It's just not in my DNA."

He believed her, but sex wasn't the only thing that broke up relationships. The adrenaline rush from being on stage had been his drug of choice—an addiction to which he had succumbed completely. He'd ridden some crazy highs while chasing his dreams, only to come crashing down under the massive guilt that he wasn't missing his family nearly enough. "It's not just about sex," he mused, half to himself. "Obsessions and temptations come in all forms."

The pizza sat between them, mostly uneaten and somewhat forgotten. It seemed they'd both sunk into a state of introspection.

"I think I know what you're talking about," she said. "It's easy to sit here in this idyllic place and imagine having it all—a life with both love and music. But deep down, I know the moment I get back to New York, my work will consume me again. Ever since I got my first guitar, I've put music above everything else, even friendships and family."

Her words were laced with guilt, and he felt a melancholy shift in her mood. But, more than that, he noticed they were speaking the same language without judging one another. If there was one difference between them, it was that Matt had finally learned to put his family first. It had been a painful lesson and full of missteps, but in the end, he felt like he'd gotten it right.

She was staring at him intensely. "I'm a little worried. I thought we were having a cautionary discussion. Mistakes to avoid. That sort of thing. But now I feel you're taking this somewhere else."

Maybe he hadn't known at the beginning either, but somewhere during the conversation he'd realized he didn't want to develop feelings for this woman, only to deal with the inevitable separation.

He hung his head. "I'm sorry."

"Can we at least think about this?" Joelle said. "Distance and careers are challenging, but people make it work all the time."

He wanted to believe those words and continue enjoying the evening and her company. Her long legs and flawless skin made it all the harder to think rationally. But this was where his experience trumped her inexperience. He knew firsthand what it was like when relationships were full of constant goodbyes.

She read his silence for what it was and slumped back in her chair. "If you're about to end this, Matt, at least give me some clarity. Otherwise, I'll be sitting here tonight, wondering what the hell just happened." Buried in her disappointment was also the message that this decision was entirely on him. She was not a willing accomplice.

"I know this really sucks," he said, cringing at his choice of words. It was an understatement that minimized his fondness for her.

She responded with a wry smile and a bit of sarcasm. "Well, if my dating history is any guide, we were bound to find each other's faults eventually. Two more dates and repulsion might have set in."

Matt doubted that and knew her words were coming from a place of hurt. "I hate to bring up another issue," he said. "And we can discuss it another time, if you prefer. It's just that Gracie adores you and—"

"Of course, she can keep coming over," Joelle said. "She already knows it's only for a few weeks. Plus, I enjoy her company."

"Thank you. I know she'll still be sad to see you go at the end, but there's no way we can put that horse back in the barn."

She rolled her eyes at his glib turn of phrase.

He felt terrible and needed to leave before he lost his resolve. "I better go. Not that I want to, but I just better."

They both got up, and she immediately wrapped her arms around him as if she could change his mind by anchoring him to the spot. He pulled her in tightly, one hand cradling her head against his chest. He felt wretched and feared that a mile down the road, he'd realize he was a fool.

Neither of them was in a hurry to let go, and he couldn't resist burying his face in her hair. She smelled wonderful.

"I'm sorry. I'm making this worse," he whispered. Finally, he pulled away and strode down the stairs. He got into his truck without looking back and drove out of the driveway.

CHAPTER 19

―――――――

JoJo

THE SUN HAD SET and the half-eaten pizza was still sitting beside her. Jojo got up and went inside to refill her wine glass, then returned to the porch.

Matt's sudden departure left her feeling blindsided. How could a guy go full speed ahead one moment and then slam on the brakes? This was why you could never really know a man until you saw him deal with adversity. The two of them had seemed perfect together, but at the first sign of trouble, he couldn't get away fast enough.

She checked her phone for the time and decided that Leah probably had the boys in bed. She called and her friend picked up.

"Are the kids asleep?"

"Lights are out, but I can't guarantee they're down for good."

"I miss them and sure could use some of their sweet hugs right now." She made no attempt to hide her feelings.

"Oh no," Leah said. "I take it the date didn't go well?"

"I don't know if I'm more sad or mad. At least we were both civil. It even ended with a hug, and I mean a long, melt-my-heart kind of hug. It was so weird."

"What happened?"

"Nothing really. It was great one moment and then it wasn't. He just doesn't want to do long distance. Period."

"Wow, that came up quick. Maybe he'll change his mind."

Jojo doubted it. "To be honest, this makes everything easier. I was ready to ditch Joelle tonight and be myself—at least around Matt. But who knows? That might have made him run off just as fast."

"It's still a bummer," Leah said. "It sounded like you were good together."

"We were. We absolutely were. But I need a guy who doesn't scare so easily—someone who won't bolt just because life is complicated."

"You'll find someone," Leah said. "Once word gets out that you're back in circulation . . ."

That sounded exhausting and right now, Jojo was tired. Disappointed and tired.

"You know," she said, "the really crazy part is that, even when we were at odds tonight, I had this totally disjointed moment when I thought, I'm mad at this guy, but I don't want him to leave."

Leah laughed. "That sounds like marriage."

If that was true, maybe Jojo was better off on her own. "Speaking of marriage," she said, "is there any chance that wonderful husband of yours would let you slip away for a weekend? I could really use the company."

"Well, I've been waiting for an invitation."

"It's your cabin, Leah. You hardly need an invite."

Leah lowered her voice, and Jojo guessed Tom might be within earshot. "To be honest, I'm desperate to come. The cabin's always great, but the chance to be there with my best friend and no little ones running around yelling, 'Mommy, where are my socks? Mommy, can I have a snack? Mommy—'"

"Okay, okay," Jojo laughed. "I get the picture."

"Unfortunately," Leah said, "they've added an all-day rehearsal

Saturday, so this weekend's out. But I desperately want to get up there before you leave. I've already hinted at it, and Tom didn't freak out."

"That would be so awesome," Jojo said. "Just having that to look forward to—"

"It's not a hundred percent, but if it works out, I get first dibs on the hammock."

"What hammock?"

"Oh, did I forget to tell you?" Leah said. "Guess I'll have to discount your rent for the first week."

"We'll get back to that later. So, where's this hammock?"

"Look inside the window seat. You need to take the cushion off first."

Jojo went indoors and discovered the entire seat was hinged. Inside were a bunch of old board games, along with a rolled-up hammock. "Found it. Now where do I hang it?"

"There are hooks on the porch. Just wait until tomorrow when it's light. You'll figure it out. It's simple. And enjoy it while you can because when I get there, it's all mine." Jojo noticed that this time Leah said *when* and not *if*.

She was already unrolling the hammock. "It looks pretty big. I bet we can share."

"I don't think so," Leah said. "Have you seen these hips lately?"

"You're full of it."

"Gotta go," Leah said.

"Give Tom a big hug for me."

"No way am I passing on any hugs from you. Last night when I came to bed, he was lying on top of the covers with a big ole grin and a T-shirt that said 'I love Jojo.'"

Jojo burst out laughing.

"I don't know what you think is so funny," Leah said. "Apparently, you gave it to him."

"It was supposed to be a gift for you. He said he wanted a size large so you could wear it as a nightshirt."

"Well, it's mine now. I stripped it off him."

"TMI!" Jojo laughed.

"Well, I wasn't going to let him wear it. It's tough enough having you prancing around the apartment on a regular basis."

"Hey! I never prance, and on a completely objective scale, *you* have a much hotter body."

"Ya think?"

"Oh spare me," Jojo groaned. "I am not staying on the line just to pump up your ego. Now go make your man happy. The fact that you have a man and I don't should tell you something."

CHAPTER 20

JOJO

THE NEXT DAY was custom-made for moping around. It rained most of the morning and, though it tapered off by noon, it remained gray and damp.

At some point, Jojo received a brief text from Matt: *I didn't say anything to Gracie.* That was it. He didn't even ask if she was okay.

She attempted to channel her feelings into a breakup song, but that felt juvenile. It would be embarrassing if the song went anywhere, and she had to admit it was about a guy she'd known for all of three days. This little pity party had to end, but for one day, she needed some breathing room and texted Gracie that she wasn't feeling well enough to play.

In the late afternoon, Jojo lay in the hammock under an old camp blanket that smelled vaguely of mothballs. She was on her back, staring up at the sky-blue porch ceiling, when her phone rang. It was Carson and she almost let it go to voicemail, but she couldn't keep avoiding him.

"Hey, Carson."

"*Finally!* Do you have any idea how worried I've been? It's like you totally disappeared."

She refused to let him rattle her. "I told you we'd talk in a few days and here we are."

"You broke up with me over the phone and then hung up." He was using his sulky voice. At least he wasn't in complete denial, which seemed like progress.

"You know these things are never easy," she said. "It's been hard for me, too. Four years is a lot of time to be together."

"How long have you been planning this?"

Now he sounded like he was accusing her of something. She didn't blame him for being hurt, but did they really have to do a full autopsy?

"It wasn't all at once," she said. "It came on slowly."

"But what happened? You've gotta give me *something*."

She wasn't in the mood for this but figured she owed him some sort of explanation. "Well, for one thing, our energy levels are different."

"Are you kidding me?! On a scale of ten, we're both nines and tens. Ask any of our friends. When it comes to energy, we couldn't be more compatible."

"But that's where you've misunderstood me. I know how to be a ten, but then I need to go home and chill."

"We didn't turn you into a star by chilling. But I know you need some downtime. That's why I've always encouraged you to keep your own apartment. See? I know you better than you know yourself."

Did he actually believe any part of that? It felt like they were speaking in different tongues and no amount of explaining was going to break through.

"Carson, I can't do this. I know it seems unfair that I'm making this decision unilaterally, but isn't that the way breakups usually are?" She was extra annoyed today and poor Carson was getting both barrels, his and Matt's. "You and I have grown in different directions and need to find a way to get past this."

The silence was so long, she glanced at the screen to make sure they were still connected. Just then, she heard Gracie's bike on the driveway.

"Carson, I've got to go. Somebody's here."

"Who? Is it a guy?"

He had no right to ask, but if she wanted to lower the heat, it was better to pacify him. "It's just a neighbor kid. I'm giving a guitar lesson."

"Are you joking? Do you need cash?"

She took a little satisfaction in his confusion. That might distract him for a while. She waved to Gracie, who waited at the bottom of the steps.

"Carson, next time before you call, please send an itinerary and we'll stick to business. It won't always be like this—just for a while."

She waited, giving him a chance to respond, but he didn't. She hated this kind of tension because it settled into her belly like a lead weight. Finally, she said goodbye and hung up.

"Sorry about that," Jojo said, swinging her legs over the edge of the hammock. Gracie had come without her guitar, so she must have gotten the text.

"No problem," Gracie said. "Are you contagious?"

"No. It's safe to come aboard."

"I didn't tell Dad how you're feeling, since I figured it might be . . . well, you know . . . cramps or something."

Despite her sour mood, Jojo couldn't help but smile at Gracie's forthrightness. "Did your grandmother teach you about that?"

She shook her head. "Dad knows the school nurse and asked her to talk to me. It was so embarrassing."

"That was resourceful of him."

"Dad always says, 'It takes a village, so good thing we live in one.'"

With Gracie spitting out folksy sayings, it was tough to stay grumpy. "So you got my text?"

"Yeah, but I came anyway, in case you're lonely or need some help. I could make you some herbal tea—if you have some."

"I don't really have cramps."

"Oh." Gracie bit her lower lip. "So, did you and Dad have a fight?"

"What makes you think that?"

"He barely spoke to me last night and then you texted about not feeling well." So much for hiding things from Gracie. "Plus, he wrote this check for twenty-five dollars and said I have to pay every time I come over." She handed the somewhat crumpled check to Jojo and then sat down. "He doesn't know your last name, so that part's blank."

What the hell? This was insulting on so many levels. Her friendship status with Gracie was being revoked and now she was an employee? And a poorly paid one at that! Did he actually think twenty-five dollars was the going rate? What century was he living in?

She looked from the check to Gracie, who was on the verge of crying.

"I thought we were like two friends jamming. That's what it felt like."

Jojo dropped to her knees in front of the child and tried to console her. "That's how it feels to me, too. That's how it is."

"But when I got your text, I thought—"

"That was just for today. Most days, I still want to jam. It's one of my favorite things."

"Really?" Gracie looked doubtful.

"Absolutely, positively." Jojo held out the check. "Tell your dad I appreciate the gesture, but it isn't necessary."

The girl shook her head adamantly. "He said you'd say that. But you're a professional and it isn't fair to take advantage of you." Clearly, she'd been coached.

"You're not taking advantage of me." Jojo's tone was gentle and reassuring. "I love every moment of having you here."

Gracie's forlorn expression persisted, making her look younger than usual. *Poor kid, she didn't deserve to be caught in the middle of this.*

Then, without warning, the girl threw her arms around Jojo and held on for dear life. "You're the best thing that's happened to me in a long time."

Jojo returned the hug and felt a wave of warmth but reminded herself this was the type of attachment Matt feared.

Gracie abruptly released her grip and brushed moisture from her eyes. "When did you get a hammock?" It was challenging to keep pace with her shifting moods.

"I just set it up. Wanna try it?"

"Definitely." The gloom magically lifted, and Gracie went over and climbed in. "I've always wanted one."

Jojo realized the check was still in her hand and it was more crumpled and even a little damp now. "Do you think there's any way we can change your dad's mind about paying me?"

"I'll try," Gracie said. "But I think I should wait a few days. Anyway, if I'm really going to take lessons from you, there's something I've been trying to figure out. I don't know how you bend the strings the way you do."

"It's a blues technique, but nowadays, lots of guitarists use it."

"Dad showed me on his electric, but it's totally different on the acoustic."

"Yeah, it's really not the same," Jojo said. "The common mistake is trying to rely totally on your finger muscles. You've got to rotate your arm slightly. I'll go get my guitar." As she went inside, she yelled back, "I'm getting a soda. You want one?"

"Yes, please. And I'm loving your hammock."

Chapter 21

Matt

Life was returning to normal in the Heston household, with two exceptions. For one, "Sweet Side" continued to inch its way up the charts. Matt knew this from Gracie's daily reports. With each announcement, he'd grouse about the likely return of the paparazzi if the song were to hit number one, but secretly, it was nice to feel relevant again.

The other exception to normalcy was Gracie's continuing friendship with Joelle. He worried the time she was spending at the cabin was cutting into time with friends her own age.

"But Dad, I still hang out with Cammy all day at camp. We're still best friends."

Even so, her attachment to Joelle had been so abrupt that it left him wondering if this was a cry for help. Was she looking for a big sister or a surrogate mother? In his uncertainty, he'd let it go on for a week, but at twenty-five dollars a pop, it was getting out of hand. So, at dinner on Friday night, he laid out a new set of rules.

"No going over on the weekend. Joelle needs some time to herself."

"But she's having fun, too. We're amazing together."

"Honey, I'm sure she enjoys it, but she's probably thinking the same thing I am—this every-day thing is a bit much. And frankly, we can't afford it. So next week you can go twice. Just pick your days and let Joelle know when you'll be there."

Her face drooped, and he prepared himself for tears or a fight or both. But he wasn't ready for utter desolation.

"Joelle wasn't even going to charge me. That was your idea."

"Because it's the fair thing to do."

The tears were flowing now. He could handle an argument, but not this look of soul-crushing anguish.

"You are such a mean . . . hypocrite!" She ran from the room and left him staring at the doorway. Like any child, she'd had her share of outbursts over the years, but she was taking this like a deep personal injury. And *hypocrite*? That didn't even make sense.

He thought of following her upstairs, but decided to give it a little time. He did the dishes and cleaned up. Then he went into the living room and took one of his acoustic guitars down from the wall. They still called it the living room and there was indeed a couch and an overstuffed chair, but after his parents moved out, the instruments and sound equipment gradually migrated up from the basement until the room more closely resembled a recording studio.

He played a song they'd been working on recently. Gracie was partial to the keyboard part because her mother had written and played it on Matt's first album. It included a long, "Layla"-esque solo.

He heard occasional movements upstairs and wondered if the storm had passed. Music had always been their way of smoothing things over. She would eventually come down and wordlessly pick up her guitar or stand at the keyboard and join in on whatever song he was playing. But tonight, there was no response.

After a while, he hung up his guitar and sat on the sofa with his laptop. He'd been woefully unsuccessful at pushing Joelle out of his mind, and it didn't help that Gracie wouldn't stop talking about her. If he was honest with himself, he guessed he was feeling a little jealous.

His fingers hovered over the laptop keyboard until at last, he typed five words into the search bar: *Joelle guitar lessons New York*. But nothing relevant appeared. He had tried those same keywords before, so there was no reason to expect new results. And then he thought about the checks and the fact that he'd been leaving her name blank. He logged into his bank account, but to his annoyance, she hadn't cashed a single one.

Unwilling to give up, he tried a different search, this time including Leah Skoby's name. Since they were friends, maybe they'd worked together, but again, nothing came up.

He got distracted by the vast body of work Leah had on YouTube. He watched one video and then another. The style wasn't exactly his taste, but he could see why they were popular.

"What are you doing?" Gracie was halfway down the stairs. It seemed some music could still get her attention.

"Do you know if Joelle has any YouTube videos?"

She shook her head. "I tried Googling her, but I couldn't find anything. Once I asked about her last name, but she acted like she didn't hear me and started talking about something else."

Apparently, he wasn't the only curious person in the Heston household. Relieved that Gracie was talking to him again, he wanted to keep the momentum going. "Joelle plays really well, doesn't she?"

"She's strong on guitar. Maybe a little better on rhythm than lead."

"I just heard her that one time," Matt said. "I also thought her vocals were good."

Gracie came the rest of the way down the stairs, losing her sullen expression. "At first, Joelle's voice seemed kind of average, but it turns out she was holding back. I think she was afraid of singing over me, but then realized she didn't have to worry."

Matt fought back a smile. Now and then, Gracie let her ego show. "So, she's even better than the time I heard."

"Yeah."

Huh. There had to be more to Joelle's story than she was telling, but he'd given up the right to ask personal questions.

"I need a big piece of cardboard," Gracie said, changing the subject.

"What for?"

"I'm working on something."

He was curious, but assumed he'd find out soon enough. "There's some folded boxes in the shop. You okay with a utility knife?"

"Of course."

"Well, just be careful," he called after her.

"Dad, I'm not a little kid."

The screen door slammed, and he let out a heavy sigh. He wasn't doing very well this evening—in the father department or as a cyber sleuth. His eyes returned to the computer. Why was he so curious about Joelle, anyway? He spent far too much time thinking about a woman who would soon be gone and out of their lives. With that thought, he closed his laptop.

———

The next morning, Gracie came to breakfast with a cardboard sign that read YARD SALE. On the back he noticed she'd originally tried to write SCHOLARSHIP SALE, but it hadn't fit. With stony resolve, she explained her plan to sell her childhood toys and any clothes she'd outgrown.

"And your intention is . . .?"

"To help pay for more lessons."

He was torn between irritation and respect for her enterprising spirit. He decided to let it play out and figured that after a couple of hours of sitting in the hot sun, she might do the math and give up.

Since the grass was still wet from the dew, he helped her spread a blue plastic tarp and then watched from the kitchen window as she neatly spread out her sale items. He even went through his sock drawer, gathering up coins and putting them in a shoebox so she'd have some change to get started.

It only took about a half hour for Matt's attitude to soften. If it meant this much to her, he hated to see her fail. His change of heart led him to the attic where three generations of Hestons had been storing their castoffs. Truth be told, he'd been wanting to clean the place out for years, and if it helped Gracie's entrepreneurial venture, so much the better. He grabbed a box and headed downstairs.

As he emerged from the kitchen onto the porch, he spotted Joelle talking to Gracie. She was dressed more casually than he'd seen her before, in a pink tank top and cutoff jeans. She waved—perhaps a little tentatively—and he smiled back. He wouldn't blame her if she excused herself and took off, but part of him hoped she'd stay for at least a few minutes. It might be nice if they could smooth things over, especially since Gracie was spending so much time at her place.

"You in the market for any stuffed animals?" he asked.

"This one's a cutie," she said, picking up a stuffed horse.

Matt was taken aback by what she was holding. "Gracie, honey, your mother gave you that."

She looked startled. "Oh, I forgot. That's not for sale." She snatched it back and held it close to her chest as she surveyed the rest of the items on the tarp.

"I think we should rethink this," Matt said. "Even if you're too old to play with some of these things, at least a few have special memories."

"But I need the money." Her jaw was firmly set.

He could only imagine what was going through Joelle's mind as she witnessed this little family drama. "You know," he said, "I found this box of stuff in the attic and there's tons more I've been wanting to clean out. Plus, there's a bunch in the basement."

Gracie looked at him cautiously, as if hesitant to get her hopes up.

"We might even make a few hundred dollars," he said. "For the scholarship fund."

As though the clouds had suddenly parted, Gracie threw her arms around him. "Thanks, Dad. And I'll do most of the work. You don't have to do a thing."

"Actually. I need you to stay out here and handle customers. I'll bring everything out."

"Can I help?" Joelle asked. "I was just on my way to the store, but I can do my shopping later."

"It's nice of you to offer," he said, "but we've got it covered."

"Have you ever done this before?" she asked.

"How hard can it be?"

She smiled in a know-it-all way. "Well, I guess you're about to find out." She turned to leave. "Gracie, I applaud your tenacity. I hope it's a huge success."

"Wait!" Gracie said. "Have *you* done this before?"

"Yup." Although her eyes were on Gracie, Matt suspected she was speaking to him. "My family moved a couple times when I was growing up and each time, we did a big garage sale. Most people start a couple days ahead of time. But fortunately, your dad is big and strong and will have no trouble hauling everything out here, while also sifting through each box to make sure you don't accidentally sell any priceless family heirlooms. And don't get me started on pricing, but I'm sure he's okay leaving that up to you, Gracie." She spun around and headed back to her car. "Good luck, guys."

Damn, she was infuriating!

Gracie tugged at his arm. "Go after her. We need her."

"We definitely don't." If his daughter had been a little older, he might have added a few choice words about patronizing city people but held his tongue.

He turned away and headed back to the house. As he climbed to the attic a second time, he was even more determined to make this sale a success. One thing was certain, he was going to get a workout today—two flights up and two flights down and who knew how many trips.

The good news was that Gracie was fired up and every time he brought her another box, she immediately unpacked it. He got another tarp from the shed and brought out two sawhorses and a sheet of plywood to create a table. In no time, cars were stopping and people were looking through stuff. The only problem was that Gracie didn't know what to charge for anything, and he wasn't much better.

On about the twentieth trip from the attic, Matt was carrying a pair of lamps and feeling winded when he discovered Joelle in the kitchen. She was standing at the open refrigerator, rearranging things to make room for a brown paper bag.

"Gracie told me to put this in here. I figured you'd be too busy to make lunch, so I brought sandwiches from the deli."

"Thank you. That was thoughtful." He may have sounded more brusque than intended, but he needed to get outside and see how Gracie was doing.

"There's some chips, too," she said, nodding to another bag on the counter.

This was all very generous, but he didn't know what more to say. He'd been clear about not needing help, yet here she was in his kitchen . . . helping.

She must have sensed his discomfort because she immediately closed the refrigerator and made a beeline for the door. "Sorry for intruding. I'll get out of your hair now."

This was precisely the challenge of dealing with women. Even when he was perfectly upfront and clear, he often ended up feeling like the bad guy. "Hold on, please wait." But she kept moving, and he followed her through the swinging door, still carrying a lamp in each hand. "Thank you again. We're going to love those sandwiches. I don't have my wallet on me, but Gracie has a shoebox with money, and she can pay you back."

Joelle whirled around so fast they almost collided. "Matt, knock it off. It hurts my feelings when you turn every act of friendship into a business transaction."

Even in the chaotic craziness, her words hit home. He should simply accept her kindness and not try to read anything into it. At the same moment, he realized the number of people on the lawn had doubled and a little panic may have shown in his eyes.

"What are you going to charge for those?" Joelle said, looking appraisingly at the lamps.

"I don't have a clue."

"First of all," she said, "you'll need at least one light bulb and an outlet so people can test them."

"There's an outlet on the porch."

"They're nice lamps," she continued, "and they look like they're in good shape. But lamps never sell well at yard sales. I'd ask for twenty and be willing to take fifteen."

He was thinking higher, and she must have read his thoughts.

"You can try thirty, but the last thing we want is to have to carry them back upstairs at the end of the day."

Somewhere in this brief exchange, she'd shifted from saying 'you' to 'we' and at the same time, Matt realized he and Gracie were in over their heads.

"Okay, you're hired."

She frowned, and he rephrased the offer.

"What if I promise not to pay you?"

"That's better," she said, taking the lamps from him. "I'll stay out here with Gracie, and you get more stuff."

"But I'm still the boss," he said, turning back toward the house.

"Keep telling yourself that."

As he ran up the two flights, he felt lighter. It was a relief to know Gracie wasn't out there alone.

He grabbed a wobbly old rocking chair and headed back downstairs.

CHAPTER 22

Jojo

THE FIRST THING Jojo did was rescue a handful of items that looked like potential keepsakes and put them aside. There was a plaster handprint that said Matt Heston, age five; a leather bag of antique marbles; and a cardboard tube with Matt's high school diploma. As Matt brought out more boxes, she kept her eyes open for anything that looked like it might have sentimental value and placed those items into a box labeled NOT FOR SALE.

Matt's guess on the value of the lamps had been better than hers. She got thirty dollars for the pair, but only after tracking down a Sharpie and coercing Matt to autograph the shades. That's when Jojo realized celebrity yard sales were a unique breed. Once people saw Matt signing stuff, they wanted their items signed as well—everything from a teapot with a chipped spout to an antique pair of snowshoes. By about the twentieth request, she worried he might have had enough of the foolishness, but he was a good sport about it. Even Gracie thought it was cool that she could sell almost anything with her dad's signature.

Jojo had never seen a kid work harder. Gracie bounced around with a smile, holding up items and yelling, "Price check!" To which

Jojo would shout back her best guess. This went on for the rest of the morning and into the early afternoon.

Around two o'clock, business slowed to a trickle, and Matt set up camp chairs beside the makeshift table. Gracie brought out the deli sandwiches and all three of them collapsed into their chairs, feeling a bit dazed.

"That was intense," Matt said. "When I woke up this morning, I never saw that coming."

"We should do this more often," Gracie said.

Matt unwrapped his sandwich. "Sorry, kiddo. We cleaned out most of the attic and basement."

A young couple approached with a mirror in an arts-and-crafts frame and when Matt named a price, they decided against it. As they walked away, he looked at Jojo for a second opinion.

"The feeding frenzy's over," she whispered. "It's time to slash prices."

Matt relayed the message to the couple, and they came back for the mirror.

"How much do you think we made?" Gracie asked. "Let's each guess a number."

"My guess is five hundred," Jojo said.

Gracie thought for a moment. "One thousand."

"Holy cow," Matt said. "If either of you is even close, I'm going into the junk business."

"Dad, what's your guess?"

"Heck if I know. I was carrying stuff all day. Do I at least get to peek in the box?"

"No!" said Gracie and Jojo.

"Okay, okay," he said. "I think it's closer to $1,600." He had a funny look on his face.

Both Gracie and Jojo reached for the shoebox and opened it. Most of the bills were gone.

Matt grinned and patted his right pocket. "You guys were nuts leaving that kind of money sitting around."

"You cheater!" Gracie said.

"Did we seriously make that much?" Jojo asked. It was the hardest she'd worked for $1,600 in a while, but it was super satisfying.

He nodded with a conciliatory smile. "And we couldn't have done it without you." She felt the flicker of a connection again.

"Is that enough for a lesson every day?" Gracie asked.

Matt appeared to think for a moment. "Honey, can you at least explain why this is so important?"

She looked surprised. "Because *you* said it's important."

He was clearly confused.

"When you were a kid," Gracie said, "you practiced every day."

"Well, I was a little older. I was fifteen when I formed my first band. Are you comparing that to you and Joelle?"

Gracie nodded.

"And is that why you called me a hypocrite last night?"

Jojo was only now realizing she'd missed Act One of this story.

Gracie lowered her eyes. "Sorry I said that. I was sad about you cutting my practice time. You said I need at least ten thousand hours to go pro and so far, I've only got about five."

Matt scratched his head. "Did I really say that? Have you been keeping track?"

"You said that's what the Beatles did. So, I've been writing my hours in the back of my song journal."

Matt looked as blown away as Jojo was feeling.

Gracie started breaking the numbers down. "Each afternoon with Joelle, I get about one and a half hours. Then, if you and I play in the evening—"

"Okay, I get it." He glanced at Jojo, who was trying hard not to crack a smile. She was picturing the day of reckoning in the Heston household when Gracie hit her goal.

A few people were still milling around the yard, and Matt seemed to need a distraction.

"Gracie, why don't you go tell those folks everything's half price. Then run inside and get us some sodas? I'll bet Joelle's thirsty, and I know I am."

Gracie rolled her eyes. "If you guys want to talk, just tell me to get lost."

"Okay, kid. Get lost."

As she walked away, he let out a sigh. "Well, that was a revelation."

Jojo sputtered from holding back her laughter. "You aren't really surprised, are you?"

"I shouldn't be. She's been beating the same drum for a while now. It's only that she's so young to be so..."

"Obsessed?" Jojo suggested.

He reluctantly agreed. "I suppose it's karma. I did it to my parents, so she's doing it to me. My father wanted me to go to trade school—either plumbing or electrical."

"My dad owns his own insurance agency," Jojo said. "He thought I'd be great at it. 'People always need insurance' is his mantra."

"I don't have any regrets," Matt said. "Do you?"

"None. But that still doesn't stop you from wishing Gracie would choose a safer path. And yes, twelve is a little young, but what do you expect when you raise a kid on a steady diet of music?"

He seemed to look inward. "I brought this on myself, didn't I? Ever since she was little, music's been our thing, so I guess my passion became her passion."

"Did I just hear Matt Heston admit that he's still passionate about music? Is that an inside scoop?" She pretended to jot down notes on an imaginary pad.

He glanced around as if someone might overhear and then leaned in conspiratorially. "Sometimes I wonder if I've still got it . . . or could get it back. Maybe after Gracie goes to college."

The news wasn't a shocker. She'd never bought into the story that he'd burned out. But he was usually so tight-lipped that it was surprising he'd say it out loud. As if realizing what he'd done, his eyes locked on hers.

"My lips are sealed," she assured him.

His gaze lingered, but he didn't appear overly concerned. Maybe it was dawning on him they could still be friends without it getting complicated. He finally leaned back in his chair, and they resumed eating. Gracie was on her knees, talking to a little boy about the purple bunny he'd picked up.

"This turned into a really good day," Matt said. "I hope it's a memory she'll hold on to."

"I know I will," Jojo said, pulling out her phone. She dragged her chair closer to his and slowly swiped through a dozen or more photos she'd taken. "This is my favorite." Matt and Gracie had been engrossed in a conversation about an old rug beater when she'd caught them unaware.

She handed him the phone, and he slowly scrolled back through. "I always forget to do this. I take photos at school concerts and birthdays, but I rarely catch this kind of everyday stuff." His expression was tender, and she realized how easily she could be drawn in again—if it was what he wanted, but she knew it wasn't.

"I'll forward them to you and Gracie."

"Thanks. And also, thanks for making today run smoothly." He hesitated and then added with a sly smile, "I'm glad you were so pushy."

She gave him the eye. "Is it really pushy when I'm right?"

In the past, they might have hit a couple more volleys back and forth, but Matt seemed distracted.

"I've been chewing on something you said this morning—about me turning acts of friendship into business transactions."

She winced. In hindsight, it sounded more severe than she'd intended.

"Is that really what I do?" he asked.

She wanted to be honest, but she tried to soften it. "Maybe just a couple of times."

He folded his arms. "I don't want to keep repeating the same mistakes. And since you seem wise beyond your years"—he slipped her a sidelong smile—"or at least think you are, what do you suggest?"

"Hmm . . . first of all," she said, "if I ever seem wise, it's only because I'm good at bluffing. Second, if we're talking about Gracie's so-called lessons, how can I charge her when I've barely taught her a thing? And third, sometimes I feel like I should be paying Gracie. If I miss a lick, she shoots me a look."

Matt chuckled. "I know that look."

"She's such a perfectionist," Jojo said.

They were both laughing when Gracie returned with three cans of soda. "What did you decide? How many lessons can we afford?"

Matt's expression turned serious. "We talked—"

"And," Jojo jumped in, "you can come over every day after camp, as long as your dad doesn't need you at home."

"Yes!" Gracie leapt a foot off the ground.

"There's more," her father said. "Apparently, Joelle has taken a vow of poverty and may have to live on the street when she returns to New York. It's still a mystery to me, but she insists she doesn't want to get paid."

Gracie looked concerned. "Are you sure?"

Jojo nodded.

"If you ever need a place to live, we have a guestroom. Right, Dad?" The offer was sweet, and Jojo dearly wanted to see Matt's reaction, but she couldn't bring herself to meet his eyes.

"So, what are we going to do with the yard sale money?" Gracie asked.

"I was thinking we could put some in your bank account," Matt said. "And some in my bank account, and maybe there'd be enough left over to take Joelle out for dinner sometime."

"How about tonight?" Gracie looked hopeful.

"As nice as that sounds," Jojo said, "I think I'll take a rain check." She figured it was best this way. They'd had a good time and the communications blackout was over. That was sufficient progress for one day. "If I go now, I can still have my afternoon swim." She glanced around at what was left of the unsold odds and ends. "And I can't say I'm going to miss the cleanup."

Matt grumbled, "Considering how much we sold, I can't believe how much is left."

Jojo was already on her feet. "My parting words of advice are to put out a 'free' sign in about half an hour." She was ready to turn and go, but Gracie caught her in both arms and gave her a hug.

"I had so much fun today. Thanks for helping and thanks for the sandwiches."

"You're welcome."

"Hold on a sec," Matt said. He ran over to the tree where Gracie had hung her yard sale sign and yanked it down. Then he spoke to a young woman who'd been going through a pile of Gracie's baby clothes and the two of them walked over together. "I asked Millie to take a picture of us."

It was a spontaneous side of Matt that Jojo hadn't seen before. The three of them lined up, with Gracie in the middle, holding the sign. It was a touching end to the day. There was another round of goodbyes and then she headed for her car.

The afternoon was still hot, and she was looking forward to cooling off in the lake. She looked down Westbury's Main Street at the picturesque yards with their pretty flower beds and the impressive maples and oaks arched across the road. Her other life seemed far away.

CHAPTER 23

MATT

WHEN MATT AWOKE the next morning and swung his legs over the edge of the bed, he felt the tightness in his thighs and calves. How many boxes had he carried? How many old chairs? How many cases of canning jars? But he had no regrets. The yard sale freed up so much space in the attic and basement, he wouldn't be surprised if the house floated off its foundation. Plus, a lot of people went home happy.

It was also an opportunity to clear the air with Joelle and prove they could still be friends. He even appreciated her leaving when she did. Spending too much time together had been their original problem.

He glanced at the clock. Usually on Sunday mornings, he'd spend an hour in the shop tidying up and getting organized for the week ahead, but today he'd earned a rest. After pulling on jeans and a gray T-shirt, he went quietly past Gracie's room, then down the stairs and outside to get the Sunday paper. There was a hint of rain in the air, and he was glad they'd finished cleaning up after the yard sale. On his way to the paper box, he exchanged pleasantries with Mrs. Davenport, who was walking her terrier, Jack. She'd retired a couple years back from the credit union in Manchester and they often traded comments about how their respective gardens were coming along. Hers was always far superior, but she was sweet and pretended not to notice.

Back in the kitchen, he encountered a surprise when he went to make coffee. Leaning against the pot was a small leather bag and a folded note.

Found these in the yard sale. Didn't want you to lose your marbles. Joelle

She must have snuck it into the kitchen during the sale. He looked inside, then read the note again and chuckled. He remembered the marbles from his childhood, but he hadn't seen them in years. They had originally been his grandfather's when he was a boy. Later, they had passed to his father and then to him. He got a dish and poured them out. The majority were standard size, but several were the larger shooters. And mostly, they were milky, with swirls of primary colors. He was grateful Joelle had rescued them. Even without asking, somehow she'd known they were worth keeping.

He left the dish of marbles on the island and went back to making coffee.

"Morning, Dad." Gracie headed straight for the refrigerator and got the orange juice, while he got down two glasses from an open shelf. "I couldn't believe how dirty my clothes got yesterday," she said.

"We raised a lot of vintage dust. You should check out the attic and see how empty it is."

She spotted the marbles and ran her fingers through them. "Where'd these come from?"

"They belonged to my grandfather when he was a boy. And speaking of dirt, there's probably eighty years' worth on those."

"Can I clean them up and put them in a jar? They would look really pretty."

He was willing to bet three generations of boys had never thought of that. "I hereby declare you the keeper of the Heston marbles. But I think I'll hold on to the pouch." He'd find a practical use for it in the shop, and it was a nice keepsake on its own.

They took their usual stools at the island, and he opened the paper, sliding the comics and entertainment sections across to Gracie. They read in silence for a while and when the coffee was ready, he got up and poured himself a cup.

"Dad, what does MIA mean?"

"How is it used?"

Gracie read from the paper. "Jojo is MIA."

"Oh," he said, wondering how Gracie might take this. "It means she's missing in action."

Gracie read on. "It's not much of a story. It just says nobody's seen her lately, and she hasn't been posting on social media."

"Well, I guess everybody's entitled to a break," Matt said.

"Yeah, that's probably it. Her tour just ended. I'll bet she's resting."

"How about French toast?" he asked.

"Yum." She turned the page, apparently unfazed by the story. "Is there any bacon?"

"Sorry. I need to go shopping." He started warming a fry pan and got the eggs and milk.

"Dad, did you know we're performing tomorrow night?"

He looked at her, hoping it was a joke. "What? But we never play this early in the season." He walked over and read the paper's calendar listing from over her shoulder. "Well, dang. Westbury Farmers Market, performers Gatt and Macie."

"That's such a stupid name," Gracie said, sourly.

"It is pretty silly," he agreed. "But you never want to take yourself too seriously."

A couple of years back, one of the market organizers put it on the flyers to keep their concerts on the down-low. All the locals knew it was them, and it became an inside joke that stuck.

He went to the family calendar hanging on the wall and, sure enough, he'd written the concert date down a couple of months earlier. He was good about keeping up with his business calendar, but he rarely checked the family calendar. Probably because there wasn't much on it.

"We're going to have to rehearse today," he said. "And you need to let Joelle know you won't be coming by after camp tomorrow."

"Bummer," Gracie said, but just as quickly, her face brightened. "We should ask her to sing with us. I bet she's free to practice today."

"I don't think so. We just spent a lot of time with her yesterday and it's good to spread things out. Anyway, our fans are expecting Gatt and Macie."

"Please stop saying that. It's stupid, and it doesn't help my brand."

Not this again, he thought. "Honey, you don't have to think about your brand for at least a few more years."

"Are you kidding?! Because of YouTube, everything's moving faster. And it's worse for girls than boys. If I don't break through by sixteen, I may as well forget about it."

It used to be cute, but this was getting out of control.

"Gracie, you can't put all your hopes and dreams into one basket. Plus, it's nuts to think you're washed up by sixteen. When did Jojo start?"

"Her early twenties, but that was her generation. It's different now."

He lowered his head. How was a father supposed to argue against everything she was seeing online? Maybe if he started his own YouTube channel, she might actually listen.

"What are they paying us?" This was the first time she'd asked that question.

He hesitated but figured she had a right to know. After all, she was a member of the band. "Three hundred."

"Perfect. Even the math's easy. You said yourself Joelle needs the money, and this will help her get noticed so she can get some Vermont gigs. And if she gets more Vermont gigs, then she can visit—"

"Honey, stop!" He hadn't meant to raise his voice, and she looked wounded. He softened his tone. "When someone's trying to break into the business, they don't spend less time in New York and more time in Vermont. Joelle might see that as going backwards."

"Dad, I get that." She looked exasperated. "I'm not a complete newbie. I just thought it would give her a reason to visit more."

Now he understood, and his heart softened. A part of him wanted to put a smile back on her face, and all it would take was a simple 'yes.' But he'd already compromised enough, and if he allowed this, Gracie would keep pushing. Plus, there was another issue. He could just imagine the talk around town if a woman suddenly joined the band. Even Joelle was likely to realize it was a bad idea.

"I'm glad the two of you get along so well," he began, trying to put it as gently as possible. "But if we're going to talk about branding, it'll only confuse people if Joelle plays with us once and then never again."

Gracie started to argue, but he held up a finger. "The matter is closed." He said it with enough finality that she went silent, though she was clearly stewing. "However, I know Joelle will want to see us perform, so it's okay to invite her."

He half expected her to sulk away to her bedroom, but instead, she buried her eyes back in the paper while he got up to start breakfast. It was several minutes before she spoke again.

"There's something I don't get. I can tell you like Joelle, and every time we hang out, you're both happy. Even when she bosses you around."

Matt couldn't help smiling. "You've noticed that?"

"Yeah, it's pretty funny."

"You would think so."

"Admit it, Dad. You like it. I can tell."

He opted to take the fifth. "I think we spend way too much time talking about someone who's going to be gone in a couple of weeks. Just please let her know you won't be over tomorrow afternoon. Okay?"

"Yeah. Okay."

It probably was unnecessary to repeat himself, but he wanted to make certain there was no confusion. "Remember, you can invite her to the concert, but don't ask her to bring her guitar. Are we clear on that?"

She groaned. "Yes, Dad."

CHAPTER 24

MATT

ON MONDAY EVENING, Matt parked the truck behind the bandstand, and they unloaded their gear. After setting up, he gave Gracie some money to buy dinner.

"Just get one and we'll split it."

"I know!" she hollered back. Neither of them wanted to be hungry on stage, but if they ate too much before the show, they'd be dragging.

For the last couple of years, he'd kept the equipment to a minimum since Gracie wasn't much help with the heavy lifting. Plus, there were never more than about a hundred and fifty people in the audience, so two mics and two amps had been enough. And for instruments, they'd gone exclusively with acoustic guitars. But Gracie was no longer sitting back and letting him call all the shots.

It started at Christmas when he gave her some looping equipment. The gear looked complex, and he figured they'd be spending most of the day reading the manual, but she'd been watching videos and had it set up in minutes. The sound was rough at first, but within a few weeks, she'd learned to loop half a dozen tracks into their songs, all of which she managed with foot pedals and a midi keyboard. It had been a game changer because now they sounded more like a full band.

On the downside, it meant there were over fifty items on the checklist to pack, move, and set up. Amps, microphones, stands, cables and more. And now, as he went around double-checking the connections, he wondered if they'd gone overboard.

"Hey, Matt." He looked up to see Joelle standing about thirty feet away, in the middle of the empty lawn. She was holding a blanket and a canvas bag. "You want to run a sound check?"

There was something different about her. She was wearing denim capris and a white scoop-neck T-shirt, which was nothing out of the ordinary, but then he realized it was the first time he'd seen her in sunglasses. It was a subtle change, and she looked rather chic.

He stepped to one mic and flipped the switch. "You have perfect timing. Check, check, check." She gave him a thumbs-up and he picked up a guitar and strummed it. One by one, he went through each mic and instrument. When they were done, she spread her blanket before coming over to the bandstand.

"I wanted to make sure I got a good seat."

He laughed. "You could arrive an hour late and get a good seat. This is as laid-back as it gets."

"It doesn't look laid-back." She was scanning the amount of gear strategically placed around them.

"I tried whittling down the list, but apparently, my daughter calls the shots now."

"I'm guessing you enjoy this as much as she does."

That was true. As much as he downplayed it, he looked forward to these evenings. "We have fun, but it was less pressure when she was little and people showed up expecting a simple father–daughter act."

"I get it," she said. "With every success, your critics raise the bar, and it feels like you're always chasing expectations."

That was it exactly, except she'd said it even better. It wasn't the first time he'd noticed how they spoke the same language.

"Gracie tells me this is her looping debut."

"Yeah. It's amazing how quickly she's picked it up. Have you ever tried?"

Joelle raised both hands as if warding off the subject. "Never touch the stuff. I don't have the mental capacity to juggle that many balls and stay connected to the audience. It's enough just to —" She froze. Just as she was opening up, she'd shut down again. He wanted to say, "Keep going" and wished he could read the expression behind those sunglasses. One thing was certain: every time her career came up, it felt like he was getting the abridged version.

"Hey, guys." Gracie appeared, carrying dinner. "I heard the sound check from the food trucks."

"Joelle helped."

"Seems like you say that a lot, Dad."

Before he could shoot her a look, Joelle hip-bumped Gracie, who in turn shoved her back.

"Hey, you two, behave." They were grinning like a couple of schoolkids. Of course, one actually was.

"Food's getting cold," Joelle said, and she and Gracie practically skipped off toward her blanket. Matt followed, uncertain whether he was the babysitter or the third wheel.

As they ate, people started showing up, and soon the lawn was scattered with picnickers, awaiting the concert. A few people stopped by to say hello and one young couple—the woman quite pregnant—came over to say they'd already re-glued the rocking chair they bought at the yard sale and that it was perfect in their nursery. As the couple walked away, Matt thought about how easily Joelle fit in.

She caught him looking and smiled. "There's something I've been wondering. Which of you is Gatt and which is Macie?"

"Arghhh!" Gracie said. "See, Dad. It's spreading."

Judging by Joelle's grin, she already knew this was a sore point and enjoyed rubbing it in.

"You're supposed to be on my side," Gracie said.

"I am. But it's such a bad name, it's hilarious."

They both turned to Matt as if expecting him to settle the matter.

"Okay, okay," he said. "I'll take it under advisement and consider a name change. But I don't think fifteen minutes before we go on stage is the right time."

The two shared a fist bump and Matt suspected he'd been played. But it was worth it to see Gracie this happy.

"Do you guys have a setlist," Joelle asked, "or just winging it?"

"A little of both," Matt said. "Sometimes we get requests."

"But we only do Dad's songs." Gracie sounded almost apologetic. Matt might have convinced himself it was his imagination if Joelle hadn't shot him a look.

Suddenly, she was digging through her bag. "I want to share something with you, Gracie." She pulled out her phone and quickly found what she was looking for. Matt couldn't see it, but Gracie's mouth fell open.

"No way!" She touched the screen and swiped down. "Dad, she's got a playlist of all your songs."

Joelle tucked the phone away again. "Long before I got into hip hop, I was a hardcore fan of your dad's music. I still am."

It was rare to see Gracie at a loss for words, but it didn't last long. "Oh, this is bad. I told Uncle Thad you're super cool and now I'll have to call him back and tell him I was wrong."

Joelle's eyes narrowed. "Ohhh . . . You're in big trouble, missy." She looked poised to launch an attack and Gracie tried crab-walking backward, but she was giggling too hard and collapsed onto her back.

"Dad, make her stop."

"Hold on," Matt said, a little sharply, and the scuffle ended before it really began.

"I was only joking," Gracie said.

"So, you didn't talk to Uncle Thad?"

"Oh, that part's true." She sat up warily, as if ready to dodge another attack. "I thought Joelle might need an agent, so I told Uncle Thad about her."

Joelle looked amused. "Thanks . . . I guess."

Matt couldn't remember Thad calling in the last few days. "When did you talk to him?"

"Ohhh . . ." Gracie looked suddenly downcast. "I forgot to tell you. He called this morning."

"Honey, he'll think I blew him off. Did it sound important?"

"Sorry. He didn't say."

Joelle glanced at her watch. "Is it too late to call?"

"I'll have to do it tomorrow when he's back in the office." It shouldn't have been that big a deal, but after ghosting Thad for ten years, this wasn't the best way to reboot the friendship. Matt hated distractions right before a show, but since there was nothing he could do about it now, he did his best to let it go.

Just then, an older female voice spoke from behind him. "Hello, Matthew. I hope we're not interrupting."

He swung around and recognized Mrs. Swank, his high school algebra teacher. Beside her were a boy and a girl, a little younger than Gracie.

He quickly got to his feet. "Mrs. Swank."

"Come now, Matt. I think you're old enough to call me Thelma."

"Of course," he said, but they both knew he never would. Gracie and Joelle stood up to join them, and there was a round of introductions. Mrs. Swank shared that her grandkids were visiting from Hartford.

"I just came over so Buddy and Sky could meet you. I'm not sure they believed me when I said I knew the man who wrote that song on the radio. What's it called again?"

"'Sweet Side,'" her granddaughter said shyly. She was eyeing Gracie with a touch of adoration. "Will you sing it tonight?"

"Definitely. Near the end of the show."

Matt got a sense Mrs. Swank was sizing up Joelle and that meant others probably were, too. This was the second time Joelle had eaten with them at the market, plus helping at the yard sale undoubtedly raised a few eyebrows. At least Mrs. Swank had the good manners not to appear nosey.

"Gracie, you have a beautiful singing voice. Your father should let you do more solos."

"We're in negotiations," Gracie said with a straight face, and the older woman did a double take.

"She's joking," Matt said. "At least I think she is."

He glanced at his watch, hoping Mrs. Swank would take the hint, but she was clearly on locals' time.

"I still remember when your father was in high school, and his band would play at assemblies." She leaned closer to Gracie. "Just between us, I think he spent more time on the guitar than on his algebra."

"Reaaallly." Gracie smirked at her dad.

"And on that note," Matt cut in, "we should probably get on stage. It was great seeing you again, Mrs. Swank."

As the woman walked away with her grandkids, Joelle was chuckling. "Darn, it was just getting interesting." But just as quickly, she put on a game face and gave Gracie a hug. "You'll be awesome." Then she gave Matt a nod as if to say "You too."

It got quieter as they went up on stage. The audience was twice as big as normal—maybe three hundred people—and Matt glanced over to see if it was making Gracie nervous. But just then, her voice boomed out over the sound system.

"Hi, everyone. I've got some bad news. Gatt and Macie weren't able to make it tonight, so you're stuck with us."

There was laughter from the crowd. Matt switched on his own mic, ready to take it from there, but Gracie wasn't finished.

"I'm Gracie and that's my dad, Matt. It's awesome so many of you came out tonight. This is our biggest crowd ever, so let's hear it for you guys!" There was whistling and more cheering.

He wasn't sure who his new sidekick was, but she sure wasn't the retiring kid he'd performed with last year. He caught sight of Joelle laughing, and she gave him a thumbs-up. When Gracie finally reached for her electric guitar, Matt managed to get a word in.

"It's great to be back performing at the market. I see a lot of friends and neighbors, plus some new faces. This first song is called 'Howlin' Wind.'" Another cheer went up. There was already more energy than usual.

From the first chord, the audience was with them. There was nothing quite like hometown fans. Some of these people had been following Matt since he was a teenager and others were friends of Gracie's from school.

And it was nothing like last year's acoustic show. Thanks to Gracie, the added layers of sound gave Matt's songs more of the kick fans loved. He'd always enjoyed their father–daughter duo in the past, but this was on a new level, and he was having a blast.

There was one face in the crowd that kept drawing his attention. Joelle had removed her sunglasses and wore the mirthful grin of a woman who had just found a pearl in an oyster. He could see her laughter bubbling over every time Gracie made a clean transition between phrases, which was no small task for a young girl managing multiple tracks.

Joelle also seemed to delight in the audience response, studying them much in the way Thad used to. In the end, it was all about the audience experience. As with most concerts at the bandstand, there was a cluster of young children gathered up front. They were spinning and cartwheeling and dancing about. A couple of little ones were even trying to dance before they could walk, aided by older siblings who held them upright with both hands above their heads and marched them around like marionettes.

Gracie had a permanent smile on her face. She'd spotted Cammy and some other friends and even dedicated a song to the kids from Newbury Village Middle School, which got another great response. She'd always shown confidence on stage, but this was different. And it wasn't just that she was reflecting the positive energy of friends and neighbors—Gracie had a special brand of stage presence. It was infectious and their audience loved it.

Since the halfway point in the show, there'd been a few shouts for "Sweet Side" and each time Matt would say, "It's coming, I promise." They had decided to close out the set with it, but on the next-to-last song, Matt broke a string. He made it through the final chorus, but then considered his options. He could take the time to change it or switch to the electric, but that wasn't what people were expecting.

Suddenly, Joelle was at his side. "Are there extras in the case?"

He nodded, and she took the guitar. "Keep talking. I need two minutes."

A two-minute string change was something he would have liked to see, but he took her advice and kept his focus on the crowd. "Hey, everybody, please give a hand to our roadie, Joelle." He clapped and there was a ripple of applause. "While Joelle replaces a string, I just thought I'd say a few words about "Sweet Side." By now you've probably heard there's a new version of the song on the radio, sung by the artist Jojo. My daughter loved it right away and I guess a lot of young people did. And I have to admit, it's been growing on me. At any rate, it's exciting to have a song on the charts again after all these years, even if it wasn't my voice behind the microphone." There was more applause. "I hope one of these days to say it in person, but for now—thanks, Jojo, for sharing my music with another generation."

He looked behind him to check on Joelle's progress. She was crouched on one knee, her hair falling across her face. Remarkably, the new string was already in place and she was tuning it. He had time to say a few more words to the audience, but the tableau of her kneeling amongst the sound equipment captivated him. Here was another example of how effortlessly she fit into their lives. His will to keep her at arm's length was collapsing. Gracie had been right. Nothing could be more natural than inviting her to sing with them.

In a flash, she was by his side, handing the guitar back, but she seemed unexpectedly timid. She wasn't making eye contact. In fact, her face was turned toward the back of the stage, as though uncomfortable under the gaze of so many eyes.

"Double-check the tuning," she said.

He leaned toward her. "Do you remember the words to 'Sweet Side?'" Likely, she did.

She nodded tentatively, but still wouldn't look at him.

"Are you okay?" He leaned down to better see her face and was startled to see her eyes were moist. He wasn't sure what he was witnessing, but he suspected stage fright and his heart went out to her. He hesitated, no longer certain he should ask, but he did anyway. "Do you want to sing with us?"

The crowd was growing restless, and Gracie spoke into her mic. "Sorry for the holdup, everybody, but it looks like Joelle's going to join us for this last song." She stepped away from the mic and offered her guitar to Joelle. "I'll switch to keyboard."

Joelle was having none of it. "This is your show, guys. You've been amazing. Now bring it home." She made it final by retreating to the back of the bandstand and running down the steps before disappearing.

Gracie shot a confused look at her father, but he had no answer. She returned to her mic and Matt forced himself back into the moment. He strummed a couple of chords, and the tuning was perfect.

"I guess you're stuck with just the two of us," he said into the mic, trying to keep it light and the energy up. And with a nod to Gracie, they launched into the song.

He saw the upside of living on the high side
Where the joy of the journey was the goal
Amplified and ringside
His life was a joyride
The crowds were feeding his soul.

She saw the flipside of living on the high side
She grew weary and tired of the road.
Alongside their bedside
She rocked as their child cried
Fearing how love can erode.

He stood on the curbside by the bus on the backside
Of a thirty-week cross-country tour.
He was fried from the downside
And longed for her bedside
For once, he was certain and sure.

He longed for the sweet side in the house on the
    hillside
With his wife and his child and a song
Put his pride by the wayside
He promised his dear bride
That home was where he belonged.

CHAPTER 25

───────────

JOJO

JOJO SAT on the couch watching and re-watching a YouTube video of Matt and Gracie singing "Sweet Side." As far as she knew, this was Gracie's internet debut, and it was a good one. Considering it was shot outdoors and probably with a phone, the video and sound quality wasn't bad. After leaving the stage, Jojo had remained behind the bandstand to hear it live. Then, when the crowd was breaking up, she'd quickly picked up her things and left.

It was Carson who'd sent her the link, along with the instructions, "Leave a comment so your fans know you're alive." She noticed the absence of the word *please*.

Her phone dinged and a text from Gracie appeared. *Missed u after the show. Thanks for coming.*

Matt and Gracie had to be wondering why she took off. She considered saying nothing in hopes it would be forgotten, but she knew Gracie wouldn't let it rest.

Sorry I didn't stay to help pack up. Feeling a little off, but sure I'll be ok by AM. Listened from backstage. U were awesome. Watching it on YouTube now. Have u seen it?

After hitting send, she scrolled through her messages, but there was nothing from Matt.

The light in the living room was fading, so she reached for the nearby table lamp and clicked it on. If only she could change her mood as easily.

She felt like a first-class idiot for running on stage tonight. It had been sheer instinct and happened so quickly she was on one knee, changing out the string, before she felt the presence of three hundred pairs of eyes and probably dozens of cameras. It was like throwing herself under a microscope, but at least she hadn't freaked. She stayed composed and kept her head down, but then Matt turned up the heat when he thanked her for sharing "Sweet Side" with a new generation. She'd done her best to hide the swell of emotion, and suspected Matt and Gracie didn't notice. But running off like that must have seemed a little psycho.

The first time she'd watched the video, she practically dug her fingers into the couch, praying the whole time that her face was hidden. Thankfully it was, and at the end, she finally relaxed. It helped to know Carson had watched the same video without noticing her.

Although she was loath to take orders from him, she liked Carson's idea of leaving a comment under the video. It was the perfect way to send a message to Matt and Gracie while being herself. She sat back and thought about what to say.

CHAPTER 26

MATT

AN HOUR AFTER THE PERFORMANCE, Matt collapsed into an easy chair and cracked open a beer. He was still wired from the concert, his senses elevated. He knew this feeling well from his years of touring, but never imagined he could get a similar buzz from performing at the farmers market. Yet something incredible had happened. It felt like a part of him was coming back to life.

He wished Joelle had stayed to share in the celebration. After the concert, he and Gracie were mobbed by friends, and it took a while before the crowd thinned out and he was able to look for her. By then, she was gone.

She had seemed herself when she ran on stage and whisked the guitar from his hands. Few people understood how stressful it was to replace and tune a guitar string with the audience noise and the pressure of time. But she'd done it like a seasoned pro, so that couldn't have been what upset her. Maybe she simply wasn't cut out to be in front of an audience. He knew it was terrifying for some people, but a musician like Joelle . . .?

If he didn't have a daughter upstairs getting ready for bed, he would have driven to the cabin to make certain she was okay. He considered calling, but texting seemed less intrusive, in case she wasn't in the mood to talk.

He was not adept at typing on the tiny keypad. In fact, Gracie was fond of saying he had the slowest thumbs in the north, south, east, and west. So, he kept it brief.

Hope you're okay.

Maybe that was *too* brief. He considered asking if she'd gotten her picnic blanket back because he'd noticed it was gone. But that felt ridiculously mundane, so in the end, he sent the text as it was.

Just then, he heard Gracie on the stairs. She came halfway down and sat where they could see each other.

"Somebody posted a video of us on YouTube." Considering the magnitude of the news, her voice was surprisingly flat.

"'Sweet Side?'" he guessed.

"Yup. Not many hits yet, and the sound quality's just so-so."

"Too bad because we sounded awesome—thanks to you."

He wasn't thrilled about his daughter being online. She'd wanted to make videos before and post them herself, but he hadn't allowed it. Unfortunately, he had no control over the actions of others.

"Joelle texted. She left because she wasn't feeling well."

"Do you know what's wrong?" he asked.

Gracie rested her forehead against the balusters. "It looked like she was crying, or maybe scared."

When she was younger, he might have glossed over the incident but doubted that would work tonight. "I think you're right, but I can't figure out why."

"Did you ask her to sing?"

"Yeah, but my timing was off." He wasn't usually this candid with her. "I should have asked earlier."

"I was wondering . . ." Gracie's words were drawn out, as though thinking aloud. "Have you ever known anybody with stage fright?"

"I knew one guy who threw up before every show, and then

he'd be fine. And my own stomach still churns a bit, even before the local shows."

"Me too," Gracie said. That was new information, but he didn't interrupt. "Maybe Joelle has it really bad."

"It's hard to say, honey, but whatever it is, we shouldn't push her to talk about it. Just be a friend and treat her normally."

She ran a hand along the railing as she mulled something over. "Maybe this is why she doesn't have a regular band."

"Let's not jump to conclusions." It made sense, though. Stage fright would explain a lot—even Joelle's reticence to talk about herself. It would be a source of great sadness to possess her musical gifts but be unable to perform live.

Just then, the house phone rang. Matt got up to answer but wanted to make certain Gracie didn't do anything rash. "Remember, you're not to bring it up unless Joelle brings it up first."

"I won't."

He gave her an earnest look to reinforce the point.

"Dad, I promise."

She went back upstairs, and he headed for the kitchen phone. Before picking up, he noticed it was almost 9:30. They rarely got calls this late.

"Hello."

"Matt, it's Thad."

"Hey, Thad. I'm glad you called. Gracie didn't give me your message until this evening, and I didn't want you to think—"

"No problem," Thad said, cutting him off and sounding upbeat. "I was going to try again tomorrow and then a few minutes ago, I started getting messages about your performance tonight. I just watched the video."

"Yeah, Gracie told me about it. I can't believe how fast stuff gets posted. We barely got home."

"That's the way it works nowadays," Thad said. "Anyhow, I was blown away and figured you'd still be up."

"I'll have to check it out," Matt said. This felt like old times—getting feedback from Thad after a show.

"That daughter of yours has charisma beyond her years. And to see the two of you up there having fun . . . I just shared it with Myra, and she actually cried."

Matt felt his throat tighten. Thad's wife was another person he'd hurt. "I think you're both biased. By the way, what did you call about this morning?"

"The record company's been in touch. You're back on their radar screen."

Considering his label had accused him of breach of contract, he was surprised they would have anything to do with him. "I thought those guys hated me."

"Riley left and went to BNI. He took Hodges with him."

"Huh. Can't say I'm heartbroken," Matt said. "Did they poach some of the talent?"

"You really don't read the trades, do you?"

"Does *Woodworker's Bulletin* count?"

"I'm not buying this routine anymore," Thad said. "Not after watching that video."

It sounded like Matt needed to watch it himself. "What does the label want?"

"Well, I know you'll probably blow this off, but as your sometimes manager, I'm obligated to let you know there's an offer on the table." Thad allowed time for his words to sink in.

"Still here," Matt said.

"That's progress. In the past, you would have hung up by now."

"Bygones," Matt said. Was Thad exaggerating, or had he really been that bad?

"Anyway," Thad said, "thanks to Jojo's cover of 'Sweet Side,' there's a new crop of kids discovering Matt Heston. Bottom line, the record company wants to reissue all of your songs as a double album set and put some fresh artwork on it."

"Is that it?" Matt wasn't sure what he'd expected, but it might have been nice to add a new track or two. He hadn't exactly been sitting on his thumbs for ten years. Then again, the label probably wanted to capitalize on the current hype and didn't have time while he futzed around in the studio.

"Yeah, tell 'em to go ahead. Just make certain the artwork's tasteful."

"Seriously? You're on board?"

"If you think it's a good idea," Matt said, "I trust your judgement. They won't remix anything, will they?"

"No remixing. I'll make sure it's in the contract and email it to you once it's ready."

"I'm glad you didn't retire, Thad."

"Well, according to my 401(k) and my wife, I can't afford to until I'm ninety-five. So, I'll be around for a while."

Gracie called down from upstairs, sounding excited. "Dad, where are you?"

"Sorry, Thad. Can you hold a second?" Matt covered the receiver and yelled back, "I'm still on the phone." He could hear her feet on the stairs. "Thad, I'm back."

"Make sure you tell Gracie I'm a fan."

"Will do." Then Matt did something spontaneous. "Do you think you and Myra would be up for a visit to Vermont?"

Gracie came into the kitchen with her laptop open and set it on the island.

"I'd like that very much," Thad said, "and I think I can get Myra to warm to the idea. She's got a big heart and, deep down, the past is the past."

That was a good note to end on and they said their goodbyes.

Matt turned his attention to Gracie as he hung up. "That was Uncle Thad. He just saw the video."

"I've been reading the comments. I think it's trending mostly because people like what you said about Jojo."

For years Matt hadn't cared what people thought of his opinions, but if YouTube could help fix his curmudgeonly image, maybe it was a useful tool after all.

"But the coolest part is this." Gracie turned the screen toward him.

He sat on the stool beside her. "What am I looking at?" There was a series of comments and she pointed to one, which Matt read aloud.

Thank you for the kind words, Matt. I love everything about your performance. Your voices blend beautifully, and of course, I love the song. I've been a longtime Matt fan, and now I'm also a Gracie fan. Keep it up, Jojo

Suddenly, the kitchen erupted in Gracie's delighted screams. She leapt into his arms, almost knocking him off his stool.

"This is the best day of my life! My first YouTube video and Jojo commented!" She released her grip on him and landed back on her own two feet. But the dancing had only just begun as she twirled around the island.

"Honey. Gracie." He tried to settle her down and get a word in. "How do you know it's really her?"

"Click on her picture."

Sure enough, there was a tiny photo beside the comment, and it took him to the home page of Jojo's official YouTube channel. As he stared at it, Gracie came around beside him.

"It looks legit," he said. "Can people respond to comments?"

"Of course." She sat back on her stool, suddenly sober. "Should we?"

"I think it would be nice, and this way she'll know we saw it."

Gracie hesitated. "But she's *Jojo* . . ."

He gave her a sidelong glance. "You're right. She probably doesn't care what Gatt and Macie have to say."

"Daaaad!" She gave him a shove, and he reeled her in and

mussed her hair. She wriggled free, her expression dead serious. "This is important. I need to think."

It was important to Matt, too. When he'd thanked Jojo from the stage, a part of him secretly hoped the word would travel back to her. He just hadn't expected it to happen so fast.

"Maybe we should sleep on it," Gracie said.

"But what if she's sitting there, waiting for us to respond?"

"You're hilarious, Dad."

He sighed. "Just humor me. And I think you should be the one to write it. You have a better feel for this social media stuff."

"Okay, but you have to help." She pulled the laptop closer and reread what Jojo had written. Then she started typing:

Hi, it's Gracie. I know all your songs by heart and have picked up a lot of guitar stylings from your videos. I want to develop my own style someday, but Dad says copying the masters is a good way to learn.

Gracie paused and her fingers hung above the keyboard for a moment before continuing.

My dad is old-school, but sometimes I catch him watching your videos, so I think he likes your music, too. He's watching me write this, and he just smiled, so I guess it's true. I would like to meet you someday. I know everybody says it, but I really am your biggest fan. Gracie

Matt was impressed. It was perfect—even the part about him.

"Should I add your name?" Gracie asked.

He thought about it, then shook his head. "No. I wouldn't change a thing."

Gracie clicked *Reply* and her words were instantly published.

CHAPTER 27

IDA

IDA STOOD on the platform at Union Square Station with her nose in her phone. The chance of spotting celebrities waiting for a train was next to nil, so she'd already switched off that side of her brain. She was all too eager to put this night behind her. It had been a total bust.

She'd had a tip that a famous supermodel rumored to be dating a newly single rock star would be catching his show at Irving Plaza tonight. Unfortunately, about twenty other photographers must have gotten the same tip. Ida took one look and decided it wasn't worth trying to elbow her way to the front of the pack. Instead, she'd hoofed it over to a posh restaurant on Fourteenth Street, but after an hour of staking out the front door, the only person she recognized was a local politician. At that point, it started to rain, and she'd sprinted for the cover of the subway station.

And now the night was going from bad to worse as she watched a YouTube video of Matt Heston and his daughter. Some local amateur had beat her to the punch. It looked like the video was shot with a phone; the image was okay, but the audio could have been better. *What a waste.* Ida's brilliant idea of returning to Westbury for the Heston girl's talent show was pointless now.

She was surprised by the number of hits and likes the video had already racked up. But the reason became apparent as she scrolled through the comments and found one from Jojo. That explained why it had popped up on her main page. Considering Jojo's recent disappearing act, this was news in itself.

Ida read the comment several more times. It was warm and personable and sounded like something Jojo had written herself, unlike the recent tweets from her Twitter account that read more like someone in PR was trying to cover for her absence.

The squeal of an approaching train turned Ida's head and she pocketed the phone.

It always hurt to get scooped, particularly when it had felt like she was onto something special. Well, at least she didn't have to drive back to Vermont.

CHAPTER 28

JOJO

BEING AWAY from New York presented some creative challenges. Normally, Jojo partnered with other songwriters and arrangers, and this collaboration kept her sound from getting stale. In the past, the process required a lot of face-to-face sessions, but this summer she was trying something new—sending audio files back and forth. She'd expected some pushback, but so far, it was going well.

Of course, these were just demos, with some of the tracks utilizing synthesizers and drum machines. Once she got back to New York, she'd meet with the band and put it together for real.

Her phone buzzed, and she glanced at the screen, half expecting Tyrell, who had just sent another audio file. But instead, Matt's name appeared, yanking her out of work mode. She hit *stop* on the track she'd been playing and headed outside, hoping the fresh air might clear her head.

"Hey, Matt."

"Hope I'm not interrupting anything."

"Not much. I was just writing another top ten hit." It was nice when she could be somewhat honest.

"Oh excellent, I wrote a couple myself this morning."

"It's not as funny, Matt, when you actually have a song in the top ten. What's it ranked today?"

"I hear it's bad luck to follow the charts."

She doubted he was as blasé as he sounded and assumed Gracie was keeping him informed. As for herself, she tried not to obsess over rankings, though Carson's frequent texts made that a challenge.

"Is it bad luck if *I* follow the charts?" she asked.

"As long as you keep it to yourself. It'll be self-evident when I wake up and there's a bunch of reporters on my lawn."

"Okay, my lips are sealed," she said. "So, considering that you've had my number for about two weeks, and this is the first time you've called, I'm guessing you had a reason."

He was quiet for a moment. "Has it really been two weeks?"

"You'd think I'd know. I've been sitting here counting the minutes . . ." She cringed—maybe that was too much.

"Hold on a moment. I think I've got the sarcasm level turned up on my phone." There was a brief pause before he returned. "Sure enough, it was set on high."

"Ha, ha."

"Actually, I was calling to see how you're feeling."

She wasn't surprised. In fact, she'd half expected it. "Turns out it was no big deal. I woke up feeling much better."

"Glad to hear it. But if there's ever a day you don't feel like having company, just tell Gracie. She'll understand."

With a start, Jojo noticed the time. Gracie would arrive any minute, and the recording equipment was on the coffee table and her Rubio was on the couch. She kept the phone to her ear as she went inside and grabbed the guitar. The case was in her bedroom, so she headed upstairs.

"Everything okay?" Matt asked.

"Yeah. I just realized how late it is. I gave the maid the day off and the place is a mess."

He hesitated. "That's a joke, right?"

"Yes, Matt. That's a joke." She kneeled as she placed the guitar in the case before sliding it under the bed. "I better go. Gracie'll be here any second."

"Be prepared for a whirlwind," Matt said. "She's still high from last night."

"I know. We've texted a few times." It suddenly occurred to Jojo that she hadn't spoken to Matt since the concert. She'd posted a comment on YouTube, but in his mind, that was another woman entirely.

"I hope Gracie told you how much I loved the concert. You guys were amazing." She sank onto the bed; her words fell short of describing how moved she'd actually been.

"Thanks," he said. "To be honest, even I was surprised."

"How so?"

"Gracie blew my mind," he said. "I don't know if it was her new equipment or the fact that she's a year older or . . . maybe the time she's been practicing with you . . ."

Jojo could hear the pride in his voice, and she regretted having run off the way she did. She could relate to what it was like to walk off stage, amped up from a show and craving feedback. At least she had Carson to talk to—she wondered if Matt had anyone.

"You're right," she said, "Gracie was amazing, but it's also the way the two of you interact. I couldn't stop smiling."

He chuckled. "I know. I was watching."

She chewed on her lower lip. Every now and then his words hinted at something deeper, but it was never enough that she could be certain. She got up and crossed to the window, looking down at the spot where Gracie usually set her bike, but there was no sign of her yet. There was still the recording equipment that needed to be put away, but one question had been needling Jojo at the back of her mind. She feared it might come out as a criticism but couldn't resist asking.

"Do you ever perform anything new?"

"People prefer the old stuff."

"Have you tested that theory? I know Gracie would like to."

He didn't respond right away, and she hoped she hadn't crossed a line. Then he surprised her with a friendly chuckle.

"I hadn't thought about it until last night, but it feels like it's time to feature Gracie on a few songs."

"It sounds like you're taking advice from Mrs. Swank."

"I guess I am. What do you think?"

Jojo was thinking a number of things, like how nice his phone voice was and how her younger self would have been in minor hysterics to think Matt Heston would call for professional advice.

"Gracie would love it. And a lot of your audience is her age."

"In the past," he said, "I didn't want to put too much pressure on her, but now I doubt that's an issue."

"Hardly," Jojo said with a laugh. "She's fearless, and it's not an act."

There was a knock at the door, and she called to Gracie that she'd be right down.

"Gotta go, Matt. It's showtime."

He thanked her for the feedback, and they said goodbye before Jojo headed downstairs to find Gracie standing inside the door, holding her guitar.

"Nice mic," she said, checking out the recording equipment.

"Yeah," Jojo said, glancing around and wishing she'd had a little more time to straighten up. "It's pretty slick. Do you have one?"

"Not portable, like yours. All of Dad's mics go through an amp first. But I've been thinking of saving up for one. I got fifty dollars from singing at farmers market, plus some of the yard sale money."

"That beats babysitting. Do you want to try it out?"

Gracie's eyes lit up. "Absolutely!" She unpacked her guitar and the two of them sat on the couch in front of the mic. "I've been working on a new arrangement of 'Flower Girl,'" she said. "What if I sing that?"

This was a first time Gracie had mentioned rearranging anything, especially one of Jojo's songs.

"You made changes?" Jojo tried to sound neutral. She'd done it many times herself—most recently with "Sweet Side." But her songs were her babies, and she couldn't help but feel a little protective.

"Of course, I love the way Jojo does 'Flower Girl,' but she's a grownup, singing like she's kind of sad and missing her childhood. So all those minor chords make sense. But it doesn't make sense for me to sing it that way, so I just thought . . ." Her momentum faltered, as if suddenly doubting herself. "Do you think it's a dumb idea?"

Huh, Jojo thought. It kind of made sense. She gave Gracie a gentle nudge with her shoulder. "It doesn't sound dumb at all."

Gracie's enthusiasm reappeared. "Good, because I think you'll like it."

Now Jojo was curious. She adjusted the height of the mic and when Gracie was ready, she started recording.

It was an odd experience at first. Each line started as usual, but whereas the minor chords normally weighed down the vocals, the major chords lifted them up. Jojo was stunned that something she sang every night on tour could sound totally fresh. Neither better nor worse, but uniquely Gracie. It was nice how the universe kept surprising her.

As the song ended, Jojo realized her eyes had misted. Gracie noticed it too.

"I was going for a happier vibe, but—"

Jojo cut her off. "It *is* happy and sweet, and I think you should always sing it this way." She pushed play so Gracie could hear it for herself, and they both slumped back into the cushions to listen. At first Gracie's head swayed a bit, but after only a few bars, she leaned forward, staring at the small external speaker as if transfixed. There was a trace of wonder, or maybe it was self-discovery.

When the recording ended, Jojo emailed Gracie a copy of the file. "I hope you share this with your dad."

Gracie nodded, but her mind seemed elsewhere. "My voice sounded different—good different. Bigger and older. But maybe your mic just makes me sound different."

"When's the last time you recorded yourself?"

"A while ago, I guess."

"Well, I'm no expert, but I think it's natural at your age."

"Cool," Gracie said.

Jojo choked back a laugh. To a child with big dreams, the revelation that her voice was becoming fuller and more resonate was probably exciting. But apparently not so much that it needed further discussion, as Gracie's focus quickly changed.

"What are all these files that say 'Tyrell'?"

Jojo glanced at the screen and winced. Any one of those tracks would give her away. "I've been collaborating with a guy in New York, sending ideas back and forth, but it's too rough to share."

"I'd still like to hear it," Gracie said, "even if it's not perfect."

It wasn't up for discussion and Jojo closed the laptop. "Let's do our usual thing." She didn't wait for an answer but walked across the room to where her Blueridge was in its case.

"It's cooler outside," Gracie said. And just like that, the files from Tyrell were forgotten.

CHAPTER 29

IDA

IDA RODE the elevator to the third floor. She hadn't been to the newsroom or to Frank's office in eons. This was the digital age and everything from her photos to the newspaper's payments were transmitted electronically. But here she was because Frank wanted to show her something and, apparently, he didn't want to leave any kind of trail, digital or otherwise.

She wound her way between the desks in the bullpen, recognizing only half the faces. When she reached his office, the door was partially open, and she rapped twice.

Frank looked up and gave her a rare smile. "Hell, Ida. I wasn't sure I'd even recognize you. You should come around more."

"Good to see you too, Frank." Then she nodded toward the newsroom. "I didn't see Felicia or Thompson out there."

"Felicia got married and stays home with her kid. Thompson went independent like you, but between us, it's a big mistake. If no one's barking at him, he's probably sitting on a barstool."

It was true. Phil Thompson could crank out stories all day as long as he had a deadline, but otherwise, he was a lazy SOB with a taste for bourbon. That had been Ida's biggest fear when she went out on her own. Not the bourbon, but the motivation. In the end, she found that a pile of bills on the kitchen table was motivation enough.

"So, you've got something to show me?" she said.

"Yeah, but let's start with your girl. What's up with that?"

She'd figured as much. People in her line of work tended to have pet projects, and hers was Jojo. She knew the singer's friends, hangouts, and habits. But she was as mystified as anyone about her disappearance.

"There's been a few tweets and a little activity on Instagram," she said. "But nothing that sounds like her. And there was no way to date the photos—they could be old. It's probably Carson or some PR hack he's hired. There was one comment on YouTube that might have been her, but who knows."

"According to Carson," Frank said, "she's holed up, cranking out material for the next album."

"But that's not like her either," Ida said. "She never works alone."

"How much of her last tour did you catch?" Frank asked.

"Just Boston, New York, and Montreal. You know touring isn't my thing—too much competition for too little return." Ida's specialty was catching celebs around town—restaurants, shops, and on the street.

"What about after she got back? From the tour, I mean. Lots of stars have trouble keeping up that kind of grind without a little . . . boost."

This was beginning to feel like an interview. If it were anybody but Frank, she would have walked by now, but he'd helped her plenty over the years and was still her best customer.

"I know where you're going," she said. "You want to know if I saw any signs of exhaustion—"

"Or pills or boozing," Frank coaxed.

"Nothing," Ida said. "If she was worn out after the tour, she didn't let it show. When that girl hits the pavement, she's all smiles.

She talks to us. Makes jokes. Not many celebs can keep that up. She is one disciplined lady."

Frank stroked his chin as if considering his next move. His focus shifted to a manila folder in front of him, and he flipped it open, revealing an eight-by-ten glossy. He pushed it in front of Ida. "Do you remember taking that?"

She looked at it closely. If it was hers, it wasn't her best work. It must have been a telephoto, because it was grainy. She couldn't even swear the woman in the photo was Jojo, but it looked kind of like her. A guy in a suit was holding a glass door open, and she was going inside.

"No recollection. But if you say it's mine, I'll believe you."

"What if I say I want to buy it for five hundred dollars?"

Ida did a double take at the photo. "Then I'd definitely say it's mine." But there had to be a catch. It was a crap photo. She couldn't even remember the location. She looked more closely for any type of sign on the glass.

"We airbrushed the signs out," he said. "But take a close look at the parking meter."

The meter was off to the side and slightly blurred. It was the kiosk type that spits out tickets. Frank handed her a magnifying glass.

"Is it in German?"

He raised one eyebrow. "That was my idea. It's all about the details. It's like the meters they use in Zurich. You ever been?"

"Nope."

"That's one reason I can't give you credit. Is that a problem for you?"

She narrowed her eyes. "This sounds like another 'dead Uncle Fred?'" Whenever Frank needed to make up a fake photo credit, he'd go with *Frederick Horowitz*—his great uncle. "I don't want to know the details," Ida said. "Just deposit the money in my account."

CHAPTER 30

JOJO

IT WAS Friday afternoon when Jojo heard a car on the gravel driveway and tipped herself out of the hammock, immediately wary of the unfamiliar vehicle. It was a blue SUV with New York plates, but the reflection on the windshield obscured the driver. She slipped on her sandals and walked to the edge of the porch, keenly aware that she had no contingency plan if she were discovered.

The driver's door opened, and Leah stepped out with a gotcha grin. "Hey, stranger. I'm looking for a friend of mine—brassy wig and heavy makeup."

It took about three heartbeats to recover from the shock and then Jojo was down the steps and racing into Leah's arms. The reunion was short-lived before she pulled back and gave her friend a good poke in the shoulder. "You scared the heck out of me."

Leah was still wearing her Cheshire cat grin. "Sorry. I forgot until the last minute that you've never seen my car before." That was true. Back home, they always let Dinesh do the driving.

"Well, we don't need a chauffeur here," Jojo said. "I think Westbury has more parking spaces than people and the closest I've come here to a traffic jam involved a turtle crossing the road."

"Gotta love Vermont," Leah said, retrieving her purse and then closing the door.

"I thought you rehearse on Fridays," Jojo said.

"It got canceled and as soon as Tom found out, he practically kicked me out the door. They're having a boys' weekend—pitching a tent in the living room and camping out."

"That's so sweet." Leah had really scored when she found Tom.

"They're planning to roast marshmallows over candles, so I don't know what kind of mess I'm likely to go back to. But for now, I'm not going to think about it."

They walked to the back of her SUV and lifted the hatch, revealing a single suitcase and a cooler.

"Did you bring goodies?!"

"You have no idea. There's enough here that we can park ourselves in the hammock and not go out all weekend." The cooler was so loaded, they each had to grab a handle and still they managed to bump every step as they carried it onto the porch. They went straight to the kitchen and started unloading. There was wine and more than they could possibly eat in two days. "I can't believe you brought all this. How long are you staying?"

"Sunday—probably right after breakfast. But I figured you might want to stockpile some things you can't find in town."

Just then, Jojo came across half a dozen tins of stuffed grape leaves and moaned with delight. "I've been dying for these." Her eyes glazed over longingly as she kissed one of the tins. "This is all I needed. You're free to go now."

"Ahhh shucks," Leah said. "Good to see you haven't changed—at least on the *inside*." She was staring, as if still adjusting to this stripped-down version of her friend. She'd seen Jojo like this before, but not often. The funny thing was that Jojo had barely thought of her appearance lately.

"Full disclosure," Leah said, moving past the distraction, "as much as I'm here for you, I'm also here to de-stress. Marzelli's turning out to be the director from hell."

Jojo realized how out of the loop she was. There was even a twinge of guilt at how much their recent conversations had revolved around her. "What's it like working with him?"

The answer came as a deep sigh, revealing just how exhausted Leah was. "Mind if I grab one of your seltzers?"

"Don't you dare ask again." Jojo opened the fridge and pulled out two bottles. "Mi casa es su casa. Oh yeah! It literally is."

Leah accepted a bottle with a weary smile and sat down at the table. "I know everyone says Marzelli's a genius, but I swear it feels more like obsessive-compulsive. Every night he goes back to his hotel and changes the score, then in the morning"—Leah put on her best Italian accent—"it's 'Oh Leah, un piccolo cambiamento.'"

Jojo looked at her blankly.

"It's what he says constantly—'Leah, just a little change.' So, we change a few beats here and a few there and suddenly I've got dancers running into each other."

"How's morale on the set?"

"So far, only a bit of grumbling and nobody's broken ranks. Professionally, this is huge on their resumes, so no one wants to screw it up."

It occurred to Jojo that she'd been known to make a few overnight changes of her own. "Do you ever complain like this about me?"

"I don't have to. You've already got that scary diva thing going on."

Jojo cringed. "I know I'm a bit of a perfectionist, but—"

"That excuse only works for men. Besides, you know I'm kidding—well, half kidding. I've never met anybody successful who isn't at least somewhat of a perfectionist. But what about this Joelle person? I bet she's no prima donna."

"You'd lose that bet," Jojo said. "Matt will tell you Joelle's opinionated and bossy."

Leah smirked. "I wondered how long it would take before his name came up."

"Don't read too much into it. He just happens to be the only adult I know for two hundred miles."

"Hmmm . . ."

"Oh, stop it. The guy lives like a monk. He only has one love in his life and that's his daughter."

"Huh," Leah said. "That's a refreshing quality in a single guy."

Normally, talk of Matt might have ended there, especially if they were on the phone. But Leah's powers of extraction were more effective in person, and unexpectedly, Jojo found herself opening up. "Actually, if I'm being honest, Matt's signals are totally confusing. He says he just wants to be friends, but every now and then, we'll have a great conversation—like a completely out-of-the-blue phone call a few days ago. And I end up thinking, 'Wow, maybe there's something more here.' But then there's no follow-up—just a total blackout for a few days. Which probably is proof that it is *just friendship* and I'm the problem for reading more into it."

By Jojo's standards, that was an unusual amount of sharing and Leah needed a moment to digest it all. "Well," she finally said, "can you at least get a song out of it?"

"Yeah, right. Because everybody loves a good *friendship* song."

She hadn't meant for the word to come out sounding like reheated squash. There was absolutely nothing wrong with friendship except when you were hoping for more.

"Can we please talk about something else?" she said.

Leah was amenable to moving on. For now, at least.

"You know, when I came up the driveway, I knew you wouldn't look like your usual self, but still it takes getting used to. For one thing, I forget how curly your natural hair is. It's beautiful. Have you ever considered just being you again? I mean professionally."

"I've told you before. Nobody paid attention when I looked like this."

"That's ridiculous," Leah said, before gently adding. "I don't mean you're ridiculous. I mean, the way talent is groomed and packaged."

Jojo wasn't sure it was fair to lay the fault on anyone but herself. It might originally have been Carson's idea, but she'd played her part willingly, and it worked. Her fans loved it.

There was a knock at the door and through the screen a young voice called, "It's Gracie."

"Come on in." She gave Leah a warning look and whispered, "Remember, *no Jojo*."

Gracie opened the door, looking tentative. "I don't have to stay if you have company."

"It's okay. I think you know each other."

Gracie was halfway across the living room when her eyes lit up. "Mrs. Skoby! I can't believe it!"

Nothing about Gracie came in half measures, least of all her enthusiasm.

"Leah, this is Gracie Heston. But I guess you two met last summer."

"You probably don't remember me." Gracie's words tumbled out. "I took your workshop at Maycroft. You totally got me hooked on dance."

It always pleased Jojo when Leah was the focus of attention for a change. Working mostly behind the scenes, choreographers rarely got their due.

"I remember you. You were really quick at picking up the steps."

"Thanks," Gracie said. "It was so much fun. Now, even if I'm having a horrible day, dance makes me feel better."

Clearly, these two were going to get along. Jojo motioned for Gracie to have a seat and got her a soda.

"Mrs. Yates told me all about your club," Leah said. "As a result, I'm adding an advanced track to my workshop this year."

Gracie beamed, but just as quickly, her smile dimmed. "I hope you don't mind. I've been borrowing a lot of your dance moves."

Leah chuckled. "How do you think I got started? Everybody borrows from everybody, but the trick is to put a fresh spin on it."

This dynamic might be helpful, Jojo thought. With Gracie looking forward to the workshop, it could help fill the void when it came time to say goodbye.

"I've been learning your choreography for 'Fast Track,'" Gracie said. "My favorite part is that hitch kick twist combination." She got up and, with no mental preparation, executed the step perfectly.

Leah gave a few claps of applause. "Nice. There's a story behind that move, if you're interested."

"Definitely," Gracie said, sitting back down and looking completely rapt.

"I had the choreography for 'Fast Track' basically mapped out, but I wanted to get together with Jojo before we went into rehearsal—in case she wanted to change anything. So, on that day, it was just the two of us in the studio."

"Hold on." Jojo's eyes narrowed. "Is this story going to require an NDA?"

"I know what that means," Gracie said smugly. "And I swear, I won't tell anyone."

Jojo had to blink twice. It was a strange world in which twelve-year-olds knew about nondisclosure agreements.

Leah looked as if she'd swallowed something amusing and was having trouble keeping it down. "I think a pinkie swear should cover it." She leaned forward and extended a hand. Gracie did the same, linking little fingers, and both turned to Jojo as the last holdout.

She groaned, but it was only faux reluctance. Part of her

enjoyed having Leah to share stories with Gracie that she couldn't. "Do we solemnly swear that nothing leaves this room?"

"I swear," the other two said in unison. Jojo added her pinkie, and they shook on it.

"So, what happened?" Gracie asked.

"Well, as I was saying," Leah continued, "I just wanted to run through the choreo. Unfortunately, Jojo was getting over an injury. Every time she did the hitch kick, she was supposed to follow with a right turn, but she was reluctant to put all her weight on her bad ankle. So, the solution was to twist the opposite way."

"When did she get hurt?" Gracie asked.

"During a show in Atlanta," Jojo said, the words slipping out before catching herself.

Gracie paused. "Sooo . . . you know her, too?"

It was too late to backtrack, so Jojo nodded.

"How could you not tell me something SO HUGE!?"

"Maybe because I'm not a blabbermouth, like *some* people."

Leah feigned indignation. "*Blabbermouth* sounds so gauche. I prefer *name-dropper*."

Gracie's mouth was hanging open. "I can't believe I'm hanging out with you guys. You have the coolest lives."

Jojo felt the impulse to take Gracie by the shoulders and shout, 'You're Matt Heston's daughter! That's pretty darn cool!' But kids rarely saw their parents that way.

Maybe this was enough sharing for one day, plus Leah had already made it clear she was tired.

"Gracie, I hope you don't mind if we skip singing today."

"Are you kidding? This was amazing."

They all got up as Gracie got ready to leave.

"Hey, I've got an idea," Leah said. "Are you free tomorrow?"

"I think so, but I'll have to check with Dad."

"Since I won't be back until the workshop," Leah said, "what if I give you some homework—some combinations you can share with the rest of the group?"

"For real?! That would help so much. Some steps in your videos are kind of hard—especially for the younger kids."

"I've got a syllabus we can work from." Leah glanced around the living room. "And if we move some furniture, we can probably do it right here."

This was turning out better than Jojo could have hoped, and it was completely unplanned. Perhaps her ego had let her believe Gracie would be devastated at the end of her visit. But it didn't need to be that way. The girl was already thrilled about Leah's plan, and rehearsing with the other kids would keep her busy and distracted.

The three of them headed outside.

"There is one thing," Gracie said tentatively. "I hope you won't feel bad if Dad tries to pay you."

Leah raised an eyebrow, and Jojo chuckled.

"I think I've cured him of that."

"Hope so," Gracie said, then ran down the steps to her bike, looking jubilant. "I'll text you."

"We'll figure out a time," Jojo called back. "Probably in the afternoon."

Gracie was pedaling away before Leah turned back to Jojo.

"Sweet kid. Hard to believe she stops by every day and still hasn't figured you out."

"A few things have slipped out—like I can't believe I mentioned Atlanta. It's as if I want her to find out. This whole charade isn't as hard with Matt because I rarely see him, but with Gracie it doesn't feel right anymore."

"She seems savvy enough and obviously adores you. Perhaps you can trust her."

Jojo was starting to think the same thing. "If any child knows how bad the paparazzi can be, it's Gracie. And the last thing she wants is for me to have to leave early."

As they stood on the porch, the pleasant reality hit home that they had nothing on their agenda for the rest of the day. Jojo took a step toward the hammock, just as Leah called, "Dibs!" and pushed past her.

"You're such a brat," Jojo said, grabbing the edge of the hammock to stop it from swinging madly. "Scooch over—it's big enough to share." Leah moved aside, and Jojo climbed in.

"I know we've got a fridge full of food," she said, "but if you want to go out, it's my treat."

Leah had closed her eyes. "Nah. Let's break into our stash. You can choose the wine." Her voice trailed off at the end, and Jojo suspected further conversation might have to wait.

CHAPTER 31

MATT

MATT PUT a scoop of potato salad on his plate and then pushed the deli container over to Gracie. "Angie got this batch just right."

"I like Gram's better."

"Yeah, hers is good, too. I should get her recipe."

"You keep saying that."

His resolution for the past two New Year's was to become a better cook. Nothing fancy. He just hadn't realized how much they would miss his mother's clam chowder and shepherd's pie, and definitely, her brownies. Yet here they were again, eating burgers off the grill and potato salad from the market.

"So, Mrs. Skoby just showed up out of nowhere and wants to help you?"

Gracie's mouth was full, but she nodded. She'd been on cloud nine since arriving home.

"And you never asked for help?"

"No," Gracie said. "She heard about the dance club from Mrs. Yates."

Here was another reason Matt hoped the camp survived. Where else would local kids get these kinds of opportunities, like a big-name choreographer donating her time?

"We should think of a way to thank her," he said.

Gracie set her milk glass down. "Too bad she isn't single. She seems like the perfect age for you."

That came out of nowhere. "Honey, why are you even thinking about that?"

She sighed as though it should be obvious. "I'm afraid you'll be lonely when I go on tour."

Not this again. He often wished there was another parent in the house, if only to reassure him he wasn't losing his mind.

Gracie continued in her matter-of-fact voice. "It's finally happening. Jojo noticed me online, and I'm getting to know Mrs. Skoby. Joelle has more contacts than I realized, and I think I'll get to meet some of them when I visit her in the city. You can come if you want. Otherwise, there's a bus that goes direct from Bennington."

Had she actually checked a bus schedule?! He was no longer pretending to eat. He just stared as she chirped on about this alternate reality.

"We keep getting more views on our YouTube video—over half a million now." She glanced up as though a new idea popped into her head. "Do you think Uncle Thad would manage me?"

"Gracie, stop! You've got to slow down. Being a kid is a gift and you shouldn't rush through it. Life gets complicated soon enough."

His tone startled her, but he didn't care. She needed a reality check, and it seemed to work because a moment later she sounded twelve again.

"Can I still do choreography tomorrow with Mrs. Skoby?"

"Honey, of course. I'm excited you're dancing and proud you organized the club." Actually, he suspected dance might be another line out of her pop-career handbook, but at least it involved time with her peers.

She got up and put her plate in the sink, then started to leave. "I'll text Joelle."

"Wait. What did you mean earlier about her having contacts?"

"She works with other songwriters and today she even mentioned—" Gracie froze as if remembering something. "She mentioned knowing people through Mrs. Skoby. She acts so normal about stuff that would blow most people's minds."

Huh. There were many layers to that woman, yet with her reluctance to share, Matt doubted he would ever truly know her.

"Are we going to play tonight?" he asked.

"Yeah. I didn't get to jam with Joelle this afternoon, so I definitely need an hour or two tonight."

He would have preferred a simple, 'That'll be fun, Dad!' But instead, she made it sound like work. If only there was a way to temper her ambitions without diminishing her enthusiasm.

CHAPTER 32

JOJO

WHEN GRACIE ARRIVED SATURDAY AFTERNOON, the living room furniture was already pushed aside and the braided rug rolled up. Jojo was emptying the dishwasher, but Leah was ready to dive in.

"If you're going to get the most out of this session, you need to think like a choreographer, so even when I'm not around, you'll be able to make up your own routines."

"But I have zero training," Gracie said. "Except for your workshop."

"Based on the conversation we had yesterday, I'll bet you know more than you think. Even watching dance videos is a kind of training. How many hours do you think you watch?"

Gracie looked guilty. "Promise not to tell my dad?"

Leah put a finger to her lips. "We're still bound by the pinkie swear. Nothing leaves this room."

"Then I guess I've probably watched hundreds of hours."

Leah nodded approvingly. "Now that's what I'm talking about. All those movements are stored up here." She touched Gracie on the forehead. "We're simply going to release them. And do you write music and understand phrasing?"

"Sure. The typical verse or chorus is thirty-two beats—four groups of eight. The bridge might be longer or shorter. But one reason I like 'Fast Track' is because the bridge is also thirty-two, which makes it easier."

Leah looked to see if Jojo was paying attention. "Are you hearing this?"

"I told you. I just wanted you to see for yourself."

"Keeping it simple is good," Leah said. "Especially for the little kids. Don't you have some six- and seven-year-olds?"

Gracie nodded. "But the older kids may want more."

"We'll get there," Leah said. "For now, we're going to start with thirty-two beats, which you can repeat as many times as necessary. After that, and if we still have time, we'll do a more advanced section for the older kids, which you could use on the bridge."

"That would help break it up," Gracie said, "so it doesn't get boring."

"Exactly. But about your song choice. Are you really sure you want to go with a Jojo song?"

Jojo stopped drying dishes.

"I mean personally," Leah continued, "I find her music a little overproduced."

"Okay, that's it," Jojo said, throwing down her dishtowel and walking into the living room. "You diss our girl once more and you're getting a time-out."

Leah was clearly amused with herself.

"Wow," Gracie said. "That's exactly what my dad said."

"Leah's just messing with us, Gracie. She has a warped sense of humor and she probably saw your dad on TV."

Leah looked a little sheepish. "Sorry, I can be a tease sometimes."

"Ya think?" Jojo said, plunking herself down in a chair and taking off her shoes in order to dance in her socks.

"Before I forget," Gracie said, "Dad and I want to take you guys out for dinner to thank you for helping me."

"Well, hell yeah," Leah said.

"Language!" Jojo said, feeling like the only grown-up in the room.

"*Sorry*. I would love to meet your dad and dinner sounds great."

Jojo hesitated. When Leah was in a good mood, her mischievous side often came out to play, and there was no telling what she might say in front of Matt and Gracie. But on the flip side, it could be really fun.

She set her shoes off to the side before realizing Gracie and Leah were waiting for a response. "Oh definitely. I was just thinking about something: I'm not sure I brought the right clothes. What kind of place is it?"

Gracie had a big grin. "It's a surprise. I can't tell you."

"Intriguing," Leah said. "But at least tell us if it's dress-up or casual."

"Definitely casual." But then Gracie backtracked. "Well . . . not working-in-the-garden casual. What you have on is perfect."

"Got it," Leah said. "So, clean clothes only. That narrows it down." It looked as though she was trying to hide her amusement. Then she glanced at her watch. "If we're going out later, we should get to work."

"Sorry," Gracie said. "I talk too much."

"Not at all," Jojo said. "We're thrilled with the invitation—especially that it's a surprise."

The three of them worked on choreography for the next hour and a half. They took turns creating eight-beat segments, and the parts fit together remarkably well. Between them, they had so many ideas, they couldn't use them all. In the end, they had an easy thirty-two beat phrase, and another that was more challenging.

When they were done, they called Matt and agreed to meet at the mystery location, with Gracie navigating. They put her bike in the back of Leah's SUV and headed to town.

"Did you work some more on that song?" Gracie asked from the back seat. "The one with that guy, Tyrell?"

Jojo caught a look from Leah and figured she should explain. "Tyrell and I have been shooting files back and forth. And to answer your question, Gracie, it's close to being done." She hoped that would be the end of the subject, but Gracie was only getting started.

"Is that the same Tyrell that writes with Jojo? I just got to thinking it makes sense since you know her."

This was how secrets unraveled, especially when spending time around a whip-smart kid. Jojo looked for support from Leah, but her friend was staring ahead at the road, wearing a bemused smirk, and probably thinking, 'I told you so.'

"Yeah, it's the same guy. Tyrell works with lots of people."

"This is *huuuggge* for you! Can I hear it? Do you have it on your phone?"

"'Fraid not. But it'll probably be ready to share before I leave next week." She meant it. Perhaps at the same time, she'd come clean to Matt and Gracie. That sounded like a good plan.

"I've got another question," Gracie said.

Leah's shoulders shook from a silent tremor of laughter, but thankfully, Gracie didn't notice.

"It's about our pinkie swear. I almost accidentally told my dad something."

Jojo's head shot around. "You can always talk to your dad about anything. Is that clear?" The last thing she needed was for Matt to think they were keeping secrets from him.

Gracie looked slightly startled, probably not from the words as much as the tone. "Even about Tyrell?"

Jojo's voice softened. "You can tell him anything and everything."

"Thanks. Not telling him felt kinda weird. Besides, it's not like he'd mention it to anybody. He's not on social media." She suddenly pointed ahead. "Turn right at that sign."

It was the entrance to the Moose Club parking lot. Jojo had noticed the sign before, but the building itself was set back from the road behind a dense row of shrubs. There were a surprising number of vehicles, and the club was a huge barn-like structure.

They spotted Matt standing beside his truck and parked nearby. Gracie was quick to jump out, and Leah turned to Jojo with raised eyebrows.

"That was an interesting conversation."

"Welcome to my house of cards."

Leah seemed more amused than worried. "She's going to figure it out."

"I'll tell them both. I just need to find the right time."

They got out to meet Matt and he extended a hand to Leah. "Thank you for helping Gracie. It's very generous."

"Actually, it gave me an excuse to come up to the cabin and make sure Joelle hadn't wrecked the place. You know how much she parties."

"We've noticed. There've been several complaints."

"Oh, I like him already," Leah said to Jojo. "Matt, you should meet my husband, Tom. We're coming up next month, and we'll have you and Gracie over for a swim."

"Thanks. That would be great."

"*Yes!*" Gracie chimed in.

Jojo felt a pang of envy, knowing she'd be gone by then.

Matt greeted her with a slightly awkward side hug. "You need to stop by and check out our refrigerator art. Gracie printed some of the photos you took at the yard sale." His eyes were warm and sincere. Maybe she'd only imagined the hug was awkward because he seemed at ease.

"Yard sale?" Leah asked.

"We made a ton of money," Gracie said.

Matt nodded in agreement. "Mostly because Joelle's got some serious management skills."

The look on Leah's face was priceless. "Glad to hear it. I mean, just in case the music biz doesn't pan out." From her cagey tone, there were sure to be more questions later.

"How did the dance lesson go?" Matt asked.

"We took turns making up sections," Gracie said. "The other kids are gonna love it." But her attention was already drawn toward the front door and she bounded ahead. "Come on, everybody. I'm starved."

Matt laughed. "In case you haven't noticed, ladies, my daughter's in charge tonight. This whole thing was her idea." Jojo still wasn't clear what the idea was, and he didn't elaborate.

As they reached the building, Gracie breezed through the door and Matt caught it and held it open. He followed behind Jojo, his hand settling against the small of her back. Warmth spread from the spot as he leaned closer. "I'm glad you guys could come. I think you'll enjoy this."

Before she could think of even a simple response, he guided her to follow the others, his hand falling away. They passed through a lobby and then into a cavernous hall. She heard Matt tell a man with a clipboard that he had two guests tonight. Long folding tables were arranged in rows, and beyond them was a large, empty dance floor. There was no sign of a band, but classic oldies were playing over the sound system.

Gracie led the way to the snack bar and listed off her favorites, which included burgers, fried chicken, and pizza. She was at home here and the woman behind the counter asked how camp was going. Once their trays were loaded, Gracie showed them to a table near the dance floor.

There were people of all ages—families with young children, groups of seniors, and a few couples sitting off by themselves. Casual was definitely the dress code.

Matt put a hand on Gracie's shoulder. "I think we've kept them in suspense long enough."

She was practically bursting to let the cat out. "Mrs. Skoby, this is to thank you for the dance lesson and Joelle for helping with the yard sale."

"And also," Matt added, looking straight at Joelle, "for being so generous with your afternoons. Gracie wanted to pick something memorable—"

"Daaaddd. I'm telling it."

"Sorry, honey."

"Since you both like to dance, we wanted you to experience a Westbury tradition . . ." Gracie paused while her father did a drum roll on the table, then blurted out, "Line Dance Night!"

Jojo laughed, not just at the surprise, but also at Matt and Gracie's obvious excitement. She was up for anything, but was less certain about Leah, who had rather discriminating taste when it came to clubbing. But she needn't have worried.

"Awesome!" Leah said. "I didn't know this was here. Back when line dancing was big in New York, there was a studio in Soho I used to go to."

"Do they teach the dances first?" Jojo asked, suddenly realizing she might be the least experienced of the group.

"That's on Friday nights," Matt said. "Tonight, it's sink or swim. But you ladies will be fine. They repeat a lot of the same steps."

"No problem," Leah said, giving Jojo a fist-bump to the shoulder. "You'll get it. It's all grapevines and jazz boxes."

Jojo suspected there was more to it, but was willing to give it a try. "I'm just curious," she said, looking directly at Matt. "Does this mean Guitar Boy can dance?"

He puffed out his chest. "I can hold my own."

"I give him private lessons at home," Gracie added.

"Wait a minute," Leah said, shifting her attention. "I smell a rat, kiddo. You told us you didn't have much dance experience."

Gracie shrugged. "It's just line dancing. It's pretty easy."

"She knows all the dances," Matt said with fatherly pride. "I've been bringing her for years. We used to dance off to the side because she was so little, I was afraid she'd get stepped on."

"But that begs the question," Jojo said. "How has this never made it into the tabloids?"

"Because the dance floor is the last place they'd expect to find me. Plus, the club is members only." He kept surprising her and what a wonderful way to spend time with his daughter, away from the prying eyes of the press.

"Dad's a special member of the Moose Club," Gracie said.

"She means honorary member," Matt said. "They waive our dues because we sing at their fund raisers for free."

"How long have you been doing it?" Leah asked Gracie.

"Since I was eight."

"We don't take child labor laws too seriously around here," Matt said. "I'd just put a mustache and sideburns on her."

Gracie rolled her eyes. "No he didn't. People like cute little kids on stage, even though my playing was just so-so back then."

"She's being humble," Matt said. "At eight, she was both cute and talented. Shame that she's just about washed-up now."

"Hey," Gracie said, and it looked like she might have kicked him under the table. "The tween years are a very fragile time for a girl's self-esteem."

Jojo almost snorted out her soda as she and the other two adults burst out laughing.

"Not buying it," her dad said.

Just then, a woman with a wireless headset announced the first dance and at least half the people in the club streamed onto the floor.

"Gotta go," Gracie said, hopping up with Leah close on her heels.

"I think I'm going to finish eating," Jojo said. She wouldn't admit it, but she was a little nervous. Learning steps one combination at a time was one thing, but picking up choreography on the fly was not her forte. "Matt, go dance. I'll be fine watching."

"There'll be plenty more," he said, remaining rooted in his chair and taking another bite of his burger.

The two of them watched for a while. It did look like fun. Gracie, of course, already knew the steps, but it always amazed Jojo how effortlessly Leah could pick up a new dance.

"Leah makes it look easy," Matt said.

"She's in her element. This was the perfect idea."

"Gracie's been wanting to share this with you ever since you arrived, but I wasn't sure where things stood between us . . ."

That makes two of us, she thought. For her part, she spent far too much time thinking about him to be just friends, but then again, they didn't spend enough actual time together to be much more.

He was gazing intently at her. This, she realized, was part of the problem. Whenever they sat and talked, he was really good at giving her his undivided attention, making her feel like she was someone special. But she had to remind herself he'd been famous for his onstage charisma. Perhaps he had a gift for making all women feel special. Later, she would need to compare notes with Leah.

He leaned closer. "I need some advice. Last night, Gracie told me she's planning to visit you in New York. She made it clear I'm welcome to come along if I want, but if not, she's fine taking a bus on her own."

Jojo flinched at the implication. "Matt I swear I would never invite her without asking you first. I never even—"

He waved it off. "I'm not blaming you. This all started way before you showed up. And actually, I was impressed—well, not at first. But later, it got me thinking. I doubt I was brave enough at her age to get on a bus and go to New York."

Jojo was at a loss for what to say.

"And that's when I started wondering," he continued. "Perhaps I'm not taking this seriously enough. Am I going to wake up one day to find a note on her pillow that she's gone and done it?"

"Rest assured," Jojo said, "if Gracie ever pulls a stunt like that, I'll put her on the next bus home." Then she shook her head. "Nix that. I'd drive her back myself."

He reached across the table and patted her hand. "I know. I only brought it up because there's nobody else I can talk to about this stuff. At least no one who gets her like you do."

She was touched by his words. "I don't think you're alone in what you're going through. Millions of girls are probably tormenting their parents with their big dreams."

"I doubt many are as relentless."

"Maybe not, but who's to blame for that? Who gave her the skills?"

He appeared to chuckle, though the sound was lost in a Keith Urban song blasting from the speakers. They'd been straining to hear one another, so he slid over to the chair beside her. She knew better than to read anything into the simple gesture, but her heart beat a little faster.

She leaned close to his ear. "At least Gracie has one advantage that neither of us had—she has a parent who knows the industry."

He grimaced. "Which only means I see the downside more clearly."

Jojo felt like she wasn't helping much. "Maybe you're looking for the answer in the wrong place. Have you considered flipping the whole thing around and focusing more on you?"

"I don't follow."

"I'm not talking about you, the cabinetmaker. I mean the musician and songwriter." He knit his brow as she continued. "When you moved back here, it may have been the right thing at the time, but that doesn't mean it's the right thing forever."

"It's home," he said. "It's friends and community."

"It's safe," she added. "And will always be here. But does

Westbury have to be your *whole* world? As well as Gracie's whole world?"

She knew she was pushing, but hadn't he given her permission? She gave him a moment to think and turned her attention to the dance floor. It was crowded, but the dancers moved in impressive synchronicity, changing direction on a single beat without colliding. The patterns emerged, and she recognized some of the simple steps.

"I'm amazed how popular this is," she said.

He seemed to welcome the distraction. "Some folks drive an hour to get here. We're lucky it's in our own backyard. That's why Gracie and I do what we can to help keep the club going."

A new song started, and he straightened up. "This is a good one, and it's not hard. I'll help you."

She hesitated, but he was already pulling her to her feet. He led her onto the floor and found a narrow space along one wall, where a misdirection was less likely to cause chaos. Matt shouted the steps over the music, and her brain raced to relay them to her feet. She surprised herself, and by the third time around, she had it.

It wasn't until the song ended that she thought about how Matt seemed less guarded tonight and was more like he'd been when they first met.

"You're a natural," he said.

It was such a little thing—a turn of phrase men often used to ingratiate themselves to women. But with Matt, it felt sincere.

Leah's voice came through the speakers. "Hi, everybody. Gracie's been choreographing a new dance and I really think you'll like it. Does anyone want to try?"

A cheer went up and Leah passed the wireless mic to Gracie, who jumped on stage, every bit as confident as when there was a guitar in her hands. Immediately, she counted out a chasse right with a crossover rock, then a rolling turn to the left. She repeated it twice before moving on. Jojo was relieved to dance something familiar and within minutes, everyone had the new steps.

The intro to "Fast Track" boomed over the sound system, and Gracie yelled, "Five, six, seven, eight."

———

Leah waited until they'd waved goodbye to Matt and Gracie and were driving out of the parking lot before letting loose. "That was amazing! I'm definitely bringing Tom next month."

"Then you'll either have to join the club," Jojo said, "or stay on Matt's friends list."

Leah strummed her fingers on the steering wheel to the beat of a song still in her head. "I wonder if I could get Gracie to babysit, so Tom and I could make it an actual date."

"Good luck getting her to babysit on a line dance night."

"Hmmm. Good point," Leah said. "By the way, I'm unfriending you because you're a total liar. You said Matt wasn't into you."

"Knock it off. We're just friends."

"Oh, come on! I was watching you two at the table—the way you kept leaning in."

"The music was loud—it was the only way to hear."

"And on the dance floor—the 'accidental' bumping into each other." Leah made air quotes around *accidental*.

"Hands on the wheel!" Jojo shouted. "I only bumped into him once . . . maybe twice."

"And giggled like a schoolgirl."

"I have never giggled like a . . ." She didn't bother finishing. It wasn't worth dignifying. "You're as bad as the tabloids."

"And you're in denial."

It was too complicated to explain. Jojo rolled down her window and felt the rush of balmy summer air. She couldn't deny there'd been a few gestures tonight that might have crossed the friendship line. Maybe even moments when Matt's hands lingered longer than necessary as he guided her through some steps. It seemed they'd come to an understanding. She liked him and he liked her and as long as they both knew it wasn't going anywhere, there was no harm in some minor flirtation.

Leah tapped a couple of buttons on the sound system and one of Jojo's early songs with a fuzz-toned bass line filled the car. The party wasn't over, and the two women belted out the lyrics for the rest of the ride home.

Chapter 33

Jojo

Leah left a little before noon on Sunday and Jojo went back to writing. It had been a perfect visit but now she needed to refocus and get her momentum back.

She checked her messages a few times, in case she'd missed one from Matt, but so far, nothing.

Around mid-afternoon, she was outside on the porch when she got a text from Gracie. *Working on new song. Will u look at it?*

Three more texts followed, each with a verse.

> *He smiles more in the morning*
> *And worries less at night*
> *He hums now when he's working.*
> *Little less shadow; little more light.*
>
> *I didn't know he was lonely*
> *I thought he felt alright.*
> *But now I feel the difference.*
> *Little less shadow; little more light.*

The future's still uncertain,
But I know he'll be alright.
There's always a tomorrow.
Little less shadow; little more light.

It was unmistakably a song about a man in a good mood. Aware that Gracie was waiting, she texted back. *Is it about your dad?*

Yes.

Of course it was. It was tempting to ask whether Matt's positive mood was recent or weeks old. But using the child to pry into her father's feelings was just plain wrong. Suddenly, this felt a little too personal—like an invasion of Matt's privacy.

I bet your dad would love to give you advice? she texted back.

He's no help. He said it's already perfect.

Jojo laughed. Her own parents had been like that when she was a kid—gushing with positivity, even though most of her early lyrics were cringeworthy. Knowing how persistent Gracie could be, Jojo decided to offer some pointers while sidestepping the more personal aspects of the song. She looked again at the lyrics before texting back. *You write like your dad. It reads like poetry.*

Thanks. He liked it, too.

Also, the repetition of the last line of each stanza is nice.

Two seconds later, her phone rang. "You sound just like Dad. Pretend you're my agent or producer. Would these lyrics sell?"

So this is what Matt had to deal with. Jojo could see why he was sometimes at his wit's end. Still, she decided to play along.

"Okay, let's say I'm a big-time record exec and my major concern is whether the song will appeal to a mass audience. Is that what you want?"

"Exactly."

"Then give me a second." Jojo scrolled back once more through the lyrics. Even working like this with adults could lead to bruised egos, so she stepped gingerly. "Whatever changes I suggest, just remember you can always ditch them and come back to your original. That way, you can be fearless and more likely to try random ideas. Are we good?"

"I get it," Gracie said.

"So here goes. I'm sure you already know that when a woman sings a song about an unidentified man, people assume it's her lover." Jojo winced, wishing she'd substituted boyfriend for lover.

"I thought that might be a problem," Gracie said.

"But that's easily remedied by adding a reference to 'dad' or 'father.'"

"Yeah, that would fix it."

"But that's not what I'm going to recommend." Jojo hesitated, worried that she might be about to kill some of the charm of the piece. "I want you to consider that even though your dad inspired this song, maybe you can give it a more universal appeal by writing it in the first person."

"But then it just sounds like it's about me."

"Yes and no," Jojo said. "The listener usually identifies with the first-person character."

She stayed silent as she heard Gracie mumbling the changes half aloud. It was her song, and it had to be in her voice. Jojo wasn't even certain she was right. Despite her successful track record, she often looked back at a song and wondered if she'd made the strongest choice.

"I think I need time to get used to it," Gracie said. "Dad says sometimes you have to let it percolate."

Jojo smiled at Matt's euphemism. Then, appropriate or not, the question slipped out. "Has he really seemed happy lately?"

"Whenever I hear him whistling," Gracie said, "that's a good sign. And usually, he grumbles if he has to work on Sunday, but not today."

"He's working?"

"Yeah," Gracie said. "He's got a big install starting tomorrow, so he's out in the shop getting ready."

Enough with the nosy questions, Jojo chided herself. If she wanted to know more, she should act like an adult and simply call him. She shifted the conversation back to Gracie's song. "Not that it needs it, but are you going to add a chorus?"

"Yeah, definitely. I'm trying to reprise the line 'little less shadow, little more light,' but so far, nothing's worked."

"Instead of using the entire line," Jojo suggested, "try inserting just a piece of it and put it in the affirmative."

"I don't get what you mean."

Jojo hoped she wasn't putting too much of herself into the song. "Begin with 'A little more light,' and then a new line that's unique to the chorus. That way, you get tie-in with the verses, while adding something new."

Gracie took her time mulling it over. "I think my brain's burned out right now. But I'll work on it."

Jojo knew that feeling all too well. "Can I stop being the big, bad record exec and just be me again?"

"Please," Gracie said, sounding relieved.

"Thanks for last night. Leah and I both loved it. Can you pass that message along to your dad?"

"It was the best time ever," Gracie said, falling back on her usual superlatives. "And thanks for helping with the song."

"My pleasure. See you tomorrow."

CHAPTER 34

MATT

Sunday was unseasonably hot, so after washing the dinner dishes, Matt suggested a walk to the grocery store for ice cream. Every summer from about Memorial Day to mid-September, the store offered soft serve back in the deli section. It was an old machine, and the internal temperature fluctuated.

"How's the ice cream running?" Matt asked, recognizing the kid behind the counter but unable to recall his name.

"Real good, Mr. Heston. Just got it serviced."

"I'll have a small maple creemee," Gracie said.

"Make that two," Matt added. Even the smalls were generous.

"Everybody's talking about your concert last week," the boy said as he filled one cone. "I had to work, so I missed it. But I saw the video online. People say you should make an album."

"Thanks," Matt said. "We had a good time."

"Do you think people are getting tired of our old stuff?" Gracie asked the boy.

Matt looked down at his daughter. When had *his* music become 'our old stuff'? But he kept his mouth shut, wondering where this was going.

"Have you written anything new?" the boy asked.

"I'm working on a few songs. They've got more of a pop vibe."

"Peak," the boy said, looking impressed and handing her the first cone.

Matt had no idea what the boy had just said to his daughter, but he intended to look it up. For the first time, he gave some thought to the boy's age. He was probably sixteen or seventeen—clearly too old for Gracie. But despite himself, Matt had to hand it to his middle-school daughter for how unfazed she was talking to a high schooler.

Before leaving the counter, Gracie assured the boy she'd let him know when their album dropped. Matt shook his head. He worried that one of these days, she was going to have a head-on collision with reality.

As they walked toward the front of the store, she continued talking about doing an album, even asking if he'd like to write a few of the songs himself. It was mostly a one-sided conversation, except that he occasionally nodded or said "uh-huh." They were just passing the cookies and crackers aisle when he realized she was holding his hand. He couldn't recall the precise moment when their fingers entwined, nor did she seem aware. It was one of those vestiges from childhood that reappeared with less and less frequency. He'd learned it was best to enjoy these moments without calling attention to them, and in this case, it only lasted until they reached the line for the register.

They licked their cones while they waited and Matt thought about how the last five minutes summed up the experience of parenting a tween—the conversation with a boy, plans to record an album, holding hands, and now eating ice cream.

One of the tabloid headlines caught his eye, and he nodded toward the magazine rack. "Is it true Jojo's in rehab?"

"Say what?!" Gracie saw the headline and read it aloud, "Jojo checks into rehab: Fans pray for recovery." She handed Matt her cone, then grabbed the magazine and thumbed through it. "This is total BS."

"Watch your language." Matt glanced around to see if anyone was listening. "You may be right," he added. "But music is a tough industry, and it makes people do crazy stuff." As soon as he said it, he realized he wasn't being very sensitive.

Gracie didn't bother looking up from the page. "Dad, she's not like that. She's talked about it a thousand times. She doesn't do drugs or get drunk." Her good mood had vanished.

"I'm sorry, honey. It's probably not even true."

"Of course it's not true. You're always saying these things are full of lies. But what if some kids believe it?"

She was so earnest. He worried sometimes about the way she'd bought into all the hype about Jojo. Until now, the woman's reputation had been squeaky clean, but if she was having problems, he wondered how his daughter would handle it.

She'd already flipped to the story and started reading aloud. "The exhaustive pace of Jojo's recent tour has led to a near total breakdown and forced her to check into an exclusive sanitarium in Switzerland for treatment and close observation." Gracie looked up from the article. "A near total breakdown? Does that even make sense?"

Matt thought about it. "I suppose you could have a near breakdown or a total breakdown. But I don't see how you could have both."

"Exactly," Gracie said. "I rest my case." But she clearly hadn't rested. "Dad, remember that story about you joining a cult and moving to Sonoma?"

Matt laughed. "Or the time they said I'd given you up for adoption."

Gracie looked stunned. "When was that?"

"You mean you don't recall the years you spent in the orphanage?" Judging by her expression, he decided not to joke about it. "The story ran years ago when you were little. But there was a happy ending. Apparently, I had a change of heart and was able to buy you back on the black market."

"That explains my emotional scars," she said, tossing the magazine onto the checkout conveyor and taking back her cone. "I've got to show this to Joelle."

"No way are we buying that rag, especially not at $4.99." He put it back on the rack.

"Then I'm buying it with my own money." Gracie put it back on the conveyor.

"You have money?"

"Well . . . not with me." She gazed at him with angelic, pleading eyes. "I promise to pay you back later."

CHAPTER 35

JOJO

JOJO WAITED until Gracie pedaled out of sight before sitting down in one of the Adirondack chairs to read the article.

The child had arrived a half hour earlier, talking a mile a minute and tossing a tabloid into her hands. Jojo felt a rise of heat at the sight of the headline, and it took great self-control to resist opening to the story and reading the details. Instead, she'd dropped it onto the porch table, pretending it didn't matter.

"It's just a made-up story," she'd told Gracie. "They do it all the time."

"That's what I told Dad. But I figured you'd know for sure."

Gracie seemed shaken, and looking into those troubled eyes, it was tempting to end this charade. It would only take a few words: *Here I am. I'm not in rehab.*

Instead, she took Gracie in her arms and consoled her. "I promise Jojo's fine and she's not in a clinic in Switzerland. She's on vacation."

Gracie pulled back and looked up, her cheeks smeared with moisture. "But nobody's seen her."

"It would hardly be a vacation if people knew where she was."

That gave Gracie pause for thought. "Okay. I guess so. But do you just *think* it or *know* it?"

There was no point in couching a response with words like *maybe* or *perhaps*. What the child needed was certainty. "I *promise*, she's on vacation."

Gracie nodded. "I'm so lucky to know you. But what about other people? Some might believe it."

That was exactly what Jojo was thinking. "I know. That's the really sad part."

They'd chatted a bit more until Gracie seemed reassured. She even laughed at the realization she'd forgotten her guitar. They agreed that was okay because neither of them was in the mood to play.

Now that Jojo was alone, she read the article from start to finish, and then dialed Carson's number. It would have been wise to cool off first, but she was ticked.

"Hey, Jojo, it's about time you called. We've got that flight to Montreal Saturday morning."

"I'll be back in the city Friday afternoon," she said, curtly.

"Isn't that cutting it close?"

"I'll be there." She still resented the interruption to her vacation and didn't mind letting him know. "But that's not what I'm calling about. I want to know why I'm looking at a picture of me checking into a psych ward in Switzerland."

"Not a psych ward," he corrected. "It's a very chichi clinic."

"I'm not amused, Carson." How was she supposed to be a positive role model with stories like this floating around? What were all those young fans going to think and, equally important, what were their parents going to think? After all, kids didn't purchase $150 tickets on their own.

"I know you're pissed," he said. "I am too."

"You don't sound it. This better not be one of those times you're thinking, 'Any publicity is good publicity.'"

"Don't get mad at me." He sounded more annoyed at her than

at the article. "I've been putting out fires all week, while you've been off doing God knows what. This is what happens when stars go AWOL."

"For the last time, I'm on vacation!"

"You don't get to take vacations!" he snapped. "The second we stop feeding stories to the press, they start making them up. So even if you're riding a ski lift in Aspen or sitting on a beach in St. John, you better be tweeting about it because if there's a vacuum for even a couple hours, they will fill it with whatever crap their little pea-sized brains can invent."

She hated to admit it, but his words rang true. And what did she expect him to do? Wave a wand and magically bestow a conscience on the tabloid industry? Those lowlifes weren't about to change.

What bothered her, though, was that Carson had always been good at heading off these problems before they got this far. Was it possible he'd let this story get traction, just to teach her a lesson?

"I want to sue them," she said, without so much as a cursory thought. "Can't we just prove it's not me in the picture or it's photoshopped or something?"

"Oh jeez." It sounded like Carson was banging his head on the desk, something she'd actually seen him do. "Jojo, do you really want to spend the next two years in a court battle? Because if you think you're busy now, try adding that to your schedule."

He had an answer for everything.

"I just wanted a break," she said. "Why is the cost so high?"

There was silence on the other end of the line. Maybe he *didn't* have an answer for everything after all—or he couldn't be bothered.

The fight had drained out of her. "Just do what you can . . . please. I'll see you Friday afternoon." With that, she hung up.

Chapter 36

Ida

Ida sat at a table in the corner of the coffee shop. Her laptop was open, but her half-warmed bagel was still tightly wrapped. Even after scrapping her plan to return to Vermont for Gracie Heston's talent show, she'd been keeping an eye on the story.

As she'd predicted, people loved the video of the kid performing with her dad. His fame and their combined talent was a potent draw. But given the public's short attention span, Ida figured the story would have legs for about forty-eight hours and then die. So far, she'd been dead wrong.

The number of views on the video kept rising and there were full-blown discussions in the comment sections—mostly about the girl, many of them looking for more "Gracie content." It was a mystery why people fixated on some things.

So now Ida was reconsidering. She couldn't predict what the camp performance would be like and didn't relish driving to Vermont again, only to find Gracie singing camp songs in a chorus of twenty boys and girls. But, given the kid's obvious talent and recent notoriety, it seemed more than likely they'd put her on stage for a solo. Catching that on video could be worth something. Plus, as long as the show was indoors, Ida knew her video would have superior audio quality.

She'd already called Maycroft, and there were a couple of minor hurdles she would have to jump. Since she was ostensibly camp shopping for her fictional daughter, she'd have to take a tour and ask a bunch of inane questions. A complete waste of time, but probably no more than an hour.

The other issue was more of a legal matter. The camp had a strict policy that parents could only post photos and videos of their own children. Even visitors had to sign the agreement. But what were the odds of them asking for ID? Probably nil. So, she could attend as Betty Shein—a pseudonym she'd used before.

As she worked through the details in her head, she'd nearly convinced herself to make the trip. Her eyes fell on her now cold bagel, and she unwrapped it. She was feeling the buzz that accompanied a hot lead. It had been a while, and she was overdue.

CHAPTER 37

JOJO

LATE WEDNESDAY AFTERNOON, Jojo floated beside the dock, gazing at the clouds. She'd had back-to-back days of solid output, with messages, calls, and audio clips bouncing back-and-forth between Vermont and her cowriters. She might have resented that her working vacation was turning out to be heavy on the work and light on the vacation, but the creative rush she was feeling made it worthwhile.

Normally, Gracie would arrive around this time, but tonight was the talent show, so she was going straight home to get ready. She'd already sent three text messages, the first showing up before Jojo was even out of bed. It was a reminder that tonight was the big night—as if it was possible to forget.

The second text followed soon after and included photos of two outfits with an all-caps message: *HELP!* And the third arrived around lunch and appeared to be a teaser, promising that Jojo was going to "love, love, love" Gracie's choice of solo music, the title of which remained shrouded in secrecy.

Jojo climbed up the ladder onto the dock and toweled off. The sun was warm, so she lay down for a while, soaking up the heat. Mostly, she'd been lucky with the weather, and it looked as if that luck was carrying into the festival that weekend—according to Carson, the forecast was good for Montreal. Nothing was worse than making the trip to a venue only to have an outdoor concert rained out.

There had also been a brief text from Matt saying he and Gracie would swing by on their way to Talent Night to pick her up. She was happy to drive herself, but he insisted.

Finally, she decided to head up to the cabin, wanting to give another listen to a track she'd just received. The tempo didn't feel right, and she was thinking of sending it on to Leah for a second opinion. Her cover-up was lying on a nearby chair. She pulled it down over her head and slipped her feet into flip-flops before heading up the hill. She was surprised when she reached the top to find Gracie standing on the porch.

"Hi, Joelle. I was just coming down to find you."

"Don't you need to get ready?"

"I can only stay a minute, but I finished the chorus on that new song and wanted to read it to you." She had only her knapsack today and no guitar.

"Come on in, then. I'm parched. How about you?"

"I'm good. This will only take a sec." Once inside, Gracie went straight to the couch and opened her knapsack.

Jojo got a seltzer from the fridge and joined Gracie as she leafed through her spiral notebook, crammed full of ideas and lyrics, until she came to the right page.

"Once I started the chorus with 'Little more light,' it all came together." She started tapping out a beat on her knee before launching into the song:

> *Little more light to start each morning*
> *Little more light to see the way*
> *Little more lightness in each moment*
> *Let it chase the clouds away.*

"That's lovely," Jojo said, closing her eyes. "Sing it again, will you?" As she listened, there was nothing she would change. It had come together beautifully. When Gracie finished, Jojo nudged her affectionately with her shoulder. "You can tell when it's right, can't you?"

Gracie nodded. "And after I got the words, the melody just came."

"That happens," Jojo said. "Sometimes I work very hard on a melody, and other times it's as if it's just waiting for me to pluck it out of the air."

"I know," Gracie said, her eyes bright with the sense of triumph. "That's how this felt. Can I sing the whole thing for you? I thought about what you said and changed a few other lines, too."

"If you've got time, I'd love it."

Gracie launched right in, singing *a cappella*.

I didn't know that I was lonely
Didn't know that things weren't right. . . .

The words flowed—wistful and earnest—instantly conjuring a broody atmosphere. Jojo closed her eyes and let the lyrics transport her. By the next verse, the gloom began to lift and when Gracie hit the chorus for the second time, her delivery had a surging sense of optimism that carried through the remainder of the song, concluding with a celebratory lift.

Jojo's eyes shot open. "That was an awesome ride! The lyrics . . . the melody . . . everything!"

Gracie's smile widened. "Even with a band, I think it would be great to sing the chorus *a cappella* once near the end. Hopefully, the audience will clap and maybe sing along and then the band will come back in for one more chorus."

Her enthusiasm was infectious, and Jojo got her guitar from where it was lying on the window seat. "Sing the melody for the chorus again." She listened for a moment, then strummed a few chords until she zeroed in on the right key, but just then Gracie stopped singing. She was staring wide-eyed at Jojo's guitar.

"You have a Sam Rubio? Aren't they super expensive?"

Damn, Jojo thought. She'd been so careful up to now. But then she paused and let her head clear. Maybe this was meant to be.

"Yes, it was expensive. It's kind of crazy to pay that much for a guitar because I spend far too much time worrying about it. I don't even take it down by the water. It is a dream to play, though."

"But I've been here plenty of times and never saw it." Gracie paused to look squarely at Jojo. "You didn't mean for me to see it, did you?"

Now that it was happening, it was moving too fast. Not that Jojo wanted to hide the truth anymore, but she would have preferred to ease into it.

"I thought it would complicate things."

"Does this mean you're rich?"

Jojo's pulse quickened as each question came closer to the truth. "Well, I have a nice apartment in the city, and I could probably buy quite a few Sam Rubios." She held it out to Gracie. "Would you like to try it?"

"Would I?! And I'll be super careful, I promise." Gracie received the instrument like a precious relic and strummed a few chords as she tested the action, working her way down the frets and then back up. "It's really sweet. Do you ever change the tension?"

"Sam showed me, but it stresses me out. I'm afraid of over-tightening it. So, I let *him* do it. I was even nervous bringing it here because of the humidity. But I couldn't bear to leave it at home."

"Is it true he only makes about ten a year?"

"Something like that. Maybe less now that he's semi-retired."

It seemed Jojo had smoothed things over. She might get away with saying nothing more and life could go on as before. But she'd misunderstood the brief interlude. When Gracie lifted her eyes, all the questions were still there, and Jojo knew it was time to explain.

"When I met you and your dad, I didn't know you very well and so I told you the same thing I tell people when I'm trying to blend in. I introduced myself as Joelle. Then we became friends— more than friends, in fact—and I knew I needed to tell you the truth, but I just couldn't figure out when."

Jojo had been waiting to see if Gracie would turn the guitar over and read the inscription. She was either afraid or waiting for permission.

"You know Sam signs all of his guitars, don't you?"

The girl nodded and slowly rotated the instrument before reading aloud. "To Jojo with love, S. Rubio." There was an unmistakable catch in Gracie's voice. She stared at the inscription a while longer, possibly rereading it until there could be no doubt. Finally, she looked up. "It's sort of like a dream, but I can tell it's really happening."

Jojo sat quietly and gave her time.

"I remember when I met you at the grocery store," Gracie said, her voice shaking. "I thought you were a fan, like me."

"I'd just arrived," Jojo said. "And I sort of freaked out because I thought you'd recognized me."

Gracie looked at Jojo as if studying her face. "You look so different."

Jojo kept her eyes on Gracie. "Even Leah says it's the weirdest thing. Of course, I usually wear so much makeup, plus the wigs."

Gracie stared at her a bit longer before closing her eyes and covering her face with her hands. Jojo felt a pang of guilt as she realized Gracie was crying.

In an instant, she wrapped her in a hug. "Oh, honey, don't cry. Are you mad at me?"

"NO!" Gracie half-laughed and half-sobbed. "I just can't believe I didn't see it." She took two deep breaths while Jojo rubbed her back. "It's a lot to take in." The child's voice was still shaky, but she was calming down.

Gracie leaned into her, but it was awkward with the guitar.

"Why don't I put this away before we crush it," Jojo said, taking the guitar and putting it back on the window seat. It had been with her on two tours and there were a lot of memories associated with it, but none could top this moment.

She turned back to Gracie. "I'm sorry I didn't tell you earlier. I wanted to—so many times."

"I know sometimes Dad would like to be invisible. So I get it. But I'm glad I found out." She sniffed and wiped her face with her hand. "It's pretty cool."

Jojo smiled. "I hope you won't treat me any differently."

"Maybe it was better this way," Gracie said. "If I'd known you were Jojo, I never would have come over here and asked you to jam. Oh my God!" she said, looking more her usual animated self. "I've been jamming with Jojo!"

That sounded more like Gracie.

"Can I call you that?" she asked. "Can I call you Jojo now?"

"No. Definitely not. Because I haven't told your dad yet."

"So, he doesn't know?"

"Nope. But obviously, I have to tell him now. I don't want you to have to lie to him.

"I'm not sure Dad will be as excited as I am." Suddenly, she started giggling as if remembering something. "He thinks you have a wicked case of stage fright because of the way you took off at farmers market."

It was a relief to hear Gracie's laughter.

"That explains why neither of you said much after the concert. You felt sorry for me?"

"Yeah. Dad thinks you might be happier as a session musician."

This time, they both laughed. But as they quieted, Jojo felt regret returning. Her single lie had created a web of misunder-standings, and while Gracie seemed quick to forgive, would Matt?

"Wow," Gracie said, thinking out loud. "If you'd sung with us, we could have blown up YouTube."

"Yeah," Jojo said. "But this place would have been crawling with paparazzi by morning and I'd be back in New York right now."

"You don't have to worry about me telling anyone," Gracie said. She was dead serious. "That would be pretty dumb."

"It won't be easy," Jojo said. "Sometimes things slip out acci-dentally. Like me bringing out my guitar just now."

Gracie shrugged, looking a little glum. "It's not like you're here that much longer."

"But I want to be able to come back," Jojo said. "And hang out like this."

Gracie threw her arms around Jojo again and then just as quickly drew back. "But can I ask a favor? Please don't tell Dad right before I sing tonight. I'm not sure how he'll take it."

"On one condition," Jojo said. "I'm dying to know what you're singing tonight."

"That's blackmail! It's supposed to be a surprise."

"Okay," Jojo said, giving in and grateful that Gracie was smiling again. "I won't tell your dad 'til later."

CHAPTER 38

MATT

THE THREE OF them arrived early at Talent Night so Gracie could get her amp and mic backstage and then meet with the dance club for a quick last-minute run-through. Matt helped carry the equipment inside and then came back out of the hall to find Joelle. A few more cars had arrived, and his eyes swept across the parking area until he spotted her at a tetherball court, batting the ball around the pole. It was an enchanting tableau—her look of determination each time she wound up to swing and the way her floral dress trailed each movement.

He headed toward her, feeling lighthearted and thinking of all the ways she kept surprising him. His fondness for her was growing, but he kept it in check by reminding himself she was leaving soon. Once he'd made the decision to be just friends, he'd stuck to it, but there were moments like this when he wished their two worlds were a better fit.

Her departure would leave a void, and not just in Gracie's life. It seemed he and Joelle never went more than a few days without seeing each other and in between, he found himself thinking of her and making mental notes of things to talk about.

He even wondered if she might return to Westbury again. It

certainly seemed that she enjoyed the town and the lifestyle. However, a woman like Joelle wasn't apt to stay single for long and would probably have a boyfriend the next time she visited. In that case, the two of them wouldn't be hanging out like this.

"Impressive," he said as he approached. There was a bench beside the court, and he sat down to watch.

"I considered going pro," she said.

"Why didn't you?"

Her eyes continued to track the ball with each rotation. "Oh, you know how it is. My parents wanted me to finish sixth grade."

"Well, you haven't lost your touch," he said.

She wound up for one last solid hit before coming over to join him.

"You've barely spoken about your family," he said. He threw the subject out there, not expecting much, but this time, she surprised him.

"I grew up outside Rochester, New York, and I think I mentioned my father sells insurance. My mother is a bookkeeper for the school district, and I have an older brother and a younger sister. Just your basic middle-class family."

That was a whole lot more than he'd known before. "Are you close to them?"

"We all get along, but I don't get home nearly enough." Her eyes had returned to the tetherball as it slowly unwound. "Now and then, I video chat with my parents on a Sunday when I know Dad's home. And I go back at Christmas, but usually for just a couple days." She looked regretful, as if maybe she should do better.

"Don't be too hard on yourself," he said. "We all get a little self-absorbed in our twenties."

She looked away and seemed to consider that for a moment. He hoped it didn't sound like he was judging her, especially since he'd been no different.

"Are you in the shop tomorrow morning?" she asked.

"Yeah, I just finished an install yesterday and started a new project today." A while back, he'd promised her a tour of the shop and wondered if she was planning to take him up on the offer. But before he could ask, she jumped to another topic. Her mind seemed all over the place tonight.

"You know," she said, her tone turning wistful, "the farmers market wasn't the first time I've seen you perform live. When I was seventeen, I borrowed my mom's car and drove with my girlfriend into downtown Rochester to see you in concert. I still have the ticket stub in a scrapbook."

He wondered why she was suddenly more open to sharing.

"The part of the show that left a lasting impression," she said, "is when you did 'Freeway'—the extended version. It was masterful the way you started out super mellow and then let it build. By the end, you were on your back, kicking your feet straight up in the air, while playing guitar and singing, and I couldn't figure out how you had enough air in your lungs?"

"It helped that you and everybody else were making so much noise, you could barely hear me."

"No," she said, "I could still hear you. You somehow managed it."

"Pure adrenaline," he mused, feeling himself transported back to that stage and wishing he could spot her seventeen-year-old self in the crowd. It was strange to think of their worlds intersecting long ago.

As though recalling something funny, she grinned. "That's the night I bought a Matt Heston poster. I took it home and hung it in my bedroom and it's still there to this day. Except it's turned into my mom's craft room and now it hangs over her sewing machine."

He started laughing—a full belly laugh, like he hadn't felt in a long time. "Please tell me I had a shirt on."

Joelle's mouth dropped open. "You mean that was an option? Can I still get one?"

Her deadpan was too much, and it sent him over the edge again.

She knit her brow as he tried to pull himself together. "Are you going to be okay?"

"We better get inside for the show." He rose from the bench and offered his hand but try as he might to sober up, he was still chuckling. "If I start to lose it again, pinch me."

CHAPTER 39

IDA

THE TALENT SHOW was in a long hall with rough pine walls and exposed rafters. Earlier in the afternoon when Ida toured the camp, she noticed a fair amount of echo in the building, but now that it was filled with campers and parents, she guessed the acoustics would be adequate.

She'd timed her arrival well—not so early that she had to mingle and make small talk, but not so late that it was hard to find a good spot to stand—at five-foot-two, there was no way she could shoot the video while sitting down. She also wanted to be in position to pan at the end of the song from Gracie to her father in the audience. The entire shoot was mapped out in her head. Still, a dozen things could go wrong—anything from the kid getting cold feet to someone walking in front of the lens at a critical moment.

Matt arrived a few minutes later and Ida fought the instinct to sneak a couple of stills. It wasn't worth blowing her cover—not when the real prize was coming later.

She noticed he wasn't alone. A pretty woman in her mid to late twenties was with him, and the way he touched her arm to guide her into a row of benches told Ida this wasn't a casual acquaintance. There might be more than one story here, so perhaps this beat wouldn't end tonight.

By the time the lights dimmed, and Mr. and Mrs. Yates came out to welcome everyone, Ida had moved to a spot along the left wall, where several parents were standing with their cameras and phones poised for the appearance of their sons and daughters. From this new position, she had a perfect view of the stage and of Matt. And now the waiting began.

An hour into the show, Ida worried that Gracie's appearance in an earlier dance number might be her only time on stage tonight. That would make the trip a total bust. But as good as Gracie was on YouTube, it was likely they would highlight her singing talents as well, probably near the end.

So far, Ida had endured several skits about camp life, a girl on piano playing "Für Elise," and a violin and cello duet that was rather impressive. And between each performance, there had been camp songs, with many parents joining in.

Finally, Gracie's name was announced, and Ida breathed a sigh of relief as she raised her camera. She'd already set the focus during previous acts, so she didn't miss a moment as the curtain opened to an amp and a mic and the girl walking onto the stage. There was a reassuring ease about her as she plugged a cord into her guitar and spoke to the audience.

"Hi, everyone. I really love doing these shows because it feels like we're all family and even if I mess up, you won't demand your money back."

There was light laughter among the parents, and Ida's expectations rose. This twelve-year-old had stage presence, but the question remained whether she could entertain roughly two hundred people without Matt's help.

"A funny thing happened about a week ago," Gracie said. "I was performing with my dad and before our final number, he thanked Jojo for singing his song 'Sweet Side.' It's funny because *I'm* the big Jojo fan, and I've sung many of her songs and never thanked her. Tonight, I'm going to sing 'Flower Girl' from her first album and dedicate it with gratitude for all the great music she's given us."

Ida's pulse quickened. She couldn't have handpicked a more perfect song. Now, if only the kid could deliver a solid performance.

There was a hushed air of anticipation over the crowd—most of whom had probably heard her before. Ida had a good feeling about this—a very good feeling.

The guitar intro alone was strong, and as Gracie started to sing, Ida had the sweet sense of hitting one out of the park. This was going to be huge, but for now, she needed to keep her hands steady and not screw this up.

The kid was nailing all the highs and lows, and her pitch was spot on. As the timer in the viewfinder passed 3:30, Ida knew the song was coming to an end. So far, no one had blocked any part of the shot, but there was the chance of a standing ovation, which would prevent her from panning to Matt. She couldn't wait any longer, and slowly swung to the right with a steady hand, catching Matt smiling proudly just before the applause erupted and everyone rose to their feet.

A pessimist at heart, Ida could hardly believe her luck when a shoot went this well. There were taller bodies all around, obscuring her view of the stage, but another round of applause signaled Gracie's return for a second bow. If Ida left now, she could beat the rush and be the first out of the parking lot.

Five minutes later, she was on the road heading to Bennington. Two bars of cell reception in the middle of the Vermont woods wasn't going to cut it, so earlier in the day, she'd checked into a motel with good Wi-Fi. She'd even tested it by sending a four-minute video to herself.

As she drove, Ida thought about the young woman with Matt. She was vaguely familiar, and Ida wondered if she might have run into her on her last trip to Westbury. She recalled seeing Gracie talking to someone in the store and was almost certain it was the same woman. If Matt had a girlfriend, it might be a decent story—not front-page material, but still newsworthy.

For now, though, Ida needed to decide what to do with the video. Her original plan was to post it on her YouTube channel and drive traffic to it with teasers on Instagram and Twitter. She had good followings on all three platforms, so the potential for ad revenue was good. But Gracie's performance had far and away exceeded expectations and the buzz around her was growing, so maybe Ida needed to think bigger.

TV seemed like the obvious answer, but Ida's contacts worked mostly in print. She could try calling around, but she'd have to wait until offices opened in the morning. Even then, she'd have to get past a slew of receptionists and assistants before she could talk to an actual producer. It would be like beating her head against the wall just to convince someone to take her seriously.

Ida ran through a list in her mind of people who might help broker the deal. She needed a heavyweight with clout, incentive, and the right contacts. That's when Carson Skinner came to mind. He had to be knee deep in the fallout from the Swiss rehab story and frankly, she was feeling some guilt about her own role in that. The Gracie video had perfect tie-ins to Jojo, and though it wouldn't kill the rehab story, it delivered the kind of warm fuzzies that might distract people for a day or two.

She glanced at the bars on her phone and decided this wasn't the place to call him. She'd wait until she reached Bennington.

CHAPTER 40

JOJO

IT WAS dusk by the time they pulled out of the camp parking lot. Gracie had been a chatterbox ever since she'd thrown her arms around Jojo and her father after the show. Somehow, she'd managed with her twelve-year-old wingspan to gather the three of them into one big hug. Jojo had been caught off-guard, and wasn't sure how Matt would respond, but he doubled down with a bear hug of his own. The familial warmth of the embrace still lingered.

She'd kept her promise to refrain from telling Matt the truth until after the performance, but now wasn't the time—not with Gracie sitting in the jump seat. Perhaps she could invite him into the cabin while Gracie waited in the truck, but she didn't want to rush it. It was a short drive and they'd reached the cabin before she made up her mind. *Tomorrow,* she promised herself. *First thing in the morning.*

Matt kept the motor running and started to get out, as if he planned to walk her to the door.

"No need," she said. "I know you've got to get home."

For a second, he seemed conflicted before settling back into his seat. "I'll wait 'til you're inside. Thanks for coming tonight."

"I loved every minute. Even that Heston kid did okay." Jojo felt a shove from the back seat and turned to wink at Gracie. "What you said about Jojo tonight was very thoughtful."

"I meant it."

"I know." She reached for Gracie's hand, and they gave each other a squeeze. She didn't want the evening to end, but it was time, so she opened her door and told them goodnight.

She made it onto the porch and was getting her keys out when Gracie hopped out of the truck and came running. "Did I forget something?" Jojo asked.

Gracie didn't respond until she reached the top step and spoke in a low, breathless voice. "You didn't tell him yet, did you?"

Jojo gave her a baffled look. "No, silly. Do you think he's acting like I told him?"

"Not really, but I thought maybe he was being super cool about it."

Jojo was close to laughing. "Are we talking about the same guy?"

"Okay . . . yeah," Gracie said. "I guess you're right. It just felt like there was an elephant in the truck."

It took Jojo a second. "You mean like the elephant in the room?"

Gracie nodded, and Jojo masked her amusement.

"I couldn't just blurt it out on the way home. Your dad said he'll be in the shop tomorrow morning, and I think it's best if it's just the two of us." She hadn't forgotten how heated Matt got in some of his interviews, and she didn't want Gracie to witness anything of the sort. "Let's hope he's not too mad at me."

"Don't worry. Sometimes he's like that at first, but then he cools off." That didn't sound reassuring. "Good luck," Gracie said, before throwing her arms around Jojo.

As the child ran back to the truck, Jojo thought of the many spontaneous hugs she'd received on this vacation. All of that affection was turning into an unexpected summer bonus.

After getting ready for bed, Jojo went back downstairs and poured a glass of wine. She'd finished the last book, and it was time for another, so she stood for a while in front of the bookcase. She thought of staying with the same author but decided instead to branch out. One title in particular looked enticing and without even reading the back cover, she took it over to her favorite comfy chair and settled in for a good read.

The story caught her right away, and she was fully immersed in the second chapter when her phone rang.

"Hey, girl," she said, putting the phone to her ear. There was a long silence.

"Ummm . . . this is Matt. The guy who just dropped you off."

She chortled. "Sorry 'bout that. Leah often calls around now."

"I can call back another time."

"No, now is fine." She might have sounded overeager and tried to rein it in. "I'm just surprised, because I thought maybe you'd forgotten how to use the phone."

There was a low growl on his end of the line "Now I remember why I rarely call you. It's because you're always bustin' my chops." There was more mirth than misery in his voice.

"Where does that expression even come from?" she said, aware that they had launched into the conversation without so much as hello.

"Hmm . . ." Matt said. "I'm pretty certain it was the first thing Adam said to Eve."

She loved this lighthearted version of Matt. "So, did you call just to shoot the breeze?"

"Would that be okay?"

Jojo sat up a little and closed the book. "I assumed you were calling about Gracie."

"Nope. I just . . ." He seemed to search for the words. "I just wanted to apologize for not walking you to the door. It wasn't like we were in a big hurry."

That took her aback. "You offered, but I knew you had to get home."

"Well, okay," he said, apparently letting it go. But she was touched by his gentlemanly concern. "What day are you leaving for New York?" he asked.

"Friday. Probably in the morning. And I might not get back until Monday afternoon." In the back of her mind, she was mulling over whether to invite Matt and Gracie to Montreal. Of course, it all depended on how their talk went in the morning. At the very least, he would need time to process the news.

"You know," he said, "after we got home, I started laughing again—just thinking about that poster over your mom's sewing machine. Gracie came downstairs to make sure I hadn't lost my mind."

"You didn't tell her, did you?"

"Not a chance. Imagine if you were twelve and found out your dad was a pin-up."

She shuddered at the thought of posters of her father hanging in teen bedrooms across the country. "Yecchhh! That's just creepy."

"Exactly!" There was an unspoken 'I told you so' in his voice. "It's not so funny when it's your own father."

"We need to make a pact," Jojo said. "This will be our little secret."

"Too late. I think your mom's already in on it." It was oddly sweet to hear him mention her mother and, for a moment, she pictured showing up out of the blue at her parents' home with Matt. They already knew she met a lot of famous people in her profession, but it might feel different to come face-to-face with someone whose picture had been hanging on one of their walls for years.

His voice yanked her back to the present. "I should go upstairs and say goodnight to Gracie, but I have one quick question. It feels weird after all this time that I don't know your last name."

Really? she thought. *Couldn't this have waited just one more day?* "I don't have one. I legally changed my name."

He was quiet for a moment. "So . . . just Joelle?"

Suddenly, she couldn't bear to lie anymore. "You know what, Matt? There's some stuff I need to tell you. You're going to be around the shop tomorrow, right?"

"Yeah, but we can talk right now, or I can call back after Gracie goes to bed."

He sounded concerned, and she regretted not sticking to her story for one more night. "I'd rather talk in person. It's been a long day and I'm tired." She knew that sounded weak.

"Huh," he said. "The suspense is going to mess with my beauty sleep."

"It's not a big deal," she said, stretching the heck out of the truth. "Perhaps I just want an excuse to come over."

There was a moment before he responded. "You're welcome anytime—no excuse needed."

She wondered how to interpret that. Did he mean specifically *anytime tomorrow* or simply *anytime*?

CHAPTER 41

JOJO

JOJO BURROWED her head under the pillow to block the sunlight. With everything coming to a head, it had been a night of anxious sleep. Today she had to face Matt, and tomorrow was the dreaded trip to New York and the unavoidable face-off with Carson. There was little chance the icy tensions between them would thaw in the next few days.

It was hot and difficult to breathe, so she pushed the pillow away. Outside, blue sky was peeking through the forest canopy, and it was promising to be another beautiful morning.

The idea of going from this tranquil existence straight into the spotlight at a major festival felt daunting. She had only three days to get mentally prepared for Montreal, and for the first time there was a twinge of resistance at the thought of putting her public mask back on.

She had never resented the time and energy it took to go full-on Jojo. In fact, it had been fun—another form of artistic expression, with endless possibilities. And she'd always sworn by the transformative power of her wigs and makeup to make her feel larger-than-life. Still, she was growing accustomed to this laid-back summer routine, and how convenient it was to roll out of bed each morning, splash some water on her face, run her fingers through her hair, and be good to go.

But perhaps she could shelve her worries for another twenty-four hours. *Nothing's going to spoil today,* she thought. First thing, she needed to talk to Matt. He'd been in a good mood last night—both at the talent show and later when he'd called. There would never be a perfect time to tell him the truth, but at least now they were in a good place.

She sat up and reached for her phone. As she clicked out of silent mode, she realized it was flooded with messages. One by one, she scrolled through congratulations on her latest number one. She didn't even reach the bottom of the list before falling backward on the bed and throwing her hands and feet in the air with a joyful squeal.

The experience never got old, and this time was extra sweet since it vindicated her long battle to get "Sweet Side" on the album and, finally, released as a single. It had been a two-year, one-woman fight against an army of risk-averse executives. In the end, she'd been right, though she knew they'd never admit it.

She scrolled through her texts again until she found one from Leah and clicked on it.

Nice work, girl! I'll bet Matt's celebrating, too. Maybe it's time to drop the bomb.

Apparently, they were both in sync today.

Jojo broke her own speed record for getting dressed and out the door, even breezing past the kitchen without breakfast or coffee. As she drove toward Matt's, she felt buoyant and fearless. Even if he took the news badly at first, their friendship had developed enough of a foundation that she believed he would forgive her. She even dared to hope they were on the verge of transcending friendship. After all, friends didn't normally call on the flimsy premise of apologizing for not walking her to the door. That had bordered on adorable—maybe even goofy adorable. And after she'd reassured him, their conversation had settled into a comfortable rhythm, his voice dropping into that easy-going, soft baritone that made her want to curl up in his arms.

It didn't seem crazy to hope this might be a new beginning, but as she approached Matt's house, the situation changed. Coming around the last bend in the road, she was met by the sight of several vans and cars parked along the shoulder. The reporters were back, and her only choice was to keep driving. She slowed enough to see the news crews weren't keeping to the edge of the road but were clustered around the porch. So much for Matt's good mood.

She pulled into the feed store lot and turned off the engine before calling him.

"Hey," he said, picking up right away. "You better hold off coming over for a while. It's a little crazy here."

"I noticed. I'm sitting in front of the feed store."

"Sorry. I should have warned you."

"No problem. I heard the news and wanted to congratulate you in person."

"Now I'm totally bummed," he said. "I guess you could try running the gauntlet if you're feeling brave."

It was tempting. She could wear sunglasses and sprint across Matt's lawn, but that would detract from his big moment. "Let's keep today's news focused on 'Sweet Side,'" she said. "You know how they'd twist it if a woman showed up. They'd start asking about your personal life."

"Like whether I have a girlfriend?" The word dangled tantalizingly in the air.

"Yeah, stuff like that," she said.

"That's a tricky question. If it comes up, how should I handle it?"

What did he mean by, 'If it comes up?' Was he flirting? "So . . . you're planning to talk to them?"

"Do I have a choice?"

She glanced in the direction of his house. From her angle it was impossible to count all the vehicles. "I don't mean to dis Vermont, but isn't there anything else worth reporting today?"

"I wondered the same thing," he said. "Turns out there's an egg farmer in Addison County who found a triple yolker under one of his hens. It was between the egg and 'Sweet Side.'"

That gave her some perspective. The good news was Matt didn't seem to be freaking out. In fact, he sounded upbeat and she suspected the reason. "By any chance have you caught a case of paparazzi buzz?"

He laughed. "Paparazzi what?"

"You know what I mean. It's when the fame goes to your head."

"You're too much," he snorted. "I'll have you know, I was in a good mood *before* I got the news—even before I went to bed." He paused long enough for his meaning to sink in. "Did you stop to consider, I might be happy because I had a good time last night?"

Was he saying what she thought? Having misread Matt's cues before, she wasn't about to make the same mistake again. "Are you talking about the talent show?"

"That was part of it," he said, "but also, I liked the before and after. The whole evening was nice. And talking like we did on the phone . . . well, I wish we'd started doing that sooner."

Her heart beat faster. These were words she'd longed to hear, but why now? Had something fundamentally shifted? She couldn't keep him on the phone much longer—he needed to deal with the reporters—but she had to ask the question, "Matt, what's changed?"

He didn't respond right away, raising her hopes that he was taking the question seriously. "I think it was that night at the Moose Club. You said some stuff about Westbury being a great place to call home, but then you asked if it had to be my 'whole world?'"

She recalled saying something like that. It had been sort of off-the-cuff and not the kind of thing she would expect him to take to heart. But he had, and now that he was putting himself out there, she wasn't prepared. Flirtatious banter, she could handle, but this was unfamiliar ground. Before she could respond, he turned up the heat even more.

"By the way, I'm still hanging here in suspense. What is it you couldn't tell me last night?"

No way was she blurting it out over the phone, especially when he was up to his elbows in reporters and didn't need a major distraction. "I want to be face-to-face for this."

"Hmmm . . . You're being very mysterious."

"You need to focus," she said, eager to change the subject. "Have you decided what you're going to say to the press?"

"You'll have to wait and watch the news." There was a playful lilt to his voice—enough to convince her that he really was in a good place.

"Now I'm the one in suspense," she groaned.

He chuckled. "Believe it or not, I've got this. They're expecting grumpy Matt, so I'll surprise them." He sounded confident enough to pull it off.

"Did Gracie leave for camp yet?"

"No. She didn't want to miss the excitement. She even picked out my interview wardrobe."

"Sounds like you're in expert hands and I'm sure you'll do great."

After they said goodbye, she started the car and got back on the road, slumping down in the seat as she drove past Matt's. She couldn't help feeling that she was missing out on all the fun.

If all went well, the news crews would leave once they got their stories and Matt would be free to come over. Until then, she'd be on pins and needles and probably good for nothing.

But, when she got back to the cabin, her day took another unexpected turn. Sitting in the driveway was Carson's BMW. Her hopes plummeted and before she could turn off the engine, her stomach was knotting up. How had he found her? And why would he drive to Vermont when she was scheduled to be in New York tomorrow? And most of all, what would it take to get him to respect her boundaries?

She was out of the car and up the steps with absolutely no idea of how she was going to handle the situation. But this was not acceptable and something had to be done.

Apparently, she'd run off so quickly, she'd left the door unlocked. She steeled herself for the inevitable and went in. There he was, sitting smugly at the kitchen table, drinking coffee, and helping himself to the muffins she'd bought the day before.

"You better have a damn good reason for being here."

"And a warm hello to you too," he said.

"Not funny, Carson. You can't show up unannounced, and you can't waltz in here like you own the place. This isn't cool."

As she stood glaring at him, he had the gall to calmly take another bite. It was as though he was egging her on—goading her to lose her temper. But she refused to take the bait.

There'd been a time when they were good together, yet now she could barely stomach the sight of him. She walked past him to the sink and stared out the kitchen window, using the lull to tamp down her emotions.

"Don't you at least want to know why I'm here?"

She steadied her voice. "There's nothing you could say to make this okay."

"Not even Switzerland?"

She reeled around. "Are you kidding? You drove all this way to rehash that insane story?"

"It turns out that story got more traction than we expected. Since you're supposedly in rehab, Montreal wants to cancel."

"Idiots!" she said, throwing her arms up. "Have they lost their minds?"

He took another sip of coffee. "The online forums are going nuts over it."

"Don't we have a contract?" As much as she might like to skip Montreal, she didn't want it at the cost of her reputation.

"What's the point in going to Montreal if there's no audience? I'm telling you, Jojo, everybody thinks you're in Europe. And it's not just the festival committee and your fans. The label has put a hold on the studio date until they fully assess the situation. That's their words, not mine."

"Are you telling me the entire world's gone crazy," she said, "because of some wacko story?"

"And because you weren't around to prove it wrong." His ego loved being right.

The fight went out of her. She pulled out one of the kitchen chairs and sat down. As if sensing victory, he got up, poured her a cup of coffee, and brought it over. Then he sat down again and pushed the cream and sugar across the table. He didn't seem in the least upset or worried.

"Here's the deal," he said. "I assured the festival you'll be there, and they agreed to hold your place on the schedule through tomorrow at noon."

"Why tomorrow at noon?"

"We have until then to turn this story around."

"So . . . what's the plan?"

"I worked my usual magic." He was gloating, clearly pleased with himself. "Tomorrow morning you'll be on *NYC Today.* You can reassure your adoring fans you've been in creative seclusion, writing the best album of your life, and you're looking forward to trying out some new songs in Montreal." He raised his eyebrows. "Please tell me you've been productive?"

"I just sent you four more tracks."

"That's all you've got?"

Her temperature shot up again. "Those are good tracks and there's more in the pipeline. But frankly, I'm okay with delaying the studio date. This pace is unsustainable. We need to slow down the album cycle by at least six months."

There was a flash across his face, and it felt like he might erupt. But instead, he set his jaw and kept his voice carefully modulated. "Suddenly, you have all the answers. Delay the album until after Christmas. That won't impact the bottom line in the least." The sarcasm was dripping off his tongue. "I'm so glad spending three weeks in the woods has made you a marketing genius."

He was way out of line—cocky and insulting. More than anything, she wanted to wipe that smug look off his face. "Carson, did you honestly think that driving three hours to insult your boss was a good use of your time?"

He visibly blinked. It had to be the word *boss* that caught him off guard. It surprised her too, but she stood her ground and didn't regret saying it.

In an instant, he transformed into Mr. Smooth. "Jojo, where's all this hostility coming from?" He seemed oblivious to his own insincerity. "The last time we were together, we were like a couple of lovebirds."

She decided not to comment on his revisionist history. In all fairness, he likely believed every word and never saw the breakup coming. Carson's sense of reality was shaped by such an overabundance of self-confidence that the breakup might have hurt him more than she realized.

Though he didn't deserve it, she cut him some slack. "So, if I show up on TV tomorrow morning, you think this problem will go away?"

"If you're sitting in a TV studio in New York, it's hard to make the case that you're in rehab in Switzerland."

"Or they'll say I recently returned."

He shrugged as if he wasn't worried, which seemed odd, since that was exactly how the tabloids would spin it.

"You'll charm them," he said. "Like you always do. And we'll take a few photos on the way home with some folksy Vermont backdrops.

"No mention of Westbury," she said, adamantly. Then, realizing how loosely he followed her instructions, she added, "I mean it. In fact, no photos and no mention of Vermont. I'll just say I've been visiting friends in the country." There was no point in doling out clues to the paparazzi.

"Fine, fine," he said, then nimbly changed the subject. "And as long as you're in the city, is there any chance of working up some new material with the band? They're available at three this afternoon." From his tone, it sounded like the rehearsal was already set.

She wondered if Carson ever experienced self-doubt. He always seemed confident of his ability to bend the world to his will. Likely, this was the very quality that made him a formidable manager. But it also made him insufferable.

As if to prove her very thoughts, he continued, "Once again, it's Carson to the rescue, and you needn't thank me. It's my job to swoop in and save the day."

She could feel the balance of power shifting. Twenty minutes was all it took, and Carson was back to running her life.

"I'm going to take a swim," she said, desperate for space to breathe.

As she headed upstairs to change, he called after her, "It'll have to be quick. We need to get on the road."

Chapter 42

Matt

Matt looked at himself in the full-length mirror—a clean pair of jeans, a white button-down shirt, and a western-style buckle. He turned to Gracie, who was sitting on the bed.

"Do I look too country?"

"No. It's a good look for you. What about shoes?"

"The cameras will probably just get me from the waist up."

Gracie went into his closet and came out with a pair of dark brown boots he sometimes wore line dancing. "I like these."

They could have benefitted from a little polish and a good buffing, but he'd already told the reporters he'd be out to answer questions at 8:30 and was cutting it close.

"Are you nervous?" Gracie asked. She sat on the bed beside him as he pulled on the boots.

"I used to do one of these in every city when we were touring. At first, I wasn't very good, and your Uncle Thad told me not to worry about being clever. 'Just be sincere and speak from the heart,' he always said. 'And smile a lot.'"

"You'll do great," she said.

"That's what Joelle said. She called earlier."

"I know. I heard you talking."

He looked at their reflection as they sat on the bed. It was a narrow mirror and yet they easily fit within the frame, much like their recent Christmas photos—just the two of them. "I think I'll stop by and see her after I drop you off at camp."

"Definitely," she said, as if it was a foregone conclusion.

This wasn't the best time to bring it up, but it kept intruding on his thoughts. "How are you going to feel when she leaves next week?"

"Super bummed. But we can still text and talk. And . . . maybe you and I can visit New York?"

For once, he didn't push back against the notion. In fact, he was warming to the idea. "Maybe the three of us could catch a show."

Her jaw dropped. "For real?"

He chuckled and hoped he wasn't getting ahead of himself. "Isn't it normal to visit friends? And New York's not *that* far away."

Gracie's disbelief changed to a grin. "I'm glad you're liking her more now."

"Honey, I always liked her. It's just that sometimes people come here for vacation and then you never see them again. At first, I thought she might be like that, but now I sense we'll stay friends." He left it there and changed the subject. "I'm sorry this thing with the reporters is making you late for camp."

"Are you kidding?! This is awesome!"

"Well, after I'm done, I think they'll clear out, and I'll drive you over." He brushed the dust off his boots and stood up. "I'm ready. Thanks for being my fashion consultant."

As they went downstairs, he had a feeling of déjà vu. He'd done at least a hundred of these, plus when the band was on the road, they'd often stop at TV and radio stations to plug each concert. A bit of that old self-confidence and a little swagger might get him through this.

"I'll be watching from the window," Gracie said, once they reached the kitchen.

"The far window. And don't show your face."

Earlier, she'd begged to join him on the porch. "I'm like your band, and I bet they'll be nicer if I'm there." Both points were valid, but he'd said no. It was bad enough that she was already on YouTube.

As he put his hand on the doorknob, he could feel his heart thumping. He turned once more to Gracie and winked. "Here I go." Then he swung the door open and stepped into the bright lights and cameras.

The crowd had grown to about twenty people and there were over a dozen microphones set up on stands at the edge of the porch, so that's where he took his position. Immediately, the questions started flying.

He lifted a hand and smiled. "I promise not to rush off, so let's do one question at a time." He pointed to a woman near the front.

"How do you feel having a number one hit again after so many years?"

"I won't lie. It feels pretty darn good. When my manager called this morning with the news, I had to sit down for a moment." He grinned and simultaneously heard the whisper of several camera shutters. More hands shot up.

"Do you ever think of making a comeback?"

"Well, I'm still raising my daughter and trying to be a good father, so I don't see myself on the road anytime soon. But all this has gotten me thinking about songwriting again."

As other questions were shouted, he held up a hand to quiet the crowd. "I want to make sure I have time to say one thing. Jojo, if you're listening, thank you for breathing new life into my music. It's as if you dusted it off and made it fresh. And for those of you who don't know, my daughter's a big fan, so Jojo's music gets a lot of play in our house."

Another hand shot up. "Have you talked to Jojo?"

"No, I've never had the pleasure, but perhaps we'll meet at the Grammys." He grinned again, and there was a smattering of laughter.

"How have the past ten years and fatherhood changed you?" someone yelled.

"That's a good question. I'm only thirty-five, but I feel like I've already done a lot of living. Maybe it's time to tell more stories—through music, I mean."

"Is there any room for love in your future?"

Matt's mind flashed to Joelle, but there were still more questions than answers where she was concerned. So, he reached further back for an answer.

"I wrote 'Sweet Side' for my wife, and she always said a life without love is a wasted life." There was a catch in his voice, and he realized he was treading on shaky ground. When he didn't add anything, there was another voice from the crowd.

"You seem different."

He laughed, in part to shake off the emotion. "It's tough to be grumpy when you've got a number one single, plus maybe I've figured out that if I'm a little happier, you people might find me less interesting and finally go away." He made a point to smile again, and it got a few more laughs. Wouldn't it be a strange world if it turned out to be true?

In the old days, Thad would have been the one to bring these things to a close, and it felt like they'd covered the major points.

"I know a bunch of you have deadlines," Matt said, "so let's wrap it up there."

CHAPTER 43

MATT

AFTER DROPPING GRACIE AT CAMP, Matt headed toward the cabin. He couldn't imagine being happier. For years, his life had moved along a predictable course, and then out of the blue, "Sweet Side" caught a second wind, and Joelle walked into his life. Either event would have been remarkable, but the combination made him wonder if he'd finally paid off his karmic debts for the mess he'd made.

He wondered if any part of the press conference was online yet. If Joelle had seen it, she'd know it had gone well, and that he was on his way. No doubt she'd have a suitable wisecrack locked and loaded. He smiled, recalling "paparazzi buzz." *How does she come up with this stuff?*

As much as he was looking forward to seeing her, he was even more curious to hear the news she wanted to share. She'd been so cheerful lately, it had to be something good. Maybe she was extending her vacation or had sold a song, in which case, they'd have a double celebration.

As he turned into her driveway, he realized he knew nothing about her morning routine. She might be out for a walk or down at the dock. What he saw instead was a man—probably in his thirties—sitting on the porch alone. And parked beside Joelle's rental was a BMW coupe with a New York vanity plate that read SKINNER.

Joelle hadn't mentioned a visitor, but perhaps he'd just arrived. Regardless of the details, Matt's good mood flatlined.

The guy was on his cell phone and had *city* written all over him. As Matt got out of the truck, the man gave him an almost imperceptible nod but continued talking in a voice that could be heard halfway across the lake.

"Mary, I want you to go back and rework the numbers. Show some forward thinking for once." Whoever Mary was, it sounded like she wasn't having a good day.

Matt considered going up and knocking on the door to see if Joelle was inside, but it seemed rude while the guy was still on the phone. So instead, he stuck his head back in the cab and pretended to be busy. That's when he got a sinking feeling.

Was it possible this was what she wanted to talk about—that she'd gotten back together with her boyfriend? Matt should have called first, but now that he was here, he couldn't simply bolt.

The small toolbox he kept on the floor of the jump seat gave him an idea. He took it out and waited beside the truck for the conversation to end.

"Do you honestly think I care about how it gets done? Just email me the spreadsheet when it's ready. I've got to go now—there's somebody here."

As the call ended, Matt approached. "Hi, I'm Matt. Is Joelle around?"

For some bizarre reason, the guy found that amusing. "I'm Carson, and *Jo-elle* is taking a swim before we shove off."

Shove off? There was a sick sort of feeling that went straight to Matt's stomach. He had hoped he was wrong, but this had to be the ex-boyfriend. Though it sounded like they were no longer exes.

"I guess congratulations are in order," Carson said, his tone anything but congratulatory. "It's not every day a cabinetmaker has a number one single."

Suddenly, it was clear Carson knew exactly who he was and might even have been expecting him. Matt was standing about halfway up the stairs, and Carson hadn't bothered to get out of his chair, so their eyes were dead even. Matt wasn't sure what he'd done to antagonize this guy, but there was something menacing in his look.

"I see you're holding onto your day job," Carson said, eyeing the toolbox. "Probably wise. It might be another ten years before someone covers one of your songs again." On the surface, his tone was casual, but the biting subtext was not.

As difficult as it would be to leave without telling Joelle goodbye, there seemed little point in sticking around. "Perhaps I should go," Matt said.

"Don't let me keep you from your work," Carson said. "What did you come for?"

Matt glanced down at his tools. "Repairing a cabinet door. The glass broke." He'd been meaning to take care of it for a while and was glad for the excuse.

Carson nodded. "Actually, this is perfect timing. You can lock the place up when you're done. Probably the boathouse, too. Don't worry about the car, though. The rental company is sending someone."

"Joelle's car?" Matt asked.

Carson scoffed again, as if there was an inside joke Matt was missing. "Yeah, she won't be needing it. We're driving the Beemer back."

Matt felt like he'd been sucker-punched. He could deal with his own disappointment, but Gracie would be devastated if Joelle left for good without so much as a parting word. "So, she won't be here next week?"

"Change of plans. This isn't really her scene. Anyway, we won't be in your way—we're already packed."

The bright and hopeful morning was no more. Matt looked toward the lake; through the trees, he could see movement in the water. It made sense now why Joelle tried to stop by the house earlier. She'd wanted to say goodbye, and he'd misread the situation.

He was tempted to go down to the dock but had seen enough of Carson to guess that wouldn't go well. Best to retain some dignity, rather than make a scene and have that be Joelle's parting memory of him.

"I'll come back later when I won't be in your way."

"Suit yourself," Carson said, finally standing and reaching for his back pocket. "I'll leave the door unlocked." He pulled a crisp bill out of his wallet and offered it to Matt.

Stunned, Matt stared at the hundred. He'd seen this before—men who marked their territory with large tips. He looked up and locked eyes with Carson. "No need. It's part of the service."

Carson shrugged.

Matt turned and headed down the steps. He glanced once more toward the dock, but still couldn't see her. It was killing him to walk away, but he kept moving until he reached the truck. A moment later, he was in the cab, backing around. If he never saw Carson again, it would be too soon.

CHAPTER 44

MATT

AT THREE O'CLOCK, Matt was sitting in the truck in the Maycroft parking lot, waiting for Gracie. It was a hot afternoon, and the windows were rolled down. There were other waiting vehicles and a few parents milling about. He spotted Cammy's mom and waved but didn't go over, unsure of his ability to make light conversation.

After driving away from the cabin that morning, he'd gone back to the shop and tried to work but had been too distracted to trust himself on the table saw. Instead, he set about straightening up and reorganizing—anything to keep his mind off Joelle and her unpleasant boyfriend. But finally, he gave up, sat on a stool, and stared out the window.

Nothing about the situation made sense. Joelle said she and her ex had broken up, and they were so mismatched, what could have possessed her to go back to him? Was it possible they were married? That might explain the secrecy about her last name. It was hard to believe she would gloss over an important detail such as a husband, but if Matt were honest with himself, it often felt like Joelle glossed over details.

Now, as he sat waiting in the truck, he fished his phone out of his pocket and checked the last message she'd sent. It appeared mid-morning while he was in the shop, and he'd already read it several times: *Something came up and I have to leave early for NYC. Let's talk tonight.*

Matt was still deciding how to respond, but one thing was certain: he didn't want to talk. He was embarrassed enough about misreading the situation and had no desire to rehash it.

If they spoke, he also feared he'd say something inappropriate about Carson. Or worse, he'd accuse her of lying or setting up Gracie to feel abandoned. From there, it was certain to spiral downward.

He started typing a response, choosing his words carefully. He backtracked a couple of times—once because the tone felt too heavy and once because it felt too light. Before he could finish, Gracie appeared at the passenger window.

"Is everything okay, Dad?"

"Yeah. Just a slow day, so I thought I'd pick you up." He put his phone away with the message still unsent and got out to help with her bike. "I wasn't sure if you knew Joelle left for New York."

"She texted me," Gracie said matter-of-factly. "She had to leave a day early."

"Oh," Matt said, lifting the bike into the back. "Did she say anything else?"

"So, you didn't go over this morning?"

"No. It didn't work out."

"That is *tragic.*"

Any other time, he might have laughed at her over-the-top melodrama, but the look on her face mirrored her words.

"Honey, is there anything you want to share?"

She held his gaze so intently that, for a moment, he was certain she was about to spill something important. But then she spun on her heels and headed for the passenger side of the cab, bizarrely taking the conversation in a new direction. "The festival in Montreal was fun last year. You liked it. Didn't you?"

"Yeah. What's not to like?"

"Then why aren't we going this year?"

He climbed in on the driver's side. "Money's been a little tight. Plus, you seem busy lately."

"Nothing's going on this weekend, and you're getting more royalties."

"You know how I feel about spending money before it's in hand." In truth, though, the bank account *had* looked better after depositing the last ASCAP check. Still, he didn't like making snap decisions. "The hotels are probably booked, anyway."

She didn't push back—not even a little—which made him wonder if she'd brought up Montreal merely to change the subject. Something was up, but he was already feeling too drained to dig it out of her.

When they got home and walked into the kitchen, the phone was ringing and Gracie got to it first.

"Hi, Uncle Thad."

Two calls in one day, Matt thought. It was nice that Thad was back in their lives.

"Dad's right here. I'll put him on."

"Hey, Thad." Matt took a seat on a stool as Gracie ducked under the cord and went to the refrigerator for a snack.

"Matt, please tell me you don't have any plans this weekend."

"Are you finally coming to visit?"

"Well, I was thinking we could meet halfway. How about Montreal?"

Matt laughed. "I know your geography's better than that. So what gives?" This was too weird. First Gracie and now Thad.

"I got a call from the festival. They've just had a Saturday time slot open up at one of their smaller venues and since you wrote the number one song in the States—"

"It's not like I sang it."

"That doesn't matter—people are talking about you. Anyway, they've already got Jojo. She's doing a huge show on Sunday."

"Huh," Matt said, "do you think I could finally meet her?"

"Meet who?" Gracie said.

It was all starting to make sense. "Can you hold for a moment, Thad?" Without covering the mouthpiece, he looked straight at Gracie. "Did you know Jojo's at the festival this weekend?"

"Why would you think that?" But try as she might, Gracie couldn't keep a straight face. "What is Uncle Thad asking?"

Matt put the phone back to his ear. "I'm back, Thad. If you didn't already know, Gracie's a big Jojo fan."

"First things first. Are you interested in performing?"

"Aren't you forgetting I don't have a band? If I had a week, maybe—"

"Not necessary. They saw your YouTube video and just want the two of you."

Gracie had come around the island and was trying to hear. "What's he saying?"

"Shhh . . ." Matt said. There was no point getting excited. He wasn't about to put his twelve-year-old daughter on stage at a major festival. Still an offer like this was rare and it triggered a part of him that he'd thought was long dead. "Do you think they'd let me do an acoustic set? Just me."

There was a brief silence before Thad responded. "I think that would be a tough sell."

Matt had figured as much. This was the point where he needed simply to decline, but he couldn't bring himself to do it. "How can they be serious? The only gigs we've done are small local stuff."

Gracie's eyes were wide. She'd obviously picked up on the gist of the conversation.

"That's the beauty of it," Thad said. "The venue they've got in mind is outdoors and fairly mellow. Just think of it as your town square—only bigger. I'm probably massacring the French, but the short name is something like Le Parterre."

"I know that stage," Matt said. "It's one of the free venues. There's a big sloping lawn and people sit on blankets and beach chairs." Of all the spots at the festival, this was the most family friendly—at least the afternoon concerts they'd attended had been laid back. The same could not be said for Gracie, who was leaning into the phone and desperately trying to listen.

"Sounds like you get around more than I realized," Thad said. "Here I was thinking you and Rapunzel never travel beyond the castle moat."

"Hey, I'm not *that* bad a father. We've gone to the festival for the last two years."

"No kidding?" Thad said. "Wish I'd known. I was there last year. Anybody ever recognize you?"

"When I'm not standing on my front porch yelling at reporters, I'm basically invisible. Ten years, a few extra pounds, and a daughter at my side and I'm just your average middle-aged dad."

Thad scoffed. "This is why you won't be writing any promotional material. So, are you in or not?"

The whole idea was absurd, and Matt couldn't believe he was even considering it. Le Parterre might be low pressure by festival standards, but it was still a huge leap from performing on the local bandstand. What if Gracie got up on stage and froze?

Thad must have sensed he was wavering and his tone turned solemn. "The thing is, sometimes the music gods grant you an extra fifteen minutes. I think you should at least consider it. You never know if it will happen again or what it might lead to."

Again, Thad's words touched a nerve. Even if this was only a one-time shot to relive the past, it was enticing.

Matt wondered what Joelle would say, but just as quickly as the thought came, he shut it down. He couldn't afford to have her messing with his head right now. In fact, he needed a distraction—something to get her out of his thoughts for a few days. Montreal might be just the ticket and it could help Gracie cope as well. It was going to be tough once she learned Joelle wasn't coming back.

"You still there?" Thad asked.

"Yeah, I just need to run it by Gracie." He wasn't sure how

much she'd heard, but it appeared she'd heard enough. "Any chance you'd want to perform at the festival this Saturday?"

She was strangely subdued. "Are you messing with me?"

"Dead serious."

"Can I have the phone?" This wasn't the response he'd expected, but he handed it over. "Uncle Thad, we'd be using their sound equipment, right?" Matt wondered how his daughter was already one step ahead of him. "So I can patch my looper right into their system?"

Apparently, the answer met her approval, and she handed the phone back, looking almost businesslike. "Let's do it."

"Did you hear that?" Matt said into the receiver. "We're both on board."

"Fantastic!" Thad said. "I wasn't sure you'd feel ready."

Can you ever really be ready? Matt thought. A part of him still suspected this was reckless.

"And it's a quick changeover between bands," Thad continued. "All you carry on are your guitars and Gracie's keyboard and pedals. Everything else is provided. I'm emailing you the details right now, including hotel info. They've got a block of rooms."

This was really happening, but one thing had him concerned. There should have been a twelve-year-old bouncing off the walls, yet Gracie was unusually quiet.

"Could you hold for a second? I want to see if my sidekick has any more questions." This time, he covered the mouthpiece. "Honey, are you okay?"

She nodded emphatically. "I'm just picturing it in my head."

"If you're nervous, we don't have to do this."

"Isn't it normal to be nervous?"

It was a perceptive question. Anyone in their right mind would be nervous.

"Just as long as you're not *too* nervous," he said.

"I'm good, Dad. You don't have to worry."

He was inclined to believe her. It felt like they were on the same page—that despite her young years, she understood the commitment they were making. And for perhaps the first time, Matt knew he would be relying on her as much as she relied on him.

He got back on the phone. "No more questions for now, but if we think of anything—"

"There is one more detail," Thad said. "They're aiming for nostalgia—hoping you'll stick mostly with old material. If you want to throw in something new—no more than one or two. And, of course, everybody'll expect 'Sweet Side.'"

"That's all fine. We'll play it safe."

"Hot damn," Thad said. "I know you can't see me, but I'm dancing on my desk."

Matt doubted that. "How long's our set, anyway?"

"Ninety minutes and it's late afternoon." His voice turned solemn. "Are you sure Gracie's okay? We could be talking six or seven hundred people."

"She's a pro. She'll be fine." Part of Thad's job was protecting reputations—his clients and his own. "I know you're putting yourself on the line by vouching for us," Matt said. "But I want this. I'm only just realizing how much I want it. And if it reassures you, Gracie and I sing all the time. Our living room looks more like a recording studio. I've taken care of my voice and, frankly, I'm a better guitarist today than I was back then. And Gracie's as solid as anyone I've played with."

"Okay," Thad said. "I just had to ask. To be honest, I wasn't sure how this conversation would go."

"Well, if you'd called a few weeks ago," Matt said, "you might have gotten a different answer. There seems to be something in the wind."

"I wouldn't credit the wind. If it weren't for Jojo, we wouldn't be having this conversation."

"True enough," Matt said.

"By the way, nice job handling the press today. I caught it on *E! News*. It reminded me of the old Matt."

"Yeah, well, I learned from the best." He had an eye on Gracie, who was still sitting quietly. "You know, I think Gracie and I should get to work on our setlist."

"Absolutely. You two have a lot of work to do."

"But we'll see you there, right?" Matt asked.

"There's no way I'd miss the second coming of Matt Heston! Plus, I'll get to see my goddaughter."

After they said goodbye, Matt turned his attention back to Gracie. "You're being super mellow, honey."

"It's just a lot to think about. I mean, I've been dreaming about it forever. But it's different when it really happens."

"That's a very grown-up observation." At times it felt like she was changing before his eyes.

Neither of them moved or said another word as the reality gradually sank in. Matt felt slightly numb. Agreeing to perform was the easy part, now they had to deliver.

CHAPTER 45

JOJO

JOJO GLANCED up from her phone as Dinesh maneuvered the car into a tight spot outside a Moroccan restaurant in the East Village. Not only was the food good here, but it was only two blocks from Leah and Tom's, which meant everything would still be hot when she arrived. She texted the restaurant that they were out front and then tried calling Matt. When she got no answer, she left a message.

"Hey, I'm on my way to have dinner with Tom and Leah, and just wanted to hear how your day went. Miss you guys. I'll try again later. Say hi to Gracie for me."

A young waiter in an apron ran outside with two large bags and she paid him through the window in cash.

When the car got to Leah and Tom's building, she told Dinesh and Russ that she'd be at least two hours. "You guys should get something to eat."

"I'll walk you to the door, ma'am, once this group passes." Several college-age kids walked by without even glancing at the car. That was one of the perks of New York—even the luxury vehicles blended in. A few moments later, Russ got out and opened her door. With a bag of food in each hand, she made a beeline for the lobby, but just inside she came upon a mother with two preteen daughters. One selfie later, and she was on her way up in the elevator. It was the first time she'd been alone since leaving Vermont.

She and Carson had arrived back in the city early that afternoon and gone straight to her apartment. An hour later she'd emerged with a blond wig, makeup, and a fabulous pantsuit she'd bought in Singapore last winter. Carson posted a few pics and the social media blitz was on. When they got to the rehearsal site, the band was already warming up. They ran through a few songs, while Carson busily tweeted and posted more photos. It quickly became apparent the band was still in peak form.

Finally, she put her guitar down. "Wow, guys, we should take more vacations. Everyone feeling good?" She looked from face to face and chuckled to herself as she finally picked up on how laid-back they were today. There were fewer circles under the eyes and even the way they carried themselves seemed looser. Instead of losing ground, it felt like the time off had breathed some freshness back into the soul of the band.

They spent the rest of rehearsal working on "Shout It Out," the title she'd given to the new collaboration with Tyrell. She could feel the mood in the room shift. After months of playing the same songs again and again, there was a raw energy as the band tapped into the creative side of their brains.

Even Carson had the good sense to make himself scarce when the band got into this head space. Thank goodness because his flitting around taking social media pics was a constant distraction. At least his social messaging was getting out. Later, as they emerged from rehearsal, there was a cluster of people on the sidewalk and at least two professional photographers. Jojo was back in the public eye.

She knocked on Leah and Tom's door and heard the patter of small feet. As the door opened, she was greeted by screeches of "Auntie Jojo!!" Tom rescued the bags of food in time for her to drop to her knees and wrap both boys in her arms.

"I'll take these to the kitchen. Leah's getting changed. She'll be right out."

"We missed you!" four-year-old Tristan exclaimed.

"I missed you guys, too. What have you been up to?"

"Come see." Each boy grabbed a hand and dragged her toward their bedroom to play with their latest Lego creations. A few minutes later, Leah appeared.

"So, how was Switzerland?"

"Not funny. It's already cost me a day at the lake. It's why I'm back early."

"Are people really that gullible?"

"Apparently. But tonight, I'd much rather talk about Lego spacemen, like this guy." She picked up one of the boy's creatures and made a whooshing noise as it flew over Josh's head, circled around Tristan, and then landed between them.

"Again! Again!" Josh shouted.

———

After dinner, while Tom was putting the boys to bed, Jojo followed Leah into the living room. They sat facing at opposite ends of the couch, and Jojo tucked her feet under her.

"When you come home from Westbury, do you find it a bit of a shock—the pace, I mean?"

"Every time," Leah said. "It starts hitting me around the George Washington Bridge and by the time we pull up to the building and get out to unload the car, all that clean Vermont living has started to rub off."

It gave Jojo solace, knowing she wasn't the only one who felt that way. "I thought I'd come home feeling more chill and less stressed, but I'm already falling back into old patterns."

Leah remained quiet and let her continue.

"If I don't learn to slow down, there will never be room for someone else in my life. There simply won't be enough hours in the day."

"Are we talking about a hypothetical someone?" Leah asked. "Or is this about Matt?"

"*And* Gracie," Jojo added, relieved to finally share these thoughts aloud. "I think I've fallen in love—with both of them. And even though we've only been apart a few hours, I feel this ache." She pulled her legs up to her chest and hugged her knees.

Leah studied her. "This is good news, right?"

It sounded like a simple question, but Jojo hesitated. "Part of me feels like dancing on the ceiling, but even if Matt's willing to try long distance, I don't know how to make it work! You know how crazy my life is."

Leah laughed. "I know that feeling."

"But you've made it work. Somehow you pull it off every day."

Leah seemed amused by the compliment. "I wish I could go back and tell that to my thirty-year-old self. Back then, I had all the same fears you're describing. I was transitioning from dancer to choreographer and busy every hour of the day, and then my marriage almost blew up when Tom announced he was ready to have kids."

As if on cue, Tom appeared in the doorway. "Hey, I thought the deal was I would put the boys down and you two would clean up that mess in the kitchen."

"Yeaaahhh . . . about that," Leah said. "It didn't happen."

"Your timing's perfect," Jojo said as Tom sank into the chair across from them. "I want to know your secret recipe for mixing career and family. You guys somehow make it work."

"There's no formula," Leah said. "Getting through each day is a minor miracle. And it almost didn't happen." Tom shot her a concerned look, and she shrugged. "I'm okay talking about it."

"About what?" There was some heavy-duty husband-wife signaling going on, and Jojo hadn't brought her decoder ring.

Leah nodded to Tom. "You tell it."

He looked as if he'd rather retreat to the kitchen and do the dishes, but after a beat or two, Tom reluctantly began. "Did you know we were separated for a while?" Jojo must have looked shocked because he didn't wait for an answer. "It was before Tristan was born, and if you think my wife's driven now, you should have seen her then. She was a lot more like you, except without the money and the fame and the fabulous voice—"

"Okay, she gets it," Leah broke in. "The point my lovely husband is trying to make is that ambition is seductive, and it sneaks up so gradually you hardly notice when it's taken over your life. In those days, it wasn't uncommon for me to work seven days a week, and I was loving every minute."

"And with dance," Tom said, "the line between work and play gets blurred. Long workdays often spill into nights."

"I was constantly checking out the newest clubs," Leah explained. "Searching for the hottest moves. And then one day, Tom up and left."

This was nothing like the romantic backstory Jojo had imagined. It was no secret they had different temperaments and levels of ambition, but she'd always thought they balanced each other in a healthy way.

"After I left," Tom said, "it took her two whole days to realize I was gone."

"*I thought he was on a business trip!* And when I finally reached him, I found out he'd moved in with a friend from college. He gave me the speech about there being no *us* anymore, and how he was tired of waiting for me to settle down and mostly that he was ready to have a family and I wasn't."

"And so she wrote me off," Tom said.

"What?!" Jojo's eyes flicked from Tom to Leah. "But you loved each other!"

"He's oversimplifying," Leah said. "There were a lot of tears and heartbreak for both of us." Tom moved from his chair to the couch, taking his wife's hand.

It suddenly felt like Jojo was intruding, and she turned her gaze to a family portrait on the opposite wall. It must have been taken soon after Josh was born because he was in his mother's arms, his tiny face barely peeking out from the swaddling blanket.

"There are times," Leah continued, her words directed at Tom, "when we're together with the boys and I get a sense of panic that it almost didn't happen. That I could just as easily be alone."

"I get those moments, too," he said in a hushed voice.

Leah laid her head against his shoulder. "You're such a good man. No matter what I say about you."

"How did you get back together?" Jojo asked.

"A couple months after the split," Leah said. "I was going to a wedding, and it felt empty being alone. There were a bunch of dancers I'd known for years, and they all had someone in their lives —a few even had kids. Some had moved back to their hometowns to open studios, teaching jazz and ballet, and instead of getting a feeling like they'd sold out, they seemed really happy.

"Since coming to New York, I'd been living in the moment, but when I looked at my life in its entirety—ten years out, forty years out—suddenly the career alone didn't feel like enough."

"For my part," Tom said, "I'd hoped we could fix things, but as time dragged on, I gave up and had my lawyer send the divorce papers."

"Jeez," Jojo breathed. It was hard to imagine them coming that close to the edge.

"That was the final wake-up call," Leah said. "That's when I realized I couldn't see my future without Tom. I begged him to take me back, but it took a while to convince him I wanted the same things he wanted. It had just taken me longer to get there."

"For the record," Tom said. "I'll be the first to admit it's easier for men—not the marriage part, but the baby part. With each pregnancy, Leah made most of the sacrifices."

"But lately," Leah said, "he's been trying to make it up to me. The hardest days are when one of the boys is sick and can't go to daycare. Tom's figured out ways to work from home and it turns out we make a good team." She nuzzled him, and he hugged her a little tighter.

"Thank you for telling me," Jojo said. It meant even more that she'd been able to hear the story from both sides. She sensed it was time to go and as she stood up, Leah added one more thought.

"I want to be honest about something. When I went back to Tom, I was still scared of messing up, but I knew I'd never forgive myself if I didn't try." She didn't have to say more; Jojo got the point.

CHAPTER 46

JOJO

ON THE DRIVE back to her apartment, Jojo watched through the tinted windows as a blur of buildings and lights passed. She was thinking of those pivotal months when Leah's life could have gone in a different direction. But perhaps the fate of many families could be traced back to a tenuous decision, a fragile moment, a leap of faith.

Jojo was at a similar crossroads. Now that she was back in the city, there was the gravitational pull of old habits. She would wake up tomorrow and follow the schedule laid out by Carson, and on Saturday, she would do the same. And if that was the path she chose, she'd stay on track for at least a few more years of commercial success.

A short time ago, that would have been enough, but not anymore. Not that she was ready to chuck it all—far from it. But ever since the night of the solstice when Matt and Gracie paddled over to her dock, she'd grown accustomed to sharing moments with them, both big and small. Some music-related and some not. Some happy and funny, and some merely everyday pieces of life. Now here she was, after a single day of separation, missing them so acutely it hurt.

Jojo emerged from her reverie with a sudden decision. Tonight, when she called Matt, she would tell him everything, including that she was falling in love. Long distance or not, she wanted to make this work. And if he pretended not to care and tried to push her away, she would go back to Westbury and camp out on his porch until he changed his mind.

She had turned her phone off to prevent Carson from intruding on dinner, but now she switched it back on. A moment later, several messages appeared, including a text from Gracie.

See you in Montreal. We got a gig!!!

If ever there was a sign from the heavens, this was it. Jojo blinked back tears of joy as she texted back. It was only nine o'clock, so Gracie would still be up.

Epic weekend! Calling your dad tonight and telling him everything. As soon as she sent it, she followed with another. *Sorry I didn't text earlier. Phone was off.* Immediately, the phone rang, and she answered.

"You're going to call him now?" It was Gracie, and she sounded concerned.

"I figure I owe him. He's got to be wondering why I suddenly took off."

"I think he is," Gracie said. "But do you have to tell him everything?"

Jojo began seeing it from her point of view. If Matt didn't take it well, the poor kid would be there alone, dealing with the fallout. She needed to rethink this. "Tell me about Montreal. How did you get a last-minute gig?"

"Uncle Thad didn't say, but I guess some other band canceled. We're playing Saturday at five. Can you be there?"

"Are you kidding? I wouldn't miss it."

"There's pictures online of you rehearsing with your band today. Is that why you left early?"

"Part of the reason," Jojo said, "but mostly I'm here to do damage control because of that rehab story."

"Dorks!" Gracie said. "I mean the tabloids, not your fans."

"Would you believe there was a shrine in front of my building with prayer candles?"

"That's messed up. Can you send me a picture?"

"My manager got it cleaned up. Other tenants in the building weren't happy about it."

"What day do you perform?"

"Sunday evening. I'll get you both backstage passes."

There was a squeal on the other end of the call. "I think my phone just blew up. Even if Dad wants to leave early, I'll hide his keys."

Jojo hoped it didn't come to that, but it was a reminder that everything still hinged on how Matt took the news. "The more I think about it, maybe I shouldn't get into a big explanation with your dad tonight. I'll just say I had to come back to New York early for something, and that I'll also be in Montreal to see you guys."

"And just be Joelle until *after* we perform?" Gracie asked.

"You're right—I'll show up as Joelle. I don't want to break his focus." It made obvious sense, and she shouldn't have needed a twelve-year-old to spell it out. "One more thing— tomorrow morning I'll be on *NYC Today.*"

"Cool. I'll be at camp, but I'll catch it online when I get home." Then Gracie laughed. "If you really want to mess with Dad, you could be like a superhero and rip your mask off right in the middle of the show."

"Very funny, but I doubt your dad watches daytime TV, so I think he's safe."

After they said goodbye, Jojo couldn't stop smiling. That was one of Gracie's gifts.

Immediately, she called Matt, just to reconnect and apologize for leaving without seeing him. Again, it went straight to voicemail. Something didn't feel right. "Hey, Matt"—she tried to sound as light as possible—"I just got off the phone with Gracie and heard about Montreal. I'm so happy for you and would love to talk about it. Please call."

She went back to checking her text messages and found an earlier one from Matt.

We don't need to talk tonight. I already understand. No hard feelings and no regrets. I wish you the best.

Now she was truly confused. To make matters worse, he'd followed up with a second, equally inscrutable message. *Will you tell Gracie, or should I?*

Tell her what? And what did he *understand* or think he understood? She went from feeling high to low in the space of about a minute. Somehow, he'd gotten the wrong impression. She could fix it, if only she could get through to him.

CHAPTER 47

JOJO

THE AUDIENCE WAS UNUSUALLY SUBDUED as Jojo walked onto the set at *NYC Today*. Ryan and Kylie were warm and friendly, but even they were not their usual exuberant, caffeinated selves.

Carson had prepped her. "If you're angry or defensive, you'll only give the haters more ammunition. Laugh it off, talk about new projects, and basically flip the story."

After shaking hands, the three of them settled on the couch. Jojo reminded herself that Ryan and Kylie weren't the enemy. Over the years, she had been good for the show's ratings and the show had been good for her.

"It looks like someone's been out in the sun," Kylie said.

Jojo gave her a mental high five. "Yeah, almost every day. I stayed at a cabin on a lake, so plenty of swimming and sitting on the dock with my guitar working on the new album."

"Sounds like a working vacation," Ryan said.

"I guess," Jojo said. "If you consider lying in a hammock, dreaming up lyrics work."

"Now you're just making us jealous," Kylie said.

Jojo was willing to bet that top-flight entertainment hosts like

Ryan and Kylie never stopped working, even on vacation. In their line of work, it was risky to be out of touch for even a single news cycle.

Kylie leaned in slightly, her body language switching into empathy mode, and Jojo prepared herself for the tough questions. "So tell us, where did you go on vacation?"

"You know how it is. I like to find little out-of-the-way spots that are private—no crowds and *definitely* no paparazzi."

Kylie smiled but wasn't giving up that easily. "Now that you're home, can't you give us a bigger hint than that?" She grinned at the audience. "I'll bet it's a fabulous spot. Am I right?"

Jojo laughed. "It was fabulous, but not in the way you'd probably expect. There was no fancy spa and no fine dining. It was literally a cabin in the middle of the woods." A quick look passed between Ryan and Kylie, so she added with a broad smile, "I have some friends there and promised not to spill the beans." She pursed her lips and mimed locking them with a key.

There were some chuckles, but mostly hushed whispers in the audience, and Jojo was tired of tiptoeing around the edges. "But in case anyone's wondering, I assure you I wasn't in Switzerland." She rolled her eyes to emphasize how ridiculous the story was, but no one was laughing.

The silence stretched for several awkward beats and the hosts did nothing to end it. Though she couldn't see Carson, he was probably squirming in his seat by now. Or was he? Perhaps this was his idea of payback. After all, he'd been right. The only thing she could think to do was totally change the subject.

"I'm very excited about a new song I just cowrote, 'Shout It Out,' and consider it a strong contender for the next album. The band and I were working on it yesterday and I'm looking forward to debuting it Sunday in Montreal."

"That's the Montreal Music Festival?" Ryan said. "For anyone who hasn't been, it's one of the biggest festivals in North America."

God bless him, Jojo thought as her body relaxed slightly.

"Ten days and two million people," Kylie added. "And we've just learned Matt Heston was added to the program in the last twenty-four hours. It sounds like music lovers to the north could get a double serving of 'Sweet Side.'"

Jojo wasn't sure if she should act surprised. The most she dared was a smile.

"No offense to you, Jojo, or the other headliners," Ryan said, "but this seems like huge news—Matt Heston rises from obscurity after ten years and plays at a major festival."

Jojo wasn't sure Matt would appreciate the hype, nor the added pressure that might come with it. "I agree it's exciting, but this isn't a reunion of the full band. It'll be Matt and his daughter, Gracie. Not that they don't put on a wonderful show."

By the way Ryan and Kylie were staring at her, she might have said too much.

"Someone's apparently in the know," Kylie said with a cagey tone. "Any chance of you showing up at Matt's concert for a surprise duet?"

"I wish I could, but can you imagine the security nightmare?"

Kylie wasn't giving up. "Or maybe Matt could show up at your show. I just have a sense there's something brewing." She looked directly at the live audience. "Am I right?!"

The audience cheered.

At least the mood in the studio had changed. But now Jojo was worried for Matt and Gracie. With the added attention, they had better bring their A game.

"And we couldn't have scripted a more perfect segue to this next segment," Ryan said, infusing his words with a layer of anticipation, as though everything up to now had been lead-in to the main event. "You just mentioned that Gracie Heston will perform with her father."

Jojo nodded hesitantly. This didn't sound like anything they'd covered in the preshow prep meeting.

"Recently, twelve-year-old Gracie Heston made a splash on YouTube," Ryan continued. "She was caught on video, playing alongside her famous father at a local concert in Vermont."

Jojo didn't like where this was going and felt her body tense like a mother cat.

"Apparently," Ryan said, "the girl has inherited some of her father's talents."

"And her mother's," Jojo added. She wasn't trying to prolong the discussion, but those three words would mean a lot to Gracie.

"That's right," Ryan said. "Her mother played in Matt's band before Gracie was born. So, this girl is blessed with musical genes from both sides of her family."

"And recently," Kylie said, "her father told the world in an interview that Gracie's a big fan of yours, Jojo. But we didn't know exactly how big a fan until we got hold of this exclusive video of young Gracie Heston singing your song 'Flower Girl' a couple of nights ago at a talent show in her hometown."

Jojo felt a stab of dread. "I didn't know about this."

"We didn't either," Kylie said, "until we saw the video yesterday. And just to remind our audience, the song describes a wedding through the eyes of a young girl who's thinking about her own future."

There was nothing Jojo could do—this was happening whether she liked it or not.

Gracie's voice emerged from the studio speakers as her image appeared on the monitor. Who at Maycroft would have done this? Gracie might not care—in fact, she might be thrilled with the attention—but her father wouldn't like it one bit.

The studio audience was entranced. Whoever had shot the video had a decent camera, a good mic, and some obvious skills. After starting with a wide shot, the camera had pulled in tight for a sense of intimacy that Jojo doubted was the work of an amateur. Had a professional wormed their way into Maycroft? It wasn't as if there was security. And suddenly the real threat hit her. If a professional shot this video, he or she wouldn't be satisfied with just Gracie. They would also want to capture Matt's reaction, and she had been sitting beside him.

She glanced at Ryan and Kylie and then offstage at the staff, but nowhere did she see signs of an impending ambush. Everyone was focused on the monitors and seemed charmed by Gracie's performance. At least some of these people must have watched the video earlier and the big question was whether they'd recognized her.

There was nothing to do except brace herself, but to her amazement, the camera never left Gracie and the image faded to black before the song ended. Jojo sat there, feeling relieved but still a bit stunned as the studio applause erupted.

Ryan and Kylie were speaking to her and, as she snapped back to attention, Kylie was handing her a tissue. Jojo hadn't even realized her eyes had welled up. Seeing Gracie had tugged at her heart, and then she'd been flooded with fear that Matt might learn the truth, not from her but from a television show.

"I know exactly how you feel," Kylie said, misinterpreting her emotions. "I was the same the first time I saw it. It's so heart-warming. I've always loved your version, but don't you agree that hearing it sung by a young voice is a precious touch?"

Jojo dabbed the tissue under her eyes and prayed that she didn't look like a train wreck. Everyone was waiting for her to speak, and she needed to hold it together. "You're right," she said, barely able to squeeze the words out. "I love what Gracie brings to it." She looked directly into the camera. "If you're watching, Gracie, *nice job*."

CHAPTER 48

IDA

IDA STOOD in the middle of the modest living room of her one-bedroom apartment, staring dumbstruck at the TV. *Why did they cut it short?* The shot of Matt at the end was a crucial part; it provided context and an arc to the story. This was one of the most frustrating aspects of her job. Once Ida sold the rights to a photo or video, she had no creative say over its use. Generally, she didn't care, but it was especially irritating when some hack editor or producer messed with a perfectly good piece.

She went to the kitchenette and got a beer while attempting to shake off her annoyance. All in all she should be celebrating. The video was another feather in her cap, and she'd been well paid. Working with Carson had been a win-win for both of them. He had to be happy. His girl had been floundering before Gracie appeared on the screen. Did they honestly think Jojo was so invincible that charm alone could turn the tide of public opinion? Ida would bet dollars to donuts the rehab story wasn't dead yet, but at least for a day or two, people had something fresh to talk about.

She walked to the window and looked down at the alley. A guy was coming out of the back door of a restaurant in the next building with a couple of bags of trash. He threw them in the dumpster and went back in.

Overall, it had been a slow month, but that was likely to change with Jojo back in town. In fact, Ida had ditched the idea of doing a follow-up story about Matt's girlfriend. Vermont was a long way to go on a fishing expedition, and who really cared if Matt Heston was dating a local girl? Even if Ida managed to get some decent photos, they'd hardly be worth the gas money, let alone her time.

She stopped mid-thought. An image of the woman sitting next to Matt had flickered through her mind again, but this time, it was the dress that jarred Ida's memory. About a month back, she'd seen one very similar—even admired it. Jojo had come out of her building one morning wearing a stunning floral print with spaghetti straps and, as usual, a reporter had asked who the designer was. It turned out she'd bought it off the rack somewhere in Asia.

Ida's laptop was sitting on the coffee table. She went over and opened it warily, hoping she was wrong. Her hands began to tremble as she pulled up the Gracie video, fast-forwarding to the end. *It isn't possible,* she thought.

Right at the last few lines of 'Flower Girl,' Ida had captured several good frames of Matt and his lady friend. The dress was only partly visible, but the woman's smile was unmistakably familiar. How could Ida have missed it? Sure, the absence of makeup made a significant difference, but she'd photographed that face a thousand times. She slumped back in the chair. *I'm the world's biggest idiot.*

After a long moment of self-loathing, she got up and went to her desk, where the contract was still laying. She'd only given it a cursory look before signing—these contracts were mostly standard. Sure enough, she'd sold the exclusive rights, including any future use. She felt another wave of bitterness and let the contract fall from her hand. If Ida tried to use the video now or even a single image from it, Carson would slap a lawsuit on her.

In a career like hers, amazing scoops were few and far between, and the payout from a story like this could have been huge. She thought back over the chain of possession. First, she'd sent the video to Carson and then he'd sent it to his contact at the show. But, of course, he must have watched it first and recognized his client. All he had to do was cut her out of the ending.

Well, he might have won this round, but if he thought this story was simply going to fade away, he didn't know Ida. Somebody was bound to break the news eventually and she had a head start, plus she knew exactly where to go.

She thought back to the TV interview. She could swear Jojo hesitated for a moment before denying that she'd be attending Matt and Gracie's show in Montreal. Of course, there was no way she'd miss her boyfriend's show, but nobody else knew that. And nobody else knew what she'd look like.

And this time, there'd be no contracts or middlemen. This time Ida would stream it live.

CHAPTER 49

MATT

FRIDAY MORNING, Matt was wound so tight there was no chance of getting work done in the shop. He did a radio interview over the phone for a station based in Burlington and then, for the third or fourth time, went over the packing list for the trip, but after that, he was at loose ends. Finally, he drove out to the cabin to take care of unfinished business. He felt bad about leaving it unlocked overnight, plus there was still the cabinet door with the broken glass. He'd said he would repair it and, even though Joelle was gone, he intended to keep his word.

While driving toward the lake, he tried not to think about her, but she'd left a cheerful message the night before that puzzled him. Why was she still calling when he'd basically let her off the hook? If she was feeling guilty, she didn't need to. He thought he'd made that clear.

This distraction was coming at the worst possible time. He needed to focus on Montreal.

Gracie was better prepared mentally than he was. Ever since the initial shock wore off, she'd been all business. She was the one who kept notes while they discussed the setlist and reminded him they shouldn't over-rehearse. He was the distracted one and needed to get his act together.

He glanced down at his phone, sitting in one of the cup holders. A few years back, he'd jury-rigged an iPod cord to his pre-Bluetooth radio and now he was playing a recording of Gracie's song "Little More Light." It was the one new piece they were adding, and they'd spent the bulk of last night's rehearsal working out an arrangement. A week ago, she'd shared an earlier version, and he'd thought it was sweet, but apparently Joelle had pushed her to dig deeper and what a difference!

He sang along as the music blared from the speakers. The lyrics were already embedded in his memory, but that wasn't enough. He wanted the words deep in his marrow, where the stress of a live performance couldn't shake them loose.

As he arrived at the cabin, he noticed Joelle's car was gone, so apparently the rental company had already been there. He wondered how much that level of service cost—two people would've had to drive up from Bennington so one could drive it back. Obviously, Carson didn't mind throwing money around.

Matt grabbed a flathead screwdriver from his toolbox. In his own mind, he was seeing this job through for his grandfather. The old man would expect no less from him.

Sure enough, the place was unlocked, and it was a quick job to remove the old cabinet door from its hinges. As he hefted it and turned to go, he spotted a guitar case sitting by the pantry. He wondered if Leah or Tom played, but then noticed the name Blueridge. If it was Joelle's, it was an odd thing to forget. She might want it shipped, but as long as she had more than one guitar, Leah could probably pick it up on her next visit.

Then, on a hunch, he checked the refrigerator. He'd been in a lot of second homes over the years and normally, the only things people left behind were condiments like mustard and ketchup. But the fridge was fully stocked—even milk and yogurt and eggs. It didn't seem like Joelle not to clean up after herself.

Things weren't adding up. He set the door down and ran upstairs, where he found more of her belongings. Her bathing suit was hanging over the top of the shower door and in her bedroom, she'd left an entire suitcase laying open and full of clothing.

He sank down onto the bed. *What the heck?* One thing was certain: Joelle was coming back. And if Carson Skinner had lied about that, what else had he lied about?

Before Matt could change his mind, he pulled out his phone and called Joelle.

CHAPTER 50

JOJO

JOJO SAT in the back of the limo, only half listening to Carson's postmortem of the morning talk show.

"Nice job staying on message. You've been back in the city less than twenty-four hours and look what you've accomplished." He made it sound like he was complimenting her, but she suspected he was patting himself on the back. "I knew some live TV would turn things around," he added.

She didn't share his confidence. Even though the show ended strong, it was hardly a slam dunk. If not for the conversation about Montreal and Gracie's video, the whole thing could have gone badly.

"Why were you certain the show was a good idea?" she asked. "It didn't change any minds on the rehab story."

"Trust me—as long as they've got something better to talk about, it's as good as dead." He sounded certain, but she wasn't.

She turned her gaze to the buildings going by and remembered she'd put off eating breakfast. "I could use a bagel and coffee."

Carson relayed the message to the front seat.

She almost dropped the matter, but something felt off. "I was totally flailing out there."

"You worry too much. The video of the kid bailed you out."

True enough, but neither of them could have predicted that going in. The video was a complete surprise. She turned back to him. "You never said how you found me in Vermont."

He smirked. "What can I say? I'm well connected, babe."

"Please don't call me that. And that's not an answer."

He looked wounded. "I have eyes and ears on the street, even in Vermont. In this case, Ida Burroughs."

The name meant nothing to Jojo.

"She's a photojournalist," Carson said. "Ida saw you hanging around Westbury and mentioned it to me."

"Where did she see me?"

"Why does it matter? And don't get all worked up. You can't afford to have your fans see you looking stressed."

"Why? Because they'll think I belong in a nuthouse?"

He shrugged. "Hey, you said it. Not me."

She felt a flash of heat. Had he actually just said that?

"Sorry," he said, realizing he'd stepped over the line, then patted her knee. "In a few months, we'll look back on this and think it's hilarious."

Not likely. She wasn't sure which bothered her more—his inappropriate humor or his hand on her knee. It took some self-control to act like everything was cool. Rather than argue, she wanted to know more about Ida Burroughs, so she let a little time go by and then casually brought it up again. "So did Ida shoot the video of Gracie?"

When he didn't respond, she stared directly at him, only to feel a sudden chill at the coldness in his eyes.

"Yeah, Ida shot it, and you can be grateful she brought it to me, or your little tryst with Heston would be huge news right now. And we both know how much your *boyfriend* loves the paparazzi. So once again, I did you a favor."

The way he practically spat out the word *boyfriend* startled her. In that moment, a crack opened in his well-groomed façade, and she glimpsed something that unsettled her. More than jealousy, there was raw anger. Right then, she made up her mind Carson had to go. It wasn't just because of the growing friction between them. He was going behind her back and keeping secrets. She couldn't work with a manager she no longer trusted.

Subconsciously, a part of her had known this was coming for a long time. But loyalty and memories of better times had caused her to drag out the decision. She had half a mind to fire him on the spot but gave herself a moment to collect her wits.

She needed to be smart. This man, who had just gone to great lengths to deceive her, possessed the keys to her entire organization. Every detail of her empire was under his control. If further provoked, there was no telling what he might do. In the blink of an eye, her life became a high-stakes poker match, and she needed to keep her cards close to her chest.

"You're right," she said, masking her agitation. "You totally saved my butt. I was so nervous when that video of Gracie was playing and kept thinking, 'Please don't pan right' and then it just faded to black." She forced a smile. "I owe you big time."

Had she laid it on too thick? But no, he bought every word and nodded smugly.

"You never have to worry about a thing, Jojo. I've always got your back. Have I ever let you down?"

"Not once," she said, doing her best to sound sincere. "And we've been in some tight spots." Carson's ego was his Achilles' heel, so she kept feeding it. "Do you remember Ann Arbor? The second tour?"

"One of my top ten greatest hits," he said. "The stadium workers threatened a strike the day of the concert."

"And you convinced them to hold off twenty-four hours and party with us after the show. That was genius."

They pulled up to the curb at their favorite bagel shop and a young man came out with their usual order. Jojo opened the privacy window to the front seat and passed a bag through to

Russ. "Hey, Dinesh," she said to the chauffeur, "can you take us around to Carson's office?" She closed the window and leisurely unwrapped her bagel, buying time as she planned her next move. "I'm meeting up with Leah to do some shopping."

"I thought you saw each other last night."

She had no intention of actually shopping, but this way, he was less likely to pester her with texts and calls for the next few hours. "Leah's new show opens in a couple weeks, and she needs a gown for the red carpet." That sounded believable. "Plus, maybe I'll find something new for Montreal."

The tension was easing as they moved to lighter topics. Even something as mundane as chewing her bagel slowed the pace of conversation and allowed time to think. "I'm feeling better about the concert. And curious to see how the new song does."

"That reminds me," Carson said, "the label believes it's time for a greatest hits album."

"Really?" This was the first Jojo had heard the idea floated. "Aren't they getting ahead of themselves? I'd like to think I've got a few more in me."

He laughed. "Don't sweat it. I'm sure there's room for more than one greatest hits album in your future. Anyway, some of the guys think it would be brilliant if you and Matt did a duet of 'Sweet Side' and make it a bonus track."

She hid her surprise. It seemed Carson would have gone cold on the idea of her being anywhere near Matt. But she was beyond understanding the machinations inside his mind. It was even possible he was testing her.

"I think that ship has sailed," Jojo said, playing it safe. "He's not returning my calls and I doubt very much he wants to get together in the studio."

Carson shrugged off her concern. "Let me take care of it. Once we dangle a little cash, he'll come running. That old truck he's driving won't last forever."

Her mind doubled back to the previous morning. "When did you see Matt's truck?"

"While you were swimming, he came by to fix some door. The poor guy looks like he's fallen on hard times."

The pieces started falling into place as to why Matt wasn't calling. She desperately wanted to know what had gone down between the two men but bit her tongue.

"You okay?" Carson said as they pulled up to his office building.

She only had to play her part for another minute or two. "I was just thinking of something funny. Maybe we could offer Matt a new truck. I don't think I've seen that in a recording contract. Anyway, I know you've got to go, and we can keep brainstorming later. I'll call you." Carson started to get out, and she added, "Oh, by the way, are you flying up to Montreal with us?"

"Of course. Jojo, I'm always going to be at your side."

She painted on one more smile as they said goodbye.

As soon as Carson was out of the car, she texted Gracie. "What's your Uncle Thad's last name? I'd like to visit him."

It was mid-morning, and Jojo wasn't sure Gracie could use her phone at camp. She thought of reaching out to Matt but doubted he'd answer.

She opened the window to the front seat. "Dinesh, just go up a block or two and pull into a side street and park. I need to find an address." The last thing she wanted was for Carson to wonder why the car was still sitting in front of his building.

"Certainly, ma'am."

"Dinesh, if you don't stop calling me ma'am, I'm going to start calling you Mr. Patel."

"That would be awkward, ma'am."

She smiled at him in the mirror and closed the window again.

Matt had mentioned his manager several times, and always in fond terms. It sounded like he was a good man, but was he also a fighter? Because the moment Carson caught wind of what she was up to, things were going to get dicey.

She tried googling entertainment managers in the metropolitan area. How many Thads could there be?

As she searched, she kept berating herself for letting this get out of hand. Carson had always been aggressive, but in the beginning that had seemed like a good quality in a manager. And, until recently, she'd believed he was always on her side. So she had let things slide, like the brusque way he treated employees—people who essentially worked for her. Too many times she'd given him a pass, and now she was paying the price.

Her phone rang. She prayed it was Gracie, but to her amazement, it was Matt.

"I'm so glad it's you," she said, unable to hide her relief.

"Are you okay?" he asked.

"Not really." She didn't mean to alarm him, but her nerves were frayed. "I've gotten myself into a real mess."

"Is it that Skinner dude?"

"Yeah," she said, wondering how he'd guessed. "I just found out you guys met."

"Are you safe? Did he hurt you?"

"It's not like that. It's business stuff. He's not just my ex, he's also my manager."

"Oh . . . I didn't know you had a manager." There was a pause, and she wished they were face-to-face and there was more time to explain. "I remember you saying it was complicated," he added.

"It is, but it's time to make it less so. That's why I was trying to find a listing for your friend Thad. Do you think he's taking on new clients?"

"I imagine," Matt said cautiously. "It's the Sawyer Agency. I can text you his information."

It was a relief to hear his voice and feel connected again. "Thanks, Matt. If you were here, I'd give you the biggest hug." She was on the verge of losing it but needed to stay in fight mode.

"Are you sure you're okay?" he said. "Should I call Leah for you?"

She hadn't wanted to worry him, but it was hard keeping everything bottled up inside. "Thad's address is all I need for now."

He suddenly changed gears. "I'm here at the cabin. You left a lot of stuff."

"You're at the cabin? How come?"

"I'm finally getting around to fixing that cabinet door, and Carson asked me to—"

"Just ignore everything Carson said. And of course I left a lot of stuff. I'm coming back Monday."

"I'm such an idiot," he groaned. "When I came to the cabin yesterday, I should have insisted on talking to you."

"We're going to have to start trusting each other," she said. "And don't feel bad about letting Carson get to you, he's a master of mind games."

"The thing is," Matt said, his voice growing heated, "my gut told me something was off."

She hated that he was beating himself up. "One of these days, we can have a long talk about it, but right now, I'm going to see if Thad can help." Her phone dinged, and she saw a response from Gracie. Ten minutes earlier, it had felt like she was alone against the world, but not anymore. "One more thing—I'll be in Montreal to cheer you on."

"That's incredible! Hey, if you can get back here tonight, we can ride up together."

Her heart soared. It wasn't just the offer, but also his eagerness. She couldn't imagine anything more fun. "That would be a blast!" She hoped the yearning in her voice made up for the fact she had to say no. "I can't make it back tonight, but please promise me we'll do it sometime."

"Definitely!" He sounded happy. "You, me, and Gracie on the open road. It's a deal." Was he still just talking about a road trip? Because he made it sound like something more. "And I've just sent you Thad's info." As he spoke, the address for the Sawyer Agency popped up on her screen.

"After your show," she said, "I'm hoping we can spend some time together. With Gracie, of course, but later, maybe just the two of us. So we can talk."

"I'd like that," he said. "And let me know how your meeting with Thad goes."

They both said goodbye, and she quickly switched screens to read Gracie's text. *It's Thad Sawyer. He's my godfather. If you meet him, say hi.*

Jojo immediately texted back. *Thanks. Just chatted with your dad. Told him I'll be in Montreal.*

I'm glad he knows, Gracie texted. *Gotta go.*

Jojo wondered what it was like inside Gracie's head today. How could a kid focus on crafts and swimming when tomorrow she'd be performing at one of the biggest music festivals on the continent?

Jojo relayed Thad's address to Dinesh. Then she thought to turn off her phone in case Carson was keeping tabs on her. The Sawyer Agency wasn't far and when they arrived, she told Russ to stay in the car and that she didn't know how long she'd be. There was even the possibility that Thad was busy or away from the office.

It was an older building—a sharp contrast to the modern high-rise where Carson worked. The downstairs marble lobby was well cared for and had a pleasant mid-century charm, and at the moment, it was empty. There was no doorman or receptionist, so she checked the directory and then waited for the elevator. When it opened, an older man in a business suit gave her a slight nod and walked past. It felt almost as though she'd stepped out of her world and into another, where even Jojo was invisible.

She traveled to the seventh floor and when she got out, it felt like she'd walked onto the TV set of *Madmen*. The wood paneling and furniture were straight out of the 1960s. She liked it. It felt retro chic.

She walked through a set of glass doors and into a small waiting room with a middle-aged receptionist. This time, she was instantly recognized.

The woman stood and smiled. "Good afternoon . . . Jojo. Is that how you like to be addressed?"

"Yes. Jojo is fine." The woman seemed unusually composed and not in the least surprised to see her.

"Mr. Sawyer is expecting you. Right this way, please."

Jojo almost laughed out loud, feeling both relief that Thad was available and amused that Gracie must have provided an introduction.

The receptionist knocked on a half-open door. "Thad, she's here." The woman stepped aside and then closed the door behind her.

It was not a large office, but it had a pleasant view of the street. The man behind the desk—probably sixtyish, in a starched white shirt and tie—stood up and extended his hand, "Thad Sawyer."

"I take it Gracie contacted you," Jojo said, shaking hands.

He motioned to a chair. "Both Gracie and Matt texted, but not about the same woman." He tapped the screen of the cell phone lying in front of him. "Gracie wrote, 'Jojo planning to stop by. She's a friend and super cool.'" He looked up from his phone.

Jojo couldn't help laughing. "It's just so Gracie—short and sweet."

He nodded. "And knowing she's a fan of yours, I assumed she was referring to you and not some other person by the same name. And how is it you know my goddaughter?"

"I've been vacationing in Westbury, and we've been hanging out—playing music, mostly. I've grown very fond of her . . . and of Matt." There was a catch in her voice, and she glanced toward the window. She was determined to maintain a strong, professional image. But when she turned back, he was nudging a tissue box across his desk.

"When I got into this business, I had no idea how much Kleenex we'd go through."

He seemed like a kind man, and she appreciated he wasn't pushing to move the meeting along. That happened all too often in New York business meetings. It was almost as if Thad's office moved at the pace of a bygone era.

"Matt's message was different," he said, raising his eyebrows. He tapped his phone again and read. "Hope you're taking on new clients. My friend Joelle is stopping by. Strong on vocals and guitar. Possibly looking for session work."

Jojo winced. She was not making a good first impression.

"So," Thad said, "I wasn't sure if my receptionist should be on the lookout for one woman or two?"

She smiled sheepishly. "I'm guessing you figured it out."

"Not entirely, but I had a hunch." He was looking at her intently, as if measuring her character. "Matt is like a son to me—more like a prodigal son, perhaps. And I worry about him, especially on the eve of a big concert. I wouldn't want anything to throw him off his game."

There were probably a hundred qualified managers in the city who would chuck the rest of their client list in a heartbeat to represent Jojo, no questions asked. But this man was more concerned about the welfare of a client whose last album was released ten years ago. Carson would have called him a fool, yet Jojo liked him already. This was the kind of manager she wanted on her side—if he would have her.

But first, she needed to do some explaining. "Do you want the long or short version?" she asked.

He leaned back in his chair. "If we're going to work together, I need to know everything."

She nodded and started at the beginning.

CHAPTER 51

———

MATT

MATT, Gracie, and Thad stood off to the side of the stage and far enough back from the speakers that they could hear one another. The band on stage, PK Blitz, was belting out another high-energy anthem.

"They can really fill this space," Gracie said.

The four young men were in constant motion and Matt remembered when he had the endurance to go two hours straight like that. He and his band had paid little attention to pacing themselves and, through the boundless energy of youth, had somehow pulled it off, night after night.

"We're going to do fine," he said, feigning as much confidence as possible. "Just do that head whip thing that makes your ponytail spin around. Crowds love that."

She rolled her eyes.

"But seriously," Matt said, "we've got our secret weapon—you and your looper. You're like a one-man band."

"One-girl band," she corrected.

"I've always liked this venue," Thad said. "It's like an oasis. Everything else at the festival is concrete and asphalt."

Looking out from where they stood, the lawn widened into a pie-shaped wedge, gradually rising into a gently sloped amphitheater. The grass was dotted with people on blankets and lawn chairs, while fifty or more hardcore fans congregated near the stage. It had a farmers market vibe, only larger—much larger.

"This is perfect," Matt said. "Thad, I'm grateful."

"Wish I could take credit, but in this case, all I did was take a phone call. It's hard to predict what kind of attendance you'll get, what with the buzz from *NYC Today*."

This was the first Matt had heard of any buzz. "When was this?"

"Didn't you see the show?" Thad looked surprised. "It was on yesterday morning."

"Why would I be watching daytime television?"

Thad's eyes narrowed. "Maybe because your daughter—"

But Gracie cut in. "Dad, I only saw it after I got home and by then we were packing, and I didn't want you to freak out."

"Why would I freak out?"

"Umm . . . maybe because somebody videoed me at Talent Night."

Matt couldn't believe what he was hearing. "And they put it on TV, and you didn't think to tell me?!"

She looked sorry. "I was saving it for the drive home."

Thad looked concerned. "Sorry I brought it up, but can we discuss it later?"

He was right, of course. They were only minutes from performing, yet Matt's attention was all over the place. Even before this thing with Gracie being on TV, he'd been looking around the crowd expectantly. Joelle had texted an hour ago that she was running late.

"It's time for a pep talk," Thad said, looking straight at Matt. "This is mostly for you because it won't be like old times. You're not twenty-five and you haven't got a full band behind you and you can't be running around the stage and definitely no body surf-ing." He winked at Gracie, who was finding this amusing.

"Hey, I was fearless in my day," Matt said proudly.

"Enough with the jokes," Thad said, gently but firmly. He'd always put on this paternal air, right before a show. "Who knows if this will lead to more gigs, but seeing as you have this rare opportu-nity, let's capitalize on your strengths—harmony and some really tight guitar skills. Gracie, when I heard you play 'Flower Girl,' I thought for a moment your dad was backing you up but then I realized you were up there alone, and all that sound was coming from you."

Thad wasn't finished. He raised his eyes to the towering bank of speakers that rose at least twenty feet. There was a matching set on the far side of the stage, and the combined output was a massive wall of sound.

"All you have to do is whisper into your mics and they'll hear you at the back of the lawn. So don't force it."

Gracie whipped her phone out and glanced at it. Matt was about to tell her to turn it off when she beamed. "She's here. She's looking for us."

Without warning, his daughter bounded up the steps that led onto the wings of the stage and looked across the area that doubled as the operations hub for sound and lighting, as well as first aid and security. She spotted Joelle and started waving her arms and yelling. In another moment, she was back on the ground, running into the woman's arms. The combined jumping around and screaming gave the impression they'd been separated by weeks rather than days.

As the two came over, hand in hand, he felt the impulse to hug Joelle, but hesitated and it turned into a kiss on the cheek. "Thanks for coming." Both the gesture and words felt inadequate.

She hovered close, in order to be heard over the music. "I know you're about to go on. Are you ready?" He nodded, but still her eyes lingered, as if making sure he meant it. Finally, she gave his arm a squeeze before turning to Thad. "And how's the hero of the hour?"

Before Thad could answer, Gracie yanked them back to the present. "They're finishing up. Everybody, hold hands."

The four of them came together in a tight circle as Thad barked out his final instructions. "Now remember, we'll have about twenty minutes to get you plugged in and run a sound check."

Moments earlier, Matt had felt scattered, but now, everything came into focus. "We know the drill." He glanced at Gracie for confirmation, and she showed no trace of wavering. During the drive up, they'd spoken at length about how different it felt to perform on a big stage. Still, there was no way to predict how she would handle it until the moment came.

They broke from their huddle as PK Blitz finished. They each grabbed some gear and stood flanking the stairs as the band descended, drenched in sweat.

"That was awesome," Matt yelled.

"Thanks, man. You need any help?"

"No. We're good, but thanks."

And then they were in motion—up the steps and onto the stage, the four of them plugging in guitars and adjusting the height of the mics. Gracie concentrated on setting up her keyboard and looper pedals. The sound check started while Thad and Joelle were still crawling around, adjusting the levels on the amps and double-checking that every jack was firmly plugged. The twenty minutes passed in a blur and Matt's once-seasoned nerves were straining under the pressure. Finally, Thad clapped him on the shoulder and gave him a reassuring nod before joining Joelle off to the side and out of view.

It looked like some of the PK Blitz fans had hung around and there were more people arriving by the minute. It wasn't at all unusual for spectators to flow freely between the venues, some-times only staying to sample a few songs before moving on. There were always several shows running simultaneously within the Quartier des Spectacles.

If any of these people were former Matt Heston fans, it looked like they'd brought their kids—it was a broad mix of ages.

With the sound check done, there were no more excuses for stalling. Matt glanced at Thad and had a flashback to all the times his manager had stood in the wings in the past. *This one's for you, old friend.*

They had decided to dispense with introductions until after the first song, so he nodded to Gracie and from the moment they started, the sound from the monitors was full and rich. He could only hope it sounded as good out there on the grass.

> *You're like a shooting star*
> *Never know quite where you are*
> *Been good to know you*
> *Been good to know you.*
>
> *You lit up my life*
> *Like a magic carpet ride*
> *Been good to know you*
> *Been good to know you.*

At the chorus, Gracie came in strong on the harmony and he breathed another sigh of relief. *That's my girl.*

The real test was to see if they could hold the audience and grow it. If people drifted off between songs, they'd never hit that critical mass where the energy flows back and forth between the audience and the artists.

He gave them a chance to applaud at the end of the song but wasted little time.

"Hey, everyone. I'm Matt Heston and this is my daughter, Gracie. This next song is off my second album, *The Preacher Told Me So.*"

He struck the first chord, forgetting that Gracie needed to switch from acoustic to electric guitar. He didn't dare meet her eyes and just kept playing. She waited until the end of the first phrase and then came in, as if they'd planned it that way. He glanced over his shoulder and damn if she didn't look a little smug. Nothing seemed to shake her.

CHAPTER 52

IDA

THE STAGE SAT in the lowest section of Le Parterre and from there the lawn rose gently toward Rue Saint-Urbain. Ida had taken a position near the street, where she could stand on a large concrete bench. She would have liked to have been closer to the stage, but this venue didn't have a designated section for the press and, at her stature, she'd be totally blind down in the crowd.

Thank God for telephoto. She'd mounted her camera to a tripod and had an unobscured view of the stage. She didn't want to miss a moment, so she was live streaming the performance and periodically panning across the breadth of Le Parterre to document the rapid growth of the crowd. There had to be over a thousand people already.

But no matter what happened next, she'd already gotten her big scoop and dozens of exclusive photos before the show even began. Her press pass had allowed her access to the staging area while the previous band was still playing. Matt and Gracie had shown up with an older man, but there'd been no sign of Jojo as the clock ticked down. It had been a frustrating half hour, trying to remain inconspicuous and wondering if she'd guessed wrong. And then Gracie had jumped onto the steps and started waving to someone. The next five minutes had been a glorious triumph. The little group of four had been so immersed in their reunion, they hadn't noticed Ida capturing every moment.

She'd posted photos and jump-started a thread, #JojoandMatt, with several one-liners spaced roughly a minute apart.

Jojo shows up for Heston concert sporting her new "natural" look.

It's rumored that Jojo spent the past month with Matt and his daughter in Vermont. Is love in the air?

Does anybody recognize the old guy? Matt's manager???

Will we see a duet of "Sweet Side" today?

In under a minute, others joined the thread and it took on a life of its own. Now as Ida stood atop her concrete perch, she overheard snippets of conversations as people hurried by.

"Do you think she's really here?"

"Someone said Jojo's hiding backstage."

"Have they sung 'Sweet Side' yet?"

And Ida's favorite quote for the day, "I thought Matt Heston was dead."

For once in her life, Ida felt like more than a spectator. She was turning what would have been a quiet little concert into a mega-event.

CHAPTER 53

JOJO

JOJO STOOD in the wings where she could watch Matt and Gracie while remaining shielded from the audience by the giant bank of speakers. Adrenaline was still pumping from the mad dash to set up the gear while keeping her face turned away from people and cameras. She breathed easier now and took a moment to peek out at the audience through a small gap between speakers. She was startled at what she saw—the crowd had at least doubled in size since the last act. Whereas this would usually be good news, she could read the concern on Thad's face. The venue wasn't set up for this size crowd. There were no barricades in front of the stage and only a handful of security.

"They didn't expect more than a thousand tops," he yelled. "I bet it's double that."

On the upside, it wasn't a rowdy crowd. They swayed and sang along to the familiar lyrics. There was a sense of nostalgia, and she hoped the positive vibe would keep everyone safe.

Thad elbowed her and pointed back toward the staging area where two security vehicles had just arrived, bringing more uniformed staff. For several minutes, they attempted to insert themselves between the stage and the crowd, shouting and encouraging people to move back, but it was physically impossible and they soon gave up.

Gracie seemed oblivious to everything other than delivering a stellar performance. She was highly animated, and a delight to watch. Performing while looping four tracks required total concentration, and she hadn't missed a phrase change yet.

Jojo felt like the relationship between father and daughter was evolving before her eyes. Gracie's unshakable resilience allowed Matt the freedom and confidence to do what he did best. He could be the lead guitarist and front man, without worrying that his little girl might crack under the pressure. And between them, they were putting on a riveting show.

However, as the concert passed the hour mark, Jojo heard her name being called out between songs. It started with an occasional shout and then turned more to a chant. Sometimes they were chanting "Jojo" and at other times "Sweet Side." She'd been afraid of this and not just because Kylie raised the possibility on *NYC Today*. That she and Matt were in the same city at the same festival had obviously raised expectations. The event directors might even have guessed that inviting Matt would stir the rumor mill and push up attendance. But if that was their intent, they'd overshot the mark.

At the end of "Working Stiff," Matt shot them a puzzled look, and she felt for him. The chants had to be a distraction, and she worried he might respond by simply announcing, "Sorry folks, Jojo's not here." She doubted that would go over well and he must have known it, too. As he turned back to the front of the stage, he simply pushed on, announcing the one new song they'd added to the set.

"We're going to treat you to something special. Gracie wrote this next song. It's called 'Little More Light,' and she's going to sing it for you."

Performing new music live was always a risk, even for Jojo, whose fans were incredibly supportive. It was an experiment, with no guarantee of positive results. And to perform a new song now, when the crowd was already restless . . . A lump rose in Jojo's throat.

Whether Gracie sensed the risk or had planned for this moment all along, she held up her hand and shouted into her mic. "Wait! Hold on! We have a special guest who's going to join us on our last two songs." As though she'd uncorked the genie of fantastical proportions, a tremendous roar rocked the stage. Gracie looked at Jojo and waved her over.

But Jojo wasn't about to upstage Matt. She gestured with both hands and mouthed, "No, no, no!"

Either Gracie didn't get the point, or she was already two steps ahead and realized only one thing would satisfy the crowd. She spoke into the mic again. "She's a little shy, so you might have to encourage her."

All at once, a throng of voices united in chanting, "Jojo . . . Jojo . . ."

She choked up as she saw the confusion on Matt's face. It felt like everything was unraveling, and then it actually did. Thad held up his phone and there on the screen was a photo of her with the caption "Jojo's new look."

He swiped at the screen and more comments appeared. "I think the cat's out of the bag," he yelled over the din.

When she looked up, Gracie had already unplugged her guitar and was running across the stage, wearing a big smile and looking unfazed. She grabbed Jojo by the hand and shouted, "Everybody knows!"

Jojo remained rooted. "No! This is your moment—you and your dad!"

Despite the growing chaos, Thad remained composed and spoke directly into her ear. "I don't think you have a choice."

From where she stood, she could feel the crowd better than see them, but Thad was right. The only thing that would placate that mass of humanity was to walk onto the stage. She relented and let Gracie lead her out from behind the speakers.

The roar reached a deafening level, but it was all a blur, as the only thing Jojo saw was Matt's bewildered expression. Through the din, she mouthed the words "I'm sorry," but the sentiment did nothing to soften his frozen gaze.

Her head cleared enough to realize the audience expected her to smile and be her usual exuberant self, but all she could manage was a halfhearted wave. Gracie handed her the electric guitar and Jojo strapped it on. When she looked again, Matt was turned back to the expectant audience. They had been waiting long enough, and all she knew was that if Matt had the strength to pull this off, then she had better do the same.

Finally, he looked over his shoulder and yelled, "Let's do this!"

She had never respected him more.

Gracie was standing behind her keyboard, her grin in total contrast to her father's serious expression. In fact, she appeared to be on top of the world. This was her song, so she counted them in, her head bobbing to the beat as her fingers leapt across the keys, adding both rhythm and melody.

Get a grip, Jojo thought. She'd been in tight spots before and yet she couldn't account for why it felt like the world was swaying beneath her feet.

The view across Le Parterre was very different now that she was on the open stage. To her amazement, it appeared the audience was overflowing the lawn and spilling onto the sidewalks. If it grew any larger, it would expand into the streets and block traffic.

Just as Jojo joined the vocals on the chorus, Thad appeared out of the wings and grabbed Matt by the arm. He was yelling frantically.

That's when she realized the rocking of the stage was no illusion. She yanked the plug from her guitar and reached Gracie at the same time as Matt.

"We've got to go!" he yelled. "It's not safe!"

Gracie had just been jarred out of her big moment and looked dazed. "I need Mom's guitar."

"Take her!" Matt yelled to Jojo. "I'll get what I can!"

Gracie resisted. "I'm not going without Dad."

There was no need to debate, as a security guard corralled the two of them toward the stairs. She could hear Matt on the mic again, imploring the audience to move back and repeating several times that the concert was over.

But his words were drowned out by a tumultuous refrain of "'Sweet Side,' 'Sweet Side.'"

"The show is over!" she heard one more time, and then he must have given up.

Jojo felt a spasm of panic as they reached the edge of the platform because the crowd had overrun the staging area. Fortunately, several more security people were waiting and surrounded them as they reached the bottom of the steps. She'd never been so grateful to feel solid ground under her feet.

Gracie was clinging to her hand, and they both had lost any sense of free will as they were bumped and jostled and pushed forward. Somehow, their team of escorts made progress, slicing through the mob like a wedge.

After what seemed a monumental effort of swimming against the tide, they reached a black SUV with a door open and waiting. Gracie climbed in as Jojo turned back to the stage just in time to see Matt and Thad at the top of the stairs. Before she could wave to them, she was shoved inside. Seconds later, the siren turned on and their driver began inching forward as their security team outside continued to push through the throng and clear a path for the vehicle.

CHAPTER 54

MATT

MATT AND THAD walked in silence up Rue Saint-Urbain. When they reached Boulevard de Maisonneuve, they stopped for one last look across the now quiet Le Parterre. The crowd had disbanded, but a dozen or more maintenance workers were inspecting the stage for structural damage.

"Do you think we'll ever be invited back?" Matt asked wryly.

"At least no one was seriously hurt," Thad said. "And I don't see how they can blame you. They might blame your girlfriend, though, and her manager. Damned irresponsible, allowing her to show up like that."

It was hard to tell from the older man's face just how serious he was. Matt started to correct him about Jojo being his girlfriend but didn't have the energy. He looked at his watch and then back at the large expanse of grass that had been covered in a roar of chaos only forty minutes earlier. He felt drained, but at least Gracie had called to say she was safe and was hanging out with Jojo at the Omni Hotel.

Jojo, he said silently to himself several times, as if by repeating the name, it could replace Joelle.

"We should get going," Thad said.

"Are you sure you want to walk?" Matt asked. They had left the truck in the staging area, where it was blocked in by maintenance vehicles. He figured most of their gear would be safe locked inside but was carrying Natalie's guitar back to the hotel. Gracie was likely to sleep better knowing it was close at hand.

"A little exercise might clear our heads," Thad said. "And the Omni's not far."

So the two men crossed the street and headed southwest, putting Le Parterre behind them. Thad was right; Matt needed time to sort out his thoughts before confronting Jojo.

"I hear you met Carson Skinner," Thad said.

The name brought back yesterday's phone call with Jojo. "What did he do to her?"

Thad must have sensed his concern because he patted him on the back. "She's going to be okay. It turns out she's got a whole stable of lawyers and accountants who were all too eager to work directly with her instead of going through Carson. As soon as they blocked his access to her accounts, we sent him a termination notice."

Matt whistled. "He's got to be mad as hell. Is she safe?"

"She's going to have extra security for a while. Plus, she insisted on giving Skinner a generous severance. I was against it at first, but she brought me around. He did play a big part in building her career and he only gets it gradually over time if he behaves himself. That was her idea. She has good instincts."

Matt laughed. "I guess I shouldn't be surprised. She did manage one heck of a yard sale."

"A yard sale? I wish I could have seen that."

Matt stopped in the middle of the sidewalk and pulled out his phone. He found the picture of Gracie, Jojo, and himself holding up the yard sale sign. "She basically took over and ran the whole thing."

Thad looked over his shoulder. "That's priceless."

It brought back memories—the three of them, smiling and

holding up the sign as if it were a victory banner. They'd been a real team that day. When he looked up again, Thad was studying him.

"And you had no idea who she was?"

"Absolutely none."

"After the way things went down today," Thad said, "I wouldn't blame you for being angry."

"Oh, I was," Matt said, "for all of two minutes. But when it went crazy out there, who did I trust my daughter to? I didn't even stop to think." He started walking again and Thad fell into step. For a while, neither spoke. They passed other pedestrians and outdoor cafés where French and English conversations spilled onto the sidewalk.

"There's something else," Matt finally said. "For years I've been dragging around a lot of guilt for the way I bailed on you. I may never square my account, but if I helped, even in a small way, to bring you and Jojo together—"

Thad interrupted. "Consider your account squared and then some."

Matt felt like a weight was lifting. After four decades in the industry, Thad finally had a client who could pay him what he was worth.

There was one last thing to discuss, but Matt had hesitated to bring it up. Now, as the hotel came into view, he realized he was running out of time. "I understand it's customary when a manager signs a mega star to clean out the deadwood."

"Are you referring to yourself as deadwood?" Thad asked.

It seemed obvious.

"Kid, you've got to stop being so hard on yourself." Thad hadn't called him that since the old days. "You're right, though, about Jojo being a full-time job. I'll have to bring on another agent to manage some of my existing clients. But as for you, you're stuck with me."

Matt was relieved, but professionally, he didn't understand

how it made sense for Thad. Perhaps his account required so little time that it wasn't worth foisting on someone else.

"Don't be so surprised." Thad turned and looked directly at him. "You've always been like family. Even during the years we weren't speaking, I always had a feeling you'd be back. The music's in your blood."

Thad had never been one to varnish the truth, so Matt took his words to heart.

"If you say so."

"I do," Thad continued. "Plus, it turns out I couldn't give you the boot even if I wanted to. Jojo made me write it into the contract."

"She did what?"

"If I drop you, she drops me."

That was a lot to process, and yet they'd run out of time. They'd reached the hotel entrance and Matt came to a dead stop. He wasn't ready to face her.

"You can't get cold feet now," Thad said. "For one thing, she's holding your daughter hostage."

"I just don't get it. She's Jojo. She's rich and talented and beautiful and smart and—"

"I get it," Thad said. "You're wondering how you can ever measure up."

Matt nodded. "She could literally have any guy she wants."

"Well, apparently she wants you." Thad placed a hand on Matt's shoulder. "Don't sell yourself short. You're a great musician and possibly an even better father. Women see stuff like that and figure it's enough to work with."

It wasn't a resounding endorsement, but it was enough to get Matt moving again. As he walked through the hotel door, his phone buzzed. It was a text from Gracie.

I'm starving. Can we order dinner?

Matt smiled. In an odd way, it felt like coming home.

CHAPTER 55

JOJO

THE SUITE HAD three bedrooms and Jojo and Gracie were hanging out in the largest. Jojo was propped up against a pile of pillows on the king-sized bed, while Gracie sprawled across the other end, speaking to her dad on her phone. She'd been wound up and talking a steady stream since the concert. Their narrow escape had done nothing to curb her excitement. In fact, it may have heightened it.

"Hamburger and fries," she said, taking her dad's order and jotting it down on a pad of hotel stationery. "And a club sandwich for Uncle Thad."

So, they were staying for dinner. Jojo allowed herself a tiny smidge of relief, though she knew this didn't guarantee Matt was ready to forgive her. He might be thinking of Gracie and how disappointed she'd be if he showed up simply to collect her and leave. Or he might be thinking of Thad and how uncomfortable it would be if two of his clients couldn't get along.

When Gracie got off the phone, she perched on her knees. "How do I place the order?"

"Are they almost here?"

"They're in the elevator."

The news kicked Jojo into gear. She picked up the hotel phone from the bedside table and set it on the bed. "Dial zero and when someone picks up, tell them you want room service and they'll either take your order or transfer you to someone who will."

She ducked under the phone cord and went to the dresser mirror to check on how she looked. They'd been jostled by the crowd and shoved into the car before returning to the hotel. She was grateful Gracie had something to keep her busy for the moment. When they'd first arrived at the hotel, the girl had been glued to the TV and her phone, in search of news and video of the concert, but the constant updates had grated on Jojo's nerves and she'd asked her to take a break.

"Do I have to tell them our room number?" Gracie asked.

"They already know because you're calling on the room phone."

"Slick," Gracie said, picking up the receiver and hitting zero. "I bet Dad doesn't know how easy this is. We usually pack a cooler from home." Someone must have answered, and Gracie's voice turned businesslike as she ordered.

Looking at her own reflection, Jojo smoothed her eyebrows and fluffed her hair where it had flattened against the pillows. Worry and fatigue had robbed her of some color so she pinched her cheeks. A little makeup would help, but she figured Matt had been through enough today and might appreciate a familiar face.

Gracie was off the phone and observing her in the mirror. "Can I watch you put your makeup on sometime?"

"Yeah. That would be fun."

"Can you also teach me?"

Jojo suspected Matt wouldn't approve, but stage lights were notorious for washing faces out. "If your dad says it's okay. But only for onstage, not for every day. You have beautiful eyes and amazing skin—"

There was a knock at the main door and Gracie instantly changed gears, leaping up and racing out of the room.

Jojo took a deep breath. This was it. They'd spoken earlier by phone and he'd been civil, even solicitous, but at the time he'd been worried about their safety. Now that the dust had settled, his attitude toward her might have hardened. She heard the men's voices and Gracie's excited greeting and headed out to the main room.

"We're all over Twitter and TikTok," Gracie was saying. "We're even on TV news. And tons of people shot videos. Most of them are—"

"Hold on," Matt cut in. "I've been worried about you. I need a hug."

He set a guitar case down before sweeping Gracie into his arms. He was facing away from Jojo and still hadn't noticed her.

"Daaaad! I'm okay. Really."

Thad caught Jojo's eye and winked, but neither of them wanted to interrupt.

"I'm so sorry we got separated," Matt said. He set Gracie down and held her at arm's length, looking her up and down. "No broken bones? Missing teeth? Missing limbs?"

She did a huge eye roll. "Dad, I'm totally okay. And when the food arrives, we have to eat fast, because there's two street concerts I want to see."

He seemed not to hear and pulled her into his arms again. This time, Gracie relented and even hugged him back. Their tender reunion tugged at Jojo's heart, and she ached to cross the few feet between them and weave her way into their embrace.

She now realized their earlier phone call had only partly reassured him, and that he'd needed this tangible proof. Finally releasing Gracie, he glanced around and turned to find Jojo.

She hadn't been sure what to expect, but if Matt was angry, he hid it well. In fact, his smile was warm and generous, as if he knew she'd be wallowing in guilt and need reassurance. She responded with a grateful smile of her own and though she'd planned to wait and apologize when she could get him alone, the words came tumbling out.

"Matt, I just want you to know how sorry I am. I never should have—"

"Sorry for what?" He looked oddly puzzled.

She hesitated. Was he being intentionally obtuse? "I'm sorry for being there today and starting a riot."

At first, he seemed to ponder her statement, but then a playful glint crept into the corners of his eyes. "Well, somebody's full of herself. It was my concert, so I figure I should get at least some credit for the riot." There was that smug expression she knew so well. Was he for real, or just trying to keep things civil in front of Gracie and Thad?

"Are you kidding?!" Gracie interrupted, startling everyone. She planted both hands on her hips and looked sternly first at Jojo and then her father. "We were doing *my* song when the stage started shaking." She managed to appear dead serious for all of three seconds before bursting into laughter. "You should see your faces."

"Nice one," Matt said, high-fiving her. "You totally got me."

"Heaven help us," Thad muttered. "Is this what it's going to be like?"

"'Fraid so," Matt said. "Hey, Gracie, maybe you should get a cold drink for Uncle Thad. He's had a tough afternoon, and he just hiked halfway across town."

"Oh, now you're making me sound feeble," Thad said. "Don't forget who's steering this ship." Even in the older man's protests, there was obvious affection.

"And while you two raid the minibar," Matt said, "Jojo and I are going to talk." Gracie tugged at her father's arm and whispered something, then headed off with Thad to the kitchenette.

Suddenly there was just the two of them. His expression was still thoughtful, and she detected no hint of tension that might have foreshadowed a stern lecture.

"Hey," he said, gently breaking the silence.

"Hey," she echoed back.

Gracie and Thad were still within earshot, so Jojo stepped back into her room and motioned for Matt to follow. Once inside, he closed the door and glanced around.

"Nice digs." Then, almost as an afterthought, "Thanks for helping Gracie order dinner. Let me know how much so I can—" She shot him a warning look, and he stopped short. "So I can thank you for your generosity." He tried to suppress a smile but was only halfway successful.

"Good save," she said. "By the way, all Gracie's talked about for the last half hour is food. I'm not sure you feed her enough."

"I guess she worked up an appetite. Plus, room service is obviously a novelty."

It felt like Matt was stalling and she desperately needed to know what was going on in that head of his. "I know you're probably mad and you deserve to be. So, if you're going to chew me out, please just get on with it."

He frowned. "What if I'm not mad?"

"Come on, Matt. I had any number of opportunities to tell you who I am, and I kept putting it off." It felt good finally to put it out there. Even so, she couldn't seem to get a rise out of him.

He sighed, as if reluctant to discuss it. "Okay . . . since you insist, I'll admit it was tough on stage today. I think I went through a bunch of emotions. First, annoyance when they started calling your name, and then shock when Gracie dragged you out. Not to mention, embarrassment at being the last person in Montreal to discover who you are."

She winced. "Possibly more than Montreal. I think someone streamed it."

He knit his brow as if attempting to scowl, but it was half-hearted at best. "Damn, woman. You seem determined to make this as painful as possible."

Was this an attempt to make her laugh? He was confusing her

with kindness, and she had to look down at the floor in order to think straight. If everything he'd just described was true, then it seemed he should be upset or, at the very least, disappointed in her.

He must have read her thoughts because he moved closer and gently lifted her chin. "Forget about the concert for a moment and think about when we met. In those first days when things between us were moving quickly, if I hadn't pushed you away, would you have told me the truth then?"

She didn't have to hesitate. "Definitely. I'd already made up my mind to tell you that night you came to the cabin by yourself."

He let her think about that for a moment. "In that case, it seems I'm at least partly to blame."

Could he be any nicer? Not only was he letting her off the hook, he was even sharing the blame. There seemed little point in poking or prodding any further at the past and how they'd gotten to where they were. If he was ready to move on, then she should, too. Finally, she did what she'd been longing to do since they'd retreated to the bedroom. She threw her arms around him, practically knocking him backward.

"Hey . . ." he said, sounding both surprised and amused. His own arms tightened around her. "It's all good. We're going to do better now."

"From now on," she said, half muffled into his chest, "no more secrets."

They stayed like that for a while—long enough for some of her anxiety to ebb away.

"I thought I'd blown it," she whispered.

"Me too," he said. "After you left Thursday, I figured I wouldn't get another chance. But we're going to be okay now. Better than okay."

"But what about the whole long-distance thing?"

"That'll be hard," he said, not bothering to sugarcoat it. "But maybe Gracie and I'll be in the city more than I thought."

Not believing her ears, she released her arms and looked up at him. "What are you saying?"

"You saw her out there today. I don't think I can hold her back anymore. If I do, she'll just rebel the way I did as a kid."

This was big, like a realignment of the planets big. But she didn't press him on it, aware that the realization was still fresh and possibly fragile. Perhaps he knew it as well because he quickly moved on.

"There's something I need to ask." From his expression, he appeared hesitant. "How much of Joelle was real?"

The question took her aback—even stung a little—because in her mind it had all been real. But she'd only just succeeded at getting Matt to open up and didn't want to sound defensive.

"The feelings were real," she began tentatively. "The stories about teaching music when I first got to New York and how I saw you in concert when I was seventeen. That was all real." She dug back, trying to remember more. "The first time you kissed me on the porch at the cabin—do you honestly think I could have faked that?" Aware that her voice was rising, she brought it back down. "And a couple nights ago, you were like a sweet kid after a first date. You called to apologize for not walking me to the door and I—"

"Uuugghhh . . ." he groaned. "Not my coolest moment."

"But I loved it." She scooped up one of his big hands and pressed it to her heart. "I really loved it."

He still looked embarrassed, and she loved that, too. It felt like every moment she found something more to cherish about him.

This time, he was a little overeager to change the subject. "And I take it you're not about to be homeless?"

"You know, I never actually said I was. You just sort of assumed." It was a weak defense, but judging by the twinkle in his eye, he was more amused than bothered.

"Well, just in case, Gracie's offer of the guest room still stands." He barely gave her time to digest the import of his words before hitting her up with another question. "And that brings us to a more serious matter . . . *Jojo*." He drew her name out for emphasis. "It's about that poster. The one above your mom's sewing machine?"

Her entire body relaxed. "Ohhhh . . . That's definitely real."

"Good," he said. "Because that was my favorite part about Joelle."

She pulled a face. "Even better than the kiss?"

He paused, as if deliberating. "That was so long ago, I barely remember."

She poked him in the ribs, and he doubled over, laughing. It was nice to see him loosening up. As the laughter subsided, the space between them turned quiet and still. They stared at each other with equal parts longing and tenderness. For too long, they'd been dancing around their feelings and pretending to ignore this magnetic attraction.

He reached out and pulled her closer. She drew in a breath as his fingers lightly grazed her cheek. At last, he leaned in, and she closed her eyes as his lips alighted on hers, flooding her with warmth. This was unlike their earlier kisses, which had been fueled mostly by passion. That earlier heat was still present, but time and familiarity had deepened their connection.

Suddenly, there was a shout from the outer room—Gracie announcing the food had arrived. Jolted back to the present, they untangled themselves.

"Do I look okay?" she said a little breathlessly.

"Yeah, great. Actually amazing, but I can't stop staring at you. I don't think I can go out there and act like everything's normal. Do we need to say something?"

"We could announce we're going steady," she said.

He grinned. "Kinda feels like it. You know, right before I came in here, Gracie said, 'Don't blow it, Dad.'"

"Ahh . . . that's sweet," Jojo said. "I guess she really is my biggest fan."

"Second biggest," Matt said, leaning down for one more kiss. Finally, they pulled themselves apart again.

"Gracie expects to go concert hopping tonight," Jojo said. "Any chance we can get Thad to take her?"

Matt looked at her slyly. "He already volunteered on the way up in the elevator."

CHAPTER 56

JOJO

THE PLACE DES Festivals rocked to the refrain of "Shout It Out" and the enthusiasm of 25,000 fans. In only three rehearsals, the band had already brought the song up to the freewheeling standards of a live performance. As they approached the final bar, Jojo lifted the neck of her guitar and then brought it down hard for a cold close. The screams erupted, and she knew it was a keeper.

She was still getting accustomed to her new look and felt a little naked without a wig. When she ran the idea past Thad, he'd been neutral.

"It will signal change, and if you do it, do it for yourself and no one else."

She'd felt nervous and indecisive that morning, staring into the mirror. But then her thoughts jumped ahead to the ride back to Westbury in the truck with Matt and Gracie, and that made her smile. This *was* a new chapter, and she wanted the whole world to know. So today she was sporting an on-stage persona that was a little less Jojo and a little more Joelle.

She'd still been unsure about it until Matt showed up at rehearsal, gave a breathless "Wow" and then tipped her back and kissed her in front of the band and crew. Once Matt Heston got off the fence, he could be a very spontaneous man.

Her eyes swept across the enormous outdoor venue and she felt renewed gratitude for her fans. The last of the daylight had faded and the light show was more impressive now.

"It's time to introduce a young friend of mine. It's been a treat and a privilege to hang out with Gracie Heston for the past few weeks. She's a talented musician and songwriter, and I have no doubt you'll be seeing a lot more of her in the future. Here she is to perform a song she wrote called 'Little More Light.'"

As Gracie emerged from behind the band, her larger-than-life image appeared on the two giant screens flanking the stage. Her smile and exuberance sent a wave of excitement across the plaza. In the past twenty-four hours, her face had appeared in news reports across the globe, along with footage of the chaotic conclusion of yesterday's concert. She had become an overnight sensation.

There was no need for Gracie to loop tonight. They'd practiced earlier with the full band, at first with Gracie on keyboard, but then Thad suggested she switch to acoustic guitar, which gave her untethered freedom. It had been the right move, bringing her infectious energy to the front of the stage.

The two of them hugged as best they could, with guitars slung around their necks. There was a lot of speculation going around about Matt, Gracie, and Jojo, but one thing was certain: their tale appeared to be a happy one. As a result, the Swiss sanatorium story was no longer selling well at newsstands.

"Hi, everybody," Gracie shouted. She was already mic'd with a wireless headset. "We tried this song yesterday and didn't get very far, so we're doing it again!" It was hard not to delight in her innocent confidence, and there seemed to be no audience big enough to intimidate her.

Jojo looked back at her band. They were getting a kick out of this as much as she was. Gracie started winning them over the moment she showed up at rehearsal, already knowing their names.

Now she counted them in, and the stage came to life with Gracie singing solo on the first verse, her pure voice resonating in the night air.

In time for the chorus, she sidled over to Jojo and they leaned together, weaving the harmony with the melody. Three of the band members added more vocal layers, giving the song a gospel feel that fit the lyrics.

> *Little more light to start each morning.*
> *Little more light to see the way.*
> *Little more lightness in each moment.*
> *Let it chase the clouds away.*

It was Gracie's idea to display the words to the chorus on the jumbotron. "They do it at Christian rock concerts all the time," she'd said matter-of-factly, leaving Jojo, Thad, and her father once again scratching their heads. The idea worked, and the audience was soon singing along.

Jojo looked for Matt and spotted him in the wings, entranced by his daughter's performance. He had to be wondering, *How did this happen?* Even with all the evenings spent making music in their living room, he couldn't possibly have imagined his little girl captivating so many while still so young.

On Jojo's signal, every instrument went silent, and the band raised their hands above their heads and started clapping to the rhythm. Gracie moved forward again to the edge of the stage and led the crowd *a cappella* through another round of the chorus. It worked as well as they'd imagined, and then the band came back strong for one last refrain.

When the song ended, Gracie soaked up the applause and then high-fived Jojo before running off stage and straight into her father's arms.

As Jojo waited for the noise to die down, she couldn't help but count herself fortunate for all the good in her life—the music, her adoring fans, and even this beautiful summer night. But now there was something new in her life—a sense of belonging. And at the heart of that belonging were people she loved.

"Now I'd like to introduce another special person in my life." There was an expectant lull as everyone in the audience knew what was coming. She felt a surge of pure joy as she looked over her shoulder and smiled at him. "Hey, Matt, come on out."

The top came off the plaza, and the cheers filled the night sky as Matt walked onto the stage and lifted his guitar aloft. It was one of those special moments in music that people would talk about for years. *I was at the Place des Festivals when . . .*

Jojo had promised herself to keep it together and not get too emotional. But he looked so fine in a white button-down shirt, black jeans, and a big silver buckle. He was even wearing cowboy boots. If Jojo didn't know better, it looked like Thad was rebranding his client.

For a moment, she was a starstruck teenager again. Back then she'd conjured this scene in all sorts of ways, but she'd always been the newcomer, striding onto *his* stage. He would look into her eyes and recognize the harmony that resonated between their souls as their voices joined in song.

What a long journey it had been between that dream and this reality. They were both seasoned musicians now, with their own tales of road-weary blues. And that was a good thing, because the miles and years had taught them what mattered most.

There was no mistaking the twinkle in his eyes as his free arm wrapped around her waist and lifted her up onto her toes. He was solid and kind and shared her passion for music. They were good together offstage, and now she practically laughed with delight at the thought of being together onstage. This was going to be heaven. Their lips met, and a roar erupted around them.

Acknowledgments

I'm grateful for the helpful feedback and enthusiastic encouragement from my beta readers Victoria Lloyd, Leanna Maglienti, Colton Orr, Kathy Orr, Ruth Orr, Amy Sayre, Kate Sayre and Linda Lyons. That my youngest beta reader was thirteen and the oldest was eighty-five speaks to the wide appeal of sweet romance.

David Williams of Aspen Limo Tours in Vancouver, Washington provided useful information about limousine services.

Susannah Nix, author of the Chemistry Lessons series of romantic comedies, kindly suggested several indie-author resources, including *The Creative Penn* podcast and *The Self-Publishing Formula* podcast, both of which opened a treasure trove of additional resources.

Kristen Tate is my amazing editor. She is thorough and exacting and can be reached at TheBlueGarret.com.

I'm fortunate to have a professional graphic designer in the family, my son, Colton, who designed a warm and inviting book cover.

And finally, this book would not have made it to publication without the tireless support of my wife, Amy. She patiently waded through draft after draft, advising me on plot points and character development. Most of all, she could sense when the tone was shifting and would gently nudge me back on course. She truly made this a better book.

Additional resources: The manuscript was written on

Microsoft Word with grammar checking by ProWritingAid. I used Vellum for the internal formatting and Canva to format the cover. I used DALL-E 2 to generate concept art for the cover illustration, though the final image was drawn digitally by hand.

About the Author

Jamie Orr is a graduate of Dartmouth College, where he also taught dance for many years. He continues to teach in the Upper Valley region of New Hampshire, while finding time to write and pursue his favorite hobby, woodworking. He often visits family in southwestern Vermont, the setting of this book. He resides in Enfield, NH with his wife.

Jamie@SwingJamie.com
SwingJamie.com
JojoUnplugged.com

www.ingramcontent.com/pod-product-compliance
Lightning Source LLC
Chambersburg PA
CBHW021134310726
48971CB00002B/319